O9-BHK-056

OTHER BOOKS BY
RALPH PETERS

. . .

Fiction

Twilight of Heroes
The Perfect Soldier
Flames of Heaven
The War in 2020
Red Army
Bravo Romeo
The Devil's Garden

Nonfiction

Fighting for the Future

TRAITOR

TRAITOR

A NOVEL

RALPH PETERS

AVON BOOKS NEW YORK

This is a work of fiction. Names, characters, places, and incidents either are the product of the author's imagination or are used fictitiously. Any resemblance to actual events, locales, organizations, or persons, living or dead, is entirely coincidental and beyond the intent of either the author or the publisher.

The views expressed in this book are those of the author and do not reflect the official policy or position of the Department of the Army, Department of Defense, or the U.S. Government.

AVON BOOKS, INC.
1350 Avenue of the Americas
New York, New York 10019

Interior design by Kellan Peck
ISBN: 0-380-97641-2

Library of Congress Cataloging in Publication Data:
Peters, Ralph, 1952–
Traitor : a novel / Ralph Peters.—1st ed.
p. cm.
I. Title.
PS3566.E7559T73 1999 98-46862
813'.54—dc21 CIP

First Avon Books Printing: April 1999

Printed in the U.S.A.

FIRST EDITION

QPM 10 9 8 7 6 5 4 3 2 1

www.avonbooks.com

. . .

To my brother,
Bruce Robert Peters,
who always knew Holmes had a dark side;
and to Henry Nowak,
''Mr. Noir.''

In the Gospel of Luke, soldiers approached John the Baptist, asking: "And we, what shall we do?" And he said to them, "Rob no one by violence or by false accusation, and be content with your wages."

. . .

Money changes everything.

—Populist philosopher Cyndi Lauper, amplifying Tom Gray's reinterpretation of the works of Karl Marx

TRAITOR

CHAPTER 1

I marched back up to the grave after the crowd faded. Washington in July. Uniform clawing at my skin.

Arlington is efficient. A mini-excavator had already arrived to fill in the hole. A workman with graying hair and weightlifter biceps stooped near the folding chairs, picking up the casings from the salute. He sensed me and straightened his back.

"Done come back for another look, Colonel?"

I nodded. A poor-man's colonel, with silver oak leaves.

"Who this gentleman be, don't mind my axing?" His face gleamed.

"General Farnsworth. Mickey Farnsworth."

"Good man?"

"The best."

The laborer showed a broken line of teeth. "We going to take good care of him for you. Don't you worry, now."

"You can keep on working. I don't mind." But I would have minded. The metal box lay still at the bottom of the hole, kissed with dirt.

"No, sir. We don't do like that. We don't never start till everybody gone. It the rule."

A black bird settled on a green branch, sun oiling its feathers.

"You just takes your time," the workman went on. "I always be glad when somebody come back. People don't come back no more. See what I'm saying? I mean, your wives, maybe. Maybe they does. For a while. But everybody get forgot about equal."

Mary Farnsworth at the graveside, struggling to maintain a dignity worthy of her husband. She stood up straight, and the ceremony was long, and I was afraid she might faint in the heat. I started in her direction when it was all over, but the generals who had lost a rival for promotion flocked around her, cooing sympathy. I could not get past their aides.

"He was a great man," I told the workman. "A hero. Nobody expected him to go like this."

"Heart trouble?"

I almost laughed. "His heart would've been the last thing to go." Farnsworth had been in better shape than a lieutenant fresh out of Ranger School. And it had been a big heart, too. I disciplined my voice. "Hit-and-run. He was jogging." I looked up and the sun narrowed my eyes. We had all thought Farnsworth would be the next Colin Powell, and now he was senselessly dead.

The workman smeared the sweat over his forehead and sighed. Looking down through the trees, across the river. Into the marble city. "We all dust in the eyes of the Lord." He gestured with a big arm, sweeping over the white lines of markers, the dead in their thousands. "This place here just like Heaven, Colonel. Everybody equal. No man's stone bigger than his brother's. Every man get fair treatment. See what I'm saying?" He looked at me again. "But people don't come back. Everybody just be forgot. That's the way of the world."

"I'll come back."

The workman smiled. "I be happy to see it."

I smiled, too, for a moment. "You don't believe me."

He shrugged. "No offense, now. I mean, maybe you come back here for a while. Then you forgets. That how it supposed to be. It all right. He still be your friend up in Heaven. Hear every word you say. Hear you right now."

"We shall not see his like again."

The workman nodded slowly. With immeasurable gentleness. "Now, that's pretty." He turned and the sun gripped him. One of his eyes looked as though milk had been poured over it. It was the sort of thing you notice right away. If you're awake.

Suddenly, I felt disgusted. With myself and with the world. I felt I was missing big things all around me. But I had no idea what those things might be. I felt stupid and angry.

"Listen here now, Colonel, sir. You ever needs anything round here, you just axe for old Rickie York. Anything at all. Hear?"

"Thanks."

"You just takes your time now." He shuffled toward the shade. "And God bless you."

There was no more time. I had to go back to work. Then pick up Tish's present before the shop closed. And waste time meeting an old friend who was not a friend anymore, because I did not have what it took to say, "Fuck off, Em. You never even return my phone calls. I'm going home to wish my girl a happy birthday."

I felt I should do something else for General Farnsworth. But the human repertoire is limited.

The heat was terrible and my eyes had begun to ache. I looked down into the grave and said, "I'll come back."

The Ivy Club is two blocks from the White House and the suits that go in and out fit perfectly at the shoulders but not at the waist. Instead of a doorman, the club has a human catcher's mitt. He looked at my uniform as though I had wandered over from the delivery entrance.

"I'm here to meet Emerson Carroll."

"Of course, sir. Mr. Carroll expects you in our bar. Do you know your way around the club, sir? The bar is on the second level."

Worn-down Persians on the floor. Museum woodwork. Smell of steamed vegetables and wax.

It was Tuesday evening and the club was nearly empty. Em sat alone in the bar, smoking a cigar over whiskey. He had been a terrible sight at the burial ceremony, and even in this softer light, his face looked ruined. I don't know whether I had been more surprised by the speed of his physical decline or by the fact that he had bothered to turn up at Farnsworth's graveside. Emerson Carroll was a second-tier player edging toward first-tier status. He was big stuff in this town. Dead generals were of no use to anybody.

"You look like Cornelius Vanderbilt," I said.

Em did not get up. He smiled without showing his teeth, and I could smell the whiskey. One of the fundamental rules of social biology is that hard liquor is especially tough on golden boys. He swept his fingers back over his ashen hair, briefly tightening the skin on his forehead. He did not offer me his hand.

"John, I do not believe for a moment that you have the slightest idea how Cornelius Vanderbilt actually looked. Sit down." He had a legacy accent from a New England China-trade family. As a lieutenant, he had been daring and fun, full of wicked stories about the Kennedy kids. He had joined the Army to piss off his father, but the novelty had faded after a single tour of duty. For all that, he had possessed a gift for soldiering, for leading. And he tossed it.

At first, we kept in touch. But the comms broke down over

the years. I saw his name in the papers. Sometimes in the political gossip, otherwise in the business columns. By the time I was assigned to Washington, Emerson Carroll was Grand Poobah for Government Relations at Macon-Bolt Industries, the largest defense contractor in the world. He was also a player on every defense panel and foreign relations committee on the Potomac. He invited me to one party. The men talked to the Congressmen they were buying and the women whispered about the Congressmen who were buying them. I failed to measure up.

Now here we were. A shaken fat man at a funeral, Em had begged me to come. He seemed to have regained his composure in the meantime. Maybe it was the booze.

"I thought you had to be dead to join this place."

Em shrugged. "It helps. But it's not a requirement." He noticed me looking at the cigar. "Like one?"

"I still don't smoke."

"Cigars don't count."

"It all counts."

His mouth was as narrow as a knife scar. "Ever the puritan. Although not in all things, as I recall. You'd do fine in this administration, actually. The President has marvelous negative capability." He stubbed the cigar into the ashtray. "Montecristo. Never the same if you relight them. Drink?"

I ordered a beer. Em tapped his glass for another whiskey.

He settled back in his chair and stared at me. "Well," he said finally, "you're looking well, John. All that clean living. Still run every day?"

"What's on your mind, Em? Or do burials just make you nostalgic?"

"Don't be a shit," Em said finally. "I *still* consider you a friend, John. If a neglected one. Town does that to people, you know. Get all caught up in this government business. Incredibly inefficient, the way we run this country. Never enough time for the important things." He considered his ruined cigar.

"Got it. So what do you want?" I had a special grudge against Em these days. I was one of the legion of staff officers sweating blood to keep an underfunded Army alive, while Em's corporation was about to sell the Department of Defense an airplane that even the official estimates said would cost us two hundred billion over the next ten years—which meant three hundred billion, minimum.

The Next-Generation Fighter-Bomber was going to do everything perfectly. It would be the most capable, survivable, and lethal aircraft in history. Except for the fact that we did not need it and could not afford it, the NGFB looked like a great deal for America. Corporate welfare as an art form.

We had soldiers and their familes on food stamps, living in pits. We didn't have training dollars and our medical care had collapsed to the Spanish-American War level. The threats on the international horizon were thugs with old Kalashnikovs and mass murderers with Elvis haircuts and peekaboo terrorists. There was no mission in sight for Em's three-hundred-billion-dollar airplane. If one popped up unexpectedly, we already had enough techno-junk to do the job. We were short of the dull stuff that mattered. Like infantrymen and trucks. The NGFB was going to break the defense budget. But Congress was going to fund it. Bugger the troops. You could feel the vote coming.

Just in case Senator Schweinefleisch got nervous, Macon-Bolt Industries was running full-page ads in the big dailies telling the country what a bargain the NGFB would be for the national defense and for mankind. It was going to keep America's sons and daughters alive. The Army and Marines would not even need to deploy. The NGFB would bomb the global village with voodoo precision. The "public service" ads were a business expense that would be charged back to the taxpayers by way of the NGFB's funding. It was the ultimate self-licking ice-cream cone.

Macon-Bolt also happened to be the nation's biggest campaign contributor. To both parties. And to every PAC with a downtown address. For insurance, the corporation's CEO, Bob Nechestny, had loaded his boardroom with retired generals and admirals who showed up once a year to earn their half a mil. They slimed through the Pentagon in not-quite-right suits, just dropping by to say hi to their former subordinates. The Mexicans had their style of corruption, we had ours.

Em shifted in his chair. "All right. Look. I'm sorry. I've been a bastard. The original thankless friend. But I do have some questions I'd like to ask you, John. Things . . . I can't ask just anybody." He looked at me with an intensity that brought back memories of better times. "I'm asking for your help. At least for the loan of an ear. I'm asking in an unaccustomed spirit of humility. You may be the only person left I can trust."

I knew Em was a con and I put my guard right back up. I wondered how many questions he had. I kept flashing on Tish and the birthday present in the trunk of my car and on sex. A snort of mortality always makes me want sex.

"I can't do an all-night bullshit session, Em. I've got something scheduled."

Em waved that away. "Won't take long. Give me half an hour." He shifted and straightened his tie. Suddenly, he looked like he was having a bad time on the witness stand. "John . . . do you know anything about the blast at that French aircraft research site yesterday?"

"The bombing?"

"Was it a bombing?"

I shrugged and drank. The beer tasted good, but I could get a beer anywhere. "So the newspapers seem to think."

"I'm not interested in what the newspapers think. Don't

give me that." Voice cold now. Impatient. Very much the corporate muckety-muck. Em was not steady on course tonight.

"Come on, Em. You want classified information? From me? I don't owe you anything, and I don't break the rules."

"I'm cleared. For Christ's sake, John. I have clearances for programs you don't even know exist. Defense industry has—"

"No way, pal. Call one of your four-star butt boys. Anyway, France isn't my turf. I don't work current intel anymore. I'm just trying to make sure we've still got an Army left when you're done grabbing the money."

"Just tell me what people are saying around the Building. What's the scuttlebutt?"

Then I got it. Or thought I did. "That's cold, Em. Pretty goddamned grim. That lab was your competition, right? The French aircraft industry." I laughed. "You blow it up yourselves? Or just have a streak of good luck?"

Em didn't rise to it. He leaned closer with his wrecked face. I imagined a different sort of life for him then, not all successes and corporate perks.

"*Please,* John. I need you to come through for me on this. It's more important than you can imagine. Very sensitive stuff. Can't you give me *any* insight?"

The answer was no. I had seen the footage on CNN, read the *Post* in the morning, and scanned the Early Bird. A high-security aircraft research facility outside Toulouse had been flattened by a bomb. Midmorning, for maximum employee attendance. Hundreds dead, including some high rollers. Oklahoma City, with red wine for lunch. But I had not read any intel traffic on it.

"All I've got is the POAC stuff," I told him. "Wisdom from the locker room. Same line you're hearing from the media. Algerians. FIS crowd. Bombs for Allah. The frogs have their hands full. 'The Empire Strikes Back.' "

Em finished his whiskey and briefly held up a finger in the direction of the bar. "Want another?"

I shook my head. I was not going to play happy hour at the O-Club with him.

"Keep me posted on this one. Anything you hear. Will you do that, John? It's more important than I can tell you right now."

"I didn't think the French were serious competition for you boys."

"They're not. Can't even build the designs they steal. Country's nothing but a museum."

"So why the interest?"

"It's not about competition."

"What *is* it about?"

"I can't tell you." A bitter look passed over Em's face. "And you don't want to know." He reached for his wallet. The effort popped sweat onto his forehead. "Here." He handed me a card. "This number's unlisted. Use it."

"Em, you've just moved from treating an old friend like shit to treating him like a dumb shit. Why should I help you out on this? Or on anything? So Macon-Bolt can extort an extra twenty or thirty billion from the taxpayer? I don't do Washington intrigue. And I don't trust you."

The bartender hovered again. Em smiled. "It really is good to see you," he told me. "Like old times. You always had that charming crusader streak." Which is why, he seemed to say, you're still only a lieutenant colonel in the Army.

"Okay," I said. "My turn. Just to satisfy my curiosity. What brought you to the Farnsworth show? I figured a major general would be flying way below your radar coverage."

"For Christ's sake, John. Farnsworth and I go way back." His eyes switched to the direct-fire mode. "All three of us do. You and I both owed the guy. Any other battalion XO in the Army would've court-martialed our asses. You would've never even made captain and the DIS boys would've yanked my clearance forever."

"You don't exactly ooze gratitude these days."

Em looked genuinely surprised. "John . . . Farnsworth and I were *friends*. Well . . . maybe not what *you*'d call friends. We didn't take the blood oath of the Templars. But I've seen quite a lot of him these past months."

That answer did not track. I had not worked directly for Farnsworth in the Pentagon, but our projects overlapped and we saw each other often. He and Mary regularly invited me to their home for dinner. At least until Tish entered the picture. Mary did not approve of Tish. But the general had never said a word about seeing Em again. Em's corporation was the Dark Side, out to reduce the Army to a ceremonial battalion so the Department of Defense could buy more solid gold toys with wings.

"He never told me that he'd seen you."

Em did not meet my eyes. "Special-project sort of thing. You weren't read on."

"Don't give me that secret-handshake crap."

He raised his face. Drawing himself up from a well of thought. "Look, I don't know why he didn't say anything. Don't let it hurt your feelings. I know he thought the world of you. He was proud of you. But the project stuff was for real. In fact, that's already more than I should've told you."

"It doesn't track." I looked away from him and stared into the windows of the building across the street. The last office workers were stuffing their briefcases.

"John?" Em said after a pause. "Please. Just close that particular folder. There's something else I need to ask you. It's . . . something even more important."

He looked ten years older than he should have. Maybe fifteen. He played with his empty glass.

"John . . . do you believe in redemption?"

"What?"

"Redemption."

"As in God and repentance and forgiveness?"

"Not exactly. I mean, yes. But in the here and now. Do you think we can atone for the things we've done wrong?"

"What kind of things?"

"Bad things."

His hands were shaking. When he saw me looking, he folded them together. But the flesh still trembled.

"Jesus Christ, Em."

I thought he was going to break down on the spot. But the air changed again. He sat up. And smiled. A smile carved into the face of a corpse. He nodded toward the entrance to the bar.

A young woman in a blue dress had stopped at the head of the stairs. Framing herself in the doorway so we could admire her. The dress was slight—a breeze would have dissolved it—and her legs looked as long as a politician's list of excuses. She carried a wispy briefcase. Her features were the precise sort that make you suspect old families of selectively killing their infants to improve the breed. Hair blond, worn short. No jewelry. Not the kind of girl whose labels stick up at the back of her neck.

She extended her pose for a few seconds before starting toward us. Theater, with plausible denial.

Em stood up. I followed his example. Without losing his smile, he whispered, "She's getting ready to leave me. You get to know the signs."

All I could think was: That girl doesn't need Em.

"Corry, I'd like you to meet John Reynolds, my old Army buddy. John, Corry Nevers."

She turned out to be shorter than the impression she created. She gave me her hand. It was dry and cool. "Emerson's told me ever so much about you."

"Corry's on Senator Faust's staff. She's absolutely in charge of defense policy on the Hill."

I glanced at my watch. Thinking of Tish. More anxious than ever to leave.

"Why don't you two just sit down and get acquainted," Em said. "You always appreciated good wine, John. Corry's a wine drinker, too. I'll go search out something a bit better than the bar blend."

And he left me with her. As soon as he cleared the doorway, she leaned in, breath vanilla, and said, "You don't look old enough to be Emerson's Army buddy."

It was one of those times when you want to say something clever and fail to say anything at all.

She leaned closer. "I suppose he's going on about his redemption thing again." She showed perfect white teeth the way another woman might have flashed thigh. "He's turning into such a bore."

One of the best things in life is a lover who is genuinely glad to see you walk in. Tish gave me a real kiss and the zipper line on her jeans plowed into my crotch.

"Happy birthday to me," she said.

"Happy birthday, Tish."

"I was afraid you wouldn't get home before I had to go."

I could smell the dinner she had made to celebrate her own birthday. "Sorry. I had to stop by and see a friend. Serious stuff."

We had not been together long enough for things to be spoiled.

"Oh? Who?" Asked with that innocence she had preserved through some miracle. Despite her choice of occupations and the tattoo on her shoulder. She hugged me again. "Sometimes I just want to squeeze you."

"Emerson Carroll. Doubt I ever mentioned him. Not really

a friend anymore. Ancient history. We used to get into trouble together."

Tish laughed. "I can't imagine you ever getting into trouble. Mr. Perfect."

"We were all young once."

Tish put on a ridiculously serious look. "You're *still* young."

The ten years' difference in our ages was a sensitive point with her. Tish did not care, but her friends were shits. About a lot of things.

"Well, old Em isn't. He's got one foot in the grave. Drinker. Big success at all the wrong things. You wouldn't approve."

"I like your friends." Which was true. Tish liked everybody. And I wished more of my friends liked her. The guys leered, while their wives closed ranks against Tish's age, and her chopped red hair, and the cat leanness of her. And the music.

"Listen, cowgirl. I want you to just turn around and face away from the door. And stay there. No peeking. I've got to get something out of the car."

She turned around as smartly as a recruit, then stood with a knee cocked and one hip higher than the other. I wanted to carry her upstairs.

I went out to the car and got her present. When I came back in she was still standing at ease.

"Okay. Turn around."

Tish had been playing the guitar since she was a kid in Indiana and she would have known this was a Gibson and the approximate model just from the shape of the case. But she was still going to get a surprise when she lifted the lid.

"John," she said. Her eyes went hyper-alive.

"Well, check it out. And happy birthday."

She undid the latches like a kid tearing off wrapping paper. Then she knelt before the opened guitar coffin, a Buddhist in front of an altar. She did not even touch the instrument.

"John . . . is that . . . ?"

"An original. For the most original woman I know."

She touched it then. Stroking the neck. Ebony fingerboard, mother-of-pearl insets. It was an old Les Paul Gibson, the rocker's equivalent of a Stradivarius. Finally, she lifted it out of the case. A Les Paul is awkward to hold unless you've got it strapped over your shoulder. Tish just clutched it against her ribs and breasts. Without even trying to shape a chord. Then she began to cry.

"Nobody's ever been so good to me," she said. "Not in all my life. Nobody."

We lay in bed with the dinner downstairs waiting. Whatever might have been incomprehensible to others about the John and Tish Show, there were plenty of good things on the program. The twilight came in the window and her white flesh shone.

"I wish I didn't have to play tonight," she said.

"Me, too."

"I've got to get going."

"Right."

She rolled closer and I held her. My nose touching the little line of earrings.

"Thank you," she said.

"Taking it with you tonight?"

"I didn't mean about the guitar. Thanks for being you. But thanks for the guitar, too. It's wonderful. You're from Fairy Tale City."

"I'm anxious to hear you play it."

She roiled her skin against me. Cool, a little wet. The ear retreated and hair rushed my mouth.

"I'll play it for you first. I'm not going to take it tonight. I have to get used to it." She flipped onto her back and dropped her head into the pillow. "It's scary, you know that?"

"What's scary?"

"The guitar. It probably cost more than my car."

It had cost a lot more than her car, which had more rust than paint. Tish raised the issue in a voice that had no greed in it, only wonder. She had lived a musician's vow-of-poverty life for a decade. Credit cards maxed out until they were voided. She was not much of a cook, but she meant well and she was a mistress of kitchen economies. Her Telecaster and amp had been her primary possessions. When I met her, she lived in one clean room.

"If you're thinking about your car," I told her, "it means it's broken down again."

I could feel her blushing.

"Can I borrow your car? Just one more time? To make the gig. I'll be careful."

"You know you can borrow the car." I rose onto an elbow, admiring the dark lines and palenesses, not wanting her to go anywhere. "You have time to eat something before you go?"

She rolled toward me and shadows moved against shadows. "I'll get a sandwich at the club. It's free for the band. There's another way I'd rather spend my time."

There were plenty of things that did not match up in our relationship. At the Pentagon, I worked the kind of hours that unions had fought against at the turn of the century. Tish played evenings, or did late shows like tonight. Her friends, who had missed the integrity of the sixties but not the prejudices, wondered what Tish saw in a fascist baby-killer. My friends were convinced they knew exactly what I went for in Tish. We blew them all off and stole every moment we could between the end of my workday and the beginning of hers. We lived for the weekend afternoons.

We met in one of those Georgetown book-and music stores where the clerks dress in black and spend their lives waiting for a break in their "real" occupation. It was after work and I was in uniform, picking up my fourth copy of Marianne Faithfull's *Broken English*. It was The Recording Nobody Ever Returned.

I noticed Tish. Couldn't miss her. Picking through the discs with that red hair and a cast-off undertaker's suit that was the thrift shop's answer to Armani. But it took me only a few seconds to file her under What-do-you-do-with-the-body-in-the-morning?

She was the one who got things started.

"Excuse me," she said. "You might not like that one."

I looked at her as though she had slapped me.

"I mean," she said, "like . . . you don't look . . . I mean, have you ever *heard* that? It's uh . . . colorful. I mean, I just wanted to be . . ."

A Gen X girl scout, helping me across the musical street.

"I bought my first copy of it on LP," I said. "In Germany. In 1979."

"I'm sorry. I wasn't trying to be rude. I mean . . ."

With an emotional sunburn on her face, Tish pushed a flame of hair behind her ear and stared at me. Waiting for punishment. When I got her full face and read the eyes, there was a vulnerability to her that made me soften my voice.

"You a Marianne Faithfull fan?" I asked her.

"Are you kidding? She's a *god*. That's her all-time greatest. It's one of the best albums ever. If I could just make one recording like that . . ."

We had coffee where they knew her and she asked me to come hear her band. The music was good enough, but not great. Tish played with passion that veered into frustration, as if she could not move the music from her soul to her fingers without losing the best of it. I told her I had enjoyed myself. And it was true. I had enjoyed watching her. She had the look, if not the gift. I pegged her as one of those minor talents damned to appreciate greatness without possessing it.

I liked the feel of the air around her. I admired her earnestness and loved the mick hair. In the beginning, I also got off on spiting her friends. Who imagined me grinding innocents between my jaws. She, in her patchy naivete, wore a *little* black dress that showed the blue guitar tattoo on her shoulder to Mary Farnsworth's dinner guests. Then she compounded her sin with a heartfelt comment about Newt Gingrich. Nobody bothered to learn that she also did volunteer work with inner-city kids and loved nineteenth-century English novels, accepting each word with the avidity of a child. We taped every BBC miniseries so we could watch them together. At night she held me as if I were the only man in the world.

"Got to go," my birthday girl said at last, kissing me once and rising.

"Wake me when you get home."

She showered and went out with her hair wet.

I listened to her footsteps on the pavement, then I listened to the city sounds. Bus grunting to a stop on the corner, dropout moms laughing with each other as they strolled home to Indian country. The urban surf of cars. Sirens. A boom box proclaiming doomed identity. The air-conditioning unit kicked back in. Capitol Hill, America's ground zero.

I pulled on my shorts in the darkness and went downstairs. Tish had made vegetarian lasagna for her birthday dinner and I fetched my plate from the setting she had arranged on the kitchen table.

There was a note under the plate. It said:

This isn't my real birthday anymore.
My life started over the day I met you.

It struck me that I should have gone to hear her play on her birthday. But my mornings started early, and we had worked out our patterns. I went to the important Saturday-night gigs. And Tish understood. But I sat there over her make-this-last-until-payday lasagna and felt as though I had failed her.

I put my food down the garbage disposal so she would think I had eaten it, and went back to bed.

More city sounds. A domestic scene in the yard of a house two doors down that had been turned into rental units. An automobile alarm. Faint jazz from a neighbor.

I could not stop thinking about Farnsworth. And about Em. I could smell Tish on the sheets, and missed the feel of her. The best nights of my life were those when she was not working. Yet I could not imagine a long-term future with her.

I lay there awake, sensing great things moving beyond my range of vision. Except for the hour with Tish, it had been a very bad day.

When I did crash, I crashed hard. I have no idea how long the doorbell had been ringing before it registered on me. I jerked up. Tish had a habit of forgetting her keys. Or her wallet. Or the be-on-time watch I had given her at Christmas. I found my shorts again and pounded downstairs, yelling, *"Coming."*

I yanked open the door and found myself an arm's length from Em's girl. She stood in the cast of the hall light, still perfect, wearing the same tease-the-peasants blue dress. But her eyes had changed.

"Em's dead," she said. "They killed him. Help me."

CHAPTER 2

Hysteria comes in almost as many varieties as love. I had seen it in men lightly wounded, and in refugees with dead families and burning houses behind them, in mobs and in mosques. Hysteria was part of the scenery in the post-Cold War Army. In Corry Nevers, hysteria took one of its quieter forms. She trembled, inhumanly taut, and could not answer a question until the third time it had been asked. Then she cascaded words.

She and Em had gone over to Lespinasse for dinner. For high rollers only, the restaurant was just off Sixteenth Street, well within the downtown safety zone centered on the White House. But as they walked back to Em's car, two men stepped out of a doorway. They had guns and said they wanted wallets. They shot Em several times and ran, empty-handed, leaving Corry screaming on the sidewalk. In another triumph for the mayor's imperial guard, the cops took her in and yelled at her for a couple of hours just in case she was the killer.

She was so spooked that she begged me to let her come

upstairs while I got dressed. Whenever I made an unexpected move, she quivered like a hammered board. I sat her down in the kitchen and made tea, which she did not drink.

I wished I had been a bit nicer to Em the evening before.

Corry did not meet my eyes. The tightness in her threatened an explosion.

"I can't believe it," she muttered again. "I still can't believe it. I should've—"

"Nothing you could've done. Listen . . . just tell me something, okay? Why did you come to me?"

"What?"

"How did you even know where I live?"

She stirred the tea she had not drunk. Gripping the spoon so hard her fingers mottled.

"What brought you to me, Corry?"

Surprise molded her face. "Em trusted you. He talked about you. A great deal. More and more often. He told me . . . he said I could count on you. If there were any problems." Her facial muscles hit trouble. "I thought he was crazy." Tears. It occurred to me that these were the first I had seen. "I mean, he couldn't have known what was going to happen." Her wet eyes searched. "Could he?"

One bad day was spilling into another. I had been hard on Em and I did not like myself very much. And I did not much like Corry Nevers. Maybe it was jealousy. Even now, she had a classic feel Tish would never possess. Tish turned heads. Corry Nevers changed lives.

"I'm afraid to go home," she said. "I know it's wrong. But I feel like they'll be waiting for me. That they might know where I live. I'm the only witness."

Random-victim thugs did not work like that. Dully, I asked her, "Were they wearing masks or anything? You get a good look at them?" The words did not penetrate. I was ready to ask again when I heard familiar footsteps on the sidewalk.

Tish let herself in and hurried into the kitchen. With all the lights on, she must have assumed I had stayed up to greet her. When she saw Corry, she really saw her.

"And who," Tish asked, "is this?"

"*I*'ll drive her home," Tish said. "You need to sleep."

I had gone upstairs to get my wallet with my driver's license. Tish followed me, in a heavy metal mood.

"Tish . . . she's scared. She'd probably feel safer if I took her."

Tish rolled her eyes operatically, but settled them back on me. "Scared? I guarantee you, that girl hasn't been scared since the day she was born. God, you're so blind sometimes."

I smiled. "Keep your voice down, okay?"

Tish leaned over the bed. "I know what she's up to."

"For Christ's sake, Tish. Her boyfriend just got gunned down in the street. She watched the man die. She might be just a little spooked."

Tish punched her fists into her hips. "Yeah? Well, how come the first thing she does is take a taxi to the house of some guy she just met? I mean, she's efficient. I'll say that for her."

"She explained that."

"I'll bet she did."

"If you want to come along for the ride . . ."

"Why can't *I* drive her home? Just what would be so terrible about that?" Tish shook her head. "I swear to God, John. Maybe you've been all around the world, but sometimes you don't understand a thing."

"Got to go."

Tish changed the climate. "Wait. *Please*. Yeah, okay. I'm jealous. Who wouldn't be?" Celtic eyes programmed for suffering. "I mean . . . I can't wait to get home. I'm just thinking about it all night, you know? And I walk in. And there's my guy all snuggly with Miss Ritz-Carlton . . ."

"Tish, I have no interest . . ."

"John, you don't *know* what you have an interest in. That first night . . . you didn't think you were interested in me, either."

"Tish . . . it's almost four in the morning."

She crossed her arms. "Exactly. If you went to bed right now, you could sleep for a little over an hour. And I guarantee you, she and your buddy were shacked up in far Northwest. Five bucks says there's a river view. You'd never get back in time."

The truth was that I ached to sleep. Too much had happened too quickly. I could not quite grasp the world around me. And Tish was dead on: Em's place was way up in Northwest. Long drive from Capitol Hill, even in off hours.

"Don't just drop her off. Go in with her, make sure she feels safe. She really is scared."

"I'll hold her little hand," Tish said.

All my career, I had been trained to pay attention to my instincts. Now, when it counted, I ignored them. All I said was, "Call me if anything seems out of whack, okay?"

Tish gave me a pitying look. "John, I swear. You really do need somebody to protect you from the big bad world."

Corry Nevers accepted the change in chauffeurs without comment, but I sensed that she did not like it much. She had used the time Tish and I spent arguing to reconstruct herself into the kind of woman who walks out of a K Street elevator and looks right through any man who doesn't make a couple of hundred thousand a year.

On the way out the door, she took me by the hand. The eyes that had been indigo an hour before had faded back to ice-water blue.

"Thank you," she said. "You've been wonderfully understanding. Em was right about you."

She held on to my hand just long enough to really piss Tish off.

By the time I got back into bed, I had less than an hour before it was time to hit the shower and pull on a uniform again. I flopped on my belly and went out hard.

I thought it was the alarm clock. But it was the phone. By the time I figured it out, I had knocked the clock onto the floor and nearly took out a lamp.

"Hello?"

It was Tish. Her tone woke me the rest of the way. Then I registered the screaming in the background.

"*John,*" Tish said. "You've got to get over here. *Hurry.*"

"Where are you? What's the matter?"

Tish was shouting now, but not into the phone. "What's the goddamned address? Tell me the goddamned address."

"Tish. It's all right. I've got Em's address. Calm down. What happened?"

Tish sobered her voice. But I got the deep fear in it. "John, just *hurry*. You need to see this."

"What is it? You called the police? What—"

"I *can't* call the police," Tish said, but the words did not sink in. All I registered was her panic. "I *need* you."

"Tish, you've got my car."

"Call a cab. Anything. *Please.*"

"Buddy," the detective told me, "you're trying my patience." He had badged me and introduced himself as Detective Lieutenant Dickey. His name almost made me like him for a fraction of a sliver of a millisecond.

"I can almost buy the blondie running to you for career counseling after her boyfriend gets popped." He wiped the back of his hand across his chin. "People do stupid things under stress. And I can figure out how the downstairs neighbor hears more than he needs to and stumbles in on this and winds up giving blood.'' He looked around the bedroom where he had isolated me for questioning. Like all of the rooms in Em's apartment, it had been destroyed. Walls knocked in, hardwood floors torn up. Quite a job for one night. ''I can even understand,'' the detective continued, ''why your old lady drives blondie home. Oh, I got that, all right.'' He pulled his chair closer to mine. ''But what I still don't get is why she calls *you* before she calls the police.'' He made a seen-it-all face. ''In this town, mister, you call the cops when you got a problem. You don't call the Army. So how about inviting me into the information age and telling me where you fit in here?''

I would have told him where I fit in, if I had known. I thought I was sitting in a chair. Just as I had thought I was just having a drink with an old friend the night before. In the reality I had not yet figured out, I was tumbling down one flight of stairs after another. As for calling the D.C. cops, the detective had a weak grip on reality. The locals were as scared of the police as they were of the criminals.

''I've told you everything I can think of,'' I said. ''You said yourself people under stress make bad judgment calls. Tish probably figured I'd know what to do.''

The detective looked at me as though he had caught me with a gun in my hand and I was trying to convince him it was a flower.

''Buddy,'' he said, ''your girlfriend does not strike me as the helpless type.''

Em's lost world lay all around me. Antiques smashed, pillows slashed. Drawers emptied onto the floor. I did not see anything that might have belonged to Corry. They could not have been together long.

Another plainclothesman half knocked and came in. Carrying papers. Dickey looked at him, and the plainclothesman smiled.

"Interesting crew, Lieutenant. Check out the redhead's record."

Tish never said anything to me about a police record.

The detective took the papers and made a performance out of looking at them. He clucked and shook his head, smiling a little smile that made me want to knock him out of his chair. I wanted to know about Tish, and he knew it.

"Well, Colonel. Looks like you're a model citizen. Not even a speeding ticket. So how'd you get mixed up with Miss O'Malley? I take it . . . you do know about Miss O'Malley's record?"

"I know all I need to know about her," I lied.

"And you don't care that she pleaded guilty to cocaine possession? That she hasn't been off probation a year? Tell you the truth, she should've done time, considering the amount." He smiled again. "But she's a looker, I guess. If you go for that long, lean type. Figure she knew what she had to do. Got a 'Suspicion Of Receiving Stolen Goods' in there, too. But you would've known all about that."

Tish had buzzed me in the front door. When I came in, she was sitting in a broken chair, staring at the body. Corry Nevers had bunched herself in the corner. All screamed out, sobbing and shaking. I called the cops immediately, too thick to wonder why the intruders had left the phone working.

Tish dropped her tough-girl act and I held her until the police arrived. She kept her back turned to the body and trembled.

There was nothing I could do for Corry. I let her sob.

I've seen corpses. Not as many as some other soldiers with a couple of decades of paper in their 201 files, but more than most Cold War commandos. I can recognize a strong hand and a clean kill. One slash across the throat had nearly taken the old man's head off.

Lot of blood in a human being.

The cops straightened out Corry long enough to learn that the dead man was the downstairs neighbor. Poor bugger probably heard noises he could not explain, and he was from a generation that did not ignore a neighbor's troubles.

I looked at the detective and said, "If you need to keep me here, I'd like to call in to work and let them know I'm not AWOL."

Dickey put his hands on his knees. As if to rise. But he did not get up.

"Buddy," he said, "you got a connection to two murders. And you got a girlfriend with a sheet. But I don't want you to worry about that. I want you to just go and put on a nice clean uniform and protect us all from the Russians or the Serbians or the fucking Canadians or whoever's coming this week." He shoved a hand back over scraps of hair. "You can go."

"What about Ms. O'Malley? She hasn't done anything."

The detective laughed. "How about interfering with the scene of a crime? Maybe even an obstruction of justice count, if I write it up smart. We even got a 'Failure To Notify' ordinance here in the District." He waved a hand. Swatting a fly. "Get her out of here. And keep her off the powder, okay?"

"And Ms. Nevers? What happens to her?"

The detective judged me again. "Thinking about trading up?"

"She's all alone."

He grinned. "A woman like that's only alone if she wants to be."

I moved to leave. But Detective Dickey was not done saying goodbye.

"Hey, soldier boy. You probably think I'm the shits. Useless fucking D.C. cop, right? Well, how about *you* try to keep this town clean with no budget and nobody gives a damn." He gave me a smile of hatred. "You guys with your million-dollar toilet seats."

They were holding Tish in the entranceway. As I walked out, two fat men in white were loading a body bag onto a stretcher while a cop ate an Egg McMuffin.

"You never told me you had a police record," I said. The morning traffic crept along Massachusetts.

Tish put her face down into her hands. "Please. Could we talk about it later?"

The Volvo idling in front of me had a bumper sticker that said, "My child is an honor student at Barksdale Pre-School."

"Yeah," I said, shifting up into second. "Later."

Tish was crying. "You want me to get out?"

We hit another light.

"I don't know what I want," I told her honestly.

She touched my forearm, then quickly removed her hand. As if she had scorched it. I kept my eyes on the traffic. But I got the peripheral of her lowered head. Hung by the seat belt.

"It wasn't my coke," she said. "And the stereo stuff. I was seeing a guy who turned out to be a bastard. He was using my place as a stash. I didn't know about the dope. Or that his gear was stolen. I swear to God. I didn't know, John. He kept the coke in a locked suitcase. He was dealing out of my place when I was at gigs. I didn't know, I didn't *know*." Her body shook. "I'm so stupid. He screwed me over so bad."

Her hand stirred, lifted, retreated. Horns blared when a car did not respond instantaneously to a changed light.

"You lied to me," I said.

"I *didn't* lie."

"Silence is lying."

She wept bitterly. "I didn't want to lose you. I was afraid. Can't you under*stand?*"

It was my turn to be silent.

"Didn't you . . . didn't you ever fall for the wrong person?" Tish asked. "Didn't you ever make a mistake? Not even once?"

A smacked-in Dodge cut me off and I hit the brakes.

"Maybe I did," I told her.

When I got into work, the guys were gathered around the television in our conference room.

"How can that motherfucker *say* that?" Scottie had just come back from Bosnia, where he had lost two soldiers to a land mine because the Army could not afford decent mine detectors.

The SecDef was on C-SPAN, testifying before the Senate Armed Services Committee. Except for Scottie's outburst, the room was morbidly quiet.

". . . no doubt in the minds of the experts, Senator. Our military needs that aircraft. And by maintaining the projected purchase quantity, we can maximize per-unit affordability. It's going to cost us, but the services are prepared to sacrifice. In terms of the American lives it's going to save on tomorrow's battlefields, the Next-Generation Fighter-Bomber is a bargain."

Colonel Maurey switched off the set. The boss, a full colonel, silver eagles and a brush cut. "All right. Back to work. Let's just try to keep the world together until the wonder-plane comes on line."

It was heartbreaking to hear the SecDef tell such a big lie. Every one of us knew we did not need that airplane and that it would break the defense budget. When you got them alone, even the Air Force and Navy pilots would admit it. But they wanted it anyway, enraptured by the technology. Invisible to radar, intercontinental reach, max payload, protective suite right out of Star Wars. The Navy would get a carrier variant. The generals and admirals were like middle-aged guys who buy Porsches when they really need family vans.

I followed Colonel Maurey into his office and gave him the

highlights of the past twenty-four hours. He was the kind of man who could have had good suits and a corner office. Instead, he wore a polyester uniform and manned a battered desk in a windowless cubbyhole.

He leaned back in his chair and said, "How much time do you need?"

"Sir, I'd like to take leave through the end of the week. Go to my buddy's funeral. Visit Mary Farnsworth, see if there's anything I can do. Think a little."

"What's on your work calendar?"

"We're clean on the suspenses. Future Conflict NIE's on track. Nick can cover the attaché reception for me. I was going to catch the shuttle down to TRADOC on Friday, but that was just for hand-holding."

"E-mail me the leave form." He put his hands behind his head. "Sounds like you're having some run of bad luck, John. Be a little careful, okay?"

"Yes, sir."

"So how was Farnsworth's ceremony? I got held up in the Watch."

I shrugged. "Chief came, Secretary didn't. Standard mix of regret and crocodile tears. Less than he deserved."

"Farnsworth . . . will be missed," Maurey said. From his mouth, those four words carried more punch than a full-page obit in the *Post*. "Call me if you need anything."

"If you need anything at all," I told Mary Farnsworth, "just call me. Please."

She looked at me gently. As though I were the one in need of comfort. Mary was a member of what Southerners call "The Other Aristocracy," and she had a fineness that would have shamed a queen. She was the only person I knew who poured coffee from silver for every visitor.

"I appreciate your thoughtfulness, John. But there's nothing, I'm afraid."

At that point, anyone else would have fallen back into tears. Not Mary. She sat erectly and spoke with the same precision with which she transferred a lump of sugar to her cup. Maintaining the calm that had always been such a contrast to the hurricane she married.

I sipped my coffee and scanned the room, half expecting to find things changed. But everything was exactly as I remembered it. Antiques from Mary's family, their wood so dark it was almost black. And Farnsworth's "Buffalo Soldiers" print above the fireplace, bad art well meant, tolerated by Mary. Farnsworth had been born in 1947 in a shack not twenty miles from the mansion Mary's family had built during Reconstruction, when corruption briefly crossed the color line. His father had worked a mule, while her mother rode Arabians. Farnsworth had been a big man, a West Point defensive lineman, and Mary had a deceptive look of fragility. Their married life had been a long smile, yet they had no children. Only the younger officers whose careers Farnsworth had guided.

Mary laughed. "John, you have always been so transparent, even to Mickey. He knew you thought that old print of his was just awful up there. I believe he thought you and I were in league." Before I could respond, she said, "And how is Tish?"

From Mary, this was an olive branch the size of a redwood.

"She's fine."

"I have been unkind to her. My behavior has been small and unforgivable." Her eyes convinced me that brown was the color of mercy. "I suppose Mickey and I have been living in a fool's paradise, surrounded all our adult lives by the military. I suppose we lost touch a bit." She sighed. "Young people these days just seem to approach life so differently." Warm, immaculate Mary. "Do you think Tish will ever forgive me?"

"She means well."

"Don't apologize. I haven't even made an effort to get to know her. And she's your girl. Our John's girl."

"She's different. It's only that . . ." The truth was that I did not want to talk about Tish just now.

"Oh, John." And now she came close to tears. "It's just that . . . Mickey and I . . . we were trying to plan your life, too. I thought I knew exactly what kind of girl you needed to marry. Just like Mickey planning your career. I wanted you to marry the perfect wife. And I set myself up as the arbiter of perfection." She touched one eye with a milk-coffee finger. "We meant well, John."

"I'm not married yet."

Mary mastered herself, correcting her posture ever so slightly. She changed the subject with her typical grace. "You must be the tenth caller today. And I dread to think of the evening. But you are the only one whom I believe *want*ed to come. I thank you for that, John."

I almost said that her husband had been a second father to me. Instead, I just asked:

"Made any plans? Or is it too soon?"

Mary turned her head to the side. She was still a beautiful woman and I can only imagine the impression she had made on a young lieutenant home for his first leave. A stopover in Baton Rouge, en route to Vietnam.

"I don't know. It's all so sudden, it's . . ." She disciplined herself again. "More coffee, John? I think I might like to teach again. In the city. Mickey would admire that."

"Mary, I have to ask you something. Did Em Carroll ever come over to the house? Recently, I mean."

Mary's face was open. "Oh, yes. More and more often. I was so glad he and Mickey had gotten over those hard feelings."

"They were friends again?"

"Thick as thieves. And those boys were up to something, let me tell you. They'd just go off into Mickey's study for hours. It started last winter. We hadn't seen Emerson for ages." I sensed her doing her social navigating. "I asked Mickey to invite him to one of our dinners. When you would've been there. For old time's sake. But Mickey said no. Some sort of little boys' secret. Their little club. I did wonder why you weren't included. You all used to be so close."

"Mary . . . do you have any idea what they were up to? It could be important."

I could see by her expression that she did not know. "They seemed to have some sort of project they were working on together. But Mickey never talked about it to me. We rarely talked business."

"Do you know which one of them got in touch with the other first?"

Mary thought for a moment. "I truly couldn't say. Not with certainty. I have this feeling that it was Em. That Em was the one who called Mickey. But I can't be sure."

"Did Em . . . seem happy to you?"

"Em has never seemed happy to me. He's not that sort of man."

"But how did he seem? The same? Changed?"

Mary gave me her eyes straight on. "You mean the drinking? Of course, you can tell that just looking at him. But he didn't drink excessively when he came by. Mickey would not have tolerated it."

"Did he say anything about work? Did he seem unhappy—"

"John, whatever is this about?"

I did not know what it was about. I was searching. With one of those hangovers you get from lack of sleep. I almost told her about Em, but could not shoot the words at her yet. I had my finger on the trigger, though.

Mary broke the silence. "Is something wrong? Is Em in some kind of trouble? That boy was always in one tub of hot water or another. Why, I remember when you—"

"Mary, Em's dead. He was shot down in the street last night. It was in the morning paper."

"That can't be," Mary said. "It's—"

"Mary, I'm sorry. I should've waited to tell you."

"I can't believe it."

"I'm sorry."

"Right after . . ."

I ached to talk about it. To say, Yeah, hell of a coincidence. The stink was already spreading. Even I could smell it, and I'm slow.

The doorbell rang. Mary closed her eyes for a moment before rising.

It was their minister. I excused myself, absorbed in my own riddles, even though I could tell that Mary did not want me to go.

"Call me," she said. "Let me know about Em's funeral."

I did not have the sense to tell her to be careful.

I called Rob Burns—Robert Mayhew Burns—and made an appointment to talk. He was gracious, if baffled by my impatience. He could not see me until six. So I drove to kill time. I did not want to go home. Not even to change. I was not ready to face Tish.

Rain swept up from the Chesapeake. Summer in the District. Rain comes down, steam goes up. I had to turn on the air full blast to keep the windows clear. Finally, I pulled into one of those scenic-view lots along the Virginia side of the river and sat. Even in the rain, there were joggers out from the Pentagon. I let the windows cloud.

Rob Burns belonged to one of those dug-in D.C. families whose members never run for office. They take law degrees, or maybe a Poli-Sci doctorate, and enter government under the wing of a mentor. The family had produced four cabinet members in a hundred years. Rob was a few years younger than I was and had already done two years as an Assistant Secretary of Defense before the administration changed. I had dated his sister—no, his sister had dated me—for a couple of months. Until I realized she was just checking a block, sleeping with a soldier the way some people sleep with a person of another race, just to find out what it's like. She rode in the hunts out in western Loudon and Fauquier counties and did not regard me as her intellectual or social equal. She was probably right on both counts, but she could not make me like it. I hit it off with Rob, though. Now he was sitting in a think tank on Eighteenth Street, waiting for the electorate to turn again.

I drove back into town against traffic. With the suburban set brutal in the outbound lanes. My uniform soaked with sweat. When I cranked up the air, it just got uglier.

Radio on. Dow up. A jetliner down. First Lady on the edge of indictment. A terminal liberal deplored the SecDef's Hill appearance, asking if all the money we were spending on weapons systems would not be better spent on education and jobs training. He whined, but made sense.

I was beginning to feel like a traitor to my kind.

I went up Fourteenth and cut left. Secretaries dashed through the rain. The homeless milled, oblivious. Men in suits held briefcases over their heads or clashed umbrellas. A taxi had broken down in the middle of Connecticut.

Nine bucks to park the car. The Army still had a no-umbrellas regulation we would not change until the Marines blinked first, so I jogged through the downpour. By the time I reached the lobby of Rob's building, my uniform was clinging to me like an old-fashioned bathing suit.

When the elevator door opened on Rob's floor, the defense attaché from the French embassy was standing there waiting to go down. We had met at a couple of the town's countless receptions, but he gave no sign of recognizing me. Maybe it was my drowned-rat look. Or maybe not. We pushed past each other.

The receptionist was heading out, but she let me pass. Rob's personal secretary laid down her papers and pretended I was worth knowing. Rob waved me in. He sat behind his desk, on the phone, surrounded by signed photos of everybody who had mattered over the past fifteen years. He motioned for me to have a seat.

I stood. Dripping.

"Yeah, Trent," he told the receiver, "I know. But he's got you outmaneuvered on this. Look at the polls. I think you should cut your losses. Right. That's absolutley right. Sorry I can't be more encouraging. Right. See you Friday."

Rob slapped the phone down and looked up. "Hard to make the Hill understand that a majority doesn't mean what it used to. It's like herding cats." He leaned toward the door. "Joanne, I won't need you anymore today, thanks. Leave the coffee on." Sitting back again, he said, "For Christ's sake, have a seat."

"I'm soaking."

"Chairs are replaceable. Friends aren't."

"Thanks for seeing me."

"Any time, any time. Even if I didn't like you, John, I'd make it a point to be seen with you just to piss off my sister."

"How's she doing?"

"Vicky always reminds me of Bob McNamara. Walking proof of the banality of evil. What's on your mind?"

"Saw de La Vere on his way out."

Rob's family ties were to London, not Paris. His private attitude toward the French was very American, and he was always glad to share it with friends:

"Poor buggers have been in a funk ever since Pamela Harriman died. 'Nobody understands them.' De La Vere's on the warpath about the fate of the Eurofighter and the possibility that Macon-Bolt's going to corner the expanded-NATO aircraft market. Bob Nechestny's turning into the king of the world while Dassault and Aerospatiale go down the crapper. You see that picture of Nechestny doing the handshake thing with Havel, by the way? When NATO's new girls get dressed, they're going to wear Macon-Bolt exclusively. Expansion's serious dollars, and the frogs can't compete. And that bombing at their research lab seems to have been quite a blow. Shook de La Vere, you could really tell. Poor sap wanted to know who *I* thought might have done it. Their intel ops must be on the skids, too. Pathetic. Don't deserve their actresses, that what's-her-name. . . ."

"Rob . . . I'd like to ask you something. Just between you and me."

"Ask. You want some coffee? It's probably stale."

I shook my head. "You knew Emerson Carroll, right?"

He frowned. "All too well. Terrible business. Hard on the family. Only son." He ran his fingers down the back side of his tie, freeing it from the tuck at his waist. "Knew Em for ages. Since Sidwell Friends. When Em's father was down here. Early Nixon period. Looking back, I'm not sure my father didn't have an excessive interest in poor Em's mother." His eyes looked at memories. "You know how it goes. Dinner parties, tennis, the usual suspects. Em's father resigned rather suddenly, if you recall. Took the family home to the north pole. Or Harvard, anyway."

"Give me your frank assessment. Of Em. Please."

Rob calculated. "You knew him?"

"Long time ago. We were lieutenants together."

He sat back. "Christ, I never even knew he'd been in the Army. Hard to picture." He cocked his head as if lining up a shot at billiards. "You want the for-real? Okay. But it stays in this office, John." He looked at my wet shirt. "I suppose I didn't share the conventional view of Em. He was supposed to be a comer, but I saw him as already on the way out. Time was when a man could be a drinker in this town, but not anymore. And Em could be surprisingly clumsy. Heavy-handed, just when he thought he was being clever. The way he cornered Senator Faust into hiring his girlfriend, for instance. You can't pull that kind of shit anymore. At least not often. People remember, the bills come due." He smiled. "Girl looks the part, though. I'll say that for her. Freezer blonde, carved legs. Ever meet her?"

I felt so bad I was ready to get up and go. But somebody turned on the batteries in my brain. "Rob, you know everybody and everything in this city . . ."

"You sound like a Congressman who wants something."

"Tell me about Macon-Bolt Industries. What's the view from inside the Beltway?"

He swiveled in his chair. The rain changed direction and smacked his window. I could smell my uniform drying.

"No secrets there. Bob Nechestny's turning into the *éminence grise* of his generation. Think those Indonesians had access? Bob walks into the White House whenever he wants. Or into any office on the Hill. That is one CEO who really brings home the bacon for the shareholders. For which he is recompensed. And, not coincidentally, Macon-Bolt happens to be the biggest campaign contributor in this country. Hard money, soft money. Bob Nechestny could fix anything short of a Supreme Court decision—and I'm not at all sure he couldn't do that, if he really wanted to." Rob smiled. "So . . . you and the rest of the United States Army just pissed about that airplane deal? Or is this personal?"

"Maybe both."

He shook his head. "Well, my advice is to accept the inevitable. You can't beat Bob Nechestny and Macon-Bolt. No point in even trying."

"The NGFB is going to gut the Army budget."

Rob laughed. "And everybody else's budget, too. Somebody whispered in my ear that even the Air Force brass are having second thoughts. Allowing for cost overruns, they're looking at an Air Force that'll consist of that airplane and not much else a decade from now."

"Think they'll do anything about it? Is there—"

"Not in your lifetime. Come on, John. You know how it works. The generals and admirals support Nechestny, and when they retire, Macon-Bolt hires them. Biggest scam in the country." He glanced at his watch. "John, it really is good to see you. But I have *got* to go. Breaking bread with a few senators from the other camp tonight. I think we're going to get a tax cut this year after all."

I stood up. "Thanks." I think I felt even worse than I looked.

"Pull the outer door shut behind you, would you?" Rob said. "Problem with street people crapping in the foyer. And, John? Do yourself a favor. Don't fool around with Macon-Bolt. It's a losing proposition."

"See you at Em's funeral?"

He made a "yes" face. "I'll probably fly up. The mother really is a sweetie. But, John . . . you're going to be surprised how few people show. If you go. It'll be an education for you. This is a hard town."

Outside the building, a man with a storm of dirty hair sat under a blanket, singing hymns and cursing. The rain had faded to swamp air. I guess thinking slowed me down, because Rob caught up to me in less than a block.

"Forgot to ask you," he said, falling into formation at my side. "Who's going to replace Farnsworth on the Futures panel?"

"No idea."

"Well, give me a ring if you hear anything, all right? You're my inside line. And, John . . . the views I expressed upstairs? Just between us, right?"

I stopped and faced him.

"No disrespect," he said. "It's just that . . . I was being extremely frank. Damn it, John, there's just something about you that makes you seem trustworthy. But in this town . . ."

"It's my lack of imagination," I told him. "Don't worry about it."

He stood there looking at me. "Of course not. I'm sorry," he said. "But let me give you some advice. From one friend to another." He expressed everything with the lower half of his face, nothing with his eyes. He, too, would be a cabinet member one day. "Don't trust anybody."

CHAPTER 3

I still did not trust myself to go home and deal with Tish. I got a takeout burger and ate in the PX parking lot at Fort Myer. The rain came in the passenger's window, but I did not bother to close it.

I had two problems: Tish, and then all the other business. Farnsworth and Em. I thought about Tish first. And last. And in between. I knew I should hand her walking papers. But I was not sure I could give her up.

I had a problem with trust. A problem the size of Texas. Maybe it comes with my line of work. Betrayal is humanity's number two pastime, and I had spent a couple of decades watching foreign murderers dressed in ragtag uniforms go at it. I could think of plenty of reasons why Tish would not have wanted to tell me about the cop business in her past. No matter what the real story might be. But she should have told me. My work depended on my security clearance. She knew the rules. Not even a joint allowed in my house. A cocaine bust rated a mention.

If she had been quiet about her police record, there were plenty of other things she might have kept to herself. I did not want to think about those things. But I did.

Through it all, I could not stop thinking about making love to her. And being with her. The rain struck and steamed.

I forced myself to focus on Farnsworth and Em. And Em's airplane. These days, conspiracy theories were everywhere. In the streets, the press, the water supply. You started out wondering if the mechanics at the garage were cheating you and ended up convinced that JFK had been murdered by Elvis.

Yet, in my career, I had not seen one scrap of evidence of a conspiracy. Not in our government. Not anywhere around it. Unless it was a conspiracy of mediocrity. And I could not imagine why anyone tied in with Macon-Bolt Industries would need to conspire. The NGFB was as good as sold. Initial funding had already been approved and the big money would start with the next defense budget. Nothing was going to change it, and cloak-and-dagger nonsense could only hurt.

There had been some bad coincidences. But, in the Army, you saw those all the time. Fate waited until you were down to kick you hard. Maybe there was some big death-dealing conspiracy out there. With Buck Rogers aircraft and hundreds of billions of dollars in the kitty. Or maybe my buddies had hit a run of bad luck.

The truth was that Em's death still was not real to me. Maybe Farnsworth's death wasn't real to me, either. Maybe I was just going through the motions. The old bugger on that apartment floor had been cardboard.

All my thoughts led back to Tish. She was real. And I hated it.

I waited until I knew she had left for her gig, then went home. The place was drenched with her. The droopy curtains, the smell of the kitchen. Every shadow. A decomposing copy of *Far from the Madding Crowd* ambushed me by the phone. Walking in that door was like getting punched.

There was a message on the answering machine from Corry Nevers. I erased it and went upstairs. The Les Paul lay centered on the bed in its little coffin of a case. With a note:

"Please take it back for a refund. I don't deserve it. Tish."

I didn't know what anybody deserved anymore.

I was not ready to have a rational discussion with Tish, but I had to see her. Her band was playing a gay club off Dupont Circle. Straights were allowed in if they paid a cover.

The military was in the middle of a witch hunt about sex. No court-martial panel would believe an officer went to a gay bar unless he was looking for a blow job, so I went upstairs, where it was dark and I could see the stage without being seen. The balcony action was grim. A kid who looked like Audrey Hepburn with facial hair asked if he could sit down, but he went away when I shook my head.

Tish never got it quite right. She had a little talent. She was good in repose, on the quiet numbers. She was meant to be a cabaret singer. But she wanted to flail and wail. She played her scarred guitar as if choking an enemy. Red hair whipped and clung to her cheeks, and her sweat flew like breaking glass. She had her leather pants on, despite the heat, and she looked like trouble. Unless you looked hard. Then she looked afraid. To me, she looked beautiful. I felt sick down in my guts watching her. Wondering what she was really all about. And if it was over.

I was afraid I could not trust her to tell me the price of a quart of milk. I had been around enough to know that such feelings can pass. Faith comes back. Mouthful of kisses, and people sucker themselves. I was not sure I wanted that. I was afraid of her in a way I had never feared fists or guns.

I left as the set ended. I did not want to meet her in the

club, did not want anybody in the band to spot me and report to her. I walked the streets for a while. With Connecticut Avenue full of people who had been unpopular in high school and who had found one another in the city. Drivers hunting parking spots clogged the back streets. Lamps lit townhouse windows. Back on the circle, a heavy girl sobbed in front of an espresso bar.

I went home. There was a message from my boss, asking if I was okay. I left a return message at his work number: all quiet on the western front. CNN told me we had just renewed China's most-favored-nation status, and a White House spokesman told the country that a big-haired woman was lying about the President. The spokesman did his job wonderfully, without actually using the word "lying." Somebody from another planet might have believed him.

I moved the Les Paul off the bed and trashed the note from Tish. I lay down in my clothes. Just for a minute. And conked out.

Tish woke me with her body. We didn't talk. We made love as if we wanted to hurt each other. Then we held one another with arms like shackles. I smelled her hair and wished the world were a different place.

I woke up again in darkness. Sensing something wrong. Tish was not in the bed. I listened, and I heard her.

She was sitting on the edge of the bathtub, crying. The raw way children cry. A night-light lit her like a candle. She knew I was standing there, but she did not look at me. She covered her face with her hands. She was naked and shivering in the heat. Finally, she said:

"I just want to die. I love you so much. I just want to die."

"It's all right," I said. On time delay. Lying.

She shook her head and wept. "It's never going to be all right. I've ruined everything. You'll never believe me. I wreck every fucking thing I touch."

I put my hand on her shoulder and she quivered. As if I had hit her. Then she jumped up and clung to me.

"Oh, God, I love you," she said. "You're the best thing that ever happened to me. Please don't make me go."

"Tish . . ."

"I love you so much." The words broke up. A bad radio transmission.

"I love you, too," I said. I hope I meant it. I think I meant it. In that moment.

She cried on. "You don't understand. I love you all the way. I love you like everything there is in love. All of it. I love you. I want to have babies and everything."

I tried to pick her up. But somehow I wasn't strong enough. Underfed Tish. She weighed more than a continent now.

"And I can't," she said. "I'll never have babies. I've done stupid things. Stupid, stupid things. I'm so fucking stupid. Oh, God. Forgive me. Please. Forgive me."

In the books we read now, people do not ask forgiveness. Everything is permitted except that. If the actions of another wound us, it is we who are inadequate. Freedom is all. Maybe it would be better if life really were like those books, if I had not felt what I had felt toward Tish. Sitting in my car in the rain, I had imagined a scene like this. Wanting it.

I could not find any more words for her. There was so much fear in me, and it was all twisted up with love and desire.

Tish clutched me until I gathered the strength to pick her up and carry her to bed. I turned my back and she laced me in her arms.

In the morning, Corry Nevers called while Tish was in the shower. She asked me if we could get together to talk. I told her I wished her luck, but did not see what we had in common to talk about.

"I'm afraid," she said.

"Don't be."

She began to sob. "It's horrible."

"You'll get through it."

"You don't understand. It's something else. They won't let me go to the funeral . . ."

"What?"

"Em's parents. They closed the funeral. 'Only immediate family.' Nobody else can attend. I called and asked. They won't let me come. His mother never liked me."

I had regarded the funeral as an unwelcome duty and I was ashamed at the way Corry's news made me feel. Pathetic, the things that relieve us. Getting off the hook is one of the basic human pleasures. I sucked a few more details out of her and eased her off the phone by promising she could call me if she ran into real trouble.

Tish came out damp and smiling. We did not talk, but treated each other with exaggerated consideration. I was not going back to work. I had the leave days to burn. And the sun was out again.

Tish and I walked over to Eastern Market for breakfast, then headed down to the Mall in the morning's last coolness. It was our private holiday. Hill staffers hurried past us in suits that stood off from their shirt collars. The women marched in solid colors and running shoes. We held hands.

I had decided that my fantasy about some great conspiracy involving Em and Farnsworth and Macon-Bolt was just that. I was not going to make any calls or poke any more anthills. Let the dead sleep in their graves. Maybe Tish and I wouldn't last forever. But we were going to make the most of the time we had. To hell with the rest of the universe. Below the Capitol, charter buses bled tourists in souvenir T-shirts. The tourists managed to be noisy and reverent at the same time. Most of them were overweight.

"I want an ice cream," Tish said.

"You just had breakfast." But I got her a Dove Bar. Walking along in her cutoffs, she had a grace that she never managed onstage. Runway legs. The freckles she hated were coming out under her eyes.

"I want you to keep the guitar," I said.

She didn't answer.

"It's a separate thing," I told her. "I want you to have it."

She stopped and kissed me. Wet. In front of two Japanese tourists.

It was a good day. We walked to all the monuments and did not see anybody we knew. We grazed through a new exhibition at the Freer and ate poisonous hot dogs from a vendor. We went home in the heat and drank beer and made love.

Tish had a rehearsal scheduled for late afternoon, and she had to go. She took another shower. And threw herself back down on the bed beside me.

"I feel like such a shit," she said.

"You are a shit."

"No. I mean . . . it's something else."

My insides tightened.

"My car still isn't fixed. Can I please just borrow your car one more time? I'll get mine to the garage tomorrow morning. I promise."

"Take it," I said. "I'm not going anywhere. I figure I'll just stroll over to the market, buy some salmon steaks, and make dinner for anybody who's interested."

Tish rolled over and made noises to which I would have responded differently with another half hour's recuperation.

"I love you for your cooking," she said. "I'll be home early."

"Drive carefully, huh?"

I watched her dress, afraid I could never give her up. She asked where I had parked the car and I told her down the block. I listened to her leaving and tried as hard as I could to postpone thought. I ached to build a fortress for two. Where nothing or nobody would ever be able to touch us.

When the car blew up, the windows shook but did not shatter.

"Give me a break, huh?" Lieutenant Dickey said. "I don't buy the crybaby shit, soldier boy."

Explosives have their eccentricities. The blast had blown my car into the middle of the street, tossing the doors into nearby yards. Yet when I got to it, the black mummy that had been Tish was still visible in the flames. Seat belts work.

The cops had been chewing on me for a long time. I don't know how long exactly, but it was already dark beyond the windows of the police station. Dickey was the only one who had not given up.

"Come on," he said. "Make it easy on everybody. You tell the truth, you might not even do any time. You can go to court in your soldier suit with all your medals and tell everybody how sorry you are. Now tell me the truth. It's all a drug thing. Right? You and your little redheaded coke freak. You been moving dope. Wholesaling it to the dumb brothers out in the hood. Right?" He made a "Gotcha" face. "So what is it? You didn't pay the man on time? Or we got a turf battle on our hands? Maybe we got a whole bunch of soldier boys in on this? Setting up their retirement jobs. Showing the gangstas how to run a real operation. Military precision and all that crap. *Plan*ning. Mind if I smoke, soldier boy?" He lit a cigarette with a plastic lighter. "You give me the names, dates. I'll do everything I can for you."

I looked at him. There was no rage in me, and no fear. Just emptiness.

Dickey filled the little room with smoke. "Come on, pal. Let's make a deal, huh? Or do we want a lawyer after all?"

"I don't need a lawyer," I said. "I haven't done anything wrong."

The detective got up and patrolled the dirty linoleum. It might have been an interrogation room in Syria instead of Washington. Everything was crude and half broken. I heard voices of disorder beyond the closed door.

"Listen up, hero. I don't know what kind of game you think you're playing. But you're tied to three murders now."

"Four," I said.

He looked at me. Mouth open like an asthmatic flounder.

"Last weekend," I said. "A general named Farnsworth was hit by a car. Over in Virginia."

"I don't do Virginia," the detective said. "Talk to me about the District."

"Everybody thought it was an accident. I think it was murder."

"Just get back to the business we got in front of us."

"I'm not sure what the tie-in is," I said. "But I—" Suddenly, I did not want to tell this man anything. He wasn't the Law. Just a bully dying of cholesterol. "Charge me, or release me," I said. "Isn't that how it goes?"

He snorted. "What? You been watching cop shows or something?" He spread his arms and planted his fists on the table. Leaning toward me. "You better step out of your dream world and start thinking hard. That was your car that went up. Now . . . maybe whoever did the wiring job had some inside information that your girlfriend was going to take it for a drive, but two and two says they were after you, soldier boy. If you're not nice to me, I just might release you. And it's starting to look like a cold, cruel world out there. What are you going to do if I boot your ass out of here? Where you going to go?" He smiled. But I was miles ahead of him. "I figure whoever did the car job isn't done. The good news is that they are in a position to save the government the cost of your trial and subsequent incarceration. Now . . . who tried to blow you up? Tell me about the drugs. Start at the beginning."

"No drugs."

"Then *what?*"

"I don't know."

"Who did it?"

"I don't know."

He folded his arms and stood above me. Every time I was ready to shoot back, Tish came to haunt me. I saw her now. Split screen. Tish beside me, red hair on the white pillow. And the black thing in the flames.

My eyes let me down again.

"What?" the detective said. "I'm supposed to pity your ass or something? Did we lose our lover girl? The great love of our life?" He tossed his cigarette butt on the floor. "Give me a fucking break. Hey . . . maybe you'd like me to call you a public defender. Then you'll do time for sure."

"Charge me. Or release me."

He leaned over the table again. "Pal. Buddy. Soldier boy. You don't seem to get it. Serious crime, serious time. I could toss you in the can for seventy-two hours just for your attitude. Hey, but maybe you'd like that? What's that fairy-tale bar you said you went to?" He made a disgusted face. "You like your bread buttered on both sides, maybe? What's the goddamned Army coming to, huh? 'Don't ask, don't tell,' right?"

I looked up at him. "You're wrong about everything," I said calmly. "You couldn't be more wrong. If I knew who set the bomb, I would have told you the minute I saw you."

"Because you love me personally? Or because you love cops in general?"

"Because I loved Tish O'Malley."

He laughed. "Nobody loved Tish O'Malley. Her own family didn't love her. Or maybe her stepfather loved her a little too much, if you can believe the sheriff out there. She was a hard case, buddy. White trash with stars in her eyes. And coke up her nose. Hey, you know what's good? Know what she studied out at Cornhole Community College? Pharmacy. Ain't that something? A girl with a plan. Maybe franchise her own chain of meth labs."

"I didn't know she'd been to college." I was instantly sorry I had said it.

"It wasn't a lasting relationship. Your sweetheart didn't have lasting relationships. Hey, you two didn't talk much, did you? What else you want to know about her?"

"I know all I want to know," I lied.

His smile knotted. "I got another idea. Maybe she double-crossed you. Yeah. Wouldn't that be just like her? Her and her retro-scene smack-pack friends. She double-crossed you on the dope, and you found out. And you took her out." He brought his face down close to mine. It was not a pleasant view. "So what happens now? You planning to move in with that little blondie? What's her name? Caddy Mercedes?" He backed away. "Well, let me give you some advice. Man to man. It won't last. She's going to marry one of those rich fucks from Great Falls. You're the kind of food she leaves on the plate."

"Think you'll ever get around to working on the murder of Tish O'Malley?" I asked.

He pinched my cheek as if I were a baby. "Gotta love those soldier boys. They're cool customers. I guess you kind of sense that I don't like you. And you're wondering why. Well, let me tell you. I don't like you smart-ass fucks who come into this city and shit all over it and then go crying that the jigaboos can't govern themselves. You think you're above the law." He reached for another cigarette and lit it with the rhythm of old habit. "This city doesn't have a fucking chance. And I love this city, you know that? I was born and raised here. And I hate people like you who come around fucking with it."

"You're still wrong."

"Oh, yeah? About what this time?"

"Everything. You've got a perfect score."

He drank smoke and said, "That so? Well, you're either an innocent man and so naive it hurts me to think about it. Or you are one vicious shit who deserves an Academy Award. Either way, you're a fucking loser." He smoked and stared through me. Then he said, "Know what? I'm going to turn your ass loose. Because I want to see what happens out there."

I made it two blocks from the police station, then sat down on the stoop of an old house that had been turned into offices. And I cried.

After a while, I sensed somebody standing in front of me. Layers of clothing, despite the heat, and a Santa Claus sack over his shoulder. A knitted cap over cascades of hair. His beard made his head enormous. With the darkness and filth, I could not tell his race.

"She leave you, man? She make you go? Women so hard sometimes."

I didn't have any money, so he moved on. I walked. A police cruiser slowed beside me. I thought they had come to take me in again. But it was only that after-midnight curiosity.

Trying to think about Tish was like staring at the sun. I could only think around her. And I kept thinking about that goddamned guitar. She had taken her Telecaster to the rehearsal that never happened, and the left-behind Les Paul had become a sort of orphan in my very unclear mind.

Quirky Tish. I had given her a James Salter novel I reread every couple of years. Yapping at her about how it captured the complexity of the human heart and the interplay of male-female relationships. She read half of it. Then she gave it back. Telling me, "I don't want to read about how people *are*, John. I *know* how people are."

I really did love her now. Now that it was safe.

I wanted to know who killed her. While trying to kill me. I wanted to know who it was and I wanted them to suffer tortures I had not yet invented.

You could read Tish two ways. As a hustler with a little talent for music and a lot of talent for sex. Or as somebody who had played her best game with a bad hand. When she played music, for better or worse, Tish gave it all she could. And I was determined to believe that she had given me all she could in the love department. The positive spin, in Washington talk. The detective had done that for me.

If Farnsworth's death or Em's had been unreal to me, then the loss of Tish was unimaginable. I could not believe I would never feel her beside me again.

A block short of my house, a car nosed in beside me. A white guy leaned out to ask directions. Born slow, I bent to help. And darkness got me.

CHAPTER 4

Tough guys, with that leanness you see in officers from the *paras*. They weren't big. But they were hard. The kid didn't speak English worth a damn, but the fortyish guy spoke it without the least sign of brain-strain. I had not paid attention in high school, so when the boys talked frog, the only words I could make out were *merde* and *mort*.

The kid had bar fighter's hands. Jerry Lewis with Gold's Gym biceps. His inability to ask questions directly pissed him off. The older one had the narrow face and close graying hair of the men who lose their wives to bad-asses in French films. But this character was a bad-ass himself. Reptile in a polo shirt. He bent down toward the chair and knuckle-punched me in the stomach again.

"Why kill them?" he asked again. "You made fools of us. Wasn't that enough? Why did you have to kill them?"

I gasped for air. As soon as I could stitch words together, I said, "Why'd you kill Tish? Fuck you." Hoping I sounded angry and not too afraid.

We had been through the Q&A before. Twice.

Cuckold backed off, disgusted. More French. The only word I understood was *amateur*.

Cuckold folded his arms and looked down at me. In the bare white room. The only furniture was the heavy wooden chair in which I sat strapped. The chair was a specialty number. And there was a big aluminum suitcase. Sometimes Jerry sat on it and stared at me while he smoked a cigarette. The French smoke all the time because it's their last competitive skill.

"My partner," Cuckold said, "does not believe you are very receptive to education."

I tried to shrug, but the leather straps held me tight. The chair had a wooden seat and two big slats up the back. It was not ergonomically correct.

More French. *Merde* again. Existentialism making a come-back. Cuckold said, "My partner is convinced your American educational system is made of shit. Have you studied logic? Or dialectics? Is the university so inadequate? Or is my assessment correct? Do you think we are so stupid you can lie to us?"

For punctuation, he nailed me in the stomach again. He was very good. I felt it right up against my spine.

By punching me in the gut over and over again, they had given away one important thing. They did not want to mark me. I figured that meant they were not going to kill me, either. I was still looking at the world as a black or white, either-or proposition.

Cuckold walked away and sat down on the floor with his back against the wall. The guy had watched a lot of Belmondo in his formative years.

Back on the street, they had not given me time to throw a single punch. I woke up in a car trunk with a hood over my head. I did not have a clue where I was when they yanked me out and walked me over gravel. Then I banged against a doorway and bounced along a corridor. They slammed me down in the guest chair. A door shut. Straps went on and the hood came off.

Jerry tossed Cuckold a cigarette. Followed by his lighter.

"Let's review. First of all, your lover. Our regrets. We had nothing to do with this . . . event. We had no interest in her. Allow me to say that she looked like an amiable woman." He smoked and his eyes narrowed in his narrow face. "Whether you *are* stupid or just playing the fool, you must see that whoever set the car bomb was after *you*. Not Mademoiselle O'Malley." He made a gesture with his fingers. As though rubbing snot away from the tips. "You must see that your own people have decided to kill you. You know too much. Fortunately, you are also disposable. Like your whole fucking culture."

I almost told him one more time that I had no idea what he was rambling on about, but it seemed pointless. The French had been jerking off like this for most of the twentieth century. Reality did not impress them.

"So what do we have?" Cuckold went on. "We have an American lieutenant colonel condemned to death. For doing his country's dirty work." He flipped his butt and it bounced off the tip of my shoe. "John Reynolds, you are being a fool. We are your only friends. No. Allow me to say it with more honesty. We *could* be your friends, if you helped us. You would have the gratitude of the government of France—which still counts for something, you know. And you would be performing an act of justice." He rolled into a crouch. Balancing on the balls of his feet. "What are you going to do? You know they're going to kill you."

"I don't even know who 'they' are, for God's sake." I had developed a wheezing speech pattern. As if my stomach had crowded up into my lungs to hide. "You've got this all wrong."

My hosts spoke French again. The younger one got angry. Whole lot of *non*. One thing that did not track was the relationship between authority and age. Jerry was still at the body-piercing age. But he was perfectly willing to give Cuckold a hard time. Different organizations, I figured.

Cuckold turned back to me. "Okay. We will simplify things. 'Lay the cards on the table,' as your people like to say. Of course we spy on you. And you spy on us. Everybody spies on everybody. But there are rules. Sometimes we fuck with you. Just like you fuck with us. But no French agent has killed an American agent. Or even an American citizen, I don't think." He made a pout and waved his hands. "Maybe we've had little problems in Africa, maybe sometimes things got out of hand down there. But that comes from dealing with the *noires*, right? You Americans should understand that, I think." He held out an upturned palm and bounced an invisible ball. "But here? No. In France? No. Everybody understands the rules."

He strode over to me and broke one of his own rules. He cupped my chin in his hand, pressing his fingers and thumb into my cheeks. It was the first time either of them had touched my head since I got thumped cold on the street. Unless you count lifting the sack off my head upon arrival at Club Med. He brought his face close to mine, a human hatchet, and his eyes managed to be angry and dead at the same time. He stank of smoke. "You bastards broke the rules. And I want you to tell me why." He let me go and stepped away, a boxer between rounds.

Jerry said something brief and sharp, but this time Cuckold ignored him. He came to me again. Smoke close. Hate close.

"Wasn't it enough? That you have made fools of us, 'the stupid French'? Why blow up the laboratory? Are you that fucking insecure? Or that vicious?" His face shook in front of me. "You *won*. And you still had to kill everybody . . ."

I'm slow. If there was a mental PT test, I'd wind up in remedial training. I still did not realize all that he was telling me. Of course, he didn't realize it, either. All that would come later.

Jerry stood up and pissed against the far wall. It offended Cuckold. He probably figured it matched the American stereotype of the French male a bit too well.

"There was no justification for killing all those people," Cuckold went on. Backing off. His voice had quieted. "None. You had your laugh. You cost us plenty." He nodded toward Jerry. "Now . . . my partner and his people believe you set the whole thing up, that you fed us the plans with the end already in mind. Knowing we'd still have to gather the best technicians in France to work the thing out. So you could kill them in one neat strike." Single-syllable laugh. "And blame it on the Algerians." He looked down into darkness, ready to drag me in after him. "I shouldn't tell you this. It's a breach of discipline. But I think you need to develop a . . . a perspective on your situation. My partner's wife, she was in that building." He looked down at me. "So far, they have identified one of her feet."

None of this made sense to me. But I did realize that, for the first time, I really did know too much. Thanks to Cuckold himself.

"Personally, I *still* don't think American intelligence is that good," he continued. "I respect your industry. And your technical intelligence means, of course. But your agents are children." His chin dimpled as he judged me again. "I think my colleagues are wrong. I do not believe you planned all this to wipe out our top people. I think it started out as something of a schoolboy prank. But then you saw an opportunity. And you moved." He put his hands on his hips. It made him look thinner, smaller. "Colonel Reynolds—John—I believe you know exactly who placed that bomb. You know the Americans who did it. And you know the filthy fucking collaborators in France. You know who, and how, and why. Hey—wake up."

He delivered the hardest punch yet.

"Oh, God," I said. Although I'm not sure my speech was clear enough for even God to understand.

"Come on, fuckface," Cuckold said. "Talk to me."

My muscles quivered. All the way up to my neck.

"Listen," I said. *"Please.* Just . . . listen for a minute. I swear to God I don't know what this is all about. I don't know anything about bombs, or plans, or anybody laughing. All I know . . . is that three people I knew are dead. And one stranger. Maybe two of them knew something about an airplane. One did for sure. But *I* had nothing to do with this. Tish had nothing to do with this. I don't know anything about the laboratory bombing. Just what was on the news. You've got the wrong person."

He surprised me. The control vanished. He went into a fury and punched me so hard he lost his aim and started working on my ribs. He nearly knocked the chair over. Jerry had to come over and pull him away.

My eyes opened in flickers and tears broke down my cheeks. Nothing to do about it. I hurt. I would have killed them both if I could have.

Jerry had his arms around Cuckold, who was sobbing. Unreal. I tasted acid and blood at the back of my throat.

Finally, Jerry came over to me. Shift change, I figured. But he just put his hands on my shoulders and stared at me.

"I understand . . . how he say to you. He tell you . . ." He spoke slowly, with the words coming painfully. "He tell you my wife, she is . . . she *morte, non*?" He gave me a Charles-Manson-goes-to-Paris smile and tapped his forehead. "A lie. Not my wife. *Non.* The wife from him. *Très jeune, très belle. Comprenez*? Maybe he kills you."

Cuckold would not turn and look at me. I wondered if he had killed Tish. In miscalculated personal revenge.

Jerry sauntered back to the suitcase. Instead of sitting down on it, he undid the latches. Inside, small mechanical devices lay embedded in gray foam. He lifted out a device that looked like a power drill with a suction cup on thc cnd, thcn fitted it against an object the size of a pack of cigarettes. Satisfied, he separated the items again and brought the drill toward me.

He snapped out something in French and Cuckold looked back over his shoulder. Face ravaged. "Last chance," Cuckold said. "Tell us what you know."

I was afraid now. I had been afraid all night, but that had been only a little fear compared to this. I did not like the look of the tool in Jerry's paw. The new fear came big and pulsing.

"Honest to Christ, I don't know what's going on. *You* know more than I do."

Cuckold stood in profile, slender, showing me his cleaver of a face. Sweating tears. "My colleague's machine leaves no marks. It's very good. But it was not designed by the best people. They were not like the people you killed. So sometimes there is nerve damage. Maybe you will be lucky."

Jerry moved behind the chair and I found out why the slats parted in the middle. He pressed the device against my spine.

The world exploded. I've been hurt a good bit—sports injuries, Army mistakes—but I had never encountered pain like this. I had never even imagined that such pain could exist. Time stopped. I could not see. I flipped like a fish in the chair and screamed. Maybe seconds, maybe minutes later, I realized that the device was not touching me anymore. And the big pain was gone. But the shock was like the worst hangover on earth.

"Please . . ." I said. "Please . . ."

Just to underscore the point, Jerry dosed me again. This time, the whole world screamed. My muscles raged against the straps. I would have given anything in the world to make that pain stop, done anything.

When my vision came back, Cuckold was squatting in front of me.

"Talk," he said.

I tried to talk and gagged. It took me a long time to form thoughts, words. "Em . . . Emerson Carroll knew something. I don't know what. He asked me about the bombing, if I'd seen any reports." I gulped air. "Nothing. I didn't see anything. Hear anything. Locker-room gossip. Everybody thought the Algerians . . ."

"Shithead," Cuckold said. Jerry taught me about pain again. I do not know for certain what my body did. Maybe I only thought I was fighting the straps. Maybe I held perfectly still. I don't know. There was only the pain and it was endless.

Years later, Cuckold asked me, "Are you ready to talk now?"

"Farnsworth. Major General Farnsworth. Futures guy. Some connection to Em. To Emerson Carroll. Old friends. All knew each other. But they didn't include me. Em was troubled, upset. I don't know." Suddenly, I found the strength to shout. *"I don't know, I don't know, I don't know . . ."*

They gave me the pain again. For years and years and years. Nothing I could do would make it stop.

"Tish," I cried.

I remember that. Because the pain had already stopped, but my body had not realized it. There was just enough unfried brain left to listen to myself.

"Don't be a hero," Cuckold said. "Talk."

Only the leather straps held me together now. I did not know anything else. I could not even make up lies. I could only gasp, far short of speech.

The machine touched me again. For an eternity of pain. I believed I was dying. Because I could not imagine such pain without death at the end of it.

I blacked out. I think it was only for a matter of seconds,

but I'll never know for sure. When I opened my eyes again, Cuckold was examining me up close. He looked bewildered.

"Shit," he said when he saw the life in my eyes, "you really don't know."

"You can get up." Cuckold's voice. He reached back over the seat of the car and helped me right myself. Then he pulled off the hood. During the pain game, I had soiled myself. Dignity was a memory. They had to be tough just to stay in the car with me.

Heading up 395. Sparse traffic. Predawn. Ahead, lights outlined the roofs of the high-rises on Skyline. I knew exactly where I was. But it was unreal, too.

"Listen to me," Cuckold said. "Try to understand. The people who blew up our laboratory. These are the same people who killed your lover. Who tried to kill you. They killed your friends." His face shone in the highway light. "No matter what you think . . . no matter what you want . . . we are on the same side now."

He was asking for too much brainpower. I did not think my nervous system would ever work again.

"They will try to kill you. They will not give up. Perhaps we can help you, I don't know. Frankly, you are not so important now. But I would help you if I could. If I can. All this killing . . ." He turned away and looked at the highway. ". . . this is madness."

"Will I be all right?"

He looked at me quizzically.

"The thing you used. Is it permanent? The . . . way I feel?"

He shrugged. "I think you will be okay. Probably. Sleep it off."

"It doesn't . . . I can't make sense . . ."

"Sleep. Think about it tomorrow. If you are still alive."

As we crossed into the District, he gave me a spiel about

working together. For some vague common good. He promised he would be in touch, but did not offer me any means to contact him. He apologized for what they had done to me, sounding almost sincere.

"We have to drop you here," he said. Jerry had pulled in along a sidewalk in Indian country. But it was quiet now. Even dopers go to sleep eventually. "We cannot take the chance. They may be waiting for you. And, by the way . . . do not attempt to run to your counterintelligence people. You have no marks on your body. No traces. There is no evidence for what you would say. And they will only kill you for your knowledge." He leaned farther back over the seat. "And we would not be friends anymore. We are the only friends you have left, John."

It was all a dream. I was just floating through it. Remembering the pain. Tish, all the rest, had disappeared. Numb, dumb me.

"Get out," Cuckold said. "You need help?"

I got myself out. Most of the way. Then he grabbed my wrist, holding me partway inside the car. I saw the lower half of his face as the lips moved.

"Bonne chance."

Yellow tape crisscrossed the front yard. "Police Line—Do Not Cross." It had sagged toward the ground and I stepped over it. Lifting my leg hurt. Then I turned again and reached down. Bending hurt. I ripped the tape free and balled it up. I figured Dickey had left it there just to screw with me.

At least the cops had locked up after themselves. I let myself in. You could feel the dawn coming up. The day was getting off to a good start. With sirens in the distance.

I ached to sleep.

The cops had trashed the place. Looking for evidence. Or maybe Dickey was just making a point. I took a plastic garbage bag up to the bathroom, stripped, and put my clothes in it. Then I got under the shower. I could not straighten my back. I crouched there until the water turned cold. I had not begun to soap myself. I hate cold water, but I could not move. Finally, I cleaned myself. Shaking. After I dried off, I pissed blood. That gets your attention. I stumbled toward the bed.

Odd, how the brain works. When it works. Despite the bad-party wreckage of the bedroom, I realized something was missing.

Someone had ripped off the Les Paul I bought Tish.

D.C. cops.

I curled up like an infant and smelled Tish on the sheets.

It was full daylight when the banging on the front door woke me. Obviously, the doorbell had not been man enough to do the job. The banging kept up, real *Don Giovanni* stuff. Body aching, I clumsied around the floor until I found a pair of jeans the cops had flipped out of the closet. A coffin of heavy air moved with me.

I blundered downstairs, shirtless and barefoot. Stiff, fragile, and beat. I had to hunt through the kitchen until I found the key where I had left it on a shelf.

My visitor pounded away.

I also picked up the largest knife I could find.

I did not believe anybody was going to try to kill me like this. Not by daylight. Banging on my front door. But a reasonable amount of caution seemed to be in order.

When I looked through the peephole, I saw Corry Nevers.

She was about to hammer the door again when I opened it. Stronger than she appeared. Health-club type.

After looking me up and down, she cat smiled and said, "Aren't you ever dressed?" Then she pointed that little marble nose toward the knife in my hand. "I'm not *that* dangerous."

"What do you want?"

"Don't be hard." A parting of the lips, a widening of the smile. Enough to make brokers and bankers swoon. "Please."

I am not a rude man by nature. But when your girlfriend has just been killed and it looks like sombody is out to kill you, when you've just been tortured, you're pissing blood, and the cops recently held a frat party in your home, your social skills deteriorate.

"What time is it?" I said. I felt like I had slept about fifteen minutes.

She glanced at her watch. Cartier tank job. "Quarter after twelve. Did I wake you or something?"

"Late night."

"The police?"

That got my attention.

"It was in the *Post*," she said. "About your girlfriend. I just wanted to say I'm sorry. She seemed . . . nice."

"She wasn't nice. She was glorious. But not nice."

She stood there in the heat. Perspiration by Tiffany's.

"That's a lovely thing to say about a woman. 'Glorious.' " Her smile withered. "I don't think anybody would say anything that nice about me. If I died."

I let her come in. Mr. Wisdom. She barely got inside the door when the trashing registered.

"Courtesy of the D.C. Police Department," I told her. "They're convinced I'm some kind of narco."

Uncertainty in that silver voice now. "Can they . . . are they allowed to do that?"

"This isn't Chevy Chase, sweetheart. Now, what do you want?"

I had misjudged her. The way I had misjudged everything else in my short-term memory account.

She began to cry. "I'm *alone*. Can't you understand? I'm scared. I don't know what to do. I tried to go back to work. I thought it would help. But I'm a basket case. I keep thinking . . ." She hid her eyes with her hand. A fly that had followed her inside circled her blond hair. She waved it away and I saw smears under her lashes. "What do *you* want? All I wanted was to talk to somebody." Sobbing now. "I read the paper. I read about your girl . . . about your car . . . I thought we were the same now."

Even crying, she looked like an ad in a five-buck fashion mag. Misery chic. I stood there in my jeans, dumb-handed, with my guts hurting so bad I just wanted to go back to bed and curl up.

I almost touched her. The comfort thing. But something stopped me. I had an inexplicable sense that she and Tish were enemies, that betrayal followed Corry Nevers like a shadow.

When I thought of Tish, I remembered something else. I had not done one of the fundamental things a human being in my position was obliged to do.

"Go in the kitchen. Find a chair. Sit down. Wait for me."

I did not exactly bound up the stairs, which gave me plenty of time to wonder whether the cops had taken Tish's papers. What few she had. I needed her address book. An item the investigators certainly should have taken, if they really believed Tish was involved in criminal activity.

The police had ripped through Tish's things. Guitar picks prickled underfoot. Dickens lay on top of Charlotte Brontë. But the cops seemed to have been interested mostly in her underpants, which covered the floor like little signal flags.

They had grabbed her guitar, but they had not bothered about the address book. It was a ragged little thing. I had always resisted the urge to page through it. Now I had an excuse.

I knew her mother's current name was Bennet and that she had moved to Michigan. Tish had not volunteered anything more, and I had not asked. You did not have to know her long to realize she had not left a lot behind when she got on the bus out of town.

I dialed the number. Hoping nobody would answer. Hoping her mother would be at work in the middle of the day. I knew I had to do this, but I did not want to.

Someone picked up on the fourth ring.

"Yeah?" TV in the background.

"Mrs. Bennet?"

"Yeah."

"Ma'am, are you the mother of Patricia O'Malley?"

"You a cop or something? That little tramp in trouble again?"

"No, ma'am. I'm . . . Tish and I were . . ."

"You one of her boyfriends? Listen, buddy, I don't know where she is. I got no idea. She don't tell me."

I could smell alcohol through the phone line.

"Hey, you," her mother went on. "When you catch up with her. You tell her something for me, all right? You tell her she's an ungrateful little bitch, all right? Tell her just what I said. Hundred dollars a goddamned month. You call that gratitude? After all I done for her? She thinks she's a goddamned Catholic saint for sending her mother a hundred bucks a goddamned month. I'll tell—"

A male voice took over the line.

"Fuck off, buddy," he said.

When I went back downstairs, Corry was cleaning up. The blessing of coffee filled the air.

"Did you know you have seven messages on your answering machine?" she asked.

No, I didn't know. And I was not ready to listen to them. I sat in a chair she had righted. It even hurt to sit down.

"Can I make you something to eat?"

"Sit down," I told her. I did not think I would ever be able to eat again. "So you went back to work?" Maybe it was the

Victorian novels in my bedroom, but I felt like the girl should be in mourning for Em.

She did not sit down. She raised the halves of a broken plate, as if in wonder. "I thought it would take my mind off things. But I'm not worth much."

"You really like your job?"

She did not understand the question. "It's great. Senator Faust is terrific to work for. I'm learning a tremendous amount. And you meet people." Abruptly, she put down the broken china and leaned against the dishwasher. "But today I just couldn't . . . I don't know. It was a dumb idea. Going in. It didn't work. I guess it was even disrespectful. In a way. To Em." A wistful smile. Maybe real, maybe practiced in front of a mirror. "Does that sound old-fashioned?"

I wondered if she was sleeping with the senator and almost asked. He was tall, still had his hair, and played well on the talk shows. Big money, lot of power. This girl's kind of guy. Em was just a rung on a ladder, and Corry was born to take the elevator.

"Corry, would you please just sit down? Don't put anything else away. Just sit down and tell me what this is all about. Please." I touched my stomach muscles and found them unfriendly. "If you'll pardon the lack of self-esteem, I don't think of myself as your type of guy. You must have friends. Plenty of them. I don't understand why you're here."

She did as she had been told and sat down. A duchess taken prisoner by the workers and peasants.

"I'm afraid," she said.

"You don't look afraid."

She hit me with those killer blue eyes. "I'm afraid to look afraid."

"Bullshit line. What are you afraid of?"

"I don't know. If I knew, maybe I wouldn't be so afraid."

"Has anybody contacted you? Bothered you?"

She shook her head. The beautiful-hair commercial. In slow motion. She was Manhattan, not Washington. "Nobody. The police haven't even called back."

"They're busy. So what are you afraid of?"

"What are *you* afraid of? Don't I have as much reason to be afraid as you?"

"Who says I'm afraid?"

"Do you always answer the door with a butcher's knife?"

"It's a frontier neighborhood."

"I think you're afraid of me. And I can't figure out why."

I tried to meet her eyes with the level of self-confidence to which she had been born. "Handle with care. The girl has a black belt in male psychology. And she does not like answering questions."

"Ask. Ask anything."

"Were you going to leave Em?"

"Em tell you that?"

"That's not an answer."

She looked at the floor, and her voice lost its confidence. "I couldn't wait to leave him."

"Why?"

"He hit me. He was a drunk. He stank. Is that what you want to hear about your old friend?"

"Em wouldn't hit a woman."

"He hit me. When he was afraid. He'd get drunk. And hit me." Her eyes stabbed in my direction. "I've never known a man who wouldn't hit a woman. When he was desperate."

"What was he afraid of? Why was he desperate?"

"It was lots of things."

"Name one."

"He was afraid I'd leave him."

"But you didn't."

"I couldn't afford to."

"Stocks have a bad year? Uncle run off with the trust fund?"

Her eyebrows climbed. "Who do you think I am?"

"Who *are* you?"

"I'd like to hear it from you. Is that what the hostility's about? Who do you think I am, John?"

I looked her up and down without embarrassment. "Cordelia Nevers. Rich girl playing at government. Waiting to marry richer guy. Fund-raiser cocktail-party wife by birthright."

She laughed. It was unnerving. Her laughter reminded me of the way Tish laughed at me when I deserved it.

"It's Corrine. Not Cordelia. The last name was Neverosky. My grandfather shortened it because Hunkies couldn't get a job outside of the mines. My mother and father had a contest to see who could drink themselves to death first. Dad won. I went to Penn State on a help-the-girls scholarship and worked summers in the last knitting mill in North America. Because I have fast hands. I could make more that way than I could on some internship with an ass-grabber. I came to Washington because I wanted to change things. But mostly I wanted to change myself. I moved in with Em two days after I met him. Because he was charming when he drank just the right amount, and he had all the things I thought I wanted, and on our second date he introduced me to the Secretary of the Treasury. In the back of a restaurant where the tips are bigger than the paychecks back home. He got me my job. And fucked me like a bully, and slapped me when the sex didn't work. Sometimes he'd disappear. Hours, days. But I didn't have much money, and I had my first real leg-up job, and I was afraid of him and all he could do in this town." She looked at me with a fierceness that reminded me of Tish slashing off a guitar solo. But Corry Nevers sat perfectly still. "Happy now?"

No. I was not happy. I think that, more than anything else,

I hated the parallels with Tish's life. And the smarter choices, the comparative success, of Corrine Neverosky.

The phone rang. I was grateful to the caller in advance. Walking the long seven or eight feet across the kitchen, I wondered if I would ever get anything right.

"Hello?"

"*John?* John, is that you?" I recognized Mary Farnsworth's voice. But I had never heard her voice like this. "John, can you come over here? Please? Could you come now? Somebody's been in the house . . ."

"I've got to go," I told Corry.

"What's the matter?"

"A friend's got a problem."

"Is it part of—"

"Corry, please. Save it. I'm sorry I've been such a dick. But, one, you're better off knowing less, not more. Two, I don't know much myself. Three, hanging around with me is probably the unsafest act you could commit." I put my paws in the pockets of my jeans and my abdomen went neon with pain.

"I'll come with you."

"Bad idea."

"Maybe I could help."

"No. I told you. I'm not safe to be around."

"I don't care. Maybe we're safer together."

"And maybe we're a bonus target whenever we're within bursting radius of each other."

"What does that mean?"

"You'd better go back to work."

"I don't want to go back to work. I can't concentrate. I can't think about anything except—"

Impulse struck. I picked up the phone.

"Information for what city?"

"Washington, D.C. Police Department. Homicide."

"Please hold for the number."

I redialed and told them I wanted to speak to Detective Dickey. The woman on the desk said he was busy. I told her I was a suspect in a murder case. She said:

"Well, he *still* busy. But I axe him if he want to talk to you."

Dickey came on the phone. "Who is this?"

"America's Army."

"Yeah? What you got, soldier boy? I'm eating lunch."

"Remember I told you about the other murder? The general I think was murdered? Over in Virginia?"

"Out of my jurisdiction. Hey, how come you haven't been returning my calls?"

"His wife just phoned me. Somebody's been in her house. Maybe the same crew that tore up Emerson Carroll's apartment."

"You a detective now? Everybody's a fucking detective. Goddamned television."

"Her name's Mary Farnsworth. She's at five-two-one-one—"

"I told you. Virginia's out of my jurisdiction. What're you trying to do, get me to blow the case on some technicality? Dream on."

"Don't you care about this?"

"You got a lawyer putting you up to all this crap? Hey, why don't you just come over here and write out a confession."

"Just tell me one thing. Just one thing, okay? I understand why your crew tore up my place. Maybe I understand it on a couple of levels. But did you know one of your boys stole a very expensive guitar from my bedroom?"

"Don't call them 'boys.' They're sensitive about the term. And nobody tore up your little drug den. And I guarantee you, nobody stole no goddamned guitar. And listen. While you're on the phone. Hyacinth needs the name of your insurance company so she can finish up her report on the car. What's more, I told you about claiming the body. You're a non-relative and you'll have to—"

I hung up.

Corry smiled at me as though I were a fool. "I wish you'd let me help you."

I turned away. This was just wasting time. I had to get dressed and go. Mary Farnsworth needed me.

I had climbed halfway up the steps to the second floor when I realized I had overlooked an important practical matter. I bent down over the railing and hurt and called, "Corry?"

In a moment, she was standing at the foot of the stairs.

"Are you all right?" she asked.

"Did you drive over here?"

She smiled ravishingly. "Need a lift?"

"The police don't believe me," Mary Farnsworth said. "They insist I'm merely distraught." She was the only woman I had ever known who could not only use the word "distraught," but sound natural doing it.

We stood in her living room. Nothing broken, nothing even out of place to a visitor's eye. I had tried to leave Corry out in her car, but Mary would not have it. Too hot, she insisted, and too rude. A flawless hostess, even in distress.

It was clear that Em had never brought Corry to the house. She was a stranger to Mary, who was trying to figure out our relationship. Mary had no idea about Tish, must not have read the papers or watched the local news. It was jarring. As though Tish were still alive in a world that excluded me.

"What made you think somebody was in the house?"

Mary looked wronged. "I don't *think*, John. I *know*." Then she softened. "I've always been able to tell a thing like that. It runs in my family. We . . . have a sense for presences."

"Were there any signs? Anything missing?"

She shook her head. Slowly. "Nothing stolen. But they were in Mickey's study. I *know* it, John. Things were ever so slightly out of place. As though the cleaning woman had gone through it. I believe they went through the rest of the house as well. But I'm certain about the study. Mickey's desk chair had been moved. You know how precise Mickey was about things. So dress-right-dress. That chair was moved. And then there was the call from the Pentagon."

"What call?"

She looked weary. Her hair was only ninety-nine percent perfect. If my own life had not upended over the past few days, I would have been on the side of the police. I still was not convinced. The crew who had been searching homes had not been quite this neat elsewhere.

"Somebody wanted me out of this house. A major called. He *said* he was a major. Brady. Terribly officious. I swear, I wanted to slap him right over the phone. He told me I needed to come by to sign for the personal effects they had cleared out of Mickey's office. He said I had to identify each item." She grazed two fingertips along her temple. "It did seem a bit brutal. But the Army has changed so much over the years, and I supposed that was how they do business now. So I drove in. But the room number he gave me belonged to some sort of Air Force recreational services staff. Nobody knew anything about a Major Brady. So I went upstairs to Mickey's office. They were *not* expecting me." She smiled at a remembrance. "The survival assistance officer had gathered Mickey's things himself. He was going to bring them to me. There was no need to sign anything."

"You told all this to the police?"

"They wouldn't listen. As soon as I said that nothing seemed to be missing, they lost interest." She glanced at Corry, then turned back to me. "I'm so sorry. I haven't even prepared coffee. Would you like to sit down for a bit?"

"Mary, for God's sake, we don't need coffee."

"I'd love a cup," Corry said.

Mary applied a smile that her mother had taught her and said, "Do please sit down. Your family name was Nevers? I believe there are quite a few Nevers downriver in New Orleans. Old stock, terribly proud of the French connection. They never recovered from being sold to the Americans."

"My family's from the north," Corry said.

"I could tell," Mary said. She smiled beautifully.

I wished Corry would just disappear. I had selfish designs on Mary. I wanted to talk to her. About Tish. To tell her what had happened. I needed to talk to somebody, and Mary was the only clean soul within range.

Mary went out to the kitchen. Corry would not meet my eyes. She studied the room as if appraising the furniture for auction. After a minute, I followed Mary.

Mary jumped when I came in. She stood at the counter, measuring coffee, and I had made her spill a loaded spoon.

I did not have a chance to speak. She turned on me, whispering in anger.

"John, I don't *like* that girl. And I'm ashamed of you. If you and Tish are having a little spat, I want you to apologize to her. You just stop on the way home and buy your Tish flowers. A *lot* of flowers. And I expect the two of you for dinner next Friday. At seven-thirty."

"Mary, I have to tell you something."

She put her hands on her hips, which was something I had never seen Mary Farnsworth do. It was a gesture from her ancestors, from the slave shacks, a mustering of strength for a fight. Her nostrils pulsed. "I swear, John, men just make me *so* mad. And you, of all people! I thought you were a gentleman. And I had *always* judged you to have a faithful heart. Why, if you were just the tiniest bit smaller, I'd put you over my knee and spank you."

I helped her with the coffee and said nothing of consequence.

Coffee steamed from Mary's silver. But Mary served it over invisible ice. She had gone as rigidly formal as if we were line dancing at the court of Louis XIV. Corry either was oblivious to Mary's attitude or didn't care.

Talk died. We drank.

Finally, Corry said, "You have such lovely antiques. It must be your hobby, Mrs. Farnsworth."

"They're family pieces," Mary told her. "John, be a dear and pour Miss Nevers more coffee."

I did exactly as I had been told, then said, "Mary . . . you said you thought whoever was in the house moved a chair? By the general's desk?"

"Yes, John."

"Could I have a look? Would you show me?"

"Certainly." She stood up. "Do stay here and relax, Miss Nevers."

I followed Mary across the hall and into the room General Farnsworth had used as his office, library, counseling chamber, and poker den. A sea captain's desk took up nearly half the room. It had been built without pillars of drawers so it could double as a table. A PC occupied half of the desktop. Military history books sandbagged the walls and floor. The souvenirs of long service—plaques and plates and banners, diplomas and signed photographs of heroes, a cadet saber and shako—made a private museum. Mary had permitted a certain immaculate clutter in this one room of her house. The general had acquired habits that looked like discipline, but Mary was the family drill sergeant. The room appeared to be just as Farnsworth had left it, but there was such a density to it that I would not have been able to tell if anything had been moved.

Mary shut the French doors behind us. "She is insufferable, John."

"Mary, there's nothing between us. She just—"

Mary Farnsworth looked at me with frozen brown eyes. "Maybe *you* don't think there's anything going on. But that's not what that girl thinks."

I looked at the desk chair. Corry had a peculiar magic. I had never known anyone who inspired such instant dislike.

At any rate, I wanted Mary to knock it off. Her talk about Tish had dumped me in an emotional slaughterhouse. I needed to tell her what had happened, but I did not have the spirit for it.

Instead, I asked, "How was the chair moved?"

Mary grew businesslike. "Whenever he finished using the computer, Mickey would tuck his chair back under the writing part of his desk. He just liked it that way. It was how he ordered his world."

The chair was centered under the computer.

"Okay if I turn it on? Just kind of check things out?"

"Go right ahead." She drew closer to me. "What do you think . . ."

But I was not listening now. I punched the button to turn on the monitor, then reached down to flip on the brains. Wondering if I needed a password.

A password would not have helped. The power lights came on. But the screen never filled. I poked keys, but nothing happened.

"Where did he keep his disks?"

"Right there on the shelf. By the—"

No disks. Empty space.

"Oh, my God," Mary said.

It was real again.

I got down on my knees. "I'm going to have a look inside this sucker. Okay?"

"Anything . . ."

"I might break it."

"Go on. It doesn't matter."

I switched off the machine, then yanked the plug. The computer was an older model, boxy, but lighter than it looked. I laid it flat on the carpet.

No tools required. The screws fell away and the top flipped off. The hard drive was gone.

"Is something wrong?" Mary asked. "Should I call the police again?"

I stared at the gutted machine, all questions and no answers. Then I snapped the cover back down and put the box back in its place.

"Mary, listen to me. I don't think you should call the police. I think you should forget we ever touched the computer. Forget the missing disks. Something's going on, and you need to stay out of it."

She cast those brown eyes down at me. "And Mickey was involved? In whatever you're talking about?"

"Please. Just forget about everything." I could read her mind: *If my husband was in it, and if it cost him his life, I'm damned well going to get into it.* "Mary, could you just go visit your family? Or some friends? Any place far away from here?"

"I'm not about to—"

"Listen to me. This is dangerous. And you can't help. Your husband didn't want you in on this. He didn't even want me in. But I'm in, and you're not, and I'm *beg*ging you in his name to get on a plane and go."

Mary didn't like it. She did not like it one bit.

"Mickey never had time for cowards," she said.

"This isn't about cowardice. It's about survival. You'd hurt, not help."

She thought that over. Wanting more information. "Who else knows about this, John?"

I looked up at her. Just beyond the line of her skirt, I saw Corry. Standing at the French doors.

Mary finally promised me she would get on a plane that evening. Corry and I left. I expected a storm of questions, but Corry just drove.

"You can drop me at one of the rent-a-car lots down on Jeff Davis."

She looked at me from behind her sunglasses. The superbabe. She belonged in a German convertible. Or a white Jag. But she drove a little Jap number. The kind of car a woman on the make could excuse as practical for an urban lifestyle. Corry had made a series of smart choices in her life. Just as Tish had made a long line of dumb ones. Corry Nevers would not have gotten a tattoo in a thousand years. And one earring hanging on each ear was plenty.

I still liked Tish better.

"You can borrow my car," Corry said.

"Thanks. I was born to rent."

She glanced over at me. Little Miss Ray Bans. You imagined wind in her hair even with the windows shut and the air on.

"Mrs. Farnsworth didn't like me very much."

"She's upset."

"I felt like she *hated* me." She locked her face toward the highway. Jewelry-ad profile. "She didn't know about your girlfriend, about what happened? Did she?"

"No. She's a media dropout."

"And she thought you were two-timing?"

I smiled, despite myself. "That's an old-fashioned expression."

"Time stood still where I grew up."

"Yeah. That's what she thought."

"And that woman *liked* your girlfriend? I mean, no offense, but I can't imagine—"

"Fuck off, Corry."

"I didn't mean it like it sounded."

"Bullshit."

"Well, I'm sorry."

I still wanted to cry like a kid when I thought about Tish. I had really humilitated her about the blue-guitar tattoo. In mean, little ways. The shit we lay on people. And live to regret.

"Truce?" Corry said. Soft-voiced.

"Whatever."

"Want me to turn on the radio?"

"Suit yourself."

She switched on NPR low. "So . . . I don't get it," she said.

"You don't get what?"

"Her place wasn't all torn up. The way Em's was."

"They knew where to look. They knew what they wanted."

Corry shook her head. "Maybe. But you know what I think? I think it could be two separate players. Looking for the same thing. Maybe they're in competition."

"And what exactly are they looking for?"

She tipped her sunglasses higher on her nose. "Whatever it is, you can enter it into a computer."

"What if . . ." I said, ". . . what if it's all the same bunch? Only they've been getting too much attention. A burst of killings. The press. The cops. Everything spinning out of control. Maybe whoever's behind them told them to put on their table manners."

"So what do *you* think they're after?" Corry asked.

"Haven't a clue," I lied. The pain in my belly and back had long since convinced me it had something to do with Em's airplane. "How about you?"

"I don't know . . . but it must have been something Em had access to. And this general guy. I just can't figure out where you fit in."

"Same as you," I said. "Guilt by association."

A cop car blasted by us on the berm. Up ahead, traffic had slowed.

"Take the next exit," I said. "There's a back way to get onto Jeff Davis."

"You really could just borrow my car."

"Listen." I reached over to crank up the radio. Martha Raddatz, voice sober-sexy, reporting from the Pentagon. There had been a massive explosion at an aircraft research facility outside Atlanta. Fires still burning. One hundred and fourteen bodies had been recovered, but over a hundred more workers remained unaccounted for. The casualties included civilian scientists as well as military advisers from the United States Air Force and Navy. The lab was rumored to have been a prime site for work on the classified avionics for the Next-Generation Fighter-Bomber.

"Goddamned frogs," I said.

"What's going on?" Corry said, all the cool out of her voice. I suppose my reaction was contagious. "Does this have something to do with us?"

"Bastards," I said.

She turned onto the exit ramp. "*Please* tell me what's going on."

I looked at that gorgeous face. Easy to admire, hard to like. I wondered how much longer she would be alive. Hoping only that things had escalated to a point where we didn't matter anymore, that we might be forgotten.

"It's a shooting war now," I told her.

Maybe Mary Farnsworth didn't like her, and maybe I couldn't let myself like her, either. But the realization had begun to penetrate even my bunker of a skull that Corry Nevers had genuine fears of her own. When she dropped me off at rent-a-car alley, she acted afraid of the dark. At five on a summer afternoon. Just before she drove off, I agreed she could come over later.

She had a way of getting what she wanted.

The economy was booming. I had to march to three rental outfits before I found one that had a car available. I got a Ford that was falling apart. At a crummy day rate.

Merging into the after-work crawl over the bridge, I searched the radio for additional details on the bombing. At the bottom of the hour, the death toll had risen by twelve. I stopped at a market to buy food I did not want and walked the aisles like a prisoner in the exercise yard. After that, I could not avoid going home any longer.

Home was Tish. And Tish was dead. Everything she had ever touched in the house was an emotional atomic bomb. I boiled water for pasta and played the recordings on my answering machine.

Several calls from reporters. I did not copy down the names and numbers.

One call from my boss. Another from Army legal affairs. It was Friday evening and I figured there was no point trying to return the calls. I could see them in person Monday morning.

A call from Dickey that had been overtaken by events.

A message from a member of Tish's band, asking her if she was dead or if it was somebody else in the papers.

And a creamy voice suggesting I change my long-distance company.

I dumped in the pasta and got out the phone book. "F" for funeral homes. I ate first and had a glass of wine from an opened bottle, then called the number on the ad that seemed the most gringo.

When I described what had happened to Tish, the voice on the other end cautioned me that it would be hard to make her look exactly the way I remembered her.

"Maybe I didn't make myself clear," I told him. "She's

cinders. No open casket. No viewing. No wake. I just want to bury her."

"Have you consulted the rest of the family on that?"

"I'm all the family she's got. I want a cemetery south of the river. Someplace clean. And pretty."

"And you'll be wanting spaces for how many, sir?"

I thought about that longer than I really needed to.

"One."

"You might want to consider the savings—"

"*One*. Listen, do they still make wooden caskets? Not cheap ones. Nice ones."

"Oh, indeed they do, sir. We have an absolutely gorgeous eternal bed in mahogany. And a top-of-the-line imported rosewood model."

"Can I have a look at them?"

"Why, of course. Certainly, sir. That's what we're here for. And you *did* specify an interment the day after tomorrow?"

I wanted to scream at him, "Just fucking bury her, all right?" Instead, I said, "Yes. And I'd be grateful if you could find a Catholic priest. The deceased wasn't a member of a local congregation."

"And flowers?"

I thought again, hating the need to think about any of this. "Roses. A lot of them. Yellow roses."

I had given Tish roses several times. But it was only the first bouquet, the yellow ones, that had made her cry.

I went upstairs and worked through Tish's address book. There were not as many names as I had expected. Mostly clubs and other musicians. Little drawings of faces by the entries. With smiles or scowls. I rated a big smile. The sight wrecked me for half an hour.

I phoned the names I recognized first. Each call was like lashing myself with a whip. Some of her friends wanted practical details I did not yet have, or needed consolation I could not give. Others, clumsily polite, just wanted to get off the phone. One bastard told me, sympathetically, that with Tish it had been only a matter of time.

"I never bought that straight act of hers," he said. "You could feel the hunger, you know?"

When I was done, I just sat with my head in my hands. Until the phone rang.

The caller identified himself as Karl Aalstrom. Big voice. Selling something.

"I'll bet you don't remember me," he said. "The basic course. Out at Huachuca. Remember old Aley Aalstrom? We had some times, Johnny boy."

We had not had times, but I did remember him now. Second Lieutenant Karl Aalstrom. He and a ring of other students had been caught cheating. The intel school should have booted them, but they were just lieutenants and the chain of command was trying to keep the attrition rate down. So they slapped their wrists and gave them extra training. Later on, I heard that Aalstrom was caught falsifying TDY vouchers and did not even make captain.

"Yeah. I remember. What's up?"

"Oh, just checking in. Old times and all. Think maybe we could get together for some chow? Or a beer, anyway? On me, Johnny boy. Life is good. I'm living large."

"It's a bad time."

"Just a few minutes."

"I'll have to take a raincheck."

He breathed like an asthmatic. Or a sex caller. "John? I'm afraid I can't take 'No' for an answer. You see, I work for some people who need to communicate with you. They brought me in from the West Coast so we could sit down and talk. They called me because they found out you and I go a long way back."

"We don't go a long way back. What's this all about?"

"John, we don't really want to talk about this over the phone, all right? Why don't we just meet somewhere—"

"I don't have time. And I'm not interested." I didn't hang up, though. And it was a good thing, in the end.

"Johnny boy. Listen to me. One old friend to another. You *want* to make this meeting."

"Give me one good reason."

"I understand you like guitars," he said. "How about a mint-condition Les Paul Gibson?"

Corry showed up at the door just as I was leaving. She didn't care where I was going. She wanted to come along.

"No. I'm meeting a ghost from the past. Wait here, if you want."

She could not think of an argument fast enough. Or maybe she read the determination in my voice and figured the fight would not be worth the ammunition. She accepted my offer. I told her to stay upstairs and not to answer the door or the phone. She nodded. Eyes gone elsewhere.

It was dusk. I got down on my knees to check the car's underbelly. Then I checked under the hood. Nothing that I could see. The neighbor kids thought I was a hoot. The adults crossed the street to avoid me.

The traffic had faded. I sailed south with the windows down. Checking the rearview mirror. If anybody was following me, I couldn't spot them. All quiet on the Potomac.

I pulled off at Shirlington. Aalstrom knew the D.C. area. He had specified a linkup in a microbrewery cafe that was loud and anonymous. GS-7s through -11s, with their ties loosened. Young women in their first business suits. Waitresses with jogger's legs and too much education to be efficient. I wondered if I would recognize Aalstrom. It didn't really matter, since he was obviously going to recognize me.

I beat him to the powwow tent. I took over a stool that

gave me an intermittent view of the door and disappointed the bartender by ordering a Diet Coke. A few of the women looked at me as if I were in the running but not leading the pack.

Aalstrom strutted in, big and blond, with too little hair worn too long. The dark shirt and linen sport coat were upscale Tijuana. He carried a good-looking briefcase, though. New York shuttle meets Brentwood. The hostess intercepted him. He pushed up too close to her.

He saw me, waved, and took the girl with the menus hostage until he had me in a booth in a corner. He handled the briefcase with care.

"Jesus Christ," he said, slapping his hands together, "it's good to see you, Johnny boy. God Almighty, I wish I still had your physique. Army keeps you hopping, I guess. Me, I got to get back on an exercise program." He tapped the swell of his stomach. "Got to get rid of the old heart-attack sack. Jeez, though, you hardly look a day older than you did out at Fort We-got-ya."

He looked beat and old. Em's car-lot cousin. I tried to remember if Em had been any closer to him than I had been. I didn't think so. But Em had always had his secrets.

"So what's up, Aley? What's this Les Paul Gibson crap?"

He looked genuinely disappointed. "Don't you want to order first? You're my guest, Johnny boy. Live large."

"Talk to me."

"They do killer burgers here—you know that? I stop by every time I'm in town. Can't get a decent burger in L.A. anymore. Fucking broccoli patties. Tofu hot dogs. Where's it going to end?" He dropped his smile and his menu. "So what're you fucking around with all this for, Johnny? It's not your brief. Why bring down all this pain on yourself?"

"I'm an unreconstructed Protestant. We like pain. Why don't we start at the beginning?"

Aalstrom rolled his eyes and gave me the polar-bear salute.

Palms held high. "Beginning? Who knows how it all began? The here and now is what matters, Johnny boy. And the future. You should think about your future."

The waitress slapped down a basket of soft pretzels and mustard dip.

"Get you guys something to drink?"

"Black-and-tan, angel," Aalstrom said. He appraised the girl as she scribbled. "I bet you're really a model. You a model?"

"I'm an economist," the waitress told him. I ordered a draft and she moved on.

"So let's talk," Aley said. "Just like old times. Now, I represent some people. Business interests. Serious players, Johnny boy. Now . . . the people I represent are the only rational actors in this whole circus. They want to put a stop to all this violence. They're disgusted by it. And they're prepared to pay."

"They want to pay *me* to stop the violence?"

His face said I was letting him down big-time. "Johnny boy, do not give me unnecessary grief, all right? I'm trying to reach out to you. You *know* what I'm saying."

"I don't have any idea what you're saying."

The waitress put down our drinks. There was too much foam on the beers. "Take your dinner orders, guys?"

"Later," Aalstrom told her. "My friend isn't hungry." When she moved on, he said, "Hey, I'll bet she's been fucked so many times her brains are fried. College does it to them, you know?" He shared his eyes with me again. Leaning in so that the edge of the table creased his gut. "How much money will it take? Lay your cards on the table."

"Money for what?"

"Get real. Talk to me."

"I don't know what you're talking about, Aley."

Another big shake of the head. "You really are the dumbest joker on earth if you don't take this money and run. So okay. I'll open the bidding. How about five million? That's still a nice piece of change. Deposited offshore—no Freddy Fuck-Around stuff. You like the Caymans? Bermuda? How about Panama? Name the bank. Shit, we can even put it in Canada for you. Make it look like you inherited half of Ontario. Treasury boys'll never find it. Hosers can't run financial institutions. Nothing but Mexicans with college degrees. Chinese are going to own the place in a couple of years. Hey, we'll even create an investment history for you. How about it? Five mil sound good? Beats Army pay."

"Five million sounds great. What do I have to do for it?"

"Johnny, would you stop this? You are alienating a true friend."

My turn to lean across the table. So close I could see the veins webbing his nose. "Just tell me straight out what you want."

To his credit, Aalstrom did not turn away. Suddenly, he looked a lot harder.

"Johnny," he said, "I see you've never been in a courtroom. Or you are playing it very fucking dumb when you should be playing it cool." He backed his big head away. As if drawing a deep breath. Then he moved in again.

"They want the disks. Every fucking one of them. Every copy you might have made trying to be clever. No more bullshit."

"I don't have any disks."

He wanted to grab me. To hit me. Maybe this was his shot at the big time. "Fuck you, Johnny. Just fuck you. Everybody knows you got the disks. Who else is going to have them? You tell me, huh?" He could barely hold himself on his side of the table. Big hands clenched and unclenched just inches from me. "They're all fucking dead, Johnny boy. All the little shits who thought they were players. Dead, dead, *dead*." He brought his eyes closer. Life had not been good to him. "Dead is forever, pal. Stay alive. And help an old friend out while you're at it."

"I don't have any disks. I don't know what I'm involved in. If I am, in fact, involved in something. Which is starting to seem like a safe bet." I surprised him. I leaned closer and grabbed his wrists and forced them down on the table before he knew what was happening. I got the tips of my thumbs right on the nerves and went deep. "But let me tell you something, Mr. Les Paul Gibson telephone bullshit. If you . . . or any of the scum who sent you here . . . if you had anything . . . *any*thing to do with the death of Tish O'Malley, I guarantee you I will live long enough to make you pay for it."

I hit his nerves hard, right where you can grind them against the wrist joint. It's a good skill. Em had taught it to me a long time before. Laughing down in Mexico. His father had hired a private martial arts instructor for him when he was a kid.

Aalstrom nearly lost it. Doing a sit-down jig. Trying not to shout. Tears crowded in his eyes.

I let him go, took out a five, and dropped it on the table.

"Should cover the beer."

"*Please*," he said, working his wrists. "Don't go yet. I have something for you."

"I'm waiting."

He looked at me. A big wounded bear. "John . . . I'm *beg*ging you. Deal with me. Let me have the disks. It'd be good for both of us."

I tried to make my voice level and real. "Aley, I'm telling you the truth. I don't have any disks. Except for the ones that go with my PC. You can have those, if you want. They're not very exciting." I puffed beer-stained air. "I just seem to have stumbled into all this. And I wish I could stumble back out." I turned my head slowly from side to side, not quite looking at him. The sight of him was painful. How people lose in life. "But I do not have these disks you're talking about. And I've already been hurt about as bad as anybody could do it. So tell your crowd to look somewhere else."

Aalstrom wasn't living large anymore. He looked smashed in. "John," he said at last, "I wouldn't tell anybody else what you just said. About not having the disks. Especially if it's true. Right about now, the possibility that you're holding those disks is all that's keeping you alive."

"Shit."

"What's that supposed to mean?"

"Just what it says. Goddamn it. You kill my girl, try to bribe me, and threaten to kill me, too. And you want to make nice."

"Maybe . . . you should *try* to find those disks."

"Aley, you're big on old-times-sake. How about doing me a favor? Just tell me what this is all about. What's on these magic disks that I don't have?"

He lowered his face. Looking at the spoiled menu. "Can't do it, pal. Got to keep on the right side of Jesus."

"Shit."

Aalstrom sighed. "You're a great disappointment to me, Johnny. But I guess you figured that out." He roused himself and reached for his briefcase. "Tell you what. Let me lay down my last card." He took out a manila envelope with a bulge. "Got something for you. You like movies?"

"Drama? Or comedy?"

"You're going to like this one. Little video. Just for you. It's an exclusive." He extended the envelope. "Somebody'll be in touch."

"What is it?"

"Just watch it. Go home and watch it. It'll put things in perspective."

I took the envelope. And got up to go.

Aalstrom smiled again. "Bet you a fifty I screw that waitress tonight."

I was sorry I wasn't a betting man.

CHAPTER 6

I did the security thing and parked a couple of blocks away, then took an indirect route home. The darkness had weight. Heat grabbed skin and would not let go. In the park, the brothers were drinking and getting Friday-night loud. Most folks out on the street after dark just have to keep an eye out for muggers. I was waiting to get shot. Or kidnapped again. Or to turn onto my block and find my house blown up.

Corry had turned up the air and the cold smacked me when I stepped in the front door. Stereo cranked. Marianne Faithfull. *Broken English.*

Changed into cutoffs and an old Key West T-shirt, she still looked Ralph Lauren. Smiling to greet me. She had not stayed upstairs as agreed.

"Turn that down," I said. "No. Turn it off. Or put something else on."

She pouted and bent over my stereo. Lean tanned legs. Her shirt climbed her back.

The music stopped. She straightened.

"Was that your girlfriend's? I'm sorry . . ."

"Why Marianne Faithfull?" My voice sounded paranoid even to me.

She looked baffled. "No special reason. I just hadn't heard it in a while. It used to be one of my favorites. In college." She held the disc case in her hand. Judging the cool-unto-death look of the cover. "To tell you the truth, I was a little disappointed. She seems so . . . obvious. I guess my tastes are maturing. Did I do something wrong?"

"Forget it."

She smiled again. "So how was your visit with your friend? Can I make you some coffee? Oh, the phone kept ringing. Four times, I think. I let the answering machine get it. The way you said."

I walked into the kitchen. Realizing belatedly that Corry had put my place back together. With remarkable skill and speed. As if she had known where everything belonged. When I left, the wires had been ripped off the back of the stereo and the CD player had been on the floor. I was glad it still worked.

I put the envelope with the video down on the counter and played the messages. My boss, voice hot. *Call me, John.* I looked at my watch and decided to wait. There were a couple of grunts from Dickey. *Get with me, soldier boy. We need to talk.* The funeral director had two cemetery plots he wanted me to look at. And a persistent reporter named Ricks from *The Wall Street Journal* had left his number again.

Corry put on Chet Baker. She sat on the floor with her back against a small suitcase, legs dolled out. Looking up at me as though our relationship was deeper than it was ever going to get. I just said:

"Thanks for the cleanup work."

"I appreciate you letting me stay here. I mean . . . for letting me sleep here. It makes me feel a lot safer."

I did not remember agreeing to anything of the kind. And

there had not been a suitcase in her hand when she hit the door earlier. But I was too beat to argue. She could stay if she wanted. My sofa had carried heavier bones. I wanted to be alone. But I didn't, either.

I offered to get her some linens, but she had already found what she needed. The upstairs was still a wreck. But she had done a good deed on the first floor.

The video would have to wait. That was private business.

What were they going to show me? Test flights of the NGFB? Sweeping fake bad guys from the sky? Were they going to appeal to my patriotism? Or demonstrate some imaginative instruments of torture?

It could wait until morning.

"I'm turning in," I said.

"Is the music too loud?"

I shrugged. "It's fine."

"I just love Chet Baker," she said as I climbed the stairs. "Why do musicians always get mixed up with drugs?"

The sheets still smelled like Tish. Like Tish and me. But the scent was getting fainter. I wondered how long I could go without washing them. Then the wondering stopped, sudden as a head-on collision.

I woke to warmth and slow movement and night. I had been way down and it took me a while to swim back to the surface. I did not come up swinging. That was either a good thing or a bad one, depending on your perspective.

Corry Nevers hugged me from behind. Still wearing her T-shirt. But nothing else.

"I was afraid," she whispered. "I'm afraid all the time now."

I pulled away. The bright city darkness worked in through the blinds and I saw her.

"This isn't part of the package," I said. "Get out of here."

She wasn't ready for that and started to cry. I sat up on

the edge of the bed, thinking that I needed to start wearing pajamas. My body was a scum traitor pig.

Corry trailed her fingertips down my back. I jerked away again. Then I stood up. Embarrassed. Even in the dark.

"You and me live on different planets," I told her. "Tish hasn't been dead forty-eight hours." My anger was not quite sane. Certainly not proportional. "Poor old Em didn't have any idea, did he?"

She was really crying now. "I thought we . . . I thought we could just . . . comfort each other. That—"

"Fucking stuff it. Knock it off, Corry. I don't know what you're up to, but leave me out of it." I wanted to throw something. Break things. Of course I wanted her. And there she was. On sheets still scented with Tish. As if Corry were trying to erase my memories, to bury the scent with her own.

For a truly mean instant, I considered getting back into bed. What did it matter, at this point?

Corry got up. I thought she was going to retreat downstairs. Instead, she fastened herself to me. With my body proving the feminists right: Men are swine.

I broke her hold and grasped her by the upper arms. Forcing distance between us.

She was beautiful in the darkness. Wickedness adorned her.

"You want me," she said. "I know you do. Please. I'm so lonely."

"No."

She was gone when I got up, but she had left her suitcase. And half a pot of coffee. Hard woman to shake. At any other time in my life, I would not havc tricd.

I brought in the paper and worked through the front-pager about the lab bombing down in Georgia, slamming myself with caffeine. Big trouble down in the Peach State. The United States had gone to war over less.

I knew too much, and I did not really seem to know anything, and I did not know where to go. This was way off the Army's reservation. The cops were no help. I was not going to go to the French, that was for damned sure. And anybody who would hire Aley Aalstrom to make their tough sales for them did not have much market appeal.

The coffee charged through me. I was still pissing blood. But it did not look quite so bad. I decided that the smartest thing I could do would be to check in at Walter Reed and let the docs earn their specialty pay. Knowing that I would not do it. I could not even steel myself to return the phone calls from the night before.

I remembered the video. I could not recall where I had put it and did not find it immediately. I panicked, cursing Corry, imagining she had stolen it.

The envelope was sitting in plain view. Where I had left it.

The cops seemed to have had a thing about wires. They had pulled them all out. Corry had not gotten around to reconnecting the VCR. I worked as fast as I could, back stiff and unforgiving. I was just capable enough to match red with red, white with white, and yellow with yellow. Then I had to find the remote. Finally, I got the video in and eased down on the carpet in front of the tube.

Nothing. I could hear the tape running. But there was no picture. Or sound.

I checked the connections. Then I tested the television. It worked fine by itself. I dug out the instruction booklet. In the end, I shook the VCR hard and did everything but smash my foot down on it. It hissed. And gave a few little grunts. But it refused to show the video.

Life was not smooth.

I got dressed, body a catalog of aches. I tried to think of friends who might be home, then decided that the last thing I needed to do was to get another non-player involved. Taking the tape with me, I locked up and headed for the rental car.

No bombs in evidence. A fat kid tried to sell me melted chocolate. I could understand only half of what she said. "Help keep youth off the streets," I think. Another D.C. hustle. I told her maybe next time. And got in the car.

Talk radio loved the Georgia bombing. The right blamed the left and the left blamed the right. A White House spokesman declared that the FBI was investigating a possible Iranian connection, but added that the President cautioned all Americans to respect the contributions of our citizens of Iranian descent. Given the guy's recent difficulties, "contributions" was a poor choice of words. The bottom line was that none of the talking heads had a clue.

I went to a discount appliance store in the near burbs. Where things are cheaper than at the PX. A young man with a ring through his lower lip asked if he could help me.

"I need a VCR. Plain vanilla. And I want to use my own tape to test it."

"Right." He judged me. "You want to go Korean, man. The Jap stuff is money for nothing. Four heads?"

"I just want it to work."

"Right." Walking me down the aisles. All the TVs were showing *The Godfather, Part II.* Only in Hollywood could Al Pacino pass for a tough guy. "Trust me. This right here is, like, the best deal in the store. And it just happens to be on special. This must be your lucky—"

"It hooked up?"

"I was just going to switch it over." He bent toward a junction box. "Slip in your vid, man. You'rc going to love this machine."

I did as he told me. I could not wait. A born fool.

Tish appeared on twenty or thirty screens. No sound. But she was sitting in a room raw as a barracks, hunched over the

Les Paul Gibson I had given her for her birthday. Holding the guitar like a martyr clutching a cross. And wearing the same clothes she had worn the last time she walked out of my door. Our door. Oblivious to the hidden camera, she looked worn and cried-out and utterly beautiful.

"Serious babe," the clerk said. "She your daughter or something?"

I bought the VCR. I would have bought ten of them. All I wanted to do was to go home and watch the clip of Tish over and over again.

But I did not go home. I needed to take inventory. I went to Arlington Cemetery.

I parked in the visitor lot and marched up through the crowds. Tourists in shorts on their way to see JFK's grave. Then snap the poor troopie sweating his rocks off in front of the Tomb of the Unknown Soldier. I cut left and climbed through the heat. The grass crunched.

Farnsworth lay on the high ground. In winter, you would be able to see all of the city's monuments across the river, but leaves blocked part of the view now. The flowers had been removed and the grave sodded. I wanted to be alone, but I had hoped faintly that the gravedigger—or whatever the politically correct term is for a boneyard worker these days—would be around. I had liked him. A lot better than I liked myself at the moment. But the only life in evidence was a bird picking at the grass.

I sat under a tree. Probably violating six different rules. And watched the general's grave as if I expected him to speak first. A jet wrenched the sky, coming down into National.

"Christ, sir," I said, "you should've brought me in. If you could trust Em, you could've trusted me. Now here I am, in the middle of all this shit, dumb as a rock. And somebody's got my girl."

The bird hopped and poked. A fly probed my defenses.

"So who's zooming who?" I asked him. "Where do I start? Give me a hint, huh?"

I felt as though a smarter man would have pieced the story together days before.

The French were scum. But that did not fall into the surprise category. By their own admission, they had stolen the plans for the NGFB. It looked like we had bombed them in retaliation, whoever "we" were. It shocked me. Because I believed it was true. And it was a massive, terrible thing. I could not conceive of any industrial secrets that were worth it. I did not want to believe my kind were capable of such an action. I suppose Tish was right—I really didn't have any idea how the world worked.

So we bombed the French. Then the French bombed us back. The French had to have done the Georgia number. Still, that surprised me, too. I would not have believed they had it in them anymore. Sinking a Greenpeace rowboat was one thing. But whacking a couple of hundred American scientists leavened with military officers was something else. There was obviously a lot more to the NGFB than the full-page ads and the Senate testimony let on. Some black program within a black program.

Something about the French—about my own personal Jules and Jim—clawed at me. They had not said a word about any disks. Even though everybody else on this side of the Atlantic seemed to be after them. But there was another thing, too. Cuckold had yipped and yapped about us making fools of them. Even before the bombing. I wondered what that was all about.

A tourist couple poked down a lower row of graves. Lost. Or hunting for a relative. The woman bobbed along the headstones as if keeping count. The man looked at the grass, then at the sky. He wore a white sun hat with the brim down and I could feel him sweat from a hundred meters away.

I brushed off my pet fly.

Em's guilt trip. I figured he knew a lot more about us bombing the frogs than he had been willing to tell me. And he knew the big secret about that airplane that was worth killing for. Em could be cynical, but, to his credit, this time around it had been too much. That triggered his redemption thing.

And it meant that Macon-Bolt had a connection to the bombing of the French lab. At least enough of a tie for Em to find out about it. And repent. It was a new level of cutthroat capitalism.

Em turned to Farnsworth because the general was the only man left he could trust who had any clout at all. The two of them probably figured they could do a good deed, for God and country. Expose the criminals. But the criminals had better intel. And an operational capability the Hardy Boys had underestimated.

Who, exactly, were the killers? Why were they playing with bombs? They certainly weren't amateurs. This was a heavyweight bout.

What was on the disks I had never seen that made them worth killing for? My mind kept flipping the channel back to black capabilities. Maybe there was some phenomenal wonder-weapon component to the NGFB. Something so revolutionary we did not want its existence known. Even by an ally. To the extent the frogs were allies.

Why kill the general and Em, but settle for just grabbing Tish and muscling me? Why rip up the floorboards in one place, but not in another?

At least I could sketch the chain of logic that put me in the game. They would have been watching Em. And he was dumb enough to ask me to share a drink, and I was dumb enough to take him up on it. They ran my ID wide and deep and hit on my old ties to Em and Farnsworth. They tore up Em's apartment, but left the phone working because they had it tapped. Tish called me. I went over. So they figured Em had done a battle handoff of the disks to me. Or that I knew where they were and grabbed them before the cops came. Now I was in the cesspool, with Tish a hostage, and no idea how to get her back.

If Tish was alive, who had gone charcoal in my car?

And where did Corry Nevers fit in?

Corry was a size-six moment of truth. If I had met her back when my relationship with Tish had been on cruise control, I probably would have taken the detour and got away without paying the toll. Pathetic, what you realize about yourself. It was easier being faithful to Tish when I thought she was dead, or now that she was a prisoner of the video lifestyle, than it would have been on any old day when we were happy.

I had never really taken Tish seriously. I always kept some distance between us. Yet I had never loved anybody the way I loved her. I did not know exactly what that meant, but I was afraid it was not good news. Tish seemed born for trouble. Which is probably a good third of why I fell for her. I had always thought of myself as a big, bold risk-taker. But I was a coward when it counted.

It's rot to say that anything good comes out of a mess like this. But it's useful to get a clear look at yourself. Buying somebody an expensive guitar is easy. The truth is that whenever I felt Tish drawing me too close, an invisible bitch from the Officers' Wives Club whispered in my ear that she was damaged goods.

Now all I wanted to do was to go home, hook up the new VCR, and watch the film of her over and over again. She was alive. And if I ever got her back, I was not going to blow it.

The only good piece of advice I had gotten from anybody

had come from Aley Aalstrom. When he told me that even if I did not have the disks, I had better act as though I did. That was as plain as the business end of a gun now.

I seemed to own that one solid fact: The disks were my shot at getting Tish back alive. And at staying alive myself.

Who had them? Where were they? Where did I start looking?

I stood up, miserable with sweat.

"I never learned anything," I told Farnsworth. "I wish you were here to help me. A lot of people are dead now."

I scribbled a mental note to call Mary and make sure she had gotten on the plane as promised. Then I headed back into the city.

As soon as I put the VCR box down by the television, the doorbell rang.

It was the Cuckold of Paris.

He did not get one word out. I grabbed him by the shirt collar and yanked him inside, kicking the door shut behind us. I hit him so fast he could not get his arms up to block.

He went down right there in the hallway. But he was tough. Instead of going out or running up the white flag, he scissored me with his legs. So hard he almost broke my ankle.

We grappled on an old throw rug. Too close to hit hard enough to make a difference. I was bigger, but he had a mean streak and more martial arts behind him. He used his legs and feet. The scumbag smelled like he did not use deodorant.

"Goddamned Eurotrash," I said. Or grunted. I broke free just long enough to hit him in the gut with all my weight behind it. Recalling the way he had hit me.

He was thin. My fist almost made it to the floor. It stressed him long enough for me to give him a jab to the snout, then deliver a big one with my knuckles going in between his jawbone and cheekbone. I could count teeth under the meat.

"You . . . fuck . . ." I was not at my most articulate. But I threw in plenty about vengeance for Georgia and what I was going to do to him if he had Tish. Not a lot of clarity of thought or complete sentences. But this was the first time I had gotten to blow off steam. When you've been everybody's punching bag for a while, it's great to get a turn in the gloves.

"Didn't . . . do . . . it . . ." he said. "We . . . no . . ."

Then he kicked me hard. Just missing the combat zone. It threw me off balance. Before I knew it, the little bastard was on top of me. Pounding away. Trying to get at my face. I rolled both of us backward. Cuckold flailed like a hostage in a trunk.

"We . . . didn't . . . do . . . it . . ." he said.

We were trying to hurt each other. Hitting hard. But it was funny. Neither of us wanted to do irreversible damage. Nobody went for the eyes, which is where you head if you're serious. We both knew how to kill somebody. This was just guy stuff.

I threw him. He crashed against the stereo stand. Which pissed me off again. I went in swinging, but I was still on my knees. You can't get leverage that way.

He threw a handful of CDs into my face. Then he punched me low in the belly.

It hurt.

He jumped to his feet and aimed a kick at my face. I moved just in time, more luck than skill, and got my hands on his thigh. Then the little shit was on his back again, and it was my turn to kick.

Even banged up, he was fast. He rolled and threw a blind kick backward that caught my hip. In the couple of seconds I spent reeling, he scrambled back to his feet.

I grabbed him again. Before he could get his footing. And threw him against a chair. He tumbled into the upholstery. This time I landed on his guts with one of my knees. It felt indescribably satisfying. It's amazing that grown men don't do this more frequently.

The fight went out of him. But I wasn't done.

"Why'd you do it?" I yelled. "Why the hell did you do it?"

He was a rag. His hands did not even close into fists anymore. His head rolled. I put one in between his eyes so hard it hurt my hand. The bridge of his nose collapsed like chicken bones in a dog's jaws. The sonofabitch shot blood onto my chair.

Somebody had been pounding on the door for a while. Maybe his partner. I didn't know. Hardly cared. I was deep into the fight, which had been going on for maybe a minute. I intended to finish Cuckold before dealing with anything else. The rest of the world could bugger off.

I heard Dickey's growl:

"Open up. Police."

"So who's this?" Dickey asked. "Your drug partner? What do we got? Falling-out among thieves?" He turned to one of the uniforms. "Keep them separated, all right?" Pointing a thick finger at Cuckold. "Get that piece of shit out of here. Now. Take him down to the station."

Cuckold had struggled to his feet. Fighting to make sense of the world. His eyes would not settle. But he stepped away from the approaching cop.

"I'm a diplomat," he said. "I have immunity. I am from the Embassy of France."

Dickey put his thumbs in his belt loops. "Yeah? You paid all your parking tickets?"

"You cannot arrest me. I have diplomatic immunity."

"Got an ID, Mr. Ambassador? Wayne, check Pierre's pockets, huh?" Dickey swiveled his big head back toward me. "Okay. My Saturday's fucked and my patience is gone. Who is he?"

"He's French. He's a spy. And a thug. He's tied in with that bombing down in Georgia. The research lab that went up."

Dickey snorted. "Not my jurisdiction. What was he doing on my beat?"

Actually, I wasn't sure. I had no idea why Cuckold had shown up at my door.

This was all too slow for Dickey. "Billy, take Pierre La Fuckface down to the station. Check if he's got dip. Make nice until we find out. But take prints. And he doesn't walk until we find out if anybody else wants him." He spit out something invisible and gave me The Face. "You're pretty good at beating up little guys, soldier boy. Ever do any debt collecting for your old lady's drug crowd? Looks like Lucky Pierre landed at least one, though. Make that two."

"This guy was involved in a terrorist act against the United States. Diplomatic immunity doesn't count in a situation like this. You need to contact the FBI."

"Right. Would you like me to call J. Edgar directly, or should I go through Efrem Zimbalist, Jr.? We'll find out if he's Yassir Arafat or not. In the meantime, you and me got some talking to do. Oh, by the way, you're under arrest. Wipe the goddamned blood off your lip while I read you your rights."

"What's the charge?"

Dickey ignored me. Doing his spiel.

As the cops led the Frenchman out, he whispered, "Do not tell them anything."

I don't know whether he meant it or just said it in front of Dickey to screw me.

Then Dickey and I were alone. The detective finished his recitation.

"What's the charge?" I asked him.

He smirked. "What do you think?"

"Come on. If you were any kind of cop you'd know I haven't done anything. Unless pounding that little shit's face in counts."

Dickey looked up at me. I could tell he did not like the physical arrangement. He much preferred me sitting down.

"'Conspiracy to traffic in illegal drugs.'"

"That's bullshit. You know it's bullshit. You *have* to know."

He smiled. "Yeah? Well, I guess we'll see. Conspiracy's a great statute, you know that? Separates your *Habeas* right from your *Corpus*. I think of it as the superpunk provision." He smiled. "I just want to hear what you have to say after a weekend in the slammer with your fellow residents of the District of Columbia."

I closed my eyes. Held up my hand. "Wait. Look. Just tell me what you really want from me. Give it to me straight."

Dickey turned toward a side wall. Shaking his head. Exaggerating it. "What *I* want from *you*? Maybe I just want to have lunch, huh? My fucking treat. I want you to *talk* to me, pal. Tell me something I don't know. Help me clear up two murders, maybe three. Or what's your latest count?"

"Tell you what. I'll do better than talk. I'm going to *show* you something."

You-can't-con-me eyes. "Show me what?"

"I just need two minutes to hook up the video."

Dickey laughed. It sounded like falling bricks hitting the sidewalk. "What you got? Hot tapes of your girlfriend or something?"

I looked at him. "That's exactly what I've got."

His mouth opened. But before he spoke, the doorbell rang again.

"You're a popular guy," Dickey said. "Open it. Invite them in." He drew his gun from beneath his jacket with a smoothness I would not have expected. He stepped back, just an inch out of the line of fire from the door.

It was Corry. Dressed for success. With a bouquet of flowers.

"I'm so sorry about last night," she said quickly. "I was a

selfish bitch." Then her eyes moved off me and widened. I did not have to turn around to know that Dickey had moved into the open. With his gun.

I forgot that Corry and Dickey had already crossed paths in the wreckage of Em's apartment. I was forgetting a lot of things. I just said:

"It's all right. He's a cop."

Corry stood in a wash of sunlight, just enough sweat on her forehead to make her human.

Her eyes were not good. She looked ready to run for it.

"Come right in, Ms. Nevers," Dickey said. "You're just in time for the matinee. Isn't that right, soldier boy?"

When I turned around, Dickey gave me a look of absolute disgust.

Showing Corry the video had not been part of the plan. But my plans did not seem to count for much at the moment. Dickey put his gun away, Corry laid down the flowers and her purse, and I hooked up the new VCR.

We stood in front of the television.

Seeing the image of Tish again hit me in the stomach harder than the Frenchman had ever done. The clip was not long, not over a minute. But I had time to replay a lot of memories.

When the screen went black, Dickey turned to me and said, "So? What's the revelation?"

I hit the rewind button. I wanted to see it again.

"It means she's alive," I said.

Dickey lifted an eyebrow. "That a fact? Buddy, all I see is a tape that for all I know is a year old. You got to show me some leg."

"It wasn't Tish in that car." I felt like a child who cannot make his parents see the obvious. "Can't you . . . do DNA testing or something? On the body?"

Dickey barked out a laugh. "He wants DNA testing! Soldier boy, we don't even have spare tires for our cruisers. I copy my fucking reports at Kinko's. And the mayor ain't the one picking up the tab." He gave another, lesser bark. Yet for all his barstool bullshit, I could sense just the slightest change in him. "So tell me about this tape of yours."

"The guitar she's playing—let me run it again." I hit Play. "Look at the guitar. I just gave it to her. For her birthday. I just picked it up last Tuesday. I have a dated receipt." I looked up from the image, desperate to see a change in Dickey's expression. "I never made any videos of her with it. I don't even own a video camera. She never took it out of this house, either. And the clothes. That's what she had on when she walked out of here the last time." I felt I should be able to convince him through the sheer intensity of the truth. "Remember when I called and bitched about your guys stealing the guitar? That's the one. Whoever grabbed her came back here for the guitar. They knew everything. Everything about us. Every detail. They knew the guitar would convince me that they had her, that she's still alive."

"You're talking trash. I don't see proof of anything."

"*Please*. Listen to me. *She's not dead*. Tish is alive. I can't explain the car. I don't know what happened. I don't know who was in it. I don't have any idea who's got her. But she's *alive*." I wanted to grab him. "Don't you want to find her?"

I wondered what Dickey's game might be. Even a D.C. cop could not be this stupid, this unwilling to consider the evidence. I stared at him, crazy for some way to convince him. Or, as a minimum, to buy time. I could not afford to go to jail with Tish out there waiting for me to unscrew things.

Dickey did not say anything right away. I took that as a good sign at last. But something else occurred to me while I waited for him to decide Tish's fate and mine. There was a third person in the room with us. And Corry Nevers had not said a word.

"All right," Dickey said. "Give me the tape."

"What?"

"I said give me the goddamned tape." He shook his head. "I must be nuts."

"What are you talking about?"

He looked at me as though he found me inexpressibly stupid. "I'm not going to bust you. Not yet. But I got paper on you. And I can drop it anytime I want. Remember that. Now give me the tape."

"Why do you need the tape?"

My intelligence dropped another rung in his eyes. "It's evidence, for Christ's sake."

"Can I at least make a copy?"

"Uh-huh. Sure. And then we go to court and some fuck in a thousand-dollar suit gets up and says, 'Your Honor, this evidence has been tampered with.' Right. Sure, I'm going to let you make a copy."

"Please. It means a lot to me."

Dickey chugged the snot back in his nose. "The tape? Or the slammer? This is not a trick question."

I gave him the tape. I felt like I was handing over Tish herself.

He wiped his forehead. Sweating in the air-conditioned room.

"Now," he said. "Speak slowly and clearly, and tell me how this tape came into your possession."

On the backbeat, I told him, "It was in an envelope. On the doorstep. This morning."

He thought for a moment. Then snorted again. "Trusting souls. Must be out-of-towners. So . . . you're telling me this French bozo has something to do with it?"

"I don't know. Maybe. I don't know who has her. I want to know." Then I remembered. "But I'd bet a month's pay he's tied into that laboratory bombing."

"Not my jurisdiction. So what did you mean, he's a spy?"

"He's got a partner. The other night—"

A fist whacked the front door and a cop voice called for Dickey. The detective answered and he and a patrolman mumbled cop codes and street numbers to each other. After a moment, Dickey strode back to me. He had a repertoire of disgusted faces that should have been cataloged by the Smithsonian.

"You and me are going to have to talk. But right now I got a twenty-year-old some hero used for extended target practice plus her six-year-old daughter with a bullet through her neck. Life in a wheelchair. If the kid's lucky. And you're probably wondering why I got such bad manners. Accompany me to the door, Colonel, sir."

In the doorframe, he grabbed me by the upper arm and yanked me outside. He was much stronger than I would have guessed.

"You fuck me," he said, "and you're going to jail till you look like Santa Claus." He turned his wrecked eyes up to meet mine. "And just for the record, I liked your old girlfriend better. Dumb fucking cop that I am."

Corry stood by the television. Posed. Perfect. I remembered the exact feel of her rubbing against me in the night.

She pushed her hair back over her ears. One side, then the other. Chin held low. Lips opening like a wound.

"You lied to him," she said. "You had that tape last night."

"So turn me in."

She smiled. The lip maneuvers were much too complex for a woman her age.

"No way," she said. "We're in this together. We're partners." She glanced around the room. "You can't seem to keep things tidy. By the way, I don't remember seeing a vase for flowers."

"There's one down in the basement. If I were you, I'd be out of here at a run."

"I don't see how either one of us can go back," she said blithely. "I *am* glad your girlfriend's all right. Who do you think has her?"

"I wish I knew."

"Does your eye hurt?"

"Is it black?"

"It looks like it's going to be. A little. What was the fight about?"

"It was a cultural thing."

She stood there in her summer suit. Proper. Real Senate Caucus stuff. No matter how I tried, I could not stop remembering. Her flesh luminous in the darkness. And the feel of her curls against my thigh.

Corry walked to the front door, opened it, looked out, and came back.

"They're gone," she said. She glanced at her watch. "I have to get back to the office. The senator wants me to take notes for him at a hearing. Can you believe Congress is working right through the weekend? In July?" Her eyes were harder than her voice. "This is not what I want to do for the rest of my life."

"I thought you loved your work."

"I've had worse jobs. Sometimes it's good. But I can imagine a better life, too."

"Corry . . . we're getting this all wrong."

She smiled, refusing my doubts. "I think we make a good team. Even if you still don't like me."

"I thought you were scared."

"I am."

"Then why—"

"You know why. And I'm not ashamed of what I feel. So don't be a pig about it."

"I'm in love with Tish."

"I'll take that chance."

"I'm going to get her back."

"I'll help you."

"You don't believe I love her."

Corry looked away. "I don't believe you'll love her forever."

"I don't trust you."

She smiled. "Don't worry. I won't embarrass you again. I'll wait."

I shook my head.

"You don't know me, John. You don't know me at all." She picked up her purse and stepped close to me. "Do you have a gun?"

"This is D.C. Only the criminals have guns."

She reached into her bag and lifted out an old *film noir* thirty-eight.

"Here," she said. "Take it. I don't want you to get hurt."

Corry walked out. I just stood there in my living room, gun in hand, a statue memorializing village idiots everywhere. The phone rang.

I figured it was my boss. I got ready for the anger. Wondering where I should start the explanation.

It was Aley Aalstrom.

"Johnny, how you doing? Is this weather, or what?"

"What is it?"

"Hey, you alone?"

I looked down at the pistol. "Yeah. I'm alone."

"Good. Great. We can talk. You seen any good videos lately?"

"Maybe."

Aley chuckled. "Want to tell me about it?"

"What do I have to do?"

"Johnny boy . . . you *know* what you have to do. There was never any question about it. Get Republican. Respect property rights. Return those disks to their rightful owners."

"I need time."

I could picture Aley on the other end. Big jaw with the bag of fat under it. Shifting from side to side.

"Hey, John. Buddy. The good fairy just handed me a note for you. Want me to read it?"

I did not answer.

" 'Dear John'—hey, is that classic, or what?—'Dear John. Miss you. I desperately need you to prove your love. Or I'm going away forever. Signed . . .' What about that? No signature. Guess she ran out of time. Bet she's one sweet piece of horseflesh, Johnny boy. Bet you wouldn't want to lose her." I heard the weight of his breath against the mouthpiece. "So what do you think?"

"Fuck you, Aley."

"That's right. Shoot the messenger. You know, you're a goddamned inspiration to me. Some people think you've already moved on. That you're jumping that little blondie who keeps landing on your branch. But I been sticking up for you. I tell them, 'No way. Our John's the last of the big-time romantics. Faithful to the end. She could rub it right over his lips and all he'd do is recite the Lord's Prayer. Lead me not into temptation,' huh?" He chuckled. "You're *great,* Johnny boy. You know that? You got star potential. Gary fucking Cooper. People be*lieve* in you. Hey, you think your redhead's ever been gang-fucked?"

He hung up. I held the phone against my ear until the line went shrill, then held it a while longer. The gun in my hand felt like fate.

CHAPTER 7

Mail smacked the hallway floor. An instant later, the flap clapped shut. I put the revolver in the drawer with the tea towels. My *Atlantic,* Tish's *Rolling Stone*. A missing-children flyer. The phone bill, counterbalanced by a promise that Publisher's Clearinghouse was going to give me a trillion dollars. No death threats or ransom notes.

The phone rang again.

I thought it might be Aalstrom calling back and answered accordingly.

"Switch off the attack mode," Colonel Maurey told me. "Go into receive."

"Yes, sir."

"When I tell you to call me back, you call me back. Got that?"

"Yes, sir."

"I want to know just what in the hell you're up to, John. But that's going to have to wait. General Gabrielli wants to talk to you. We've been trying to get through to you since yesterday morning."

"Sir, I'll march upstairs first thing Monday morning. Sackcloth and ashes."

"Monday morning won't cut it. Write this down." He gave me a phone number. "That's his aide's pager. Call immediately. The guy's hot."

"Know what it's about?"

"Colonels don't ask three-stars for explanations."

"Yes, sir."

I had briefed Gabrielli a few times. The Army's procurement czar, General Buy-it. He was typical for his rank. Laminated with humility, vain to the bone. His staffers claimed to like him but spoke disloyally after the second sentence. He had led a brigade in the desert under a slow, careful corps commander and had managed to keep his tanks perfectly on line. Pentagon gossip said he was plugged in across the river.

I feared the coming conversation.

I dialed the aide's pager and got a swift callback from a cell phone. The aide introduced himself as Major Ripley, the tone of his voice making it clear that, due to his position, he outranked all but a few lieutenant colonels. Yet he did not fail to say "sir."

"I understand General Gabrielli wants to see me."

The aide responded in a muffled voice. "Sir, the general's putting right now. Can you hold?"

"Isn't it a little hot for golf?"

"Golf is the general's passion."

"He winning or losing today?"

"General Gabrielli never loses."

"Is General Ripley your father, by any chance?"

"Yes, sir."

It figured. You saw a lot of generals' kids go through the Pentagon as senior captains and junior majors. Punching that ticket. The system was so closed and smooth it made the Mafia look sloppy.

"Colonel Reynolds," the aide said. "Hold for just a moment, sir." I listened to voices, indistinct words, white noise.

Ripley came back on the link. "Sir, the general will be at his home on Fort McNair at eighteen hundred. He'll be expecting you. You are not required to be in uniform."

The uniform business, at least, was a blessing. Given the weather. The world's finest Army clothed its officers in polyester, the miracle fiber. Hot in the summer, cold in the winter. Probably because, back during the first confusions of the sexual revolution, a Chief of Staff's wife told him she wasn't pressing any more of his goddamned trousers.

I straightened a bit of the mess Cuckold and I had made, then took another shower. The water stung my lip. Which was swollen, with a nice crack in it. Lilac mark just off my left eye. On the positive side, my urine had faded to pink.

I stood in front of the full-length mirror on the back of the door. My body was black-and-blue and bent. When life was normal, I worked out hard. Staying in good shape was one of the things of which I was proud, a fundamental duty. Now I looked like Grandpa after he wrestled the bear. I pulled on a polo shirt and khakis. On the way out, I rang the funeral home and told the answering machine that the customer had risen from the dead.

I popped onto the freeway at the Sixth Street ramp, blending with the lazybones Saturday traffic. Heat blurred over the city. I got off before the bridges and followed a tourist bus down toward the waterfront restaurants. At McNair, the MP on the gate checked my ID.

Fort McNair sits on the best piece of real estate in the District, a sanctuary thrusting out where the Anacostia River empties into the Potomac. At the tip of the little peninsula, the National War College occupies a magnificent, wasteful building that goes back to the days of Teddy Roosevelt. But the fort's serious occupants are the generals in the row of old brick homes that look out on the river. The view is a developer's dream.

Gabrielli's nameplate had been fixed on a two-story that would have passed as a mansion a generation before. Now most of the single family homes in suburbia were as big or bigger. But the Route 7 crowd did not have a water view.

The aide let me in and guided me through a couple of rooms furnished with the frilly crap bored wives buy on bus trips to factory outlets. The air-conditioning gave the place a basement smell. Gabrielli waited in a study that caught some of the river light, still in his golf clothes. Orange polo shirt with a V of salt stains on the chest. Green-and-white plaid slacks. General officers should never be allowed to dress themselves off duty.

Gabrielli was a big man. Taller than I was. His greeting sounded as though he was clearing his throat. His hand was wet, with strong fingers but a pulpy palm.

"Sit down, sit down. Want a Coke? Dan, get Lieutenant Colonel Reynolds a Coke, would you? And call the Army and Navy Club. Leave a message for Punchy Hunt. Tell him Gail and I might be a few minutes late."

Gabrielli sat with his back to the westering sun. It dropped shadows on his face. He did an appraisal.

"Lieutenant Colonel John Reynolds. I appreciate you taking the time out of your weekend. You appear to be a very busy man. Your boss couldn't track you down for love or money." He smiled just a little. "Poor Maurey was really jumping."

"Sir, I was on leave."

He waved that away. "Water under the bridge. Now, John, you've always struck me as a talented soldier. Good briefer. Self-assured. Knowledgeable. Had a battalion command yet?"

"No, sir. I'm a FAO. I'm not on the command track."

"Well, you never know. Things happen. Understand you have a pretty good record?"

I made the mush face required in response. The aide put down a glass with ice and a can of Coke, and left again. I let the drink stand.

"You strike me as the sort of officer who really loves the Army. Who really found a home in it. Not just passing through."

"The Army's been good to me, sir."

"Love your country, too, I'll bet. Not just words. Real commitment."

I shrugged, and nodded. The truth was that my country seemed far away at the moment.

His jaw lifted like a dozer blade. "It's a great country. Greatest in human history. And the Army . . . well, the Army's been good to all of us. Damned good." He canted his head and a shadow slipped over his face like a veil. "Have to be realistic, though. In times like these. An officer can have a spectacular record—spec*tac*ular—and still find himself passed over for promotion. It's gotten unpredictable. I've seen it with my West Point classmates. Even on my own staff. Army's getting smaller. Not everybody survives the cuts. I'm sure you've seen plenty of your friends and colleagues go down." He sighed. It sounded like a snore. "We just can't hold the line anymore. Hill doesn't understand us. White House hates us. Except when it's time for a photo op. And the American people are ungrateful. They've already forgotten how different the world looked just a few years ago. We did our part—and we're still doing it. But . . . a career . . . well, it's just not the secure thing it once was. A man has to have Plan B." He leaned forward, as if to straighten a badge or ribbon on my invisible uniform. "What's *your* Plan B, John?"

I had semi-formed thoughts. Possibilities. But they had receded over the past few days. My concerns had been more immediate.

Gabrielli sat back again. "You remember General Hunt? Punchy Hunt?"

I had never met Roscoe "Punchy" Hunt. But I had heard plenty about him. Snake-eater. Jungle junkie. No spot too hopeless. As a young officer, he had supposedly bitten away the throat of a North Vietnamese captain who tried to jump him. While shooting down the man's comrades with his forty-five. Sometimes you heard six dead Vietnamese, sometimes seven. Another story had him strangling a CIA man he pegged as a sellout in El Sal. He was the kind of soldier who had a classified personnel file that leaked legends. A few years back, he had retired, abruptly, as a three-star, with honors piled up in front of him and whispers behind his back.

"I've heard about him, sir. But our paths never crossed."

"Know what he's up to in his retirement?" He gave me a little space in which I was not expected to fit an answer. "Punchy put his own team together. Drawn from the best of the best. Officers recently retired. A few NCOs he knew personally. Some talented special ops boys who decided to hang up their uniforms a little early. Just to work for Punchy. He calls them 'The Hunt Club.' Oh, there's some incorporated name. All alphabet soup. But 'The Hunt Club' is the draw. Now, I don't want to start talking business and naming names, but old Punchy's got himself a charter from one of our largest defense corporations—real patriots—to do the sort of things active-duty officers are unable to do these days. Special foreign liaison missions. Investigative scouting. Negotiations at the sub-media level. Media management, for that matter. His people are doing a tremendous amount of good for this country—and you never hear a word about it. And, I might add, they are very well compensated financially. Old Punchy always took care of his subordinates. Really good care." He smiled without showing teeth. "Think of it as payback for all those cold nights on the German border or wrestling rattlers out of your fartsack down at Hood. Might be something that would interest you. If you were looking for a job."

He bent his torso forward, passing into a deeper shadow thrown by a rolltop desk. "You see, John . . . the country might forget us. The people out there don't care about anything but money and transient pleasures. No values, no sense of honor. I mean, just look at them." He gestured toward the city's heart. "No pride in the important things. Slovenly, unscrupulous, selfish little people." He brushed his nose with a knuckle. "But we still have friends. Friends we can count on. In defense industry. They need us. Just as we need them. We won the Cold War together. Crushed the Russian economy. We could have fought the bastards, had it been necessary to do so. Now we need to do everything we can to keep our guard up. With the Chinese on the horizon." He raised a heavy eyebrow in the darkness of his face. "Russians, too. You never know. They could come back. They are a people drenched in evil."

"Sir . . . the Russians are going to be flat on their backs for half a century. And the Chinese—"

He held up a big hand. Directing the conversational traffic.

"John, I don't want us to get bogged down in a philosophical discussion. I have other commitments. Although I would be delighted to discuss these issues with you in depth at a later date." He slanted his head at a boxer's angle. The late sun burned his skin and lit the stubble along his jaw. "Now . . . this business in the newspapers. Plus all the innuendo. Not good for the Army, John. Not good at all. Officer's car bombed. Police involved. A woman dead. A woman of . . . questionable compatability with the Army family. And I've heard rumors—nothing definite, let me be clear about that—that you've gotten yourself mixed up in matters even more . . . troubling." His big head swayed like a cobra rising from a basket. "Serious stuff, John. Sort of business that could ruin a promising career. Or worse. The Uniform Code of Military Justice can be ferocious."

"Sir—"

"Don't interrupt me. I'm trying to help you." He shifted in his chair and brown shadows climbed toward his eyes. "I made a decision to keep the lawyers off your back. In light of your past record. I intervened personally on your behalf. The Army doesn't need another scandal, John. Can't afford it right now." I saw his eyes. Glowing in amber, the only part of his face not in darkness. "Do you want to hurt the Army? When we're fighting for our lives on this goddamned budget thing? Do you want to crap on your friends and comrades and everything you've ever stood for?"

"Sir . . . what . . ."

"I'm not asking you to do anything contrary to your conscience. Do not misunderstand me. I just want you to do the right thing. Support this country's defense." He grunted. "Don't goddamned betray it."

"Sir, what is it you want me to do?"

He looked at me and straightened himself in his chair. Torso rising into the light. I thought of the cobra again. But there was anger now, too. A lot of it. His expression, even his posture, conveyed passion. Well beyond the normal range. John Brown dressed for eighteen holes.

"You know what you have to do," he said. "That's all I have to say, Colonel Reynolds. The choice is yours. Take care of your country—and your own future—or take us down the road to ruin."

"Sir, if this is about those disks, I've got to—"

He leapt out of his chair. As if a phantom Frenchman had hit him with the tool they used on me. "I don't know what you're talking about. I don't know any of the details. This was just a counseling session. For your own good. We're concerned about you. Now, if you'll excuse me . . ."

He banged out of the room. In seconds, the aide reappeared to take out the trash. He looked at me pityingly.

"Christ," he said. "Whatever he wanted, you should've just done it."

I didn't look at him. I stole one last view of the river from a general's mansion. The sun had turned the brown water into gold fields strewn with diamonds.

"General Gabrielli always wins," the aide reminded me.

Man does not live by fear alone. I drove back to the Hill and turned onto Pennsylvania Avenue Southeast. There was a little Greek place where Tish and I had acquired a regular table. Although I knew it was foolish, I intended to have more than one glass of wine with dinner. Had I been on the *Titanic,* the divers would have found my skeleton in the champagne cellar.

Gabrielli had shaken me badly. The door had shut on my last refuge. At the back of my mind, I had always counted on the Army being there for me. But Gabrielli *was* the Army. And he was going to make sure he was someplace else when I shot the red star cluster.

I grabbed a parking spot down from the restaurant. The evening simmered. The few human beings on the sidewalks looked like they had no place else to go. I locked the car and took a deep breath of city.

As I turned, I saw the Peugeot. Brown, rat-bitten job, it sounded like a garbage disposal. The car pulled in at an angle, corralling me between its passenger side and my own car. Cuckold jumped out of the backseat. With a gob of white gauze and tape over his nose. And a 9mm pistol held low.

"Get in," he said. His voice sounded as though he had pinched his nostrils shut. "Or we will kill you here."

He made way for me to get into the backseat and nudged

me once with the gun barrel. Jerry was behind the wheel, drumming his thumbs and checking the mirrors. Cigarette organic to his lower lip. Cuckold jumped in beside me. Jerry put the pedal to the floor and the car gargled down Pennsylvania Avenue. Heading away from civilization.

"You really do have diplomatic immunity," I said. "So . . . do you work for de La Vere, or does he work for you?"

Cuckold parked his 9mm against his leg. "That was stupid. Very stupid. What you have done today. You are a fool. And your police are shit. I wanted to help you."

"Everybody wants to help me."

Jerry turned up by the combat Safeway, then cut right again. Working the back streets. In a couple of minutes we were in a part of town you did not want to be in after dark. Jerry was either trying to lose a tail or making wrong turns. We pulled in across the street from a cemetery. I knew the area from my early-morning runs. When the gangbangers were getting their beauty sleep.

"Get out," Cuckold told me. "Look happy. Walk between us into the cemetery."

"Sounds happy to me."

When we got out, the folks cooling off on their porches stared at us as if we had arrived from Mars. A little girl in cornrows let her jumping rope go slack. An old man shook his head. Cuckold had his pistol in his pocket, but he wasn't fooling anybody on this street.

"I hope you both brought weapons," I said.

"Shut up. Go inside. Follow the path."

Cuckold had called me an amateur the night we met. But I was not even playing. Cuckold and Jerry, on the other hand, were supposed to be pros. And they had gotten it hopelessly wrong. I pegged the cemetery as a dead drop they used with agents. When everybody else was doing it over the Internet.

The headstones were old and vandalized. A noseless, stub-winged angel presided over a litter of malt-liquor bottles and a pink condom. Jerry led the way behind a mausoleum and we tripped over a pair of terminal dopers sprawled against the granite. They did not even lift their eyes when our shoes struck them.

We turned away to find another spot.

A service building stood at the end of a line of graves. Cuckold said, "Over there. Sit down."

I sat down on a low stone bench. With Cuckold standing over me and Jerry squatting as though he had grown up in Indochina. I had questions for *les frères* myself. But I wanted to hear what they had to say first.

"Listen now," Cuckold told me. "France did not do this thing. We did not put the bomb in your laboratory."

"Right."

"It is the truth. You must listen. We cannot fight. There is no time." He held his hands out in front of him, palms up, fingers clutching air. "We are not the bombers. It was a great surprise to us. We would not be so obvious. It would not be so soon." He looked at the dying sky. "We want to . . . stop the people who hurt us. Not just to make a body count. That's the American way. Not ours."

"And I'm just another gringo dumbdick."

"No. Oh, perhaps you are a fool. But you can still help us. And help yourself. How can I make you understand that we have not done this bombing?"

"If you didn't, who did?"

On a low ridge, a line of figures in baggy shorts blacked against the sunset in a medieval dance of death.

Cuckold looked at me with that earnestness that makes the French so comical. "We do not know. We do not understand it. My partner believes it was the same people who made the bombing in our facility. Perhaps it's true. I am uncertain."

"Just for the sake of cafe conversation, who would these people be? *Who* did both of the bombings?"

Sirens in the background. Maybe one of the locals had called the cops when they marked the big bulge too far to the side in Cuckold's slacks. But I doubted it.

"We don't know," Cuckold said. "It is a great mystery. We don't know why your people attacked us. And now you have made an attack against your own laboratory."

"You believe Americans did both jobs? That we blew up our own people? Come on."

He looked dumbfounded by my naïveté. "Who else? Nothing else makes sense. Only we do not know which Americans."

"I thought Europeans always blamed the CIA."

The bandages on his nose rumpled. "The CIA is not so brave now. Too much bureaucracy. Everyone watches them. And we are French, not Europeans."

A shot popped in the distance, followed by two more. Cuckold jumped. But Jerry did not.

"Listen to me," Cuckold said, stepping closer. The air had thickened with shadows and he wanted to see my face. They had picked a truly dumb spot for the meeting, unless they planned to leave me here. But that did not feel like the case. These boys were desperate, but they wanted results, not more trouble.

I still believed they had bombed our lab.

A piercing voice from the background cried, "Shit, bitch. Do it now."

Jerry and Cuckold conferred in French. I could not get any of it. Little black flies found us. Cuckold and I swiped at them. Jerry ignored the bites.

Maybe Gabrielli had done me a favor. By giving me a reality check. I had long regarded the Army as the last refuge of virtue, but at least one shining three-star had shit on his shoes. Lot of thinking to do later.

I certainly did not like these cowboys. But I had reduced my life to one clear goal now: Get Tish back alive.

I knew two things. First, for all their dramatics and pistol-waving, Balzac and Dumas were not interested in hurting me. At least for the moment. Second, they really needed my help.

Cuckold stepped back toward me, wiping out an old crack vial. More efficient packaging had made the vials all but disappear. A couple of years back, they had been all over the sidewalks during my morning jogs. They crunched like roaches.

"My partner," Cuckold began again, "he says he does not know how you can think of yourself as a man. He says it is obvious. The people who have made the bombings are also the ones who have killed your lover. But you do not care. You let them kill her and see no requirement for vengeance. He would not want you near his sister."

"Does she shave her legs?"

It's easy to be flip once you realize you don't have to be afraid. I was far more spooked by the neighborhood than by Belmondo and Delon.

"Do you feel nothing for her?" Cuckold asked. "Nothing for the loss of such an amiable woman? Have you already accepted this blond woman as the replacement? And Americans call the French cynical."

I made a decision.

"You're reading yesterday's papers, pal."

"What does that mean?"

"You haven't heard the news. She's alive. You're not in the loop. You need to hire a good consultant."

Cuckold looked at Jerry. And oozed out some French. Then he snapped back to me.

"Who is alive?"

"Tish O'Malley. My girl."

They really were not in the loop. Depardieu could not have done surprise so convincingly. Cuckold fired off more French.

Jerry caught the surprise epidemic and moved closer to me. Aching to speak for himself.

"You should have paid more attention in school," I told him.

"How do you know this?" Cuckold demanded. "What are you saying? Everyone knows she has died. It is in the newspapers."

"You trust the media?" I shook my head exaggeratedly. "Come over here. Take notes, if you want. She's alive. I've got a videotape. Or had one. She was unmistakably alive on that tape, and the tape was unmistakably made after the car bomb jacked up my insurance rates." I looked at him. "A man named Aalstrom handed it to me in a burger joint last night. Karl Aalstrom. A-a-l-s-t-r-o-m. Claims he's out of L.A., but I don't really know where he's bunking these days. He's been running errands for some tough hombres. Maybe the people who bombed your lab. So why don't you go find out? Now let's get on our horses and ride out of here before the scalping party arrives."

Cuckold looked down at me. With darkness rolling over us, it really was time to go. Pistols or not. Around here, pistols were for the fourteen-and-under crowd. The real bangers carried AKs or better.

"You're lying," he said. "You have created this story to confuse us."

"Right. But I'm supposed to believe you didn't toss the firecracker down in Georgia? You're begging for information, and here I am giving it to you. And *you* don't believe *me*?"

"Describe this man. This Aalstrom."

"Medium height. Forty-two waist stuffed into size thirty-eight slacks. Figure it out in metric. Too much sun and too much bad living on his face. Forty, but looks fifty. Thinning blond hair. Dresses like Eurotrash. You'll love it. Probably wears sunglasses to bed. If you've been tapping my phone, you've got his voice."

"We are not listening to your telephone."

"Then you missed your shot. Somebody is."

"If you lie, it helps nobody."

"I couldn't make Aalstrom up. His nickname's Aley, by the way. You can't miss him. He's every European intellectual's image of American manhood."

"Where do we find him?"

I smiled. We were having a contest for dummy of the year. "If I knew, I'd put you on his ass this minute. He has it coming. But don't worry. You'll find him, unless you flunked the basic course. He's so stupid he's using his own name."

"Maybe we will find him."

"Listen to me . . . and no bullshit. Aalstrom's a small-timer. But he's working for big boys. He's a garbage collector in a fancy neighborhood. If you can roll him up, I suspect he'll be extremely informative." I looked at Jerry. "I'm being straight with you guys. All I ask in return is this. Any information on Tish O'Malley, you help me out. I'm not sure how much I really care about what you've done or haven't done, at this point. I just want Tish back. Alive. And undamaged. Deal?"

Cuckold shrugged. "We have no interest in the girl. If we find her, you can have her. If she truly is alive."

"And any information about her. You share with me, and I'll keep on sharing with you. But no more freebies."

More French.

The background noise had risen like the water level in a pool. Bad voices and ripples of sounds you did not want to investigate.

"Boys, we really ought to get out of here," I said.

Cuckold squatted down a few inches from my face. "All right. We will make the deal. Now, there is something else.

There are rumors about computer disks. Perhaps you know about these, too?"

"No idea. What's on them?"

Cuckold's nose patch held an echo of light. But his eyes were black.

"Perhaps the information is important. There are no details." He glanced up at the dark shape of his partner. "But I will make you an offer on trust. If these disks present themselves to you—I think you will know what they are—in such a case, the government of France would help you. In return for the disks. We would provide you with money. So that you and your lover could begin life again. Someplace discreet."

"Sorry. I don't know anything about your disks. But . . . just for the record . . . how much are you offering?"

Cuckold fingered his chin. Reading the braille of his stubble. "Let us say . . . one hundred thousand U.S. dollars? It could provide you with a new beginning . . ."

France really was on the mat.

"Can we go now?" I asked.

We went. The cemetery was an all-purpose community center after dark. Party zone. Love nest. Target range. I walked fast and made Bocuse and Escoffier keep up. Somebody had brought in a boom box. It rapped pure hatred. I figured the owner must be a tough customer if he could bring his electronics in here and not expect to get stripped. Near the gate, I felt sure we were going to face a lineup of gangstas, but the shadows turned out to be kids. They might have taken on one of us, but not three.

"Man, you got a dollar?" one of the smaller kids asked me.

"Shit," an older boy laughed, "he ain't give you no dollar, motherfucker."

On the street, the coming of darkness had driven the porch sitters inside. The blinds were down. On a lamplit corner, a punk did jive-and-slap with a couple of his road dogs. I felt better when we were in the car.

The Peugeot would not start. Jerry cranked it several times, then punched it, then got out and checked under the hood. After a minute's wait, Cuckold climbed out after him. Martin and Lewis. I made it three.

Whole lot of *merde.*

"Boys," I said, "I recommend you lock it back up and we walk fast for that bridge down there. Don't worry about the car. These kids have their pride."

Cuckold looked at me pathetically. "But I have signed for this car. From the embassy."

CHAPTER 8

I parked my rental close to the house. Illegally. Aiming for speed. Scared. And feeling plenty stupid.

I had wanted to ask Cuckold what he had meant about us making fools of the French even before the bombing of their research lab. It had become a mental itch. Yet I had gone brain-dead when I had the chance to put the question.

I needed sleep. R&R. A way out of a problem I still could not define.

Corry sat on my front steps. You could do that on my block, when you were not mixed up with bombers, kidnappers, and murderers. She looked like a kid sitting there. Until she stood up.

"I was worried about you," she told me. She had her 900-number voice on.

"Let's take it inside." I undid the locks as quickly as I could.

"Is somebody after you again?"

I ignored the question and shut the door behind us, hoping there were no hidden surprises behind the refrigerator. I started up the stairs, then doubled back. I went into the kitchen and opened the towel drawer.

"Here," I said, forcing the thirty-eight into her hand. "I must've been nuts to let you drop this on me. Where the hell did you come up with that thing, anyway? You borrow it from the mayor?"

She raised her eyes to mine. "It was Em's."

That stopped me. "Em wasn't a pistol-packer."

"He was scared. I told you. I didn't know what it was all about. I was afraid he was going to kill himself." She paused. "Or me." Inching closer. "Everything had gotten so bad between us. I hid it."

My eyebrows just about touched the ceiling. "You *hid* it? Right. And naturally, little Corry did such a good job that the demolition crew that took Em's place apart couldn't find it. Come on, Corry."

She squared her shoulders. "I didn't hide it in the apartment. I hid it at work."

"You hid it in a Senate office?"

"Wasn't that a good place?"

"You couldn't have gotten it past the guards."

"The X-ray machines are for the tourists. I have a pass."

I shook my head. "Corry . . . my dad warned me about girls who play with firearms."

"Oh, get off it, John. You don't know what it was like. You've got this fluffed-up romantic picture of Em. Well, he was a prick's prick. And he drank like a Russian. Half the time, he was bouncing off the walls. Or bouncing me off the walls. And I was a money slut for staying with him. Send me to the penitentiary."

"I don't want to hear anything else about Em. You know, he was buried today."

"How many sympathy bouquets did *you* send? You think I'm this black widow or something. Well, how about this scenario? I'm scared. I'm really scared, big Mr. Soldier. And I know more about Em's funeral than you do. He was buried at ten o'clock this morning. Whittier Cemetery. Old Massachusetts families only. The Right Reverend Francis Barlow presiding." She twisted up her small mouth. "They knew Em. They weren't about to be embarrassed by a low turnout. So they preempted it. Told the world to screw off. 'The Carrolls do not require the sympathy of the masses.' Ever met his family, John? They treated me like pond scum because my dad wasn't in the social register. They were *terrified* he was going to marry me."

"Was he?"

"No."

"Yeah?"

"He asked me. I told him no. I knew I couldn't take a whole lifetime of Em." Her face fell into bitterness. The real thing. "Try hanging with an alkie sometime. You can't even use the bathroom for half an hour after they've been in there."

"Save it for your autobiography. I've got to go." I started up the stairs again.

She followed me. Gun in hand.

"Where are you going? What's going on?"

I charged into my bedroom. With Tish's panties and books still scattered on the floor. I got out a suitcase the cops had tossed around and began loading the necessities.

"Where are you going?"

"Careful with the gun, all right? I don't know where I'm going. I just need to get out of here. Too much traffic. I need to think. Sort some of this out."

"Let me come. I can help."

"Sorry [illegible] military briefers always prepare three courses of action for the boss to choose from." I picked up a clump of socks from the floor. "First, the one you want the boss to pick. The second option is one you can live with, but that is clearly not as good as the first. The third one is so stupid, you know the boss wouldn't pick it in a thousand years.'' It was hard to tell brown socks from black in the crummy light. I threw them all in. ''Taking you with me would be course-of-action number three.''

''Please. You don't understand how afraid I am.''

''You didn't look afraid sitting on my steps. You don't *smell* afraid, sister. And I don't see anybody after your ass. Except the usual suspects, of which there are thousands in this town. Tens of thousands.'' I settled for three crumpled pairs of jockey shorts. I did not know if I would be gone one night or weeks. I was due back in the office Monday morning. But I was not optimistic about the future. And I knew I would do whatever it took to find Tish. ''Corry, I suspect that the only thing you have to be afraid of is proximity to me.''

''I'm afraid by myself.''

''Call Senator Faust. Bet he'll put you up. And put that gun down. Guns are serious medicine.''

''I can't call him. I mean, I don't want to call him. I *can't* call him.''

I hit the bathroom, emptying shelves into an old canvas shaving kit. ''I thought Faust was on the most-eligible list? Big ladies' man? It's your shot at the brass ring, baby.''

She sat down on the bed. Which had not been made in a very long time. She skated the gun across the mattress and lowered her face into her hands.

''I've been trying to explain. You never give me a chance.''

I stopped. ''Okay. Last chance. What's this all about, Corry? I frankly don't see this as your preferred option for a Saturday night.''

She looked up. With the intensity of a woman in love. Maybe fear and love do the same thing to you.

''Somebody came to the office today. To see the senator.

That never happens on Saturday. He doesn't permit it. Not even when they stay in session."

"White House intern?"

"*Please,* John. I'm sorry about last night. I'm *glad* your girlfriend's still alive. But I'm not expendable, either. I'm a person, a human being. Just like you. And her." The color bloomed in those wet blues. "This guy. He was just . . . so out of place. Maybe Las Vegas. But definitely not Washington, D.C. He and Faust were in there for, it must've been an hour. It didn't make any sense to me. Faust is just so . . . fastidious about people." She raised her face to the light. "The guy stopped by my desk and introduced himself on the way out. Mr. Angstrom or something. He said he knew you, John. He said it in a way that meant he knew a lot of other things, too. It scared me. I mean, it really scared me. I wanted to ask the senator about him, but he took off like a rabbit. Right after this Angstrom guy. He nearly knocked me down on his way out the door." Her stare nailed me. "Who was the guy, John? What does he want from us?"

I looked down at her. And at her gun.

"Your suitcase still downstairs?" I asked her.

We headed out 66 and stopped at a fast-food joint in Manassas. The burgers of Bull Run. Corry talked with food in her mouth. Something Tish had never done. It was as if she had forgotten who she was for a moment.

"So you think Senator Faust is mixed up in all this?" she asked. Touching away a fleck of mayo on her upper lip. For a woman who looked like an aerobics instructor, Corry had a serious appetite for junk food. "I mean, that guy looked like *somebody's* problem. Your friend."

"Why not? Everybody else seems to be wired in. And Aley Aalstrom is not and never was my friend." I bit, chewed, swallowed, and asked, "The senator's been a big supporter of the NGFB, hasn't he? Mr. We Need It Now?"

Corry almost finished her mouthful and said, "He's big on defense. Period. Faust never met a weapons system he didn't like." She licked her teeth and remembered. "He and Em were tight. Em used to put together these dinners for him at a gazillion dollars a plate. All corporate types. Faust would give them fifteen minutes on Mom, apple pie, and armaments. I used to have to go to all of them. Em liked to parade me. Feel me under the table. Then we'd go home and nothing would happen. Later on, I went to work for Faust. Em fixed it. I let him. I told you about that. I figured it was a big step in the right direction."

One thing I had noticed about Corry—you could ask her about chaos theory, and by the fifth or sixth sentence she would have the conversation back on herself.

"I'm not a Hill junkie," I said. "Don't even watch C-SPAN. So tell me. Is Faust for real? Or is a strong posture on defense just a moneymaker for the guy?"

She popped a last brown French fry into her mouth. "Oh, he's for real. Even has his own personal gun collection. He showed it to me at one of his parties. The guy's a barrel stroker. Real Freudian stuff. Asked me if I wanted to go shooting with him." She wiped her mouth. "He's a case. Loves to visit military bases. Kind of a hobby for him. If not an obsession. He doesn't have a lot of defense industry back home, so he prides himself on his impartial credentials. Defense industry loves it. They can't get enough. They could care less how he votes on Medicare or education. As long as he pushes the big-ticket acquisition stuff." She wiped her mouth a second time, although it was already clean. "Em used to laugh about him. When he was drunk. He said that once Macon-Bolt got Faust up in an NGFB prototype, his committee would double the order. And it was more than that. Em and Bob Nechestny were betting on Faust as a potential number two man on the next ticket. Regional balance. Listening to it all made me feel like a member of the inner circle. It was exciting. I admit it. It still is."

"Ever met Nechestny? Mr. Macon-Bolt?"

Corry looked surprised. As if I had asked a very dumb question. "Sure. Em was his boy. All the parties. Do we have time for coffee?"

"Get one to go."

I stood up. So did Corry.

"I've got to make a stop," she told me.

"I'll get the coffee. How do you take it?"

"Black."

I got in line behind a scrawny guy in jeans and a worn T-shirt. He had a ratty ponytail, a rattier beard, and a trucking company cap. He talked country. Maybe never wore a tie in his adult years. Commuters wouldn't see him, except when he came by to cut their grass. But I knew guys like him from the Army. He was the kind of man whose great-great-grandpappy wore gray and clubbed the shit out of the Army of the Potomac until Grant came east and sat on him with the full weight of the Union. He counted out pennies to pay for his McNuggets. Born knowing Washington was out to fuck him. He fought our wars anyway.

I waited by the door for Corry and handed her the coffee. "More on Bob Nechestny, please."

The parking lot stank of truck exhaust. The car had an air-conditioner sourness. I had tuned the radio to a college jazz station before we stopped, and I let it continue playing low.

"Bob's a smoothie," Corry said. "Type who bought his manners when he joined his first country club. He knows the world jumps when he gives the order, so he doesn't feel like he has to make a lot of noise. Terrific suits. Knows how to work a crowd. Makes senators look like mannequins. God returns his calls. And probably worries Bob will be too busy to chat." She leaned into the seat belt to sip coffee without baptising herself. "I don't know what else to say. If he ever dies, they'll probably lay him in a temple instead of a grave. Nobody knows how rich he is."

"What did Em think of him?"

"Em admired him. Worshipped him."

"I never knew Em to worship anybody."

I turned off onto 29 South. With back roads in our future. Where I could register headlights following us in the dark.

Corry edged into her coffee again. "Maybe 'worshipped' was too strong. But Em was dazzled. The money . . . the access. The deal-making. He used to say, 'I don't know how the guy does it.' From Em, that was serious praise. And I think he was a little afraid of Nechestny, to tell you the truth."

"Why?"

Invisible shrug in the darkness. "Who isn't afraid of the boss? Nechestny was the ultimate boss."

"You said Em was going to pieces over the last several months. That things were going downhill between the two of you. That he was drinking."

"We didn't have much of a hill to go down."

"Can you tie it to any events? The decline? Anything out of the ordinary happen?"

We bounced over rail tracks and Corry lifted the coffee high. A floodlit gas station flew a Confederate battle flag.

"Life with Em was never ordinary," she told me. "I don't know. He was traveling a lot. We were best together when he was spending a lot of time on the road. You know how that is. I do remember one time. He'd been out at one of those hush-hush test ranges in Nevada or Utah or someplace. He came back from the airport already hammered. Absolutely stinking. That was the first time he ever hit me. It was so sudden. I never expected it."

"Why didn't you leave him? When he hit you?"

She waited a moment to answer. I turned onto a rural route. Mazing our way to the west.

"Well . . . I told you. About the opportunity I thought he represented. I thought I needed him." She sipped at her coffee again. Then again. I had her white face in my peripheral vision. "I guess this is going to sound sick," she said at last. "But I think a part of me thought I deserved it."

The jazz station was breaking up. We were well into the Piedmont. I turned up the volume and scanned through the channels. The Ford had a crappy radio.

I don't think either of us wanted silence. I settled on a DJ with a salesman's voice and a Nashville playlist. I did not listen to country very often, but I felt like I had heard all of the songs before. Then the hustler said we were going to get another news update from Atlanta.

It did not make the night any better. The Atlanta cops, the FBI, and the ATF had an Iranian immigrant holed up in a condominium. It sounded like a real siege. The reporter on the scene said the man was the prime suspect in the bombing of the aerospace research facility whose loss had been such a tragedy for area families and the nation.

I pictured a very frightened rug smuggler hugging the floor and wishing he had a flying carpet.

I did not believe an Iranian had done it. Unless he had been hired to mask the local talent. I still could not say who was behind the bombing. But I did not believe for a minute it was anybody with a turban and bushy eyebrows.

A number of nasty things had gathered for a jamboree in my stomach. I was beginning to sense how very small a chip I was in this game.

Small meant disposable.

I stopped at a motel in one of those Shenandoah Valley towns that live off agriculture and Civil War tourists. Corry came into the office with me. When I specified twin beds, the night clerk looked at me like I was king of the fools.

It was after midnight. Corry shut herself in the bathroom while I watched CNN. The condo siege in Atlanta was the big story. Corry came back out in a T-shirt, but she had panties on this time. She got into her bed and switched off the lamp on her night table. I lowered the volume but kept watching. With a sick feeling that I knew what was coming. Death live.

A little after one, the Feds and a local SWAT team stormed the Iranian's place. There was enough gunfire to make it seem like revenge for Desert One. They killed him. No officers down. I didn't wait for the commentators to start second-guessing. I turned off the TV and went in to brush my teeth.

I stumbled to my bed in darkness. Exhausted. But sleep was not on the program. Too much to think about. Too little clarity. And Corry's steady breathing.

After a while, she got up to go to the bathroom again. When she came back, she stood between the two beds. As if trying to make up her mind.

I closed my eyes like a kid afraid of the bogeyman. After maybe a minute, I heard her crawl under her sheet.

We were both worn down. Corry snored. No sleep for me, though. Jagged thoughts. Stabbing and retreating. Answers that dissolved when I reached for them. Soldiers are trained to take the initiative. I was just a lab rat.

Then, in the darkness that's been haunting us since our cave years, revelation hit. The kind of thing beyond logic and reason. When you just know something.

Something bad.

I got up—very quietly—and felt in my travel bag for the pistol she had given back to me. Insisting we might need it.

John Reynolds, crouched down like the fool that he was. Champ Stupid. Bare feet on a gritty rug.

I drew the weapon out by the barrel, took it into the john, and shut the door.

The motel was not going to put the nearest Hyatt out of business. The fixtures were fifties white porcelain and the light was hard. I rolled the chamber. Then I opened the gun and dropped the bullets into my hand. I flicked it shut again and tried the action.

Click.

Okay. Whom did she expect me to shoot with it? I did not believe her story about how she had gotten her hands on the thing. I had not believed much of what she had told me. But I had not thought her through. Call Freud, Jung, and Adler to ask why, but she had become a blind spot. I wanted to cordon her off, to keep her at just the right distance. But there was no right distance. And there had to be more to her than a clinging case of nerves. Or even poor taste in men.

What was the gun all about?

I am not a weapons junkie. But I've been around enough of them. I went over the revolver thoroughly. Pretty simple piece of metal. Everything worked fine.

Then, as an early-morning afterthought, I checked out the bullets. At first glance, they looked normal. But something was off in the vegetable bin.

I put the pistol and the rest of the ammo down on the floor, then held one of the rounds up to the light. Squinting. Measuring with my eyes. Then I inspected each of the others. After that, I just sat for a long time.

Finally, I reloaded the thirty-eight, shut off the lights, and went back into the bedroom. My eyes needed to readjust to the dark and I went slowly. Quietly. I walked up to Corry's bed, bumping it a little, then stopped. Her snoring session was over, but she lay in the stillness of sleep. Her hair shone white.

I pointed the gun at her head. Holding it eight or ten inches back. And I pulled the trigger.

I pulled the trigger again and again, listening to six claps of the hammer and the following silences. Corry moaned once, but did not wake. She had given me a working weapon. But the bullets had been doctored. The first time I pulled it on somebody, I would have been dead.

My morning-after had come early.

When I could not bear looking at her anymore, I put the thirty-eight back where it had been sleeping in the luggage and slipped outside. I sat against the motel wall in my jockey shorts and T-shirt, watching the occasional car go by.

I went inside when the horizon began to crack and got a couple of hours of bad sleep. When I could not lie there any longer, Corry was still dreaming contentedly. She truly was a beautiful woman.

I showered and dressed. The noise lifted her eyelids a little.

"There's a diner down the road," I said. "I'll walk down and get us some breakfast."

"I don't eat breakfast." Voice husky with nightness. "Just coffee. Please. Black. And maybe some juice. Are you all right?"

I left. I wanted to keep on going. To leave Corry and all the rest of it in a cut-rate motel room.

The motel sat at the edge of town, where signs pointed off to the interstate. It was Sunday morning in a green world. Cars and pickups went by with families. Church-bound. Back in D.C., this was the hour to bagel-out and read the papers.

The diner was a bastion of contrariness. Old guys in suspenders, a couple of bikers. And a time-machine waitress. A family in their Sunday best sat in a corner booth. The smell of frying meat and coffee thickened the air.

I took a stool at the counter. Figuring I would eat first. I was in no hurry to go back to the motel. The waitress brought me coffee without the asking. The menu was not health-oriented.

It was hard to believe that entire civilizations had existed without coffee. The diner did it sharp and on the thin side. But hot.

Two old men laughed in their private world.

I ordered big. I was way beyond the chickenshit despair that steals your appetite. While the cook was doing the heavy lifting, I got change and bought a Sunday *Post* from a machine out on the sidewalk. The edition had closed too early to include the end of the Atlanta condo siege.

I drank more coffee. Amazed at the normalcy of the rest of the world. I was already dead to the newspapers, ancient history. Tish had been a blip. I ate fast, piggish, and even finished up the little packets of jam with the toast.

A burly guy sat down on the stool beside me. Arms cut off his T-shirt. Little Devil tattoo on a construction worker's bicep. He was as shaggy as a mountain man, beard and mustache dirty with gray. He looked just on the edge of unstable. Typical diner dweller on the American byways.

The waitress brought him coffee, topped me off, and went to pick up a plate of pancakes from under the warmer lights.

"Much in the paper?" Mr. Muscles asked me.

"You can have it."

"Thank you kindly." He reached for his wallet and dropped a twenty on the counter. "Breakfast is my treat. Now get the fuck up, walk out that door, and get in the white van."

I put down my mug. "And if I don't?"

He could take me. I had a soldier's muscles. He had real ones. And he did not look like he would succumb to elegance of form.

"Well, then," he said, smiling under his mustache, "I'll have to kill you right here." He looked at the big pink bow on the waitress's backside. "Have to kill her, too. And a bunch of these other good people. Just to make it look right." He took a quick sip of coffee. "Girl in the motel, too. And that redheaded wild woman of yours."

A big hand closed over my upper arm.

"Moment of truth," he told me. "All this shit has reached a point where we either achieve resolution . . . or clean house. Your call, Colonel."

CHAPTER 9

"Sit over there." My escort pointed to an arrangement of deck chairs by the pool. The big-buck surroundings made him look like an escaped jailbird. "He'll get to you when he's ready."

I sat. Under the shade of a blue-and-white-striped umbrella. In the pool, a man swam laps. Savagely. Doing a breast stroke, he thrust a tanned, shaved head up from the water. Followed by monstrous shoulders. I had seen plenty of swimmers with better form, but none with more ferocity. The guy was in a grudge fight with nature.

After a last heart-attack lap, he climbed out. Dripping. Hogging the North American oxygen supply. He stripped off his goggles, tossing them onto a table meant to hold long drinks. Coming toward me, he reminded me of a minotaur.

Scars webbed his body. Skin gouged and horned. He looked as if he had been taken apart and reassembled.

I stood up.

A big hand shot out.

"Roscoe Hunt. Call me Punchy. So you're the stud who's been pissing off everybody from the Buddha to Jesus Christ."

He wasn't a bully about the handshake. He didn't have to be. Firm, wet paw. Up and down and done. He turned half away and ripped an enormous towel from a stack on a bench. Rubbing his scalp, then fitting the towel over his head like a monk's hood. He crouched and stripped off his trunks. Grunting, he dried himself in the sunlight.

"Mind if I call you John?"

"Do I have a choice?"

He cocked an eyebrow. It rippled the bare skin above it. "Hell, everybody gets a choice, son. Life *is* choice. Free goddamned will. We just have to be prepared to pay for our wrong choices."

"Call me whatever you like."

He dropped the towel on the flagstones and pulled on a fine blue cotton robe. With the logo of the Oriental Hotel, Bangkok. A pitcher of water waited. The ice had faded to feathers. He picked up the pitcher and drank, ignoring the glass.

The back of his hand wiped brown lips. The skin around his mouth looked as if it had been charred.

"Truth be told, I wish I didn't have to call you anything," Hunt said. "Wish I'd never heard of you. You're a pain in the butt." He looked at me with green eyes hardened by intelligence. "But here we are."

I cocked my head toward the big house. "Not a bad place to be."

"I like it," he said. "Well, come on inside. We'll get us something to drink." He walked as though he really wanted to run. Too much energy for one body. "Magdalena," he called. "Magda*len*a."

You sensed immediately that Punchy Hunt was the real thing. He was what all the blustering Gabriellis wanted to be and could not bring off. He raised your fears, while the others just raised their voices.

My escort had brought me—after two changes of vehicle in wooded areas—to a horsey estate between Route 66 and Middleburg. The area was a theme park for millionaires. Nobody blindfolded me or played rough. It did not seem to matter that I saw where we were going. My escort and the succession of drivers seemed concerned only about being followed.

The estate was one of the serious ones you can't see from the highway. Just a turnoff with brick pillars and a "Private Road" sign. Arcades of trees. White fences as long as Third World frontiers. From a low hill I saw a small lake and a private airfield, wind sock dead in the heat. The house of white-painted brick looked like it had been built in the eighteenth century for a serious player. Every other generation had added a wing or a floor. It was big, gracefully imperfect, and unattainable. The kind of place that made a good citizen feel like a loser.

The back of the house had been redone with a lot of glass. A door slid open and a black Lab darted toward the general. Followed by a Hispanic in a maid's costume. She was plain enough not to cause trouble in the barracks.

"Let him out and he always wants to jump in the goddamned pool with me," Hunt said. I thought the dog would leap up on him. Just short, it stopped, sat, and showed its tongue.

"Good boy, Castro. All right. Come on." The general slapped his thigh and the dog closed on him. "Can't swim with a goddamned dog. Love the little mutt. But I don't want to go swimming with him. Magdalena?"

"Sí, señor general."

"Get us up a pitcher of gin and tonic. Like gin and tonic, John? Only damned drink for this weather. Hungry?"

"I had a power breakfast."

Hunt grunted. "Just as well. Can't have a serious talk over food. That's Washington bullshit." He grunted again, with the dog heeling. "Fuckers never talk about anything serious anyway. You like that goddamned town?"

"It's an interesting place."

"No goddamned place for a soldier. Pick up all sorts of bad habits. Get sloppy. Worst thing that can happen to a man. Lose his discipline." He regarded me. "Looks like you keep yourself in pretty good shape."

"I do what I can."

"One of my boys do that to your eye?"

I shook my head. There had not been much swelling or discoloration where Frenchy had nailed me. But Hunt was accustomed to reading all the signs.

"A foreign relations seminar got out of hand."

He grunted and led the way inside the house, showing me his back. A man who had forgotten how to be afraid, Hunt was an exception among exceptions. If it had not been for Special Forces, I doubt he would have survived in the military. There was just too much of him. Probably wrestled the doctor when his mother gave birth.

The air conditioning felt wet on my skin. I followed Hunt down a hallway lined with hunting prints and the loot of an overseas career.

"Come on in," he said, opening a door. He held it for me. When I passed by him, I realized how much shorter he was. It was startling. He was shorter than I was, but bigger in every way that mattered. He could have ripped me apart.

He made the dog stay in the hallway and it flopped dolefully. Hunt shut the door. "Sit down, sit down." We were in the handsomest library I had ever seen that did not come with a tour guide. I sat in a brown leather chair of a quality I would never be able to afford. Even if I survived long enough to make another major furniture purchase.

The maid knocked and the general told her to come in. The dog whimpered for attention, but did not cross the threshold. The maid laid down a silver tray with a pitcher and the proper glasses. Then she got out of Dodge. She had known exactly what Hunt would ask for and had it ready.

"Good worker," the general told me. "Brought her up from El Sal. Whole damned family massacred. By our side. Roberto was scum. But he was our scum."

"That your way of telling me Aley Aalstrom's working for you?"

The general laughed. One big rush of noise.

"Hell," he said, "I knew you and I were going to get along, John. Yeah, well. 'This thing of darkness I acknowledge mine.' Can't run a foreign policy without folks like Aalstrom, and you can't run a business without them, either. When's the last time you bought a car off a Mormon elder?" He smiled, but did not laugh again. "You're smart enough to see the uses of somebody like Aley. Don't pretend otherwise."

The library was magnificent. Not huge. But big enough for a fine old desk with carved pedestals—dogs and stags chasing each other—and a quartet of gents' chairs. The expensive editions in the bookcases looked cherished and read. The shelves closest to me held several different sets of Shakespeare, none of them new. As in the hallway, the paintings were of hunting scenes, or of dogs or game.

I was just about to tell the general exactly what I thought about Aley and anybody who would employ him, when he stood up. He had followed my eyes.

"That's a Landseer," he told me. "Real thing. Hell, maybe it's not art the way Constable or Turner were art. But *I* like it. All those fag critics can bugger off."

"Landseer's respected."

"Hell he is," the general said. He poured two gin and tonics. "That Philly exhibition back in the eighties? Know why they did that? Bunch of Landseers were coming on the market. Drove the prices way up. It's business, John. The buck is the final arbiter of beauty. Follow art, do you? Most soldiers wouldn't know Landseer from a landmine."

I shrugged. "I've been to the big city. Didn't like everything I saw there."

He held out a glass and I accepted it. Figuring it couldn't hurt.

"I like the art trade. Better than Vegas. More substance. But take it from me, it's all about the money. And nothing but. Lay down enough auction-house money, the Metropolitan would stage a black-velvet painting retrospective. With a ten-pound catalog full of scholarly commentaries. 'Elvis as Allegory.' Ever read Marx?"

I nodded.

"Bugger didn't like to wash, know that? Same thing as goddamned Che Guevara. Wish I could've been there when we nailed his dirty ass. My personal theory is that Communism went down the tubes because the sonsofbitches had no sense of hygiene. Good hygiene is a hallmark of the disciplined man." He took a powerful drink. Able to inhabit fully whatever he was doing at the moment. "Cruelty isn't discipline, John. It's a manifestation of inadequacy, of failure—I've always seen it as a last resort, no more. When I go cruel, you know I'm serious. Frustrated. But let's stick to Marx. Now, that smelly-ass sonofabitch was no dummy. Understood greed. The way things really work. Just couldn't accept that greed wasn't a monopoly of the moneyed classes. Hated what he knew, romanticized what he didn't. Typical goddamned intellectual. But valuable, nonetheless. I find him instructive. Read Max Weber?"

I nodded again. I had been an excruciatingly dutiful student.

"Good for you. Weber's my boy. Greed isn't what brings

us real wealth. It's the sense of duty. Of calling. The tirelessness of the true believer. The pursuit of a grail. Like being a soldier. Greed is for second-raters, John. Like that bitch with the hotels."

The gin and tonic was first-rate. And unreal.

Hunt gave a smaller laugh. "Now . . . I used to preach that the United States Army officer corps was the last surviving Calvinist institution in the Western world. Folks thought I was crazy. 'Old Punchy's had one too many grenades go off between his ears.' But you can turn that to advantage." He slapped a paw down on his thigh and the short sleeve revealed a crocodile-hide wrist. Burn scarring. "And the Air Force . . . they're nothing but goddamned Jesuits. Jesuits without God." He drank and waved his free hand. Sitting back down. "Now, I admire Calvinists, John. In their place. All that sense of duty. The discipline, the clarity of form. Conviction of being one of the elect. All twisted up with a terrible fear of failure. Makes a great officer." He looked at me with eyes that had seen more than I could imagine. "Trouble is, all that crap makes for a dumb shit of a civilian following retirement. I have personally seen my friends fail right and left when they took off their uniforms and tried to make a go of the business world. Reality breaks 'em like glass." He held up his own glass and I noticed he was missing two fingers on his left hand. "Me, I've really come around on the Air Force. Little shits are in touch with the spirit of the times. Do absolutely anything to get what they want. We need to study those boys."

He finished his drink and parked the glass. Leaning toward me. "Don't be a dumb fucking Calvinist, John. You don't have to go before your Maker in a robe of shining white. Minor transgressions are forgiven in the church of real life." He grinned. His teeth were too even. I wondered which enemy had claimed the originals. "Hell, look at the goddamned President."

"I believe in right and wrong."

"And so do I, John. So do I. But life's not as neat as we'd like it to be. How about a top-off?" He bounced out of his chair and poured another round. "Had I regarded the world as a domain of absolutes, I would have been dead before the end of my first combat tour. My career would have been short and not at all sweet. Goddamned failure to boot." We both drank. The Lab made a dog-dream sound beyond the door. "Well, I survived. And prospered." He shook his head over memories. "*Not* because I embraced that which was wrong. Hell, no. Because I recognized that sometimes it takes a sequence of small wrongs to get to a big right. I *do* believe that the end can justify the means. After all, that's why we have a military. Kill our fellow man so a greater justice will prevail. Right?"

"Where's Tish?"

"She's safe."

"You have her here?"

"You know better than that, son."

"What happens to her?"

He smiled. A rugged little smile. "That's up to you. You have the fate of many people in your hands. You screwing the blonde, by the way?"

"No."

"Didn't think so. Too much of a Calvinist. Now, if I were you, I'd fuck her brains out. Looks like a thoroughbred. And life does not give any of us an excess of chances. Fuck her. Enjoy it. You'll be forgiven." His smile broadened slightly, as if someone had twisted a screw at the back of his head. " 'Down from the waist they are Centaurs,/Though women all above:/But to the girdle do the gods inherit,/Beneath is all the fiend's.' You one of those poor sonsofbitches who're afraid of women, John? Most men are." His smile quirked, marking private thoughts. "Know why I love Shakespeare? Because the bugger had the balls to kill that self-righteous little bitch at the end of *Lear*. All she had to do was make her poor old daddy feel good. But she was just too much of a goddamned puritan, one of those little tin saints who have to turn out all the lights." He looked at me with forty-five-caliber eyes. "Saints and puritans fuck things up for all of us, John. Shakespeare understood how the world really works."

"Who was in the car?"

He didn't get it.

"Who was in the car?" I repeated. "My car. The body that was supposed to be Tish."

His lips formed a burned and broken shell. A sort of smile. "That shouldn't bother the Calvinist in you. Any more than it would a Marxist. She wasn't one of the elect. Strictly *Lumpen-proletariat*. Homeless. Mad. Worthless. Shopping-cart sweetheart. No one's missed her. Calvin himself had no patience with beggars."

"Save the Wal-Mart theology."

He made a kill-you-if-I-feel-like-it face. "All right. Let me put it to you straight. You don't give a shit about that homeless woman. You're just glad it wasn't your girlfriend in that car." He grinned with the suddenness of an air strike. "Occurs to me that Miss O'Malley's a crackerjack Catholic. Understands repentance. And forgiveness. The efficacy of works. Charity. Faith, too. Great big buckets of it. But that's just more—what did you call it? 'Wal-Mart theology'? I like that. You've got balls, son."

"Even if I didn't care about the woman, I'd care about the law."

"God's law? Or man's? Can the bullshit."

"What about Farnsworth? And Em Carroll? They're missed. They weren't worthless. What about all those people at the lab in Georgia?"

Hunt put down the glass he had emptied a second time.

"Avoid romanticism, John. It destroys your operational effectiveness." His face was serious, not mocking. Almost priestly. "That . . . those deaths were inexcusable. My people had nothing to do with them. *I* had nothing to do with them. I deplore them." His chin lowered, but his eyebrows climbed. He fixed me with those bayonet eyes. "I was called in because the whole business was getting out of hand. Run by amateurs. Clowns like Gabrielli." He caught my surprise and smiled again. "Oh, yes. Our friend the general. Horse's ass. Worse. Can't see past the dollar signs. To the damnation at the end. Not every man in Army green's a good Calvinist." Grunt. "Gabrielli's a fraud even unto himself. If he even has a goddamned self. Pretty typical these days."

"Why should I believe you? That you weren't behind the killings?"

Hunt made a face like a kid forced to eat broccoli. "You really think I'd be that sloppy? Hell, if Gabrielli and his bluesuiter buddies were still running this, you would've been dead days ago. And your girlfriend. And blondie. Whom you really should fuck. Cowardly not to. When you really want to." His smile returned. "Tell me you don't think about it."

His robe had slipped open. He stood and retied it. "Men don't *think,*" he said, scanning his bookshelves. "They do not consider the ends of things. Or the sources, for that matter. We live our lives in a fog. Imagining lights just ahead of us. Hallucinating moral systems. For which there is no biological justification." He ran his fingers along a set of green books whose titles I could not see. "We believe in things that are perversions of logic. Even as we reject our most powerful desires. We reason away opportunity."

He turned to face me again. Cinching the blue robe tighter. "The truth is, we're cowards. Man is born afraid. Fear is his constant companion. Only fear is with him at the end." His lips turned up delicately. A rose opening. "When you grasp that fundamental truth, everything else makes sense. Religion. Civilization. Law. Government. You name it. Everything is a fortification erected against the fear that threatens to overwhelm us."

He took down a book and paged through it, but still spoke to me. "Fears come in two kinds, John. General and specific. The fears we all feel . . . and those peculiar to an individual or time and place." He snapped the book shut and replaced it on the shelf. "When you understand a man's specific fears, you have him." He looked at me again. "You know me. I mean, you know a little about me. The stories. Rumors. I'm sufficiently vain to assume you've brushed up against my reputation." He stood erect. The minotaur again. "Credit those stories, John. Believe in them. None of them captures the full reality. If driven by necessity, I could inflict so much pain on Miss O'Malley that she would truly go out of her mind. And I would have you there watching. Where she could see you. Don't lead us down that road, John. Exercise your free will for the good."

I looked down at my drink. Not a time for brave words. "What do you want?"

He stepped over to me and put his hand on my shoulder. "You know what I want. The disks. All of them. Every single one of them." He lifted his hand. Unaccountably, I felt the loss of the human connection. If Hunt was human. "Give back the disks . . . and I'll give you back Miss O'Malley. I won't hurt either one of you. Or anybody else involved."

He sat back down in his chair. A high judge on his bench. "And there's more. My employer—who is a genuinely great American—will pay you ten million dollars. Aalstrom was telling the truth about that."

I don't know if he caught my reaction. It wasn't much. But I distinctly recalled Aley offering five million. I began to understand my old non-friend's intense interest in the transaction.

". . . and here's what's going to happen," the general continued. "You're going to agree to take that money. And I'm going to be the middleman. I'm going to handle the deposits. You will actually receive two million, sufficient for your needs. I will retain eight. You will say nothing, because you will be grateful for your life and that of your beloved. As well as for your newfound wealth. Then you and I will have something on each other. A mutual guarantee of good behavior. In time, all will be forgiven."

"And if I don't have the disks?"

"That would be unfortunate."

"If I don't play? If I give them to somebody else?"

"You wouldn't make it across the street."

I was slower. But my second drink was empty now, too. I settled the glass on the carpet. "The disks . . . have the plans for the NGFB on them, right? Everything? The black stuff? All of it? Correct?"

The general nodded. "Is one of us surprised?"

"What if I turn out to have a martyr complex? What if I believe that airplane's a bad deal for my country? What if I *do* beat you out the door? And across the street. And put those disks in somebody else's hands?"

"Like most martyrs, you would die for a dying cause. For a *dead* cause. And you would effect no good whatsoever. You would destroy the lives of those around you. Out of vanity, not virtue. Your choice, John."

He walked across the room and laid his hand on an antique globe. Turning it a little. "I find romanticism the enemy of all that is good—and I do believe in good, my friend. We disagree only on the substance, not the concept. Washington is a city tragically prone to romanticism. No. That's wrong. 'Tragic' is too grand a word for the sordid nonsense on the banks of the Potomac. Washington is *pathetically* given to romanticism."

"You think it's romanticism to buy a three-hundred-billion-dollar airplane we don't need?"

Hunt was a master of his own reactions. He did not tweak a facial muscle. All he did was spin the globe under a big hand. Strategic roulette.

"No, John, it's not romanticism." Spoken in the calmest of voices. "I believe buying the Next-Generation Fighter-Bomber is sheer realism. To oppose the purchase is romanticism."

"We don't need it. We can't afford it. And you know it."

He lifted his hand and shooed off a slow, invisible fly. "On the contrary. We *can* afford it. This is a very rich country, son. Richest in history. And we are spending a lesser proportion of our GNP on our national defense today than at any time since the Great Depression. And you might recall where that led." He patted the globe. As if it were a good dog. "There's plenty of money out there. Don't worry about it. Now . . . as for *need*ing that airplane . . . of course we don't. Not in the sense you mean it. We don't need it strategically." He looked down at the globe. Choosing a country to invade. "But we need our defense industry. That's our strategic ace in the hole." He spun the globe again. "Defense industry beat the Russians. Not our armed forces. Defense industry beat those sorry-ass Iraqis. Not twits like Gabrielli who move tanks at the speed of tricycles and worry about scratching the paint jobs." Huge shoulders rolled under the tree-bark skin of his neck. "Our defense industry is the most feared institution on earth. I would starve people to keep it going. I would starve infants to death, John. Defense industry is what keeps America on top. And I am determined that America should stay on top." He crossed his arms and pointed his full attention toward me. A minotaur with the eyes of a snake.

Suddenly, he grinned. "You're a hardhead. Aren't you? Here I am offering you salvation, and you just refuse to have faith." The grin decomposed. "Like weapons, John? Guns? Fine ones?"

"They have their place."

"Exactly right. Come on. Let me show you something." He retied his robe with a snug knot this time and led the way back out into the corridor. The dog rose and followed us. We entered a lower-ceilinged area. Probably part of the original structure. Hunt opened another door.

Stairs. Going down. I wondered if this was the trip to the torture chamber. Anxious to stay close to its master, the dog nearly knocked me down the steps. Hunt pushed on along a passageway to a vault door. He bent to an electronic combination lock and worked it quickly.

The room was twice the size of the library. It was full of guns. And edged weapons. This was no nutcase arsenal. It was a museum. Hundreds of muskets and rifles—and some automatic weapons—waited in long cherry racks. Some behind glass, others ready to hand. Swords, from Bronze Age fragments to modern ceremonial sabers, hung below the crown molding and gleamed in a fan on the far wall. There were crossbows, longbows, pikes, and axes. Helmets and breastplates. Carved clubs. Oriental weapons in the shape of animals.

Hunt took down a double-barreled shotgun that looked as though it had been worked by silversmiths. He cracked it open and held it high. Squinting into the barrel. Then he took two shells from a drawer, loaded the weapon, and laid it on a glass display case full of old military revolvers.

For a few seconds, he just admired the weapon. "Holland and Holland," he said. "A thing of beauty." Then he turned back to me.

"John . . . we are privileged to live in the greatest country in history at the greatest time in history. There is not an enemy who can threaten us at present. None on the horizon." He looked down the gleaming rows of wood and steel. "No, my friend, we're on top of the heap. And it is our mission—yours and mine—to make sure we stay there. To defend the new American empire that none of the politicians will even admit we possess. *With* the indispensable support of our defense industry." He laughed his longest laugh of the day. "We're the next best thing to gods."

"Senator Faust ever see your collection?"

Hunt grimaced. "Hell, it was all I could do to keep him from jerking off in front of me." He picked out a rapier and prodded the air, testing the weapon's balance. Then he hung it back on its pegs. "But let's stay on-message here. Those disks. They matter so much because of two things. First, for the short term, we don't want our secrets lying around so the bad guys can figure out where our vulnerabilities are. Longer term, it's about industrial superiority. Tens of billions of black dollars already went into that aircraft. And even we can't afford to give the technology away for free. Even if those who stole it could not build it, they could model beyond it. In fact, that would be the smarter strategy by far. Don't imitate, counter. We're in a constant state of virtual war with our former allies, everybody trying to outmodel everybody else. Looking for the big breakthrough. Our allies are envious creatures, John, small men and evil. They hate our superiority, our success. And they hate us. More deeply than do our nominal enemies. The Europeans would ruin themselves to spite us. The Japanese remain the monsters they have always been." He ran his fingers over a samurai sword displayed in a wooden cradle. "There are capabilities built into the NGFB's technology you can't imagine. Paradigm-shattering capabilities. Even now, I can't share them with you. And we don't want to share them with anybody else."

"What you're trying to sell me . . . is that defense industry is more important than the military."

He lifted a hand to his chin and more reptile skin emerged from his sleeve. "Yes. You don't have to like it. But it's the truth. Companies like Macon-Bolt protect us today. G.I. Joe's an anachronism."

"You say that? After all you've been through?"

The general smiled indulgently. "I enjoyed what I did. God knows what would have become of me had I not found the military. I would likely have come to a bad end young. But I loved my work in our country's service. I had an aptitude for it, a calling. I thrived in conditions that broke other men. I loved that which was forbidden to those of lesser strength." He shook his head. "But I will not pretend my career was more important than it was. We lost most of the fights I was in. Truth is, we didn't need to be in them in the first place. The age of the warrior is over. Done. And it isn't coming back. I'm a dinosaur."

"Christ," I said. "Look at the papers. It's all machetes and rusty machine guns out there. With the odd cell phone thrown in. It's Cain and Abel warfare. It's nothing *but* warrior stuff. How does the NGFB fit into that?"

He blew those considerations away like dust. "Do any of those fights threaten our country? Come on, son. That's all busybody stuff. Pimples on the ass of the world. We get involved because we're bored. If it ever got serious, we could wipe them out. We're just beating our meat."

He picked up the shotgun he had loaded.

"John," he said, "I really thought you'd be more mature than this. I've tried to reason with you. But you're beginning to wear on me."

He pointed the gun toward his Labrador and pulled one of the triggers. The sound punched through my skull.

The dog exploded across the carpet. Its head bounced off the far wall. Blood splashed my jeans.

The shot echoed. My ears ached. Hunt stared at me with such force that it drew my eyes away from the animal's death.

"I just want you to understand how serious I am," he said. "You have forty-eight hours to produce the disks."

I drove back toward D.C. with the end-of-the-weekend crowd. The woman who had set me up to die with a gun full of useless rounds sat beside me. She didn't speak, but I sensed her brain going like a hard little computer. What did she know? What did she want? When they delivered me back to the motel, she had been sitting on her bed. Watched by two gunmen. I guess her charm was wearing thin, because it did not look like they had established much of a rapport.

The desk clerk made me pay for an extra day since we had overstayed checkout time. He had no idea what was going on, probably did not want to know.

I knew more than I wanted to. But not enough to make anything good happen. I felt like roadkill. With a deadline to meet and no idea where to start. People I did not know were watching me and I had no idea how to hide. I did not know if I was being followed at the moment, or if they had wired my rental car with a locator, or both. For all I knew, the bastards were tracking me with satellites.

The green hills lowered into the outer burbs.

"Listen to me," I said to Corry, breaking the silence. "And don't interrupt until I'm done." I watched the road ahead and kept my voice low. "I don't know what you're all about. I still can't figure your angle. But I know you've got to be working for somebody. So let me give it to you straight. And you can report back to God Almighty or the Chinese or whoever pays your laundry bill."

A four-wheel-drive crammed with Sierra Club wannabes cut me off, but I had no anger to spare. "I don't have those goddamned disks. I don't even know what's on them. Oh, I'm just barely smart enough to realize there's some deep, dark secret swirling around the NGFB, but I don't know what that secret is. And I don't care. A week ago, I might have cared. Now I just want Tish back. Alive."

I let a mile pass. It was hard to speak to her, hard to know what to say. Maybe silence would have been better. But we're talking animals.

"And just for the record, don't say another goddamned thing about Em and what a shit you think he was. I've about got it figured out that he was a hero. Him and Farnsworth. The two of them. *Her*oes, baby. Whatever's on those disks, they thought it was rotten enough to risk their lives over. I don't care if Em drank. I don't care if he pulled the wings off flies and kicked your little gold ass—although I suspect that was a two-way street. All I know is that he was trying to do the right thing. To say nothing of Mickey Farnsworth. Those guys carried the flag up the hill, right into the machine guns. And I can't do it. And won't do it. All I want is Tish. And my own life. I'm as selfish as they come, lady. Maybe even more selfish than you. I'm scared shitless, and I want to live, and I don't know what to do. So pass it on to whoever you're working for. If you think it'll help."

Route 66 had entered the cash canyon, with malls on one

side, office buildings on the other. The exits led to Volvo country.

"You're wrong," Corry said.

"About what?"

"About me, for one thing."

"I don't think so, sister."

"I really am attracted to you, John."

"Just how stupid do you think I am?"

"You don't know *any*thing. You just refuse to understand. The first time we met, I had a feeling about you. You were so . . . solid."

"The word is 'thick.' "

"Stop it. You don't understand how much I need somebody I can count on. Somebody . . . I don't know, just somebody who isn't out to use me." She laughed minutely. "If you want me to put it bluntly, somebody who doesn't just want to fuck me on the cheap."

"You're overestimating both of us."

We passed the headquarters of the National Rifle Association and I thought of Punchy Hunt's arsenal.

"You don't know how attractive honesty can be."

I howled. "And you do?"

"You're crueler than Em. You're just slower about it."

"Definitely slower."

"And you're wrong about me 'working for somebody.' I'm not working for anybody."

That was the lie that pushed me over the edge. I shouted at her.

"*Fuck* you, Corry. Just fuck you. I'd shove you out the goddamned door, but I'm not going fast enough to make it worthwhile." I glanced at her. Briefly. Just long enough to hate that ineradicable beauty. "I know about the gun. I know about the goddamned *gun*, Corry."

. . .

She had great timing. She gave me just enough space to collapse back into a muddle of anger and helplessness.

"What . . . are you talking about?" she asked. With a very different tone in her voice.

"Go to hell."

"Please. Just tell me what you're talking about. I don't know what you're talking about."

I was blasting past BMWs. "The bullets. The *bul*lets, Corry. Don't give me that shit about how I'm your love supreme. You know goddamned well the first time I pull that gun on somebody I'm dead."

"No."

"Yes."

"*No.* Please . . ." The girl was Meryl Streep going for her hundred-and-first Oscar. She was good. Even now, her voice was believable. As if she really had not known. "What do you mean, you would've—"

"The bullets are no good. They won't fire. Don't pretend you don't know."

I don't know what I expected. But it wasn't what I got. Corry sank into an arctic quiet just long enough for me to pass a semi. Then she began to scream. Kicking the dashboard, the floor. The hard life of a rental car. It was a stunning performance. Had I not known her better, I might have bought it.

Just before the turnoff for the Vienna metro stop, she found her way back to language.

"You're lying," she muttered. "You're lying to me. You don't know what you're talking about."

I ripped across the lanes and hit the exit ramp like a teenager with Dad's Corvette. Fishtailing through the maze of metro parking lots. Sunday-empty now, toll gates open. I pulled into a satellite lot behind a wall of shrubs and aimed for the far corner. Slamming on the brakes just in time to stay out of the trees.

"Get out," I said. But I didn't give her time. I jumped out of the car and ran to her door. Yanking at her. Forgetting the seat belt. I dragged her out as far as I could, then went back in for the buckle. Feeling her. Smelling her. Hating her. I pushed and yanked at her until she was on her knees on the macadam. Crying.

I went into the trunk, into the bags. The bully boys had not taken away Corry's artillery. I drew it out and walked back to her.

She cringed. Looking up at me.

I pointed the gun at her. With the late heat rising from the blacktop.

"Don't," she said. "Don't."

I pulled the trigger. Again and again and again. Listening to those chickenshit little clicks. Then I tossed the gun at her. And followed up by throwing her suitcase out of the trunk. I flung her purse against her shoulders.

When I looked in the rearview mirror, she was still lying on the ground.

Weekend repairs had shut down the in-bound lanes of 66 short of the river. The detour shunted into Rosslyn and I crossed over to Georgetown, which was a big mistake. The traffic was a mess even on Sunday evening and the sidewalks were dense as Calcutta with people who looked as though they figured the next person's life had to be better than their own. The crosswalks streamed.

I waited out the light at Wisconsin and M behind three muscle boys in a jeep with a roll bar. A medieval beggar-woman meandered between the lanes, holding up a sign warning us all against hormones in meat and world government. The light changed and one of the jeep boys grabbed the sign out of her hands and laughed as they pulled away. I almost hit her and caught a blast of curses.

A cop cruiser—one of those Crown Vics D.C. could not afford—flashed me before I got to George Washington University. I did not know if it was about nearly whacking the witch back in Georgetown or playing with guns in public places or the bigger stuff in my life. I pulled into the most expensive gas station in the universe and killed the engine.

"Out of the car," the cop told me. Inevitable sunglasses. Marks on his forearm that could have been scars. Or a gangland tattoo from the days before he switched sides.

"What's wrong, Officer?"

"You got an expired registration."

"This is a rental."

"Get out of the car. Now."

I got out of the car. His partner took my place behind the steering wheel.

"Get in the cruiser," Cop Number One told me. "Unless you want me to put you in it." He opened the door. There did not seem to be any real malice in him. Just a guy doing a shit job at the end of a hot day.

He drove me up to paleface Northwest, to one of those pockets a little too close to the danger zone for the lobbyists and SES types. No lights, no siren. No information. He worked the radio briefly, but I don't know the cop codes. He stopped the cruiser behind a school with a parking lot full of family vans and mothers with dark circles under their eyes. The cop let me out and pointed toward a sports field where gradeschoolers played soccer by the herd.

"Lieutenant Dickey's over there somewheres." The light was fading, but he still wore those sunglasses. "Don't come up on him from behind. He don't like that."

Dickey was halfway up a stand of bleachers. One of the few males making the scene. On the field, kids ran and collided while their mothers shrieked like Romans at a Christian-eating contest. Dickey held a portfolio open on his knees. Pen in hand.

I did not come up on him from behind. I climbed the bleachers, apologizing to mothers with bloodlust in their eyes. Dickey saw me, but went back to his work. I stood just below him. Finally, he shut the portfolio and zipped it. Gesturing to me to have a seat beside him.

"Fucking fag sport," he told me. "American kids ought to be playing football."

"Your son?"

He looked at me. "My daughter. But just look at those wimpy little boys out there, would you? She chews 'em up and spits 'em out. I mean, this coed shit has gone way too far. I worry about the future of this country."

He looked heavy and worn in the bleeding light. Almost human.

"So tell me about the blonde," he said abruptly.

I looked around. "Here?"

He waved a paw at a mother's back two rows down. "They're not interested in us. Listen. I fucking hate this. But I'm beginning to get this deep-down fear that there might be a remote chance I owe you an apology."

We both watched the kids. I tried to figure out which one had sprung from Dickey's loins, but it was hopeless. They all looked too normal. "So what's the apology for?"

"I'm not apologizing yet. But I want to talk like gentlemen. And see what happens." He half rose from his seat. Yelling. "You see that? You see her? Go get 'em, Kath. Give it to 'em, you hear me?"

I had her now. A lanky girl with brown hair. On the hormone express to being a teenage knockout. She looked briefly in her father's direction, then trotted down the field with a smile on her face.

Dickey settled back down. And his voice hardened. "Tell me about the blonde."

I told him. Everything I could remember about her. I might as well have been some old Italian mama in the confessional. I surprised myself with my need to talk. Wondering all the while if Dickey might not be a much better judge of animals than I had given him credit for.

I was just a beaten old dog. Responding pathetically to the slightest sign of decency. Not good for much.

The field lights came on. His daughter ran over little boys who would run over her heart in a couple of years. While Dickey heard me out. I was ready to tell him all the rest, too. But I made myself stick to the subject of Corry Nevers. One sin at a time. I told him about the gun. And even about the metro parking lot scene.

When I was done, we sat for a while.

"You know," he said at last, "I worry about my kid. I mean, how can I not worry? Her growing up in a world like this. I mean, I'm a goddamned cop. And I know I can't protect her from the crap that really matters." He looked almost as lonesome as I felt. "I just hope I can keep her off the goddamned drugs, you know? Kids got no sense."

"She looks like she's going to be a very pretty girl."

Dickey snorted. "That worries me, too. Anyhow. We're both dumb fucks. You and me both. Must be godddamned genetic." He began unzipping his portfolio again. "I checked you out. Really good this time. And your redhead. You're clean." He grunted. "Both of you. Looks like she took a shitty fall. Poor judge of roomies. And you're too goddamned dumb to make a drug dealer. And don't give me any I-told-you-so crap." He opened the portfolio on his lap and carefully moved his paperwork to one side. The heavy bureaucracy of copdom. He dug his big fingers into an interior pocket. "I play fair," he said. "As fair as I can, anyway. Here. Have a look at these." He handed me half a dozen photos.

" 'Corry Nevers,' my ass," he said. "Try 'Karen Aalstrom.' "

The first picture was a mug shot of Corry. With a slammer number. Not looking her best. And, yeah. It read "Karen Aalstrom." The second picture was of Corry and Aley holding hands on a beach. Flowered shirt over his gut. Corry in a bikini. Matching sunglasses. It had an FBI stamp.

I handed the photos back to him without looking at the rest. And laid my face in my palms.

"Born Karen Hinkel," he said. "Sacramento, California. December fifteenth, sixty-seven. A little older than she looks. Teenage runaway. Off to Hollywood. Nailed for very ambitious shoplifting. Tearful homecoming. And back to L.A. Calls herself an actress when she does paperwork. Had a couple of parts in movies a generous person might call art films or something. Busted for raiding the petty cash at a Mercedes dealership where she worked the desk. Cruising for Mr. Right, I guess. Charges dropped. And I wonder why."

I looked up at the high-summer sunset.

"Remember that big hooker ring out there?" Dickey asked. "Couple years back? Gal with the kraut name? And those movie stars? Our girl was the pride of the stable. Eleven charges, and she walked. Then the Malibu cops pop her for reckless driving in somebody else's car. Cocaine in her purse. Way above the 'personal use' level. And a cute little automatic, thank you. Sweetheart walks again. Oh, and this is all *after* the marriage to Mr. Aalstrom, who is another fucking story. I mean, can you imagine it? Letting your wife work as a hooker? Must be some kind of California thing."

He looked at a photograph. I looked, too. "I guess maybe she's a pretty good actress, after all," Dickey said. "Just never got her big break. Until now, at least. The 'Corry Nevers' trail was the best I've ever seen. Great papers. All the way back to birth. Blondie's working for real pros this time."

He shifted his butt on the hard bench. "Husband's trouble. Fraud charges. Extortion. Multiple counts of assault, and not all against men. Resisting arrest. Jails are crowded out there, so he only did fifteen months total. Got some very unappealing friends down in Mexico. And suddenly he's a straight arrow for the last couple of years. Jimmy fucking Stewart. And don't that make you wonder?"

The game was over. The kids muddled about as though the last thing they wanted to do was hook back up with their moms.

"I bet you're trying to figure out a guy like that and a looker like her," Dickey said. "Me, too. But believe me, it really does take all kinds. Try my job for a couple of days." His daughter punched a little boy on the upper arm, then strolled toward the bleachers. "Must be a hell of a marriage, though. They beat the L.A. stats for longevity. Maybe the guy's a sausage king. Anyhow, they got plenty of history between them. And an ocean view in Redondo Beach they can't afford. Two-year-old Jag just a car length from the repo man. California living. But the Feds put the tax man on him, and damn if the bugger didn't come up clean. And people think clean don't smell." He grunted and stood up. "I figure you'll excuse me at this point. I don't want my daughter any closer to this. Cruiser'll take you home. We'll talk tomorrow."

"We *need* to talk," I said.

"I been telling you that for days, soldier boy."

"Please. Just a minute." A little girl with huge gypsy eyes was closing on us. Feminine now. Skinned knees and all. "I need your help."

He looked at me. With his overcooked eyes. "I been telling you that, too. Now get out of here. And try not to turn up dead."

* * *

I was starting to feel at home with the dead. You're not supposed to be in Arlington Cemetery after hours, but I did not care anymore. All my life I had played by the rules, and all it got me was this. A home away from home in a boneyard. My girl grabbed by a Shakespeare-shitting goon with billions of dollars and the arsenal of democracy behind him. Dead friends. I sat by Farnsworth's grave with my back against a tree wide enough to swallow my shadow.

"So what's on the disks, sir?" I asked the headstone. "What's the big secret? What was worth dying for?"

I had imagined that I possessed a redeeming degree of self-knowledge, a perspective on my limitations. I had never realized what a hopeless case I was until Dickey showed me the photos of Corry. Or Karen Aalstrom. The one of her and Aley holding hands on the beach was beyond pornography.

Everybody was lying. And I actually had been on the verge of believing Punchy Hunt when he told me he had been brought in on the case just days before to clean up the mess.

Bullshit.

Bullshit, bullshit, *bullshit*.

If Corry was hooked up to Aley, and Aley was hooked up to Hunt, even I could figure out that Hunt had been in on all this at least since Corry hooked up with Em. This was a setup of long standing.

Poor old Em must have looked like a security risk to the black hats a long time back. Lonely old Em. With his life gone to shit and a bottle on the next pillow. Corry would have seemed like an angel. In a very literal sense. He had not suspected a thing. She had played him so beautifully that his big worry was that she was about to leave him.

Corry had killed him. I would have bet my life that she led him out of that restaurant after his last supper and guided him down the street to where fate was waiting. She had known exactly what was coming. Maybe it was even Aley who pulled the trigger. And Hunt had blessed it. That was certain. And Bob Nechestny was Em's boss. He would have been in on it, too. Em had grabbed the disks. He was about to hand them over. To somebody who could John Law the big boys. With Farnsworth working as a go-between. But Corry had blown the whistle. Then walked arm in arm with Em until the bullets hit him. She had treated me kindly in comparison.

An ant wandered up my wrist.

There was still so much I could not understand. Corry and her husband were working for Hunt, who had to be working for Bob Nechestny, Mr. Macon-Bolt Industries. And Corry had to know I did not have the disks. Yet Aley figured I had them. And Punchy Hunt thought I either had them or knew where I could get my hands on them. There was money on the table, and everybody wanted his share.

I thought I had Corry's pistol figured out now. I was supposed to carry it as protection when I turned over the disks. The bad guys would set things up to make me nervous, and I'd reach for the gun like a country boy on the streets of Laredo. My share of the money would lessen considerably.

Hunt was going to rip off Nechestny and Macon-Bolt for eight million. Or ten, if he killed me. Which seemed likely. Aley didn't realize that Hunt was working the same scam on a higher level and he was ready to settle for five. So he and Corry could live happily ever after in Mondo Redondo.

So why didn't Corry tell him I didn't have the disks?

The frogs were another story. Day late and a dollar short. Talking a hundred k when the kitty had run up to ten mil. But they had been right about a few things. Among them, that our own people had laid down the bomb at the lab in Georgia. I was convinced that The Hunt Club had done the deed. It gave a new twist to the old Groucho Marx joke about not wanting to be associated with any club that would have you as a member. But I did not know *why* Hunt's boys had hit the lab. I could not make the key connections. And I still wanted to know why Robespierre and Danton thought our side had played them for fools. I should have asked, but didn't.

A jetliner's position lights floated down toward National. The boneyard crickets were so loud they covered the sounds of the aircraft and the city. I kept very still, watching for the least change in the shadows. I had sneaked out of the roof hatch of my own house, working down the block like an amateur burglar. Any place but D.C. and I would have been busted. Then I worked the alleys over to Pennsylvania Avenue Southeast. Took a cab to Dupont Circle. Where I surfed the crowds. I strolled in the door of a late-night bookstore and hustled out the cafe entrance at its rear. I took another cab. Across the river to the Marine Corps Memorial. Cabbie thought I was nuts. And he was right. I climbed over the wall into the cemetery. And worked my way through a hundred and forty years of dead soldiers to Farnsworth's grave. Still worried that somebody had tailed me all the way.

The night held still. The nearest movement I could see came from the headlights bridging the Potomac.

I could have slept. Maybe should have. But there was more to do. I just wished I could make my brain work. My body was a lost cause.

If Hunt was a stickler for timetables, I had about thirty-six hours left. And not a single clue to the location of the disks.

I wanted Tish back. Doing the right thing would have been nice, but I was ready to settle for considerably less. They could have their NGFB, if that was the price of Tish's life. I could swallow it. Em and Farnsworth were dead, and dumb heroics were not going to bring them back.

The thought was bitter.

Dickey was the only one of us who really gave a shit about justice. At least the only one still alive.

I needed allies. Any I could get.

Publicity was out. I had no doubt that a public move on my part would kill Tish immediately. She was prime evidence, and Hunt would make sure she went away. But I had decided to work with Dickey, if I could do so quietly. It was a forlorn hope, considering that the D.C. cops could not even crack the gang that was chopping the heads off all the city's parking meters. And, against every shred of patriotic pride I had left, I was even going to take a chance on the French.

I said goodbye to Farnsworth and left the cemetery by a different route. I walked up to a little row of Third World feed troughs between Henderson Hall and Route 395. And I called the French embassy from a hooded pay phone. An earlier user had conjugated the Spanish verb *chingar* on the nearby wall.

The weekend duty officer was a typical junior dick afraid to bother his superiors. He did not want to give me Colonel de La Vere's home number. Until I told him I knew who bombed their research lab.

De La Vere was sleeping. For the first thirty seconds, he was stupid. For the next thirty, he played dumb. Finally, I said:

"Listen, fuckhead. Just tell your sorry-ass buddies Lieutenant Colonel John Reynolds is going to be waiting for them at the far end of Pentagon North Parking in half an hour. If they don't know where it is, explain it to them. Tell them I'll wait thirty minutes, then the deal's off. Screw this up, and you'll spend the rest of your career in Djibouti."

I hung up. And started walking.

Cuckold showed up in one of those big Citroëns shaped like the stuff that crawls out of drains at 3 A.M. I got in the passenger side. We drove.

"Where's Frère Jacques?" I asked him.

Bandage pale on his snout. He kept both hands on the wheel. As if the car might have a mind of its own.

"Working. Your friend. This Aalstrom. We are watching him."

"Turn right," I said. "You found him?"

"There is always a way. He has an arrangement with a waitress. In Arlington. But we have seen no movement, no activity."

"He'll move. Just wait. He thinks he's playing for big stakes."

I guided him to the mud flats behind Crystal City. Scummy, infested. When they built the Pentagon, they dumped all the waste there. Now weeds would not grow. We parked at the edge of a construction site. There was a partial view of the city. Blocked by highway bridges.

"So," Cuckold said, "what is so important? What is it that cannot wait?"

"Plenty. But first I want you to tell me something."

He shrugged. The French have a way of shrugging that makes you want to crush their little shoulders.

"On our first date," I began, "you said something about the Americans making fools of you. I was under a little stress, and my recollection may not be perfect. But I think you said something to the effect that we didn't have to bomb your lab because we'd already made fools out of you. What was that all about?"

"It's true. You did not have to make the bombing. This was a terrorist action. Of great viciousness. For nothing."

"How do you know it was for nothing? You shits stole the plans for the NGFB. Tens of billions of dollars' worth of research. Now, maybe my fellow Americans tend to be creatures of excess, but I think I can see why they might have gotten angry that you ripped off Uncle Sam's most expensive secret."

Cuckold laughed. Everything about him made me want to smack him. My new ally.

"I don't know," he said. "Maybe you are a fool. Or maybe

a liar. Or both things. But if I must say it out loud, I will say it. Yes, you have made fools of us. Terrible fools. This was our most important program, to find out the secrets of this airplane. And you . . . give me the English words . . . you 'set us up.' You made us go through all of the steps, spend all of the money, so much time. But you cheated us. You gave us false plans. Then you watched us build the program to copy your technology, and you laughed. You knew all along that what you gave us would not work. So we were already the big fools. There was no need to kill so many people. There was no need . . ."

I felt sick. I got out of the car because I thought I was going to vomit.

I understood now. I had it. And it was worse than I thought.

I didn't throw up. I just stood. Dizzy. Staring up at the bug-ugly high-rises of northern Virginia.

"Oh, Jesus Christ," I said. A plane roared overhead. We were just a gunshot from the runway at National. "Oh, Jesus."

Now I knew why they wanted the disks back. Now I knew why it was worth so many lives. Now I knew why Em and Farnsworth had risked everything.

Cuckold came up beside me. Tough little sucker. Good on his feet in the dark.

"Fuck off," I said. There were tears in my eyes, but I did not think he could see them in the bad light.

"And you can go to fuck yourself as well," Cuckold said. "Are you all right?"

"No." I did not think I would ever be all right again.

"You know something. Tell me what it is that you know."

I fingered the corners of my eyes and waved my head. "You already know it. We're all dumb shits. I should've figured it out on day one."

"What is it that I already know?"

I turned and looked back across the river. Broken view. Some light, lot of darkness. I thought briefly about Corry. Because even that was easier than thinking about what I had just learned. I looked at my city and realized that Em had not gotten Corry her job on the Hill. He just thought he did. Faust was wired in with Nechestny and Hunt. My think-tank bud, Rob Burns, had it exactly reversed. The senator had been working Em. Faust and Corry were sharing the same hymnal. And God only knew how many scumbags in uniform like Gabrielli were involved. Plenty of them had to know. How many Air Force generals were involved? Had to be a bunch. If it spilled over to touch the Army. This was enormous. And where did it all end?

Tish and I were bread crumbs.

"What is it that I must know?" Cuckold said.

I looked at him. "You're all shits. I'm pissing pink lemonade because of you."

"And I must wear these supporting things for my kidneys. And my nose is very bad. The nose is very distinct in my family, and now it is ruined. I think we are even."

"There's no such thing as even."

"What do you want to tell me?"

I toed the ground, dawdling like a kid. I was about to tell him one of my nation's greatest secrets. Something I had not known myself five minutes before.

"Don't you get it?" I finally asked him. "Don't you *see*, for Christ's sake? They *had* to blow up your lab. *Because* the plans didn't work. We didn't slip you fake plans or doctored ones or anything else. You had the real thing. And we had to destroy every last trace of it, all the evidence." I could not look at him. "The goddamned airplane doesn't work."

"That . . . makes no sense."

"Hey. I thought the French were supposed to be so cynical." I laughed. It was the sound of an animal dying. "All of this . . . it's all because the Next-Generation Fighter-Bomber's nothing but a great big fraud. It's all lies. It's a fake."

"That's not possible."

"The hell it isn't. We've got B1 bombers we couldn't use in the Gulf war. We've got B2s that have to live in intensive-care wards. This isn't a first. It's just bigger this time."

"I think you are lying. You are trying to fool us again."

I wanted to grab him. Almost did. "Okay. Your turn again. Tell me. What was wrong with the model you were copying? What made you so sure the plans were bogus? How did you know it wouldn't work?"

Cuckold made a puffy little sound. Like a kid pretending to smoke a cigar. "For one thing, the matter of stealth was questionable. Our computer models indicated that such an airplane would be detected by the latest-model radars." He thought for a moment. I wondered if he was censoring himself. "And the composite materials. This is your big secret, I think? The thing you most want to hide? Well, our scientists did not believe the materials to be stable. That is why they believe you have made fools of us. The compound would begin decomposing in . . . I think they have said five years. A few more years, and the aircraft would be worthless. Melting. Like the ball of wax, you know? We thought you were trying to bankrupt us, then leave us defenseless. So we would need to turn to America for everything."

I stood with my head bowed and my hands stuffed into my pockets. "That's it, pal. Capitalism at its finest. Just think about it. We build that goddamned airplane. And by the time the production run's ending, the fleet's already rotting away." I looked at him. With my whole face twisted. "And then what do we have to do?"

"You would need all new airplanes."

"And it won't matter that Macon-Bolt took us for three hundred billion. It'll be the only contractor left standing. The

NGFB contract's going to put all the other defense aerospace players out of business. Macon-Bolt will buy them up for ten cents on the dollar. Or less. And the patriots at Macon-Bolt will say they're sorry about the NGFB and they don't know how it could have happened. And we'll give them a contract for six hundred billion to try again. It's fucking beautiful. From a business point of view, it's a hell of a lot better than building something that works and lasts."

"This cannot be true."

I held out my hands, palms up. "Believe what you want. I'd bet my life on it."

Cuckold leaned back against the car. "I think you are already betting your life. You cannot put the same chips on different numbers."

"Skip the Cartesian shit. You know what I mean."

"If you are right . . . this is a terrible thing."

"I'm right, pal. And your scientists were right. You did everything right. You grabbed the secrets. Your boys cracked the code. And now you've got me standing here at zero dark thirty spilling the beans."

"If this is all a true thing . . . tell me why they have made the bombing of your own laboratory."

I looked down at the chemical mud. I was shivering. Not from cold. But from the sort of fear that hits you when you are truly weary and lost.

"I don't know. Not yet. Could be any number of reasons. Maybe a whistle-blower. Maybe parallel research that came up with the wrong answers. I'm going to find out."

"If you live. I think now they will want to kill you very much. When they look in your eyes and see that you know."

"I'm going to live. And I'm going to beat these shits. And you're going to help me."

I came to my senses in that poisoned lot in Virginia. When I realized that the NGFB was the biggest scam in history.

I am a creature of doctrine and training. But the two had come apart on me. My doctrine held that those in uniform could be trusted all of the time and that our government could be trusted most of the time. I held a fundamentalist's conviction as to the virtue of those I served. I *need* to believe in something. I think belief is the most basic human need, even more irreducible than the impulse toward sex. Like most of the faithful, I rejected evidence that threatened my beliefs. Luther had the psychology of my kind down cold when he wrote the hymn "A Mighty Fortress Is Our God." I need big, thick walls. My training, on the other hand, had conditioned me to attack: You could not decide an issue in your favor without going on the offensive. Throughout my career I had attacked mentally, at least—those who slighted that which I revered. The collapse of my beliefs left me on the defensive, stunned, and reacting to enemies I could not identify with certainty.

Now I knew my enemies. The fallen angels. And I was going to attack.

Like most military people, I am also a creature of fear. I lived for two decades in the safety and comfort of regulations that divided good from evil with transcendent clarity. Yet all the while, fear shaped my life: the fear of failure, of not measuring up, of losing the regard of my comrades, of taking the incautious step that leads outward from the garden, of revealing the imperfections I recognized in myself. A thousand years ago, I would have been one of those dull-witted Crusaders who kept plodding eastward while the smart guys had fallen out to loot Byzantium.

Now I decided to throw away the regulations, to break the rules, and to shift the fear into the lives of others. It was time to stop worrying about losing and start trying to win. The first step, according to my hundreds of thousands of dollars of taxpayer-funded training, was to identify the weak spot in the enemy's defenses.

That part was easy.

We stopped to pick up Cuckold's sidekick. He was on stakeout. Keeping tabs on Aley Aalstrom. Cuckold rapped the window of the rat-bite Peugeot with his knuckles. Hands flew up in a martial-arts defense, striking the steering wheel. Sidekick had been snoring. He was embarrassed as only a Frenchman can be.

We left the Peugeot and lumped into the Citroën. With me in the backseat like Grandma. Heading north to the city.

"Listen," I said, "if we're going to work together, you need to tell me your names. Or make some up."

Voltaire and Rousseau glanced at each other.

Dummy quiet.

Then Cuckold said, "I am Henri. He is Gerard."

"Delighted to make your acquaintance. Here's the deal. I

know which street he lives on. And I have a fair idea as to the block. But—"

"There is no problem. We know where he lives." Henri the Cuckold wiped a finger below his nose. Cleaning an invisible mustache. I wondered if he had shaved one off for this job. "This is a long affair. All of these people who are involved. Perhaps not all. Many. When we first became interested in the airplane, we watched them. Only we made a mistake with this one. We saw only the women. Always the women. We decided he was not a serious man. We have not watched him for some time. We had stopped even before you bombed our laboratory."

"*I* didn't bomb your lab."

"Before your people bombed it."

"They weren't my people, either."

"Your countrymen, then."

Yes. My countrymen.

"I find it strange," Henri went on, "that in the great land of democracy, where all men are created equal, such men live in ways no longer permitted to the aristocrats in France."

"It's just money," I said. "His family owns an entire state."

We crested Arlington ridge. Washington lay before us. City of stars fallen to earth.

"We need to talk terms," I told him.

"Tell me your terms," Henri said. Wary.

"You do everything you can to help me rescue Tish O'Malley. Anything happens to her, it's a deal breaker."

"But you do not know where she is."

"I'll find her."

Henri thought about that. Maybe he did not believe me. "This is agreeable. We will do everything to help that is not foolish."

"The foolish stuff, too."

"Maybe not so foolish. No absurdities. But I think we will agree. More?"

We pulled onto the bridge. Bright banks of lights. Nighttime construction work. Traffic lifelined down to one lane.

"You get the disks. If and when I locate them. But you promise me that the government of France . . . or somebody . . . will publicize the fraud. Tell everybody that the goddamned airplane doesn't work as advertised. Knock Macon-Bolt in the mud."

Henri and Gerard spoke French to one another. Gerard shrugged muscular shoulders, then lit a cigarette. I opened a rear window.

"I think this will be all right," Henri told me. Turning his head to talk. Glancing back at the freeway between phrases. "France will be glad to embarrass these people. I would say 'to shame them,' but I think they have no shame. So there will be an embarrassment in public. I believe it will be so, but I cannot promise, of course. I must refer it."

"Then refer it. Next point. I'm not going to be popular around here when this is over. You get Tish and me out of the line of fire. You set us up someplace where we can rebuild our lives." I knew I was at their mercy on this one. Maybe they would just give me a bullet when they had what they wanted. There would not be a diplomatic protest.

More French. Big, smoky gestures from Gerard. Younger and dumber, he still seemed to be the final authority.

Henri ran his hand back over his close-cut hair. "This is not such a problem. You have my word. If you help France, France will help you."

"Last point. You offered me a hundred thousand. That's bullshit, and you know it."

"How much do you want?"

"Five hundred thousand. Dollars, not francs. And this is not a payoff. I'm not selling you the disks. That's separate. But

I'll need money to set up a new life with Tish. If she wants to hang around. And I'm not going to have a lot of handy credit references."

Another conversation between Ravel and Debussy. Gerard turned, gave me a suspicious look, and muttered something I could not hear.

"I think this will be approved," Henri said. "But I must refer this, too. It is a great deal of money."

"It's fucking peanuts."

Henri canted his head. I could imagine the expression I could not see. One eyebrow lifting higher than the other. A slight pucker of the lips. The eyes counting ghost bills.

"I will ask," Henri told me.

"Ask hard."

"I will try. It is not so easy today. In the old days, there was always extra money for such purposes. But now . . . you see how things are."

We crossed the Mall on Fourteenth Street and hit the downtown government ghetto. Monumental buildings, lit up for nobody. After midnight, the streets were as dead as an archaeological site.

"All right. Do what you can," I said. "Now let's review. You're committed to help me get Tish back. Alive and kicking. If necessary, you'll get us out of here and help us make a fresh start. You'll ask about the money, and you'll confirm the business about publicizing the flaws in the NGFB. In return, I hand you the disks. If and when I get them."

"And . . . if you do not find the disks?"

"You still help me get Tish back."

"I think I am not making such a good bargain."

"Bullshit. If you do get those disks, you've got your arms around the world's biggest secret. Real comeback for *La Belle France*. And revenge for the lab bombing. I get crumbs."

Suddenly, Gerard spoke. In French. That spitting tone. He

flicked an empty hand toward me. Then he tossed his cigarette butt out of the window and dropped back into his sulk.

"What's the matter with Maurice Chevalier?" I asked Henri.

That Gallic shrug. "Oh, he just thinks you make plentiful demands. For someone who has so many enemies and no friends at all."

We stopped at a stucco-front mansion in Kalorama. No brass plate, but I figured it had some connection to the French embassy. Gerard went inside while Henri and I stayed in the car and crafted the questions he would ask our target.

"We need something concrete on the Nechestny connection," I told him. For the third time. "Not logic, not insinuation."

" 'The smoky gun,' " Henri said.

"Yeah. A smoking gun. Details. And why did they hit the lab down in Georgia? That's big. We need a chain of evidence we can tip to the media. After we get Tish back."

"No media," Henri told me. "Not this kind of publicity. Not yet."

"Okay. We'll defer a decision on that. But we need the story on that lab."

"I think you need this more than us."

I shook my head. "It all fits together. You can't separate it." I rubbed my eyes. Exhausted. Moving, I was okay. But I could not take much more waiting.

A police cruiser rolled by. More bored than curious. I really was anxious to talk to Dickey. I intended to play multiple hands. To do whatever it took.

Gerard came back out lugging a small rucksack in his left hand, fresh cigarette in his right. Tools of the trade, I figured. I had expected to see the metal suitcase with the little pain machine they had used on me.

In the car, Gerard handed Henri a 9mm-sized pistol, then cleared his own and rammed in a fresh clip. He did not offer me any artillery. But he did toss me a dark rag. It took me a couple of feels to puzzle it out. Commando mask. Made out of a synthetic fabric. Holes for the eyes and mouth. Lot better than hacking the leg off a pair of panty hose. As we pulled out, he threw me a pair of gloves, too. Material thin as a condom. And even more sensitive. No fingerprints.

Short run over the buffalo bridge into Georgetown. Even in the bottom hours of the night, parking was a problem. We cruised, with Henri and Gerard cursing in turn. My ear had tuned sufficiently to understand Gerard's complaint that this was worse than Paris.

We parked six blocks away. There was nothing closer that was also legal. The Citroën did not have diplomatic plates and it was not the time to get towed.

Three bad customers prowling residential streets. No dogs and no leashes. Well past the Wilson Pickett hour. Nobody would have mistaken the guns shoved under Cézanne's and Monet's alligator shirts for colostomy bags. Plus Henri's bandaged nose. A good cop would have sniffed us a ward away and busted us on smell alone. The best we could hope for was that an observer would read us as three gays still sorting out the dating game and look the other way.

"It is on the next block," Henri told me. "Come. There is an alley. We must be quiet now."

I'm good at quiet. I've done the night patrols and the bedroom exits. But I was clumsy compared to these boys. Serious training behind them, and *beaucoup* experience. They moved with vacuum silence. The tension of their bodies had changed magically. As if the bones and muscles had downshifted. I watched their backs intently. They seemed on the edge of evaporating into the darkness. We eased past a row of garbage containers and the smell had more weight than my companions. The frogs were so good it jarred me. Like finding out the Sunday-school teacher is also an exotic dancer.

The city sounds came back to me. Sirens. Snake-pit hiss of traffic in the distance. Music, mostly drums, from a bad neighbor. And the insect prickling that haunts our world.

One high lamp in the alley. Taking the lead, Gerard shied around it. But I saw the shadow of his forearm dip into his pack, emerging with the hand disfigured and extended. They really had worked the site before. He moved directly for a metal box mounted on a pole, snipped it open, and went to work with a mini-light clasped between his teeth.

Henri closed his wire fingers around my bicep. With his free hand, he pointed toward the back of a pale house built to imitate the townhomes in his part of the world. Freestanding, though, with little rat-catcher alleys on each side. From the back, the house was four stories. Up on the street side, it would be three.

He lifted his chin, as if his hand did not provide direction enough. "There," he whispered. "You see?"

I looked. Trained to be observant. Yet I had not noticed until cued that there was a soft glow behind a pair of blinds on the top floor.

"Listen," I said. "This guy's got an artillery collection. Serious firepower."

"Be quiet. Do not worry. His guns are locked in a room with an alarm. He is afraid of them."

"You hope."

"When we go inside," he said, "there will be stairs. Always the stairs. You must walk with a spreading of the legs. The feet must touch only the sides. Lightly." He judged me in the darkness. "Perhaps you are thinking too much."

I was. This was the point of no return. The beginning of the counterattack.

"I'm crossing a line," I told him.

Henri stood so close to me that I could smell the long day on his breath. "I think you have crossed this line sometime before," he said. "But now you are aware. Put on your mask. And the gloves." His voice was almost fatherly. He understood people, too. I aped him as he prepped for action. His face, the pale bandage, disappeared.

Gerard came up. A spook. Mask on, head like a chunk of dark metal. There was no wet, no light, where his eyes lurked. We followed him over a slat fence, one at a time. Maybe I had thumped him around, but Henri went over like a young cat. I did not hear either one of them land on the far side. I did my best, but I was bigger and less trained. And a lot stiffer. I came down with a paratrooper thump.

Gerard was already across the garden. A tiny light traced a section of basement wall, then stopped at another utility panel. Bell Atlantic was going to have a serious repair job on its hands. Security systems only stop amateurs. Of course, in D.C., where breaking and entering is just another teen sport, that's usually enough.

While Gerard handled the comms and sensors, Henri climbed the steps to a screened-in porch and let himself inside. The boys were quick. I let Gerard follow him, then brought up the rear. Keeping enough distance to allow reaction time.

I wondered whether, if the night went bad, one of the 9mm rounds might not turn out to be for me.

We entered the house. A heavier darkness. The sound of three men breathing in a hallway. And music, downbeat jazz, from an upper floor. I sensed Gerard smiling. The music made everything easier. Although it also meant the target was probably awake.

Our eyes tuned, enriching the surroundings. The silhouettes of my new partners. The vertical pool of a mirror on the wall. Beyond an archway, the nighttime blue of kitchen appliances.

We began to move.

I followed them up the stairs. Moving as I had been told. When I put my hand on the banister for steadiness, the wood was wet. Then I realized that the wet came from my own palm. Sweating in the glove.

The music grew louder. On the second-floor landing, I heard other sounds streaming from above.

Senator Faust was living up to his reputation.

Maybe monks are never surprised by burglars. But some trade-offs are not worth making. As soon as he picked up on the level of activity upstairs—the moans and the guy grunts—Gerard galloped up the remaining flight of stairs. Followed by Henri. I waited a few seconds and reached the bedroom door just in time to catch the senator's delayed reaction to the intrusion.

He was fat. Not just hefty the way he looked in his well-cut suits in the photos or video bites. His belly and thighs and cow tits covered so much of the bed that at first I could not see the girl under him. Then I saw a foot and a calf. And another foot, a slender arm. The woman was lying belly-down.

Faust lifted himself, fell back clumsily, then finally succeeded in separating himself from his lover. He plopped on his rump beside her, eyes huge, mouth chewing fear. He made no attempt to protect the girl. Instead, he struggled up off the bed and stood with his back to a window blind. As if jumping were a consideration.

It takes far longer to describe this than it took it to happen. Action goes fast. Gerard leapt behind the senator like a panther and got a paw over the man's mouth. His other paw stabbed a pistol in Faust's ear.

For the first time, the woman on the bed moved. She had a fine, glistening body. Even flattened and splayed, it possessed an elementary clarity that you might see once or twice in your lifetime. If you're lucky. She pulled a muss of sheet and pillow toward her. Covering herself. But instead of covering her nakedness, she tried to shield her face.

She was too slow. I saw her.

It was Corry Nevers.

I watched. Useless. Henri slapped Corry—or Karen—out of the bed. Plenty hard enough to earn respect for his seriousness. She did not bother with the sheet at all now. Maybe she thought nakedness was her best armor. Or maybe she wasn't thinking at all, caught off balance for once. She probably was not accustomed to being the one on the receiving end of bad surprises. I wondered, stupidly, why she did not look at me or ask for my help. Forgetting that I wore a mask.

Henri got a fistful of the hair at the back of her head and steered her from one door to another, opening each. A bathroom. A shallow linen closet. The last door before the one by which we had entered was exactly what he was looking for. A walk-in closet. Without windows. In a masterfully coordinated gesture, he let go of her hair and gave her a knee between her ass cheeks. She stumbled into the darkness.

"Do not make a noise," he told her. "If you wish to live."

I could have told him she was too smart to scream. Except when a man wanted her to.

He shut the closet door.

Faust was not wearing much senatorial dignity. He stood naked and shaking with fear, dick shriveled, paunch trembling. Astonishing, what money can do. He had been linked with actresses and anchorwomen, and he had the reputation of being the town's most eligible and irresistible bachelor. Nothing but an overripe pear on stumps. A skinned pear. His flesh had the whiteness, almost the translucence, of the great slabs of lard the butcher sold to poor people when I was growing up. Lard, with curls of matted, colorless hair. Where his thighs and belly came together, his body creviced softly. It almost had the look of a maw, of something that devoured the small and vulnerable.

His eyes were the worst, though. The eyes of a true coward. You could see that Corry had disappeared from his mental horizon. He would have helped pitch her out the window if it would have saved him a pinch on the cheek. His eyes were self-concerned without intelligence, vicious without strength. When Gerard dropped his hand from the senator's lips, a strand of drool trailed like a skein of spiderweb. The mouth showed a big emptiness of the kind you see when people remove false teeth. But I kept going back to his eyes. Colorless chips. Shifting from one of us to the other. And back again. I wondered what he saw.

Henri and Gerard tied the senator's hands with a necktie that had been tossed over the back of a chair. Then they sat him down in the chair, on top of his discarded clothes. His love handles contoured to the wooden arms.

"Please don't hurt me," he said. In the voice of a ten-year-old. Then he began to cry. "You can have anything you want. Money. You can have the girl. She's—"

Henri struck him across the mouth. Very, very hard. Blood burst from Faust's lower lip. The words stopped.

When they grabbed me that first night, they had not touched my face.

Henri bent close to the man's snout. Grabbing fistfuls of the man's cheeks, distending his face. It looked as though the meat would rip away from the senator's gums.

"You think . . . how is it you think I would touch a woman . . . who is dirty with your filth? You think we are thieves? You are the no-good fucking thief. You are a filthy thief, a pig. And you will be the dead pig if you do not help me."

He let go of the senator's face. Red-and-white flesh showed where the gloved fingertips had been.

"Please," Faust said. "Anything. What do you want?"

"Is it true that this airplane, the Next-Generation Fighter-Bomber, does not work?"

I saw the first glint of intelligence return to the senator's eyes. "Oh, now . . . it's a damned fine . . . it's . . . there's only a few little problems . . . see, it's—"

When you punch a man, you don't wind off one of those Hollywood haymakers that fill up a screen. Unless you want to be the first one on the deck. You get in and jab short and direct with a recoil finish that reloads your arm like an automatic weapon. But slapping somebody is a different art. A slap can go for the long arc, the buildup of force.

Henri reached over his left shoulder as if to scratch his spine, then brought the backs of his knuckles down at the back of Faust's jaw. Jumping teeth. I could feel the crack in the man's ear. Faust must have weighed two-fifty, but he nearly spilled out of the chair.

Before the senator could recover, Henri thrust his hand in between the man's legs. Grabbing balls. Not a job I would have wanted. Faust began to scream, but Gerard slapped a hand over his mouth again. The senator wriggled and jumped, clamped his eyes shut, and nodded his head in short jerks. Sweat exploded from his skin.

Henri let go of the guy's glories and wiped his glove clean on the bedsheet. *"Cochon,"* he muttered.

Gerard let the pain calm just enough, then he removed his hand from Faust's mouth. Wiping the blood from his glove on the drapes. He stood ready to clamp back down.

Henri returned to the discussion. "Listen. You are a man with alternatives. You can make a stop to the pain now. Or I can finish so that there is no more lovemaking for you." He smiled harshly, lips closed. Then added, "No fucking the little girls, huh? Would you like such a life, you mountain of shit?"

"Please," Faust said. Sweating. Panting. Still unable to fully open his eyes. *"Please."*

"Tell me about the airplane. Tell me how it does not work."

"I don't *know*. I'm not a scientist. I don't understand—"

Henri sent a fist straight into the man's nose. It was a beautiful jab. Better than anything the guy had used on me. Bone crunched. The instant the fist withdrew, blood streamed downward, joining the slower flow from Faust's lip.

"I am not a scientist, either," Henri said calmly. "So you will not need the technical langauge. I think you should talk to me."

"I'm a United States senator," Faust cried.

Henri laughed. Then Gerard laughed, too. Gerard gave the man's ears playful little tugs. Then he closed his fist around the left ear and tore it away from the senator's skull. As if doing a magic trick. He closed a glove over the man's mouth again.

I had never seen such a thing done. My stomach twinged. I was not remotely capable of playing in the same league as these boys. And I did not want to play against them.

I do not know if Faust fully realized what had been done to him. He got the pain, though. He bent forward hugely. Rocking. In agony. Face all tears and blood. Gerard bent over the chair, following the senator's misery, hand clamped firmly over his mouth. He tossed Henri the ear.

Henri dangled it in front of Faust's eyes. And the eyes changed. Several times.

This is something you do not want to see.

Faust finally understood that things were going mortal. United States senator or not. Gerard tentatively freed the man's mouth. And Faust got away from him. He collapsed onto the carpet, blood draining onto pale blue pile.

The ear thing spooked me. I did not know how you could ever make such a thing right. We had crossed another border.

Henri tossed the ear onto the bed. He knelt beside the senator.

"You pig," he began. "Do you know how many French citizens have died in your explosion? How many lives are ruined? So many families? Children without the father? You have done this to us . . . and all we ask is that you talk to us in return. That you tell us about this airplane. And why you have made the bombing." Slowly, as if the world had ground down, Henri looked up at me. "And about this bombing in Georgia. This killing of your own people." He turned back to Faust. "You must talk to me now. It is my last offer."

"I can't hear," Faust moaned. "I can't hear."

Somehow we all knew that he could hear. He was not lying, though. He just did not understand what had happened to his body. The stump of his ear must have hurt ferociously. Maybe there were big sounds in there that were hidden from us. He kept reacting to Henri's words, believing all the while that his hearing was gone. I worried that he was beyond the possibility of sensible thought or speech.

"I will take the other ear," Henri said. "Then your eggs. Maybe your eyes. I will take you apart into pieces."

Faust cuddled himself. Going fetal. Weeping. But he began to talk at last.

"I never wanted . . . to do it. Nechestny. He did it. He paid. Gabrielli. And Hunt. Hunt's a madman. Crazy man. He loves to kill things. Kill anything. The airplane's too soft. Melts like a popsicle. But they can treat it . . . make it last long enough . . . the full production run. Other things. Systems. The electronics. Nothing really works. Not the way they say. But the stealth. That's the worst. The skin." He cried harder, pawing his skull with bloated hands. Then he gathered himself to speak again. "French stole it. You stole it. You're French. I know it. You knew everything. Whole deal could have collapsed. So much money. Macon-Bolt . . . everything riding . . . once-in-a-lifetime deal . . ." He sobbed himself down to a level no man should ever reach. Maybe people get there in concentration camps. "Had to kill the French. Kill them all. All the French. Kill everybody who knew. Hunt wanted to kill more . . ."

"And the other bomb? In your own laboratory?"

Faust began to shiver. Going into shock, I figured. Henri smacked him across the face. An awkward blow, the angle bad. But it was enough to bring the senator back to the realm of the living.

"Tell me about the other bomb."

"GAO. Fuckers. Fucking goddamned bastards. Goddamned shits. Running their own . . . their own goddamned tests. Using our labs. Our people. Behind our backs. They were on the trail. General Accounting Office. Bastards every one. Think they're God's gift . . . had a team in the lab. Had to get them. Get everybody who might have known. Could have spoiled everything. Hunt said we had to kill them all."

Henri had begun to pant. "And where are the disks?" he asked Faust.

"Don't know." His voice rose. "Oh, God. I don't know, I don't *know*. Everybody wants them. Kill for them. Hunt's going to find them. But I don't know anything . . . nothing else . . . please . . . "

"Where are the disks?"

"Please don't hurt me anymore . . ."

Henri rose and planted a shoe at the bottom of the senator's belly. Flattening him on the carpet. Blood and lard. Ruination of the divine gift. The Frenchman moved his shoe down to the senator's crotch.

Faust screamed. The shoe jumped to his face. The great

body went into convulsions. Until Henri kicked it back to stability.

Faust's eyes stared through the ceiling.

"There is nothing . . ." Henri said, allowing the first genuine emotion into his voice, ". . . not a thing I could do to you . . . no thing of adequate horror . . . to punish what you have done." He shook his head. "I wonder if it is real to you even now. All that you have killed and destroyed. In your filth."

He drew a switchblade from behind a trouser pleat and landed like a hawk.

"Forgive me," the senator begged. In a shrunken voice. Eyes unseeing. Time all fractured. "Oh, God. Please forgive me. I'm sorry. So sorry. Don't hurt me anymore."

Henri began at the pulp where an ear had been and traced the knife into the fold between Faust's double chins. The blade must have been extremely sharp. It cut smoothly. I had heard that a man could not feel his own throat being cut, but I still do not know if it's true. Faust did not reveal what he felt. He closed his eyes and his bloody lips trembled.

I had not expected this. But I did not move to stop it, either.

We stood and watched him die. It was hyper-real, yet fantastic. I could not accept this as a scene in my life.

Blood slopped into the carpet.

I came back to life when Gerard moved toward the closet door. I knew what was coming. And I spoke for the first time.

"No."

Gerard stopped. Both Frenchmen looked at me. It crossed my mind that maybe I would be left lying here, too. But I was not afraid now.

"No," I repeated.

Maybe there was something new in my voice. Or maybe Gerard had just been showing an excess of initiative and was unsure. He made no further move toward the closet. We stood suspended in time and that room. Waiting for God to make a decision. I needed Henri to back me up. Even if Gerard was somehow in charge, I hoped that the two of us could stop this.

I feared their training and their rules, their habits and desires. Even now, I could not let Corry die. Just like that. She was too real to me.

"Leave the girl," Henri told his comrade finally. "She has no importance."

He was wrong about that, of course. But I was not going to tell him. Maybe I should have.

"That wasn't part of the deal," I said. "Killing him."

The Citroën bugged from traffic light to traffic light on Massachusetts. Gerard snoozed. As though the business behind us mattered less than a pizza delivery. Henri drove. And thought about what I had said.

Caught in the web of signals by the Convention Center, he turned his face back over the seat.

"You're right," he said. "This is not part of the deal. It is not included and not excluded. But I think he does not matter to you."

"Killing matters."

The light changed. We hopped to the next signal. On the corner, a creature in a smeared track suit bent into a waste container. Puking or searching.

"That is naive," Henri told me. "But you are not naive. You lie to yourself. You do not break free of the things you are supposed to believe. Sometimes I think you are like a slave. A slave to the pleasant beliefs. In Africa, I have seen so much death it became boring. I walked through corpses the way a child wades in the sea. Without a thought. Rice is worth more than the lives of men and women, John. Water is worth more." He stopped, but began again before I could respond. "I have seen the bodies . . . slaughtered like the cow. The beefsteaks cut from them. Men eating men. And in Paris, they lie. Like they lie in London, in New York. They will not put this in their newspapers. Because it does not match their philosophies, their educations. Think of it. Men who will discuss with you the merits of the flesh of a child, why it is better than that of a grown man. Men who laugh with their great white teeth. While they roast a woman's buttocks. You think killing matters? Then you are a child. Humans are thrown away like the toilet paper." He flung an arm at the windshield. "Look at this city around us."

"Killing matters."

The Frenchman shook the back of his head at me. Driving again. I imagined a hard little smile on his face. "Oh, yes. It matters. But not in this way that you mean. It matters because such a man deserves to die. He has earned his death. There is always a price to pay in life. But his life . . . the life itself . . . that is unimportant."

"No."

We drove past a ruin where the rear wall had been lopped off an old tenement. Behind Chinatown. On the left, the National Public Radio building slept, dreaming of the good causes of its youth.

"And what should we do?" Henri asked. Anger denting his accent. "Should we collect the evidence? Chase this man with the law? Ask your government to judge him?" He laughed. As though laughing hurt. "I think there would be no justice. Only great lies. Deals, perhaps. But there would be no justice."

It was my turn to think. As we rounded Union Station with its spotlit facade, I said, "Your government . . . was his murder authorized? Did you actually have permission to do that? Or were you just inspired?"

He shrugged. "What does it matter?"

"You didn't have permission. Did you? It was just your call."

"There is no justice. There is no justice anywhere." He made a right turn. "Men must make their own justice. Men of courage. Otherwise . . ." He lifted a hand from the wheel and snapped his fingers. *"Le déluge."*

Gerard roused briefly, then lolled again.

"And the law?" I asked. "It doesn't matter at all?"

We came up beside the Capitol. The dome glowed through the trees.

"I believe in the law," Henri said. His voice had calmed again. "Until it interferes with justice. I believe in the law for the minor concerns. Does your law protect the small against the great? Can you say this with honesty? Would this man have come to justice?" He turned up East Cap. "Suffering is for the small people. For people such as us. For the people in these laboratories. For their families. But for the great, there is only scandal. Then there is a book and a new wife. A fresh start. *Merde.*"

He understood America.

"Stop here," I told him. "I'll walk the rest of the way." We were in front of the Folger Library. White marble glowing in the hot night. As good as civilization got.

Henri curbsided. "So now we are done. Until tomorrow. Be careful. You have the pager number, the telephone."

"The whole world's watching," I told him.

"What?"

"A mantra. From an age of belief."

He grunted. "I think you are a stupid fucking dreamer. But we must work together now."

"You're wrong, you know. I do care that he's dead. Not for the sake of his personality. I believe the law is all we have, in the end. Even now, I believe that."

"The law will shit on you."

I shrugged and cracked the car door. "Probably. And I'll still believe."

Gerard stirred again. Henri looked at me with the eyes of a revolutionary on the barricades. "You must be ready to fight."

"I'm ready to fight. But murder takes getting used to."

"Listen, John. There will be more death. Expect it. Only hope it is not your death." His tone of voice carried no threat. I believed him. There would be more death. I was ready to participate in it. But I did not have to like it.

"We'll see," I said, moving to get out.

"No," Henri told me. "*You'll* see."

I walked up East Capitol toward home. Broken brick sidewalks. You had to pay attention even by daylight.

I reminded myself of a woman who has made up her mind to have sex but still feels obliged to protest her innocence. I knew Henri was more in the right than I had admitted. But I hated it. Faust had it coming. If anybody did. A great trust betrayed. But I still would not have done it myself. Not like that. Maybe it meant I was a coward. Maybe it meant I was the weak link.

The truth is that I was meant for a middle-class life and church on Sunday. June, Wally, and the Beav. I believed in God—especially when I wasn't thinking about it—and critical thought did not come naturally to me. I would have made a lousy Frenchman.

In the interval between two streetlights, a figure stepped out in front of me. A figure with a gun.

"Give it up, motherfucker. Come on. Give it the fuck up." Soft voice filled with hatred.

He was a veteran, not just a kid out to finance a new pair of sneakers. He kept enough distance between us to prevent any countermoves. And he stood with his legs set apart and staggered, like a fighter. Ready for any crap life might throw back at him.

"Okay," I said. "All right, now. My wallet's in my back pocket. I'm going to reach into my back pocket."

"You just shut up and give it the fuck up, motherfucker. You just toss that thing right the fuck over here."

I lobbed the wallet at his feet.

"Now get the fuck down," he told me. "Get down on you fucking belly."

I got down on my belly. I did not believe he would shoot. He seemed too organized, too smart. But life is full of surprises. It struck me that it would be one hell of a twist if, in the middle of all that was going down, I got waxed by a mugger.

"Shit, motherfucker," he said. "This all you got?"

"That's everything."

"You ain't even got no fucking phone cards."

I did not answer. Let him roll.

"You be one sorry-ass poor motherfucker," he said. "Ought to cap you and put you out of you misery like a goddamned dog."

"There are two credit cards in the pocket."

"Shit. You think I'm that dumb? I don't want you damn credit cards." A flying wallet hit me on the top of the head. "You stay there, hear me? You stay right the fuck there, you sorry motherfucker."

I stayed right there. I listened to his footsteps pick up speed until he was fading at a sprinter's pace.

When the sound died, I rose and picked up my wallet. Wearily, I gathered the papers and cards he had scattered. It was the least exciting thing that had happened to me in a week.

CHAPTER 12

Blood painted my dreams. Until the phone woke me.

I jerked up. Caught in a twist of sheets. The bedding was soaked with nightmare sweat. Daylight scoured the room.

I had a hangover head. Without the pleasure of drink.

The phone cord had twisted. I dragged the cradle onto the floor, firing needles of noise into my ear.

"Hello?"

"You awake, soldier boy? I wake you up?" Dickey's voice.

"Yeah. I'm awake."

"That's a good thing. 'Cause we got serious business to discuss."

"My phone isn't secure, we shouldn't—"

"Shut up and listen," Dickey said. "You just listen to me a minute. I got a dead senator. Throat cut like a poor little lambie. And that ain't the half of it. Looks like the guy was tortured by serious sickos. Unless he was maybe impersonating that artist fuck with the ear cut off."

"Shouldn't we wait and talk—"

"*You* wait. I'm not done. So I got this dead senator, right? And me and my new Army buddy just happen to have a mutual acquaintance who has been working for this senator. As a staffer, they tell me. Working her little tail off, I bet. Ain't life in this town rich? And here's where it gets really interesting. Me and my bud happen to know that she is one naughty girl. With a hit-and-run sheet that goes back to her training-wheel days. And what, you are about to ask me, does this have to do with saving the taxpayer the cost of a senator's pension? Well, just coincidentally, there are blond hairs on this dead senator's pillow. And elsewhere. And if a cop with a basic understanding of human biology can trust all those nasty stains on the bed, there was a totally different sort of activity going on before the senator's reelection bid got canceled. Yet there is no blond body, living or dead, at the scene of the crime. And this fuck did not commit suicide, let me tell you." Dickey let off one of his don't-this-world-stink? whinnies. "Me, I got FBI snots fresh out of college crawling all over the place because it's a goddamned senator, and they're so smart they know everything. Except they don't know what me and my Army buddy know. Now let me ask you something, your heroship. Are you awake enough to put these simple facts together and guess who those blond hairs might belong to?"

"We need to talk."

"You keep telling me that."

I was afraid. Shocked awake. Afraid with layer upon layer of fear. I was an accomplice to a murder. Among other things. And Dickey had just told the big, bad world that he and I had a meaningful relationship.

My thoughts rushed, but my thinking was glacial. Dickey knew exactly what he was doing. And I failed to get it.

"Just tell me when and where," I said. "Name the place."

Dickey gave me another nose honk. "I'll get back to you. Right now, I'm up to my ass in self-righteous J. Edgars and meat-eating reporters. But don't take off for Mexico, all right? And you might want to steer clear of Miss California. Don't you go aiding and abetting a felon on me."

He hung up. I flopped back down on the bed. I just wanted to think for a minute, to reconstruct something that resembled a viable future. I had, at best, a day left until the deadline Hunt had given me. And everything was coming apart instead of coming together. The disks were as far away as ever. I was in serious trouble, no matter what happened. And the woman I loved was a lot worse off than I was. Had she been lying beside me, I would have held her so tight it would have taken God and an army of angels to pry us apart.

But even Tish and dead senators and Dickey and blond hairs on a pillow could not hold me in the land of the living. My body foreclosed on the sleep debt. Which was massive.

I blew it again.

The next time I woke, it was twilight. Corry sat by the bed. With a gun in her hand.

"Wake up, sleepyhead," she told me.

"What?"

Corry smiling. But not making nice. "I was hoping you'd talk in your sleep. That you'd call my name. It would have meant a lot to me."

"What do you want?" The sheets were brinier than ever. Despite the air-conditioning. I sat up against the back of the bed, drawing the sheet with me. Shy. Or just scared.

"Maybe I want to thank you. I owe you my life." She wagged the gun slightly. "By the way, I changed the bullets."

"I don't know what you're talking about."

She smiled. A girl born to win. At any cost. "Don't treat me like a fool. I know it was you. I knew it was you the instant I turned around. The way you move. The cut of the shoulders—you know you have nice shoulders, by the way?

I've seen a lot of shoulders. I know it was you, John. I'll always know you."

"Want to fill me in?"

Corry still smiling. "And your voice. I know you so well. You don't realize. I heard you say, 'No.' Then you said it again. I knew what was happening. I know that you saved my life."

I just wanted to go to the bathroom and piss. "I would've hated to see a great marriage come to a premature end, Mrs. Aalstrom."

It took her a moment to absorb that. But she managed it. "I knew you'd find out sooner or later," she said. "It was inevitable. But that doesn't mean you understand."

"Can I just go to the bathroom for a minute?"

"No." She lifted the gun a little. She did not hold it like a girl. Corry was loaded down with medals from the battle of the sexes. "I want you to have a sense of urgency."

"I thought you came to thank me."

"Among other things." She filled her chest and gave a soap-opera sigh. "I suppose I need to clear the air. About Aley. And all that."

"'And all that.'"

She looked at me with Actors Studio tenderness. "I suppose I'll never be able to make you understand completely. You want me to be Salomé. The ultimate bad girl. Damned forever. Beyond redemption. And you think you're John the Baptist. You want it all to be so clear. Good and evil. Wicked or wonderful." She smirked. "You're just such a *guy* sometimes. But it's not that easy. Sure, I've done things I'm not proud of. But I'm not necessarily ashamed of them, either. Those things were about survival. Sur*viv*al, John. And getting ahead. *Try*ing to get ahead. I hustled. You don't know what work is until you've lived that life. Rich kids are the lowest life form in the universe. Yeah, and I stole. From other people who stole. And Aley . . ."

She smiled. But her voice turned as bitter as a mouthful of aspirin. "I was young. He seemed . . . he seemed like a guy who had everything. Everything I wanted." She allowed herself a different kind of laugh, a very small one. "Yeah, he had it. He just didn't know how to pay for it. Neither of us did." She was good at meeting my eyes. But this time she looked away.

The gun held steady, though.

"You live and learn," she said. "It took me a long time to learn. You keep thinking, This time it'll be different. This time I'm really going to make it. And you do foolish things. There was a time in my life when Aley and I deserved each other. We were perfect . . ."

I shifted my back. More sweat. "And?"

"And now," she said, "there's you."

"Corry—or do you prefer Karen?"

"Corry, please. I've begun a new life."

"All right, Corry. Just how stupid do you think I am?"

Cat smile. "Oh, your stupidity may be immeasurable. It's one of your many attractive qualities, John. I've had plenty of men who thought they were smart."

"You know I'll never believe another word you say."

She lost her smile. And leaned toward me. "That would be sad. Even tragic. Because we were made for each other, John. You're everything I always wanted. Only I didn't know it. You're a white knight. An honest guy. Loyal."

"I just happen to be loyal to somebody else."

She waved it away. A queen dismissing a fool whose wit was slower than hers. "That won't last. She won't hold your interest. There's too much of you and too little of her. You're baby-sitting."

"I'm going to marry her. When we get through this."

"*If* you get through this. If *we* get through this. And . . . maybe you should ask her first. I don't think she'd go for it.

She'd say yes, then she'd freeze up. She'll fade on you. Disappear. She's fluff. And deep down inside, she knows it. She's afraid of you."

The light was dying. Tish was dying. I had no time.

"So . . . I should just forget about Tish? And marry you?"

"You could do worse. I'd make you happy. Once you got your devils under control, I'd know how to make you happy. I'm strong enough for you. And it wouldn't have to be marriage."

"Of course, there is the matter of the living, breathing husband."

"The one who gave me a gun to protect myself? With dummy bullets? Who's so fucking greedy he wants all the money for himself? The husband who wants me dead?"

"Every marriage has bad patches."

"John, this is serious. You and I . . . we could make it. We could bring this off. We could beat them all."

I shook my head in wonder.

"*Lis*ten to me," she pleaded. "We're talking ten million dollars. *Ten*. Tax-free. Do you have any idea how much money that is? How much did Aley offer you?"

"He said it was five."

"See? Everybody's lying. Except me. John, even if you don't want to be with me . . . do this with me. Help me. Even if you don't want to be with me at first, I'll give you six million. No, seven. That's fair, isn't it? Seven million dollars? All you have to do is help me a little bit. You won't regret it." A woman pleading, with a gun in her hand. Another new experience. "I have what you want, John. I have what you need."

I lost it. You just hit a point and you snap. We are not rational creatures. I barked something and jumped out of bed and stood there in my birthday suit. Too angry and frustrated to give a damn anymore.

"I'm going to the bathroom. Shoot me, if you want. But

let me tell you once and for all, sister. You do not have one goddamned thing I want or need."

Her eyes held me for a moment. Those great eyes. The kind of eyes that ruin men's lives with false candor. As I was turning away, she said:

"How about the disks?"

"There's not much time," she told me. "You have to really listen."

I was listening.

"Aley's going to call you. This is it. The big one. It's his last chance. He's desperate. He knows Hunt will cut him out if he doesn't produce this time. We can turn that against him."

"Where's Tish? Where are they keeping her?"

Economical shake of a blond head. "I don't know. And that's the truth. Hunt keeps everything in separate compartments. Aley doesn't know, either."

"Why should I believe that?"

"I swear to God," she said.

I lifted a corner of my mouth. "You don't strike me as the religious type."

"Please listen. He's going to call soon. You have to get it right. Agree to meet him. But you say where. And set a tight deadline. Cut down his reaction time. And don't go to meet him, or Hunt, or anybody, on their turf. Once they know you have the disks, they'll do anything it takes to make you tell them where they are. Then they'll kill you."

"How will I prove I've got the disks? Or that you've got them?"

She reached into her purse. Without shifting her eyes from me. She tossed a disk onto the bed. It landed halfway out of its jacket.

"Give Aley that one. It's the real thing. Then talk money."

"And Tish."

"He'll lay out how they'll do the funds transfer for you. In return for the disks. He'll give you the number of an account in the Caymans and the matching codes. So you can verify the payout." She switched the pistol to her left hand and stretched the fingers of her right. "Aley's got a triple cross set up. He's going to tell Hunt you're the one insisting on using the Caymans account, that you've been working a scam all along. Hunt won't like it, but he'll release the funds. It's small change to his crowd. Although he is one stingy sonofabitch." I wondered if she had enjoyed a close relationship with Hunt as well. "Then Aley cues the account so that your confirmation query triggers another transfer. To Panama this time. Into an account even Hunt won't be able to track. And it'll look like you did it. Hunt kills you in revenge. Aley keeps the money."

"Wasn't it supposed to be Aley and you?"

"That's why he gave me this." She lofted the gun. "With the sandbox bullets."

"And?"

"The money?" She smiled. It was an ugly, sincere smile. "Fuck Aley. That shit. I know more about offshore banking than he ever will. The instant the money hits Panama, it's out of there. Straight to Luxembourg. Straight to us, John." She leaned toward me in the early dusk of the bedroom. "He'll think Hunt screwed him after all. But he won't be able to do anything about it."

I looked at her. Looking for holes. "Except Aley's bound to wonder why his dream girl is suddenly gone. Don't you think he's going to suspect you?"

She prodded the air lazily with the gun. "I'll be too disappointed. No, I think I can make his life sufficiently unhappy that he won't suspect a thing. I figure if I stay with him . . . say six months . . . then file for divorce over one of the countless other reasons he's given me . . ." She straightened her Sunday-school posture. Little Miss Prim. "Besides, that'll give you time to wrap up the thing with your girl. More than enough time."

"You're a confident woman."

"I know you, John. I know her. There aren't more than a dozen different types of people."

"And how do I know you won't do a job on me? Or kill me, for that matter? Maybe pay somebody a couple of bucks to do the dirty work. How do I even know that disk is real? You've got so many angles, this could be a setup within a setup within a setup."

"Have an alternative?"

"I could wait."

"Until your redhead strolls down memory lane? For keeps?"

"Listen . . . I don't give a damn about the money, Corry."

"Everybody cares about money."

"I don't."

"Yes, you do. You will."

"Six months pass . . . and you're ringing my doorbell, ready to hand me seven million bucks? And give me a kiss besides? I'm supposed to believe that?"

"I'll give you a lot of kisses. I'll kiss you like you've never been kissed."

"I'm going to do what you want. In the short term. You know that. But don't imagine that I trust you. In any respect. Don't confuse necessity with volition."

"You'll learn to trust me, John. I'm trusting you with that disk. With my life. They'd kill me. Aley would kill me. He'd make it ugly."

"What about the disks? Where are the rest of them?"

"I have them."

"But you don't trust me? Not enough to tell me where?"

"It's better if you don't know. In case anything goes wrong tonight."

"That's reassuring."

"It's practical."

"Okay. At least tell me how you got them. When everybody else has been digging tunnels to China trying to find them."

She canted her head. Posing for a magazine cover. Hair wandering across her cheek. She probably would not have made it as a model, though. Successful models all have some little flaw.

"All right. I don't mind telling you that. I got them from Em. He had them."

I hung my head. Hit from the front, back, and sides. I should have seen it on day one.

"Em was going to go public. Wasn't he?" I asked her. I wanted to hear it from that perfect little mouth. "Or turn them over to the GAO? Or to somebody else?"

"Em was stupid," she said.

"That makes two of us."

"Em was stupid in a different way."

"A better way."

"A useless way," Corry said. "Don't romanticize him. Em was a shit. He was a fucking drunk with so much on his conscience he was afraid of dying."

"Was he dying?"

"Yeah."

"Cirrhosis?"

"Cancer. He hit the jackpot."

"You're cold."

"Try realistic."

"I never know what to believe."

"Try trusting me."

I laughed. "Like Em did?"

"I'd do anything for you."

"Then tell me something. When they killed Em . . . you didn't come straight here from the police station. Did you?"

"No."

"You went back to the apartment. And grabbed the disks. That's why they tore it up. The disks were supposed to be there. Only you saw the main chance. And you had your own key. And you were quick." I admired the tactician sitting in front of me. Wondering how she would turn out as a strategist. "So who did it? Hunt's boys? His goddamned Hunt Club? You grabbed the disks and stashed them and showed up sobbing on my doorstep. While your teammates went nuts hunting for the goods."

"Yes. Now do you believe that you can trust me?"

"No. Where'd you stash the disks?"

"I won't tell you that."

"Who shot Em? And don't give me the big-bad-black-boys crap you gave the cops."

"Aley did. Aley shot him. It was the first time he killed anybody. He panicked. He ran. That's when I knew I had to grab the disks myself. That I couldn't depend on him."

"And you knew it was going to go down. You walked Em right into the ambush?"

"Em had it coming. He was a shit."

"Let's just agree to disagree on that. So . . . how'd you do it? Did you get him to bend over and kiss you? To distract him? Or was it just supposed to be a miracle meeting on the streets of Washington, Em and his old Army acquaintance Aley Aalstrom?"

Corry brushed stray hairs back over an ear and leaned toward me. "John, do you know that your girlfriend can't have babies?"

"Don't change the subject."

"Would you like to know why she can't have kids?"

"No."

"Then we both have to accept that some things are best left buried in the past."

"Leave Tish out of this."

"You're the one who's so intent on including her in our lives, John."

"Tish has had a hard-luck life, Corry."

Corry laughed. A human being should not be able to laugh like that when he or she is still young. "We make our luck. She doesn't understand that. Or anything else. I know the type. She probably did this big remorse number on you. All weepy. 'Oooh, I can't have little babies for you . . .' Get a grip, John. Her kind doesn't feel remorse. She's just sorry she got caught."

"Go to hell."

"You believe in the image you've created of her. She's just a slut on temporary good behavior. Because she thinks she won the lottery. And she wants to make sure she gets the payout. If you did marry her, it wouldn't be six months until she was down on her knees giving a blow job to some agent or promoter. Or maybe just the paperboy."

"You're poison."

"I'm honest."

"No. You're not. You're the devil."

"John, do you know what happens to romantics? Their kids come out looking like some other guy."

The phone rang. And we both stopped. As it rang for the second time, Corry told me:

"Tell him you have what he wants. Tell him you'll meet him. On your turf. This is our chance, John."

It was a woman who introduced herself as Melissa. She offered me a special low introductory rate on a new MasterCard.

I hung up. "Telemarketer."

Corry had a way of sharpening her eyes that made me think she was getting a sight picture on an invisible rifle. "It was that policeman. Wasn't it?"

"No. It was a credit card offer. Really."

"John, we need to discuss this. What have you told the police?"

"Next to nothing. Just what I had to tell them to get them to put me back on the street."

"Was the cop the one who told you? About me and Aley?"

"Yes."

"What else does he know about me?"

"He thinks you're trouble. He warned me to stay away from you."

"Is he watching me?"

"I suspect he'd like to. But this is D.C., sister. The cops are in a round-the-clock sewer diving competition. We're small stuff."

"Has he made any connections?"

"No. Not really." I had, though. Corry was too good for Hollywood, but for once, I had more information than she did. That told me she was not plugged in all that tightly with Hunt and company. Who had been tapping my phone. Hunt wasn't sharing the power information with Corry. Or, I suspected, with Aley. I liked it like that. But I also believed that Hunt would see Corry as one hundred percent disposable. Thanks to Dickey's phone call, Hunt knew the cops had connected her to the Faust murder. Which was not a Hunt-approved action. Hunt might just be anxious to talk to Corry about that.

The stakes were going up and up.

"Don't tell the police anything you don't have to," Corry said. Voice earnest. "It won't help."

"Corry, I'm at the point where I'm afraid to talk to myself."

"And that other one. The French guy who was here. The

one you fought with. Has he tried to get in touch with you again?"

I wondered if this was a test question. If it was, I was ready to fail.

"No. I think the cops scared him off. The frogs are still hot about the lab bombing. But even the French are smart enough to figure out that I'm not connected."

"Stay away from them," Corry said. "Don't talk to the French. Don't talk to anybody. I'm the only one you can trust, John. Believe me."

The phone rang again. We both jumped.

It was Aley.

"John. Hey, Johnny boy. The clock has been fucking ticking. Ticktock. So you got good news for me, or what? Moment of truth."

"Maybe."

"What the fuck is that? 'Maybe.' *Talk* to me."

"Not over the phone."

"Don't waste my time, Johnny boy."

"Fuck you, Aley. I've done enough of an analysis of the situation to figure out that you need me a lot more than I need you. You're a flunky. So can the bad-boy act."

"John, you remember all that shit about snuff films? You know, where they gang-fuck some babe and torture her? Kind of cut her up piece by piece? Then kill her? Right on camera? Well, I am here to tell you that cinema verité is not just a legend of our time. They make 'em right across the border. Little ranch down the highway from TJ. Your redhead's got star quality."

"Doesn't work, Aley. Try sugar."

"Try getting real. The curtain comes down in the morning, Johnny boy."

"Here's the deal, Aley. I've got something you want. And I'm prepared to give you a taste. If you say, 'Please.' "

"Tell me you got them, John. Say it."

"Meet me at Monsieur Paul's. Pennsylvania Avenue. Southeast. I'll be at the bar. In half an hour. If you're late, I'm going straight to General Hunt. And you can go make Mexican movies for a living."

I thought I had it all sorted out at last. And I had already begun to shape a plan. I walked out of the house. Into the concentrated end-of-the-day heat. Leaving Corry upstairs in her web. I turned the corner fast. Heading for Monsieur Paul's, where Capitol Hill gets strange.

A kick-ass energy surge powered me. I imagined myself taking charge of the whole mess at last. For the first time, I had cards *and* chips. And I was ready to cheat like a Congressman in a tight reelection campaign.

Then I recognized Mary Farnsworth. Bent over. Locking the Cadillac Seville that had been the general's pride and joy.

She saw me. And barely kept her excitement within the bounds of decorum. Queen Mary. The last person I wanted to see mixed up with desperados. I wondered if anything would ever really go right for me again.

"I don't know *how* you live here," she told me. "Parking is just an impossi*bil*ity."

"Mary, you promised me you'd—"

She hushed me with a fine, small gesture of the hand. "Oh, I did every last thing you said. But . . . do you understand what Louisiana is *like* this time of year? Besides, I could not stop thinking about Mickey. And I began to feel like the most shameless coward. Just running away. *Flee*ing. Just like that. Without even knowing what I was fleeing from."

"Mary, this is serious."

Her bearing changed. She reared like a drill sergeant confronted with a cruddy pair of boots on parade.

"My husband's dead, John. I think I can appreciate the seriousness in that."

"You shouldn't be here. It's dangerous."

"And what about *you?* I kept thinking about you, John. I thought you might need a friend. To stand by you."

"You can't help me now. You have to leave."

Her eyes surprised me. Reserve melted into yearning. An ache to do something, anything, in the face of immeasurable loss. "I don't want to burden you," she told me. "That would be the last thing. It's only that . . . given all that's happened . . . I didn't know if it would be safe to telephone you. You see, I found them."

"Mary, you need to get out of here. Now. Please."

"But I found them. Those disks. I thought you might need them."

I hurried Mary into an alley. Not a crack dealer in sight. Or anybody else. Gray birds pecked garbage.

"Stay in the shadows. Away from the light."

"I just thought you'd want to know . . ." She was confused now.

"You bet. Tell me about the disks. How many? Where were they?"

Mary shook her head. As if looking around for answers that had slipped from her mind. "I was . . . John, you have to understand. With Mickey . . . I mean, I was so terribly upset. *Dev*astated. I wasn't thinking at all. But when I came back, I had to go to the bank. To our safe-deposit box. For our personal papers, records." She wrinkled her fine mouth. A shadow twisting within a shadow. "It should have been obvious. I should have thought about it immediately." She touched at the sweat that covered every forehead in the city. "I was just such a fool. You see, we always kept a big safe-deposit box. I had to keep all my jewelry in it. Mickey insisted. He had that dread of crime soldiers seem to acquire. Well, wasn't it just the most obvious place in the world for him to keep those disks?"

"How many of them are there? Is there any writing on them? Where are they now?"

She shrugged. "Oh, there must be dozens. I don't know. I didn't count them. I was so excited. Perhaps . . . oh, would sixty or so sound right? That's just a guess, now. But you can come over and count them. I brought them home. They all have Macon-Bolt stamps on them. With a lot of numbering. And they're marked 'Top Secret.' Was Mickey supposed to keep anything like that in our private box?"

"Mickey—I mean, General Farnsworth—was a hero. He knew exactly what he was doing."

She regarded me with a sorrow the new darkness could not mask. "Then why is he dead? I miss him so, John."

The customer next to me at the bar looked like Gertrude Stein in a biker's jacket. Monsieur Paul's had a core gay clientele, but it was open to other human variations. Tish and I had gone there a few times to hear friends of hers play jazz. Of all the establishments I could have picked for the meet with Aley, I figured Monsieur Paul's was the likeliest to surprise him and keep him off balance. Besides, the kitchen did a good club sandwich.

I had the third triangle in my mouth when Aley came in. Funny to watch him. L.A. boy or not, the atmosphere hit him hard. He saw the crowd, not me.

Management kept the bar dark. During the day, the sunnies ate at the sidewalk tables and drank bottles of beer. At nightfall the vampires came out. And plenty of victims drifted in. The joint provided good people watching at all hours. I enjoyed watching Aley.

I left the last quarter of the sandwich and worked toward him through the performance-art boys. He finally saw me. A what-the-fuck-is-this? expression split his lips.

We did not shake hands.

"You hitting from both sides of the plate now?" he asked me.

"Your problem," I told him, "is that you never met Mr. Right."

"Up yours, Johnny boy."

"You're going to fit right in. Have a seat. Over in the corner. It's more romantic."

I let him lead the way. Shirt too shiny. Jacket expensive but loser-snug in the armpits. Padded shoulders. With organic padding at the butt of his trousers. A heavyweight in the heat. No weaponeering, as far as I could tell.

"So what's with the circus?"

A splendid human specimen with a West Indian accent loomed. "What going to be your pleasure?"

"Two drafts," I said. "Whatever."

"You're deep in the shit," Aley told me. "Right down to the wire. So talk to me. You got the goodies or not?"

It was strange as hell sitting there. Wondering how much he knew. Thanks to Mary Farnsworth, I knew Corry was out to beat me. But were she and Aley playing as a team, after all? Or was she out to beat him, too? The disk she had given me had some alpha-numerics printed on its label. It looked convincing if you did not know what you were looking for. But it did not look like the disks Mary had described.

Who knew what the real disks looked like? Hunt had to know. Did Corry and Aley really believe they could bluff the big boys? I did not rule out the possibility. The scent of money makes folks stupider than the prospect of cost-free sex.

I had the aces. Or I would have them as soon as I got across the river to Mary's house. But no matter which way I turned, I was sitting with my back to a door or a window.

If I was going down, I was not going alone. It was going to be a fight. Keeping Tish alive constituted a clear and worthy mission. Maybe we had a chance. But I could not expect to outmaneuver everybody else—I had to let them outmaneuver themselves.

I tossed the disk onto the table and watched Aley. I expected him to grab it. But he only stared at the thing.

"How do I know it's real?" he asked me. "That could be something you picked up at Computerland."

"You don't want it, I'll go." I reached for the disk.

He flattened a swollen hand over it. "Just fucking wait. You listen to me. If it turns out you're blowing smoke, I'm going to introduce you to misery like you never imagined. To say nothing of your trash mick bitch."

"Aley, you're more impressive when you keep your mouth shut. And that's just what I want you to do. Until I tell you to open it again."

The waiter brought the beers. I suspected the guy was one of the bar's key attractions. He floated away, muscles and air, twirling his tray on an index finger.

"The disk is good," I said. "And you know it. Now let me tell you how we're going to work the battle handoff. You are going to give me a phone number. And you are going to be standing by that phone at a quarter to five tomorrow afternoon. Sixteen-forty-five, pal. At that time, I will designate a location within the city of Washington. You will be there at six P.M. Eighteen hundred on the dot. I will name a very public location, with more witnesses than even Hunt could take down. Tish O'Malley will be there. And she will look as healthy as Tarzan. General Hunt will also be there. Make it happen. Accept no substitutes."

Aley opened his mouth and raised both hands.

"Save it," I told him. "My deal, or no deal. And I've got it fail-safed. Any of the Hunt Club boys try to move on me between now and tomorrow afternoon, the disks will be in French hands before the HOV lanes open up. And one more attendee. General Gabrielli will be there. In uniform. Tell Hunt to make it happen."

"What's that monkey Gabrielli got to do with the great apes?"

I sipped my beer. Acting calmer than I felt and hoping it came off. "Insurance. If Gabrielli's there with all those stars and his nameplate, he won't want any rough stuff that might get him dirty in the public eye. We'll keep the swap clean that way. No double crosses. And I'll have backup."

Aley snickered. "My ass. You're so deep in the shit you couldn't find backup to sing harmony at your funeral. Get real."

"Know why I invited you here, Aley? Because you never were anything but a pussy with hormonal confusion. So let's talk money. Ten million. Not five. Hunt told me. Yeah, you're master of your emotions, all right. I wish I had a mirror so you could see your face. So smart. So tough. Well, let me offer you the break of your life. It's a deal. I'll settle for the five. You take the other five. And I won't feed you to Hunt." He really was small-time. Corry was a thousand times more accomplished as a hustler. "Your turn to talk. Tell me about the money. How it's going to work."

He shook his head in disgust. "Just fuck you. It'll go to the Caymans. It's all set. Here's how it happens . . ."

Aley laid it out. Exactly the way Corry said he would. I could not get a constant fix on how much anybody really knew, but Corry seemed to know more of whatever there was to know than Aley did. Maybe they were still in it together. But I was starting to buy Corry as a triple-crosser. Maybe going for a quadruple.

There were so many layers of lies, a Southern belle could not have kept them straight. I let Aley talk. Then I let him pay for the beers. And I made him add to the tip. He started to stand up, but I got a foot behind one of his chair legs and yanked it in behind his knees.

"One more thing," I said. "You killed Farnsworth. Didn't you?"

"What the fuck? You wired or something? You're talking shit."

"Truth or consequences. I just want to know. Let's see some eyes. Talk to me, Aley."

"What does it matter who killed him? Fucking nigger busybody. They in short supply this week?"

"I'm just sentimental. Tell me you killed him."

"John, we are talking ten million dollars. And that's just the trickle-down effect for the little people like you and me. The old shit was on the heart-attack express. Old and in the way."

"Just say you killed him. I don't even need the details."

"You wearing a wire? What is this?"

"No wire. But here's the deal. You try to beat me out of my five million, and I'll put the Farnsworth murder on you. Fair's fair."

Aley smiled in recognition. "Shit. We all have our price. Don't we, John?"

Mary Farnsworth's kitchen. With the blinds closed. The disks lay on the table between us. They looked real. Felt real. I was going to bet my life that they were real.

"Mary, you're sitting in front of three hundred billion dollars. Give or take a few billion." It was the kind of thing she did not need to know. But it was also the kind of thing you can't resist saying. "If you let me take them, neither one of us will ever see a penny of it."

"I don't want money."

"I know. I'm just talking. It's a human disease."

Mary smiled. But the valiant attempt at warmth faded. "More coffee, John?"

"Please." I had driven the most convoluted, back-assward route imaginable to get to Mary's place. Then I parked several blocks away. I gave the neighborhood's sensor lights a workout. Slipping through backyards. Thanks to the leash laws, there were no dog problems. When I arrived at her back door and gave the triple-secret club knock, she had coffee waiting. On Judgment Day, Mary would be out there serving iced tea to the damned.

She poured me another cup of her New Orleans roast. Blended with chicory. She refilled her own cup, parked the pot with her customary grace, and sat back down like a woman with something to say.

"John . . . are you a Christian? Forgive me for being so awkward. I mean, do you con*sid*er yourself a Christian? I suppose it's a terribly personal thing to ask . . ."

I reached for words. "My church attendance has been pretty spotty."

"But do you be*lieve?*"

I looked down at the disks. This was not something about which I was comfortable talking. Nor had I expected to talk about it. Death, disks, and theology. I suppose it all matched up.

"Mary . . . I'm not sure I'm the kind of person who really knows what he believes. I'm a trial-and-error kind of guy." I smiled, a real lemon-biter, thinking of a long sequence of errors. "I just may be the sloppiest believer on earth. But . . . at the end of the day . . . I guess it's there."

"We all need faith, John. I wish you faith. *Strong* faith."

"Don't worry about me."

She gave me those wonderful brown eyes. "Oh, I don't. Not really. Not that way. You strike me as a natural believer. The sort who has the faith but not the habits. And that's what's important. Not the rituals, comforting though they may be. God is . . . ultimately unknowable. We're too small for God. I have always seen you as a worshipper, though. In your way. Sometimes plain human decency is a form of worship. Perhaps a very high form." She scrubbed her hands together. Not a very Mary-like gesture. "This is *so* awkward."

"Is there something you need me to do?" I drank the piercing coffee.

She placed her hands flat on the tabletop. As though she had suddenly regained control of them. The nails shone unpainted. "John, you know Mickey and I were always active in our church."

I nodded. And drank.

"I have always considered myself a good Christian," Mary said. "I have been blessed with faith." She rolled that beautiful face slightly to the side. "I have counted many blessings. I know I am an imperfect being. A *very* imperfect being . . . and I have certainly been guilty of the sin of pride . . ."

"What is it, Mary?"

In the thin light, her eyes looked like long, dark hallways.

"I always assumed," she continued, "that I adhered adequately to the tenets of my faith. It was vanity. I see that now. A lack of self-evaluation, of the critical faculty applied where it is most needed. I *believed* that I believed in the Christian virtues."

I tried a smile. "Mary, you're probably the most saintly person I've ever met. If sheer kindness counts for anything . . ."

She shook her head. "No. No, that's not true. My soul . . ." She leaned toward me and her voice dwindled to a whisper of bones. "My soul is filled with sin. And I can't help it." Her eyes held me. Their grip was just short of physical. "John, do you know who hurt Mickey? Who killed him?"

"I think I do."

She gentled a hand toward the disks. "Can you use these to hurt whoever it was?"

"Yes. I can do that."

I would never have believed her face could change so. Or that any face could change so. Those precise, drawing-room features took on the bone-thunder look of a vengeful prophet.

"I want them to suffer," she cried. "I want them to pay. I don't care if I'm damned for it." The granite began to crack, to melt. Tears burst through, water from the rocks. "I want them to hurt the way I hurt. I want them to hurt the way Mickey hurt. And I don't care about anything else in the world."

To my amazement, Dickey had a listed home number. I had been prepared to work my way through layers of police bureaucracy to reach him, but the recorded voice read me his number and would have dialed it for me if I had not been calling from a convenience-store pay phone in suburbia.

I called, he answered.

"It's John Reynolds," I said. "I need your help."

"You bet you do. What're you doing calling me at home at this hour? Wake up my daughter and all."

"Please. This is important."

"And it just can't wait till morning, right?"

"It can't wait until morning."

"You got rocks, I'll say that for you. What's your major malfunction this time?"

"I need a phone number. It's unlisted. For a Roscoe Hunt. Retired general. A.k.a. Punchy Hunt. Ever heard of him?"

"We move in different circles."

"He's got a big spread ten or twelve miles out of Middleburg."

"So that's where our defense dollars go."

"Some of them."

"All right. Jesus. I'm going soft, I swear. Give me the name again."

"Hunt. First name Roscoe. Nickname's Punchy. Horse farm about—"

"Yeah, yeah. Got it. Call me back in . . . give me twenty minutes. The whole world's asleep."

"Thanks. I owe you."

"You got debts Bill Gates couldn't pay." He hung up.

I figured Dickey would come through. Anticipating, I got back in the car and headed west. Thinking about an Elvis Costello song. A favorite of Tish's. With the line "I can give you anything but time."

I knew where I was going. I simply did not want to be shot when I arrived. I was going in clean. No real wampum to trade. Mary and I had hidden the disks inside the empty PC casing in her husband's library, the one that had been looted of its hard drive. I figured it was the safest place in her house. The disks sure as hell would not have been safe with me.

File me under "Unprepared for the Twenty-first Century." I never had a car phone or a cellular to call my own. Now I saw the value. I had a bad time finding a pay phone in the yuppie belt off 66. I had to push on to a gas station where Route 50 hits 15 and the big rigs backroad down from Maryland and parts north.

When I called, Dickey had the number for me.

"I'll phone you in the morning," I told him. "I pay my debts. At six o'clock tomorrow evening, you'll have all the murderers you can handle in one place. But they're not going to go gently into that good night."

Hunt did not answer his own phone. A guard dog voice just said, "Hello," and waited.

"This is Lieutenant Colonel John Reynolds. I need to talk to General Hunt."

Fido did not respond immediately. I began to wonder if he had hung up. But the phone noise did not change. Finally, he said:

"You're not on the list. Call back during business hours."

"I need to talk to him now. Tell him it's John Reynolds."

"You're not on the list, buddy." I could feel the phone pull away from his ear.

"Wait," I said. Or yelled. "Three hundred billion dollars. Computer disks. Tell him."

"What is this shit?"

"Hunt's going to lose a lot of money if you don't get him on the phone. And I guarantee you he'll lose his temper, too. You know what happened to that Labrador of his?"

"Stay on the line."

I stood in the almost-cool of the night. Watching a big gal with a time-warp Charlie's Angels hairdo pump gas into a pickup. The truck had a bumper sticker that said, "Impeach the President—and her husband, too."

Hunt's voice came on like a storm.

"Watcha got? What is it? That you, Reynolds? Start talking."

"It's me. I want to see you."

"You have my disks?"

"No."

He blew the rhythm. After the pause, he said, "Aalstrom just told me you did."

"I need to see you. You're being scammed. I'm on Route 50, fifteen minutes from Middleburg. Headed your way. I'd like to make it inside the gates alive."

Hunt laughed. Then chopped off the sound with an invisible axe. "Reynolds, you got more balls on you than a fifteen-foot Christmas tree, you know that? You tell me you don't have my disks, but you want to drive right on into the belly of the beast. You trying to run some kind of scam yourself, boy? Or are you just crazy?"

"Try me."

"Damned if I won't. Come on out here. Let's have us a talk. If you're fucking with me, I'll kill you with my bare hands."

The gates to Hunt's estate stood open. I did not see any guards. But I was certain Hunt's boys saw me. I followed the country road that served as a driveway for about a mile, with a gauntlet of trees black on the flanks of my headlights. The road was flat but gave the illusion of a descent into an ever-thicker darkness.

Suddenly, the landscape opened and climbed. The car crested a low ridge. Across a field I picked out two silhouettes carrying those jagged, chopped automatic rifles that look like pieces of modern sculpture.

In the background, a pair of red lights floated up above the trees. I cranked down the window. Engine noise confirmed it: A plane had taken off from Hunt's private airstrip. I wondered if it had to do with my problem or with some other grand scheme to take over the world with guns and money.

Another defensive line of trees. Slight movement, perhaps imagined. Good soldiers waiting for an enemy to attack. I half expected to see the outline of dug-in tanks.

Bright windows marked the big house. I braked hard at the

last minute and stopped just short of a steel swing gate. I didn't remember it. But there had been a lot on my mind during my last visit.

Three boys in black emerged from the shrubs. One stood behind the gate. Directly in my headlights. Pointing a weapon as angular as a swastika at my windshield. The other two spooked along the side of the road. A big voice said, "Get out of the vehicle. Clasp your hands behind your head." No malice in it. The tone was as routine as the kid at the Burger King drive-through.

One of the boys patted me down, intimately enough to make a positive impression back at Monsieur Paul's. Real high-security prison frisk. Then they went through the car. And under it. With flashlights.

Out in the big-bucks peace of Middleburg, Hunt had a little army of commandos. In black uniforms. Faces mottled dark with camouflage. These were not weekend warriors. When the reception committee was done with me and my rent-a-Ford, one of them just called out, "Clean." The guy with the minimalist automatic pulled the gate open.

I drove up the rise to the house and parked next to a pair of four-wheelers. More security around the parking apron. By the time I got to the front door, Hunt filled the opening, a minotaur black against the lights of the entryway.

"Wondered if you'd pussy out at the last minute," Hunt said. "Then I figured, Naw, this boy's gone to too much trouble. He's going to play out his hand. Come on in."

He turned and marched down the hallway. A red dragon reared across his back. Hunt went barefoot, with massive, scarred legs pumping under khaki desert shorts. The black hairs had been burned off the muscle of one of his calves. Those legs were an encoded history of the man's life. But my eyes pulled back to the dragon. Emblazoned on seductive blue silk, writhing over Chinese characters I could not read. The wrap was cut like an old-fashioned smoking jacket and tailored to fit. Above the collar, a purple scar meandered down the back of Hunt's skull. But every line of his body seemed to converge on the dragon.

I got the same impression as the first time I saw him: a man who had been blown apart and reassembled.

"Hell, let's just use the library," he told me. "Still haven't got the goddamned armory cleaned up to academy standards." He pushed open a door. The lights were on over the bookcases. He had known exactly which room he would use. He was the kind of guy who knew exactly how much ammo to hump and who never forgot the spare battery for the radio. A two-canteener. "Sit down, sit down. Want a drink?"

"I'm driving."

He smiled at that. "Maybe. And maybe the boys'll have to bury you out back before sunup. Sure about that drink?"

I shook my head. "I'm not much of a drinker."

That got a snort. "Hell, son, a couple of days ago I would've said you weren't much of anything." He looked at me with eyes of pure jade. "Now I'm not so sure. You don't mind if I have one, I take it?"

He bent to a cabinet. Hidden mini-fridge. A bottle of Stoli bobbed up in his right paw. His left drew out a can of V8 Juice. "Nothing but goddamned vitamins," he said. "Take care of your body, your body takes care of you. Make me happy and tell me you were yanking my chain on the phone. Tell me you have my disks."

"I don't have the disks."

"Aalstrom told me you did. What happened to them?"

"I never had them. Aley's a liar."

"Why'd you tell him you had them? He says you even gave him a taste." He dropped into one of the leather chairs that fit you like a lover. It looked like he was drinking blood.

"He's got a disk," I said. "It's bogus. At least, I think it is."

"You don't fucking know?"

"His wife gave it to me. To give to him."

One of Hunt's eyebrows lifted a notch. Like the range slide on a rifle.

"I think they're out to screw each other," I told him. "But I'm one hundred percent positive they're both out to screw you."

Hunt dimpled his chin and looked down into his glass. "You know, that woman has the makings of a great courtesan. Just lacks patience. Haven't been fucked like that since I left Thailand." He smiled with half his mouth. "Figured I ought to test-drive it. And I guess you still haven't?"

"Not my type."

"Hell, boy, she's everybody's type. You're dumber than dogshit, passing that up. So she gave you a disk? To give to Aley? To tease me with? Now how about explaining that to an old soldier who's been hit upside the head a couple of times too many?"

I leaned back in the big chair. Half expecting iron clamps to leap across my chest and lash around my legs. But I only got that glorious softness.

"Here's my take on it," I began. "You be the judge. Either she's out to beat everybody, including Aley. Or she and Aley are working together on the double cross. No matter which way I cut it, though, they're both out to use me to blindside you. For the money. I'm here to bet my life that the disk Corry gave me is a fake. They're setting up a hand-off scenario in which you have to transfer the money. Temporarily, as far as you know. So I can confirm it and feel secure. So I can imagine I'm in the driver's seat. For a millisecond. Only the instant I make the call, another electronic transfer occurs. International borders pop up like fire walls. The ten million disappears. And we're both cut out. Thanks to the wonders of information-age banking."

Hunt's face locked up.

"You wouldn't realize what happened," I went on. "Not immediately. You'd have other things on your mind. Fires to put out, dragons to slay. Accounts to settle. By the time you exit the battlefield and get those disks into a computer for a look at the contents, they'll be high in the sky and over water. And you won't have the code to follow the money. They only need a couple of hours. Maybe less."

"I'd find them," Hunt said. Voice of stone.

"Sure. But they don't believe it. They think they can bring it off. She's sure of it. I suspect she's even ready to toss you Aley. Not much of a sacrifice. And so what if you do find them? The damage is done. You've blown your shot at crisis management. And you look like a horse's ass. Scammed by a drunk-tank hustler and a slut for all seasons."

I concentrated on keeping my voice sober and firm. Although I probably sounded like a prisoner begging his executioner for five more minutes.

"They've spotted your one weakness." I avoided his eyes when I said that. Looking just to the side. At the blue silk on his shoulder. The way you avoid locking eyes with a really mean dog. "You're overconfident. And they are not as dumb as they seem. What Aley lacks in table manners, he makes up for in his knowledge of international banking. And she knows more than he does. A lot more. She could pick the devil's pocket and make the poor bugger smile in the process."

I tested his eyes again. And found them opaque. He might as well have been an idol carved into the wall of a cave. "They've got it figured. An excuse for every move. Cover stories for their cover stories. The deal goes down. They fade on you. As if they're just plain scared. After all the carnage. You're supposed to blame me for the bad disks and the missing money. I'm dead, you're out ten million, your credibility's in the sewer, and Macon-Bolt goes shopping for a new security messiah."

Our faces were two masks—mine a crude wooden thing meant to hide fear.

Hunt rubbed his thumb back and forth across the side of his glass. A look of amusement had grown on his face. It was the kind of look that was just a hair-trigger short of fury.

"Well, fuck me," he said. "Now . . . just what's to stop me from killing you and that redhead of yours and tidying up the sandbox? Before I look into the Aalstroms' family values?"

I leaned forward. "Two things. First, I expect you to live up to your reputation. The O-Club stories claim that, in addition to being the meanest sonofabitch in the gutter, you were also a guy who paid his debts. Who never left a comrade behind. A young SFer lieutenant who got shot to shit in the Laotian highlands carrying out the corpse of a CO he personally hated."

His eyes had changed again. He could have stared down lions.

"Maybe I'm a chump," I said. "But I figure you owe me. For the preemptive info. I'm saving you ten million bucks and a major embarrassment. And all I want is my girl back." I wished I sounded more confident, more convincing. "She won't say a word. She'll do what I tell her. You set the rules. Just let her go."

Hunt drained his glass and pawed his lips dry. "Reynolds . . . that gal of yours must be one hell of a screw. Or else she's the possessor of talents as yet undivined by old Punchy Hunt. You know, she asked my boys for pen and paper. Wanted to write you a little old letter. Just in case she didn't make it back to your loving arms. God Almighty, I feel like I'm in the presence of true love. Now, I still might kill you. After all, you are one hell of a security risk. But I'm thinking. You said there were two reasons why I shouldn't cut your throat and throw you in the cookpot. Try number two."

I wished I had taken him up on the drink offer. I had been trying to appear rigorous, macho, clean, confident. Now I was ready to drink straight from the bottle.

"You need me to play through the scenario. To give you the walking, talking proof. I told Aley—"

"I know what you told Aalstrom. Just talk to me."

"All right. Tomorrow evening, at eighteen hundred hours, Corry—or Karen, or whatever her name is—she and I will link up with Aley in Union Station. Then we'll meet you in the main hall for the handoff. She and Aley don't know the location or the specifics yet. I've been holding it back. As if I'm afraid and clinging to my only card."

I looked into the mask of his face. Maybe it was a trick of the lighting, but his cheekbones seemed to have climbed. To barricade his eyes. He looked like a devil in an Oriental pantomime.

"One of us will be packing the bogus disks," I went on. "Probably Aley, by the time we meet you. He'll grab them from whoever has them. Sheer nerves. I'm not going to call him till sixteen-thirty or so. So he'll be sweating. And pissed. After I call, he'll spend a couple of minutes wondering just how close he can cut it with you. Afraid you'll try to set up your own double cross. Then he'll panic. Afraid he's going to blow the whole deal. And he'll call you. Say just before five. To pass you the location for the transfer. And to make sure you've transferred the funds. When we're all on-scene at Union Station, he'll be nervous as a whore in church. And she'll have her eye on him, not on you. He's the one she doesn't trust. But you have the intel in advance. You can set it all up, preempt the bank transfers, grab Ozzie and Harriet on the way out. Or follow them. However you want to do it. You'll have them red-handed."

Hunt rubbed his jaw. Heavy beard. Unshaven since the previous morning. I could hear the whiskers crisp under his fingers.

"What if you're wrong, boy? What if Aley already put that disk in my hands and it's sound as the Federal Reserve?"

"He didn't."

Hunt grinned. Showing those replacement teeth. The originals would have been brown with coffee stains and tropical medicine. "No. He didn't. But what if he does?"

"He won't. Not if he's in on the scam with Corry. And I think he thinks he is. Although she's probably angling to triple-cross the double-crosser."

"Gets kind of fuzzy, doesn't it? Kind of like applied morality."

"Ask him to deliver the disk I passed him. He'll make every excuse in the world to delay handing it over."

"But . . . if you're right . . . and I press him . . . he'll run for the jungle."

"Which is why you need me. To walk the line. At eighteen hundred."

Hunt stood up. And calmly set his glass on a table loaded with photographs of a young soldier with lost colleagues. I noticed one photo in particular. I was glad Hunt's back was turned. So he could not see the stunned look on my face. The last linkage had just fallen into place.

Hunt walked over to the Landseer doggie painting and stared at it. Back still to me. Feet planted apart, roots embedded in the floor. The dragon fidgeted on his back. As though his muscles were wrestling under the fabric.

"'His captain's heart,'" he said, "'which in the scuffles of great fights hath burst the buckles on his breast, reneges all temper . . . and is become the bellows and the fan to cool a gypsy's lust.'" He groaned. A speared beast. "That bitch."

With slow arms, he lifted the painting from the wall. He tossed the frame into the air.

I never saw anything like the performance that followed. Not outside of a Jackie Chan preview. As the painting fell, Hunt punched through it and caught it. His hands and arms moved so quickly my eyes could not tune. He chopped and hacked at the frame, keeping it up in the air. Juggling. Smaller and smaller pieces. He screamed. And smashed the splinters ever smaller. Flipping them high. Double-cutting them with the edges of both hands. Howling.

After maybe ten seconds, he stopped cold. Leaving a mess of wood chips and shredded canvas on the floor. He had a new career waiting as an art critic.

He flopped back down in his chair. Gasping. For the first time, he looked old.

"The bitch," he repeated. "That little bitch."

Suddenly, he mastered himself again. But his face remained pink. He had done the unforgivable. He had lost control. And it embarrassed him. As every man will, he tried to make a joke of it. In his sandpaper fashion.

"My theory of art valuation," he said softly, still searching for oxygen, "is that there is a finite supply of the salable. Each time a piece of value is destroyed, the relative value of the surviving pieces climbs. Followed, if erratically, by their selling price." His face shone rose, with spots and lines of darkness. "Think of it as creative destruction."

He looked down at his hands. One bled along a finger. He watched the blood bead and streak. "Aging teaches us the laws of entropy. On a very personal level. Still, the notion of killing a piece of womanflesh as fine as that little blond bitch does not appeal to me. I have . . . I've had to do many things in life that do not appeal to me. My survival was conditional upon it. Can you understand that?"

Yes. I could understand that. Still I said:

"You wouldn't have to kill her."

His eyes gave me two seconds of pure disdain. Then he shook his head slowly and said, "I'm tired. This should have been a small job. Nothing at all. I want to end it." The jade eyes were flawed now. "You really don't have any idea where those disks are? The real ones? I could make you a rich man."

"Sorry."

He grimaced. "Nechestny's a horse's ass, of course. Greedy. Could've made an airplane that worked. More real potential. Could have sold the services a pretty good one now and a better one later on. But no. Old Bob had to go for the big kill. It's all a game to him." The martial arts display had been dazzling. But now Hunt's lips were purple and black. There were unexpected spaces between his words. "I don't expect you'll credit this, John . . . but I have always believed honesty is the best policy. This world's so goddamned crooked . . . honesty is like a suit of shining armor. Oh, you might move a little slower. But you're more apt to get there . . . alive." He stopped to glut his lungs. A dying minotaur. "I am a violent man. It has been my trade. But I don't like to think I'm truly a dishonest one. There are roles . . . to be played. Jobs to be done. Certainly, you might conceive of honesty differently than I do. But . . . "

He snapped back to being old Punchy Hunt. "Hell, boy, it's all crap. Every bit of it. I'm tired and talking trash. So you just listen to me. You hit the goddamned lottery. I don't know if it's brains or balls. But I'm going to see to it that you walk. Redhead, too. *After* you deliver my two little scumbag shit traitors into Daddy's loving arms." He pawed his cheek. Streaking it with blood. "Union Station, huh?"

"Safest for me. The crowd. Witnesses."

Hunt laughed. His lungs had come back on line. An act of will. He smacked a big bare knee with his palm. "Damn, you're not as dumb as you look. Now . . . what's all this bull Aley was laying down about how you want Gabrielli there? In uniform?"

"More security. Gabrielli's scared. If he's there in his greens, the center of attention with all those stars on his shoulders . . . I figure he won't want you doing the damn-damn on anybody. Where it might turn into the ultimate photo op."

He smiled. A pondering smile. "Why not? Good experience for old Gabe. Lay some fear on him. Goddamned therapeutic. Don't know how we ever let a craven shit like him pin on all that rank. Goddamned peacetime Army."

"And Tish."

He nodded. "Yep. And the instant those disks change hands, I want you to un-ass the area of operations. ASAP. Tow your girlfriend right on out of there. Don't wait for permission. Leave that building at warp speed. I'm going to have things to discuss with our friends from California."

"And call off Gabrielli. I want to go back to work."

"Don't worry about Gabe. He's fully booked. Now . . . tell me one more thing. Are you happy in the Army, John?"

I shrugged. "It's been good. Tastes a little sour at the moment."

Hunt puckered his lips. A thinking gesture. "Tell you what. You decide you want to pack it in . . . retire . . . you call me up. This wild bunch I got working for me could use an injection of sanity. You've got balance. And balls. I'd have plenty of work for you. Good work. Not like this Nechestny crap. Christ, I'm sorry I ever hooked up with the guy." He stretched out a paw. Handing me an invisible gift. "Don't jump to conclusions. I know you're sitting there thinking, Screw this ape. I wouldn't work for him in a million years. But think about it. Let it simmer. Till all the present danger passes into the cavalcade of memories. I'd take care of you. And the work's not all covered in slime like this one. Our country needs good men who can work in the shadows."

"I'll remember the offer."

He smiled. More fake white teeth. "Diplomatically put. But let me just lift the blinds one little bit for you. The world is not as it seems. At least, not as it seems to the common man. We're reconstructing this country. Streamlining it. Key people . . . from industry, government . . . the military . . . we want to ensure that talent continues to be rewarded, that America not only remains the world's leader, but widens that lead."

He gave a dismissive wave. "Now, I'm not talking right-wing political crap. Or left-wing, either. Politics is for people who lack power and don't really understand how to get it. Politicians don't run anything. The people who run the politicians call the shots. Like it or not, that's the truth of it. No, what I'm talking about is a core—an expanding core—of people who understand what needs to be done, people who have the money, the power, the vision . . . the talent. The guts. People who understand that the Constitution, while a beautiful document—and I'm the first to admire it—folks who realize that the law does not always extend far enough. People . . . who would do anything for this country."

I did not know what to say. But he did not expect me to say anything.

"And don't waste another minute trying to stop the Next-Generation Fighter-Bomber. It's going to happen."

"I hate that airplane," I said.

"Well, channel your hatred more constructively. I understand you, John. We're not as different as you think. I know you're thinking about your dead friends." He opened his arms like a priest giving the blessing. With the blood drying on his face and hand. "Well, they're dead. Can't bring 'em back. We all have dead friends in this business. You have to move on."

He put his paws on his knees and levered himself out of his chair. "Now get out of here, son. Before my mood changes."

I got out of there. But with the gate closed behind me, I made the mistake of thinking about what he had said. About his crowd of insiders running things. Even if it were true, I did not want to believe it. Self-delusion has its place. Anyway, I had more urgent things on which to expend my dwindling brainpower. Or so I tried to convince myself.

New possibilities haunted me.

Middleburg looked expensive even at two in the morning. The fox-hunt crowd. They wanted to be English in the worst way. And they were English in the worst way. Riding britches and Range Rovers. Overcooked food. Acres of pastel hats at the Gold Cup. Overdressed women with time on their hands. And pet polo teams. Now and then an heiress shot an Argentine horseman. It made Karl Marx seem pretty sympathetic.

On the other hand, I was not in condition to render an impartial judgment on anything.

I thought of Tish. I had no guarantee that Hunt would turn her over to me, or even that she was still alive. I decided I should have demanded proof. Then turned on myself for even thinking something so stupid. I had pushed Hunt as far as I could. And I had gotten off easy.

So far.

I tried as hard as I could to believe he would bring Tish to Union Station. And that she would break into a great big smile when she saw me. Tearing away from her captors, running toward me—I could see it as though it were already a memory.

I just wanted her alive. I no longer cared about her past. Anyway, mine was nothing to lay on a snow-white altar cloth. What mattered was that I loved her. We could improvise from there.

I stopped at the gas station where I had used the phone

on the drive out. I tanked up, bought a Diet Coke and a pack of cupcakes, got a couple dollars' worth of extra quarters, and ate supper on the hood of my car. With my hands shaking. My body had stood by me when it counted. But the pent-up fear was spilling out now.

I had one more call to make before I went home. A couple to make after sunup. And a friend to betray. As he had betrayed me.

I dialed an emergency number the frogs had given me. Henri the Cuckold answered.

"It's John Reynolds. Tell me when you're awake."

"I am awake."

"You don't sound awake."

"I am listening."

I pictured him rubbing his hatchet face. Blinking his eyes away from a bedside lamp.

"This one's for Lafayette," I said. "You need to be standing by this phone at four-thirty in the afternoon. At that time, I will give you a location in the city of Washington. If you are there promptly at six, you will see me or one of my companions hand over a bag to a couple of military-looking men. The computer disks you want will be in that bag. The men receiving them will be the people who blew up your research lab."

"You have the disks?" He was awake now. "Why not—"

"No. I don't have them. But I *will* have them. It's complicated. And no, I can't pass them to you ahead of time. First, I won't have them until the last minute. Second, this is the only way I can get my girl back. You promised you'd help me rescue her."

After a little too much hesitation, he said, "We will keep the promise."

CHAPTER 15

I knew Corry would be waiting for me when I got back. To hear my take on how it had gone with Aley. And she would damned well want to know where I had been since I left him.

That was fine. I wanted her on edge, worried about losing control of the whole scam. Corry with a clear head was an enemy of mankind.

At first, I thought she had fooled me and gone. Dead quiet on the home front. I found her upstairs, racked out on my bunk. She did not react when I switched on the overhead light. So far gone she was mouth-breathing.

We were all worn down. That was good, too. Unless it made somebody jumpy on a trigger.

Corry lay curled up like a child. Pistol loose in her hand. I could have snatched it and thumped the crap out of her. But I'm a sucker for the social rules.

"Get up," I told her. In my best drill-sergeant imitation. "My bed isn't part of the deal."

At last I found a weakness in Corry Nevers, alias Corrine

Nevrosky, a.k.a. Mrs. Karen Aalstrom, nee Karen Hinkel. She could not find her way back to sensible life. Too damned tired. She flapped and half rose, dropping the pistol, then reaching frantically to recapture it, eyes flashing open and quitting again. I gave her my reading light full-face. It turned her into Dracula's favorite bride.

For one bad instant I worried about the gun. She gripped it fiercely in that small hand. Fingers so stressed I thought she might start shooting blindly. Instead, she shook her head and shoulders, determined to conquer herself, and forced those blue eyes open.

"Where were you?" she demanded. On brain delay, she looked at her wristwatch. That made it worse. "Where the hell have you been?"

"Walkin' after midnight."

She raised the pistol. This girl clearly needed time to put on her cosmic makeup.

"Pull the trigger, Corry. And you'll be back in L.A. screwing deadbeats for dinner. If you're lucky."

She closed a second hand over the gun. Steadying the aim. I suppose Corry had been thin in the self-control department for a while. The tantrum in the car should have tipped me. What conned you was her ability to carry herself with royal confidence when she had a grip. You figured her for the world's strongest human being outside of the steroid set.

"I want to know where you've been. And don't lie to me."

I flopped down in the chair she had occupied the evening before. "Arlington Cemetery. Thinking. I'm not as quick as you. Or as confident. I had to consult a friend."

That wild streak of panic in her eyes again. *"Who was it?"*

"A dead man."

"Who did you meet? You're so goddamned stupid, I should never—"

"Your social skills are deteriorating. I didn't meet anybody. Except your loving hubby."

"What were you doing? Don't fuck with me, John."

Remarkable that a face so full of hatred and mottled by sleep and pillow lines could remain so beautiful. After you banged up against Corry Nevers, you would always read history with a different eye. Understanding the follies of great men. And the siege of Troy.

"Kill me and we're both going to have a bad day. I did exactly what we agreed. And Aley said exactly what you said he'd say. Then I went to Arlington and sat on my ass in the dark. Talking to my ghosts. We all have our little quirks."

"Did Aley believe you? Was he—"

"He took the disk. He'll be standing by the phone."

She dropped the gun to her side. "Don't try to do me, John. I'll come through on everything I promised you. Don't blow it for both of us."

"It's up to you now, sister. You'd better be able to produce the rest of the disks. Or there is going to be a serious tide of unhappiness."

"Don't let me down, John."

That earned a smile. "Just honor your part of the deal. And I don't mean the money bullshit. That's all yours. I just want to walk away with Tish self-propelling next to me."

"She'll stumble on you. She'll always stumble."

"Then I'll pick her up and carry her."

Corry left. Stroking the thirty-eight in her purse. Any muggers working the graveyard shift were going to get more than they had bargained for.

I was beginning to feel good and warned myself not to get overconfident. It seemed like I had it wired at last. I had even known she would leave. Because she needed to link up with Aley, to lay out a different set of lies. Maybe she had to report in to Hunt, too. And she would need to refine her airline reservations, now that the timeline was set for the deal. She would have to fetch the rest of the phony disks that were supposed to make her rich and leave me dead. All before meeting me in the bar at the Dubliner at five-thirty in the afternoon.

I had not told her any more than that. Just, "Meet me at the Dubliner. It's a yuppie boozer on Massachusetts. Bring the disks." That enraged her. But she had tried not to show it. I was performing according to her script. More or less. And she did not want to blow it now.

I went to bed. Allotting myself four hours' sleep. I dreamed in basic black. When the alarm went off, I was homicidal. I hit the john, then pulled on my running gear. Not exactly my preferred activity after a short, bad sleep, a week of deprivation, and a couple of beatings. But this was a special run.

I jinked through traffic and down alleys. With the heat raising its fist. I was sure somebody would try to follow me. Probably in a car. But I knew the one-way streets, the vacant lots that cut across blocks, the old tradesmen's passageways. I did a pair of underpasses, doubling back both times so a trail car could not follow. It was the wildest dash in D.C. history that did not involve street crime.

At the end of it, I walked into the shabby fortress where Dickey hung his hat. The desk sergeant judged me sufficiently strange to merit a handoff instead of a brushoff. He called Dickey, who came out of a hallway looking even more swollen than usual.

"What the fuck?" he said. That translated as "Good morning."

"Time to talk," I said. "For real."

He looked me up and down. And snorted. "Nice legs. I hear you were back in fag country last night."

"I'll tell you all about it," I said. And this time I meant it.

* * *

We sat in his office. Drinking lukewarm brown vinegar that only cops and old NCOs would call coffee. I told him everything I knew. All of it. As clearly as I could. He turned out to be a good listener once he got what he wanted. I wondered again how much of his spiel was the real Dickey and how much of it was the persona a smart cop had crafted over the decades. Looking like a fool has its advantages. If anybody knew that, I did. Of course, the difference between Dickey and me was that I had been the real thing.

"Christ," he said at the end of it, "it's enough to make me wish I was on the mayor's bodyguard detail."

"I couldn't lay it out earlier. I didn't have all the pieces. And I didn't know who I could trust."

He treated me to a smile. "Now you figure you can trust me?"

"If you were on anybody's payroll, you'd wear better suits."

He let the remark go by and sat back. "I should bring the FBI in on this. By all rights."

That scared me. I should have seen it coming. But my thinking had been so blurred, I had imagined Dickey would want to handle anything going down on his own turf.

I did not want any other players in on this game. Especially not *federales.* The field was already too crowded, the score too close. And I had committed too many fouls myself. The FBI was not going to award me a trophy as Most Valuable Player.

Before I could come up with a counterargument, Dickey said, "Thing is, they'd just bitch it all up. At this point. Come stomping in like elephants. The fucks." He chewed into his cheek. "I got to tell them. But I don't see why I got to tell them just yet."

Dickey sipped cold coffee. The taste made his double chin quiver. "So I got one question. And it's serious. Why Union

Station? Sounds to me like Mr. and Mrs. Commuter could find themselves in the middle of the O.K. Corral. There's a serious public-safety issue."

I nodded as though I had thought it all through. But I had not. For all my training in plans and operations, I had been as sloppy as a second lieutenant. And my selfishness embarrassed me. I had chosen Union Station because of the crowd, ignoring the fact that the crowd was made up of real people. The truth was that I had forgotten that Tish and I were not the only people on the planet. Maybe I was becoming a real Washingtonian.

I could not change the swap site. It was too late and the tolerances were already too close.

"This town's got enough of a problem with headlines," Dickey said. "I don't go for this Union Station business one bit."

"I had to pick a public place. If I tried to do it in private, they'd kill me for sure. And Tish. And everybody else."

"Sounds to me like these bad boys might do it anyway."

"I don't think so. Not unless it all goes to shit. The common denominator of all the players left standing is their desire to avoid more publicity. The bombings . . . the killings . . . it all got way out of hand. There's no rug big enough to sweep any more trouble under. The industry pricks, Hunt and his boys . . . the French . . . to say nothing of Frankie and Johnny from L.A. . . . nobody wants to end up in the spotlight."

"But they're shooters."

I pulled at my running shorts. They were almost dry. And sticky as a spilled margarita. "I figured you could handle that. Anyway, they're not sloppy. They hit what they want to hit with the first shot. No debris."

Dickey looked at me. Face scrubbed of any expression. "Listen, partner. You're overestimating me and my department. I only know two officers who hit on the first shot, and they're both certifiable. A setup like this takes skill. And planning. Rehearsals, if you want to do it right." He looked at his watch. "And you come in here giving me less than eight hours to stage the invasion of Normandy. It's going to be a miracle if nobody gets killed."

I hung my head like a beaten prizefighter. In a cop's shabby office, in the slam-dunk morning light, my plan looked a lot shakier than it had the night before. I ached to believe it still could deliver success. But faith slips.

Dickey's eyes were different, though. There was life in them now. Detective Lieutenant Dickey, the original pissed-on cop. His thoughts had moved beyond me. Maybe he was dreaming of one last great bust to cap his career.

The best I can say of the two of us is that we believed, in our different ways, that things might just work out. Against all odds. People don't understand how idealistic cops and soldiers can be. All the public sees is the uniform and the face you learn to wear above it. Dickey seemed to me to be fighting the good fight in a city committing suicide. I felt like I was duking it out with the whole world. I figured we both wanted to do what was right. It was a lousy combination.

He let me out the back door of the station and I made my way between squad cars down for lack of spare parts. He signaled to the patrolman on motor-pool duty to let me pass. I faded into the heat of the side streets.

I went home. Showered. Dressed for success in khakis and a polo shirt. And treated myself to a crabcake sandwich at Eastern Market. The Last Lunch, since there might not be a Last Supper. For good luck, I put a big tip in the plastic bucket. Then I lingered over my plastic tray. Struggling to war-game everything that could go wrong. The truth is, I was thinking like a punk. Short-horizon stuff. I could not get beyond my reunion with Tish. It's a good thing I could not foresee all that was coming. I would not have been able to go through with it.

Panhandlers on the sidewalk, then metro limbo. I headed downtown underground. Riding with the gentlemen of leisure who had figured out the secret of summer afternoons in the city. A guy with a deep scar down his cheek wore a T-shirt that read, "Just because I'm black doesn't mean I'm a criminal."

I had one more loose line to reel in. And I had to do it in person. The bastard would not have taken a phone call from me. Not now. So he was going to get the living, breathing, unhappy John Reynolds. I was playing the politics of inclusion. No deserving party was going to be left out of the game.

A sax player blew old Broadway hits by the metro exit and a Central American pushed flowers in the heat. Office studs moved fast along the sidewalks, hurrying through the exhaust haze in shirtsleeves and ties, too young to be so soft around the middle. A few old-schoolers dehydrated in their suit jackets. Women in pearls wore a wet shine on their foreheads and a hatred of panty hose in their eyes. The whole K Street hustle.

The lobby was so cold it startled you when you came in. But I stayed hot. I came out of the elevator like a fighter coming out of his corner at the beginning of a round.

"May I help you?" the receptionist asked.

"Check with Burns before you call the cops," I told her and the flock of secretaries.

I banged through the door to his office.

All those handshake, shoulder-hug photos. Couple of Presidents. And the ex-cabinet members who rewrite history and take consulting fees from dictators. Shortage of females, but the town had been late to change. Corry Nevers would have brightened up the walls. Shame he had missed her.

My friend and betrayer, Robert Mayhew Burns, opened his mouth wide enough to swallow a cannonball.

"Yeah, fuckhead. It's me."

It is a wonderful thing to see fear in a man born of fine lineage. It's a very democratic event.

Rob Burns was a fitness-club type. Just like his sister, who had dated, drained, and dumped me. But I was bigger, stronger, and a lot meaner than Mr. Think Tank. He did not have time to get all the way out of his chair. I helped him up with one hand on his throat and the other blasting into his gut. When he hit the wall, books tumbled.

His secretary was in the doorway. I did not have to see her. I could hear her, feel her. I knew precisely the look of rupture she would have on her face.

"Tell her if you want her to call the cops. *Fucking tell her.*" I loosened my grip on his neck.

He gasped. Talking in separate words. "It's . . . all . . . right . . . nothing . . . friends . . . shut . . . the . . . door, Joanne . . . all right . . ."

"Mr. Burns—"

"Shut the door."

"Don't shout at the help, Rob. What would Granddad say?"

The door closed. And I was alone with the last traitor in the pack. A guy I had really liked. Who had sold me out to Punchy Hunt on one side, and to the French on the other. He was going to make a brilliant cabinet member someday.

I wondered how thick those office windows were, whether I could send him flying down to the street if he played it wrong.

I threw him back into his chair. Then I sat on his desk and put my foot on his chest. Rolling him back against a credenza where family photos stood isolated from the upstart trash.

"I'm one dumb sonofabitch," I told him. "It's really unbelievable. I was so dumb. But you were stupid beyond belief, pal." I shook my head. "Jesus Christ, it couldn't have been money. Or is the family silver in hock?"

The punch just above the belt buckle had been one of the few perfect things I had accomplished in my life. He still could not breathe properly. And he was terrified of this sudden contact with reality.

"Don't . . . be a fool. Power, John. Only thing this . . . town understands. Got to be connected. Never meant to harm—"

I was never a bully, except emotionally, and my fights tended to be eruptions, not sadistic choreography. This was a new experience. I had time to plan exactly where and how I would hit him. Time to shape the fist so I would not sprain a finger or my wrist. Time to come down off the desk at an angle that gave me maximum leverage. I aimed where his left canine would be hidden at the corner of his mouth.

Bonus play. I got two of his teeth. He spit them into his hand, dropped one, and began to cry.

I had never realized it could feel so good to hurt another human being.

"Yeah," I said, "that's me. The dumb fucking soldier. First your sister fucked me, then you did. I bet your family reuses toilet paper." I was as angry at myself as I was at him. I had really believed this human being was my friend. If only in a Washington kind of way. "De la Vere almost screwed it all up on you. Showed up unexpectedly. Right? Looking for results. Christ, you must have panicked. Just couldn't get him out of your office fast enough. And then I showed up too soon. But I was soaking wet and blind and thick as day-old cement. You danced circles around me. You'd make a great con, you know that?"

He looked at me. Bleeding. Thinking too much. I realized I was being stupid again.

"Hell, Rob. What am I talking about? You *are* a great con. In a city of master criminals. You were the information clearinghouse, tipping the frogs to Hunt and selling out Hunt to the frogs. And giving me up to everybody after I strolled by asking the wrong questions. You're the man who can't lose." I had thought of myself as cynical before all this began. Now I was amazed at how naive I had been. "So tell me. Who do you think is going to be more anxious to kill you? De la Vere and his boys? Or Punchy Hunt?"

Do not believe the saints and sociologists. Fear can be a beautiful thing. When you see it in the right pair of eyes.

"Don't . . . you can't . . ."

"The hell I can't."

"Please."

"Man . . . does it hurt when you say that word? Say it again."

"Please."

I folded my arms. I was not worried about Rob striking back. He was a worm caught on the sidewalk after the rain.

"Great riff," I told him. "I admire it. All that Anglophile crap. Family history as a cover story. Brilliant stuff."

"Please, John. We can work this out. Please. General Hunt doesn't need to—"

I gave him a little openhanded tap on the side of the mouth where I had punched him. He shied.

"That's my decision. Who to tell and what to tell them. It's my turn now. Although, as a military man, I have a soft spot for people who obey orders."

Anxious eyes. "What do you want me to do?"

I wasn't ready to tell him yet. I wanted him to hurt a while longer. "Why the French? I've figured out the Hunt connection. But why sell everybody out to the frogs? Tell the truth now, Robbie."

He looked down. Probably wondering if a chump like me could understand the calculations of policy at the strategic level, the nuances of the international order. He spoke to me in a lecturing tone, a professor with blood on his chin and shirt. I let him yap. The poor bugger did not know how to talk any other way.

"The Brits . . . are backing off on European integration. The single-currency thing. France is going to lead. All of Europe. Germans are rich. But they're afraid. Afraid to lead. France . . . is the key. We've got to play the French card. If we want leverage in the new Europe. Trade. The military thing. The Mideast connection . . ."

I snorted. "You are a no-go at this station."

"What?"

"That is the dumbest political analysis I've ever heard. You sleeping with a French girl or something?"

"France is going to—"

"Can it. That's enough. The answer is that you wired yourself in with the French because you're stupid. Now let's talk about Em." I tossed him the box of tissues from his desk. "Not a bleeder, are you?"

"I don't know a thing about Em."

I would have liked to hit him again. It felt so good. But I did not want his face to look any worse. He had a public appearance coming up.

"Bullshit. Ever been in Punchy Hunt's library?"

Rob shook his head. Patting his hurt little mouth.

"Didn't think so," I told him. "Hunt has his own kind of social standards. So let me tell you about his library. Lousy art that costs a bundle. Leather-bound sets I think he actually reads. And memorabilia aplenty. Photos. He's got this round mahogany table right by a big leather chair. Table's covered with framed photographs. Some of the frames are works of art in themselves." I glanced around Rob's office, at his photo display. "He's more selective than you. But then, he generally knows who's going to come through his door. Anyway, there's a photo of Hunt as a lieutenant colonel. Wearing a big shit-eating grin. Standing beside your old man. Back when Daddy was doing the OSD ticket punch. I didn't notice it the first time. Hunt's so damned impressive. Riveting. But last night I saw it. And everything fell into place. Brother, you should have stayed on Hunt's side. Exclusively." I smiled. With all of my own teeth. "Got a spare shirt in a drawer? Maybe in a closet? You seem like that kind of guy."

Rob nodded.

"Good. Because you're going to need it. But we'll get to that." I leaned down toward him. "I couldn't figure out how the bad guys made me as a connection so quickly. They seemed too good, too aware, too fast. They were waiting for me every time I went to the john, ready to hand me the soap." I looked at the frightened little man in the chair before me. He was not that small physically, but he was miniature in spirit. "I should have figured out the French connection. But Hunt . . . that was another matter. I'm not a genealogy expert. Then I saw that photo. And I got it. The real Hunt Club isn't those thugs with war toys he's got patrolling his spread. It's a blueblood thing. Hell, your families probably really did hunt together, back before genetic decay set in. I'd forgotten, you see. One key part of the Punchy Hunt legend. Kid from rich family goes to West Point. Volunteers for Vietnam. Folks in my line of work worshipped Hunt for that. For the self-sacrifice. The guy did great things for his country. Back then."

"He's still doing good things, he—"

I lifted his face in both my hands. As if about to kiss him. Instead of a smooch, I worked my thumb through the skin into the brand-new gap between his teeth. "Save it. I have a deep-seated need to communicate. So there it is. Hunt. You. And Em. God knows who else. Old money getting a plus-up. And yeah. Power. Does Bob Nechestny really run Macon-Bolt? Or is he sort of a puppet? Your little pet risen from the lower classes." I let go of his snout.

"Nechestny's naive. He doesn't know what it really takes in this town."

"Thank you. Now back to my little story. Money and power and old families. The stuff that made America great. But Em got an attack of conscience. He did the unforgivable. He broke ranks. Tell me—did it bother you more that Em was trying to expose your three-hundred-billion-dollar rip-off, or that he was doing it with a black general? I don't expect you to answer that. I'm allergic to platitudes."

"What do you want?"

I raised my eyebrows as theatrically as I could. "What do I want? Maybe good government? Integrity? Peace in our time? An honest return on the defense dollar? You're bleeding again. Hey, I'm a simple guy. All I really want at this point is my girl back."

"There's nothing I can—"

"Wrong. You're going to help. You're going to do exactly what I tell you. Or I'm going to let the frogs know you've been playing a double game on them with Punchy Hunt and Company. Then I'm going to let Hunt know you've been triple-crossing him. They'll kill you, Rob. And they'll make it hurt on the way."

The man was so frightened he could not speak. His lip bubbled pink spit. And he began to shake. With the spirit upon him.

"All you have is a walk-on role. At six o'clock, you are going to be standing by the Center Cafe in the main entrance hall of Union Station. When I'm gone, go down to the john and run cold water over your mouth. It won't hurt much. Then put on your clean shirt. If you don't have a clean tie in the office, go around the corner to Brooks Brothers. I'm sure you've got a charge account that goes back a century."

"What's going to—"

"Shut up. Or I'll break your nose for shits and grins. I am not a happy man today."

"What if I don't—"

"I'll make two phone calls. And the race will be on to kill you. Six o'clock. Make that five of. If you're late, the deal's off."

"What do I have to do?"

"Look important. Make your family proud of you."

I really did want to hurt him some more. I liked myself less with each passing hour. But getting past decency and mercy also has a wonderful lightening effect. You can loathe your behavior and feel really good about what you're doing at the same time.

At the door, I turned around one last time and looked at the coward in the desk chair.

"Aren't you even a little bit ashamed?" I asked him. "Your kind used to sacrifice for this country. First to volunteer in war. Dollar-a-year men in peace. Obligation. Responsibility. *Noblesse oblige*. You were the best we had."

"Don't kid yourself," he said.

I had two hours to kill before my bar date with Corry. So I went to the National Gallery. To see my second-best girl.

I figured the National Gallery was safe and close to Union Station. It did not attract many killers. It had pay phones. And I needed a dose of civilization. With all its discontents. I needed to believe that something of worth might be salvaged in the end. That it wasn't all ugly.

The girl was my secret. It was possible that I had shared her with only one other man. In over a hundred years. High-schoolers on class trips yawned past her, and women in glasses with graying hair pinned up admired her for all the wrong reasons. While my number two redhead just stood there with her American Mona Lisa smile, waving her goodies. Winslow

Homer had painted her. The picture was formally titled "Autumn." The real name had to be "Fuck me."

Maybe Homer shared the joke with a couple of pals. Or maybe he kept it to himself. The armies of art historians never realized what he had done. Despite a recent retrospective that analyzed the guy to a second death.

We see what we expect to see. That flaw had damaged my ability to compete with Corry and company. One old girlfriend told me I had rose-colored contact lenses glued to my eyeballs. But she had a doctorate, and thought about what she was going to say a day in advance, and could never sustain relationships. I seemed to have better luck with redheads.

I stood in front of that painting, trying to zen out my jitters, with the air-conditioning not quite working and tourists slumping by like plague victims. In the winter, when the all-in-black crowd came out to pose, I had seen the tragically hip blow off my sweetheart as Homer at his weakest, sunk in his Norman Rockwell mode. My second-best girl wore the laced-up, exclusionary clothing of 1877, a black hat and snug black velvet jacket, with a heavy oyster-gray skirt. She stood on a damp forest path, surrounded by leaves the color of Tish's hair. A white-gloved hand held the ruffle of her skirt up to her waist. If you did not crack the code, you just figured she was holding the cloth up out of the mud. But if you knew how women looked—if you knew how they felt and smelled and a little bit about how they thought—you saw that Homer had played the greatest erotic joke in the history of painting.

The damp, fleshy folds of cloth and their shadows form an image as explicit as a rotten-hearted porno mag. Only Homer did it with style. The model must have been a hoot. I bet Homer never got over her. When you finally figured out her smile, she made Corry Nevers look like a schoolgirl at a pajama party.

I never told anybody about my gallery girl. Not even Tish.

I was afraid word would get around and some Bible-beater from the Hill would have my alternative darling imprisoned in the National Gallery basement, where I would never be able to see her again.

I broke my communion to make my calls from a pay phone by the men's room. Tipping the players to the Union Station meeting place and the six o'clock be-there-or-be-square linkup time. I staggered the calls and trolled the galleries in between. Giving everybody just the right amount of time to fight the traffic, park, and rush to the grand hall. Now and then I got an attack of the shakes.

I even called Colonel Maurey, my boss at the Pentagon. I left a message on his answering machine. Promising I would be in for work at the usual time in the morning. I did not qualify it by adding, "If I'm still alive." None of us can really imagine his own death. And I had gotten my fill of theatrics.

Everybody was anxious. Everybody wanted to play. Homer had his joke. Now I was going to have mine.

The best call was the one to Aley. He was squirming. Dying to get the deal done. His response to the Union Station location was, "What is this shit you are laying on me?" Followed by a suspicion as natural to him as weakness to the flesh. "So what is it, Johnny boy? You planning to get on a train and ride or something?"

His macho spiel sounded about as tough as cellophane now. He could not wait to dump the financial data on me.

"So, Johnny boy? You prepared to copy? You got a call to make. Confirm that you're a rich man. Make sure nobody tried to screw you at the last minute. You got to look out for number one."

I pretended I had a pen and paper. Watching dads lead their anxious sons into the men's room. Aley read off a list of numbers. A phone code for the Caymans. The bank access number. An account access number. More codes to unlock the deposit information. Financial numerology.

"You need me to repeat any of that?" he asked me.

"I've got it."

He repeated it all anyway.

"Call in, Johnny boy. This is the ultimate Dialing for Dollars. Do it now. And don't trust anybody. Confirm that deposit."

The moment of truth was coming. Everything Aley had longed for. The pressure put him in competition for the title of Jumpiest Man on Earth.

I was another contender. Scared as hell. As the time ran down, my palms started getting damp. The hairs prickled on my forearms. And my feet were sweating. I worried about Tish. And about myself. Dickey had me concerned now about a slaughter of the innocents during rush hour. I had made some remarkably dumb decisions. I could only hope they had been less dumb than the decisions made by everybody else.

That was just possible. Soldiering teaches you a few basic things. For example, battles are not won by the most competent army, but by the least incompetent. Murphy the Lawgiver is the patron saint of mankind. And there is no bomb as unstable and volatile as the human heart.

Just before it was time to link up with Corry, I went in to look at the Renoirs. I hate Renoir. In a couple of minutes I was in a sufficiently brutal mood to face what was coming.

The Dubliner is one of those bars that fake history. Dark wood and dark beer. The windows are small and the rooms are deep. It's always twilight inside. The food is bad, in keeping with Irish tradition, but they know how to draw a Guinness or a Harp. In the evenings, different Irishmen take turns singing the same songs. Kids who work on the Hill come by after work to romanticize a heritage their ancestors were only too glad to leave behind. But a drinker could do a lot worse. In this town.

Corry sat at the backmost table under a print of the Easter Rising. She was drinking a whiskey sour. In an Irish pub. The girl really had no shame. She saw me and froze for a moment. As if she had not really expected me. When I sat down beside her, I smelled the earlier drinks on her.

"How many of those have you had?" I asked her.

Corry shifted a big soft purse that could have served as a weekend bag. The kind of thing women who can't make choices lug around. She moved it from my side of her chair to the other. Letting me know how protective she felt about the disks.

"You don't understand," she said. With drink in her voice. Almost enough to make the emotion real.

"Buck up, girl. You need to be ready for action."

She laughed. "Look who's talking. When were you ever ready for action? I could've given you the best action of your life."

I moved the whiskey sour across the table. She moved it back.

I wanted her edgy. Not falling-down drunk.

"Corry . . . these people don't fuck around. You don't want to—"

She threw the drink in my face.

"You think you're too good for me," she said. "Fuck you, John."

There were only half a dozen other people in the bar. But we suddenly attracted far more attention than I wanted.

I wiped my face with a paper napkin. Wishing the sting of the alcohol out of my eyes. Just walking from the National Gallery to the bar—allowing for a few side-street doglegs—had soaked me in sweat. The drink added sugar. Like glue. On my shirt. In my hair.

I kept my voice down. Although I would have been glad to punch her. "Corry, you can straighten your ass out right now. Or I'm walking."

But her emotions were ahead of me. She barely listened. Wetness in her eyes. And fear. Confusion. A sinner on Judgment Day.

"It's time to go now," I told her. "Get straight. We're going over to Union Station. It's the last stop."

"I have to go to the ladies' room," she said. And she stood up. With reasonable competence. Scraping her chair back.

She knew where she was going, so it was not her first trip to the can. I wondered how long she had been sitting and drinking.

She swayed a little. In handsome linen slacks. Baby-blue blouse precise at her shoulders, with a slight drape at the waist. Good clothes for traveling.

Just before she turned the corner, she wheeled and looked at me. With a smile you never want to see on your wife. Or even on a transient girlfriend. Not a ghost of trust in the girl. She walked back toward our table. With the steadiness that comes of great concentration. She grabbed the purse. With her genuine, authentic, fake computer disks.

It was a nice touch.

I watched her walk away again. Even now, I did not know her. Had she planned to throw a drink at me all along? To complete the effect? Was she that good? Was she far less drunk than she was acting? If so, the girl was wearing a whiskey-based perfume. Was there even a sliver of real emotion in that woman?

The one thing I believed about her was her fear. I guess I never learned to recognize love. But I knew fear when I saw it.

She had gotten the world just where she wanted it. And now she was afraid of what she had done.

A waitress brought me ice water and a stack of paper napkins. Unbidden. Maybe there is understanding and kindness in the world.

"How many drinks has she had?" I asked.

The waitress thought for a moment. She was largish and blond in a way that drives Arabs nuts. With dropout's eyes.

"I could check at my station. I think five or six."

Lot of afternoon booze for a small woman like Corry.

"It's all right. I'll get her out of here as soon as she comes back. What's the tariff?"

"Let me get the bill."

I dipped and wiped and wished away the whole past week. The boys along the bar had lost interest when Corry disappeared, but the barkeep had a nose for trouble and kept his eyes on me. I would have liked a drink myself. But there was no time now.

I paid and tipped big. Just before Corry came back. She marched in like a mean little soldier.

"Time to go," I said again.

She looked at me with those deadly blues. "Couldn't we just sit for one more minute?"

I checked my watch to make her happy, but I already knew we were out of time.

"Got to go," I told her.

"But it's right across the street."

"We're not going in the front door."

"I need a minute."

"This is it, Corry. Now or never."

"I need a minute with you."

"Thanks for the drink."

Her eyes did not waver.

"I love you, John. Can't you see that?"

"You'll get over it."

CHAPTER 16

At the back of Union Station there is a multilevel parking garage built to bankrupt tourists. You can slip in from the H Street bridge over the rail yards. We did just that. Avoiding the regular entrances.

Getting there was a minor trial. Corry still had her walking skills. But barely. And she would not trust me to carry the bag with the disks. I wanted to move fast across those prairie-wide avenues. Corry was good for only a funeral march.

The heat smelled. So did I. Corry had whiskey on her breath. I had it caked into me. Along with a sugary lime smell. We passed a squatter dressed for January. His resident flies deserted him for me. That's how I went to Armageddon. Leading a drunken beauty who thought lying was mankind's basic mission. Waving flies away from my face.

The gasoline air in the big garage sat a few degrees cooler than the day outside, but Corry found the up ramp hard going. She still would not trust me with the bag full of disks.

I let her struggle. Pissed. I maneuvered through the level

where they held the rental cars for the Amtrak crowd. Figuring that was the approach my fans would least expect me to take. I looked hard for the bad boys. Hunt would have scouts out. Dickey, too, I hoped. Maybe even the French. But nobody in the garage had that trouble look.

I had the pulse. The rush. Any fly that sucked up my sweat was going into an adrenaline frenzy. I had been here before. A few times. Bad times. In that moment, Union Station blurred with half a dozen shitholes scattered around the world. Where the U.S. Army does the quiet things that let our fellow citizens live the sweet life back in the Land of the Big PX.

Corry came up beside me. Lopsided with the bag weight. Sweating jewels.

"Something the matter?" she asked.

I shook my head. "Just stay up with me."

"I can't go so fast."

"Just stay up with me. Keep it together, girl."

I knew she would listen now. Frightened people are easier to steer than a kiddie car. If they think you are unafraid.

A carillon chimed. Six. We were late. But the gang would hang. I had no idea what their various plans would be. But every last hustling shitbird would have one.

Hunt. The frogs. Dickey. And Aley. Maybe even Mr. Think Tank. And Corry all whiskey, fear, and greed. Planners. Schemers. Dreamers.

Our lateness bothered me. It was one more part of my plan going off track. Like Corry's unexpected appetite for booze. I had tried to do everything with Command and Staff College precision. Forgetting that all that Leavenworth junk works only with other Leavenworth types. When it works at all.

"Wake up," I said. "Get alert, girl."

"I meant it," she told me. "What I said. About the money. Your cut."

"Save it for your marriage."

"I'm coming back. In six months. I mean it."

"Worry about the next six minutes."

We made it inside the rear entrance, mezzanine level. No shooters or grabbers by the automatic doors. There were rows of boutiques, left and right, shopped by travelers too early for their trains. I had told Aley to meet me in the store that sold the Disney paraphernalia. It was my private joke. On a Mickey Mouse kind of guy.

I stopped just short of Uncle Walt's capitalist legacy.

"Wait here."

"What?" Corry asked me.

"Just stand here. I'm going in to get your beloved."

"Don't leave me alone."

"Do what I say. Stand right there against that wall. Keep away from the windows."

"We should stay together."

"No. I don't want you trapped inside. If it all goes to hell. I'll be right back."

What I really meant was that I wanted her available. If Hunt and his boys had decided to screw me and do a premature grab. I was not going down for this damsel if I could help it.

Aley stood behind a rack of cartoon-figure ties, watching for me. He had positioned himself against a camouflage of colors and wore a windbreaker three months ahead of the weather. The jacket was zipped halfway up. I had no doubt that he had a gun under it.

"You make that call?" he asked me.

I nodded. "We're good to go."

He sighed. Then he registered my empty hands.

Panic burned his eyes. "Where's the merchandise, Johnny boy?"

"Your wife's holding it."

He looked at me. Calculating. And twisted up his face. "I wouldn't trust her with a dump I took last week. Let's go."

"Where's Hunt?"

"Downstairs. You'll see."

"Tish?"

"Too much fucking talk, all right? Everything's like little Johnny wanted. Your birthday party, okay?"

He was shaking. Trying not to show it. But he was shaking like a prisoner under an icy shower.

We were all afraid.

"Let's just fucking move," he said.

I led the way.

"Bitch better be there. If she—" Then he saw her. Where I had parked her. And he laughed. "Ain't she just a package?"

"She's a package."

He bumped against me and sniffed. "Hey, you fucking stink. You been hitting the sauce or something? That fear thing nibbling at you?"

"Your wife shared her drink with me."

We came up to Corry. Aley got a really good whiff. "Fuck, Karen. One hell of a time to fall off the wagon."

"Yeah? Show me your veins, you goddamned junkie." She turned to me. "You know he's a needle boy?"

"Could we postpone the domestic bliss? Let's just do this. All right?"

Aley gripped me by the upper arm. There was real strength in his hand, meanness. If he was into syringes, it was meth, not heroin. I let him hold on to me. Fighting the instinct to put him down on the marble floor. I wanted him certain that he was in charge.

He spoke to Corry. Or Karen. Surprising me one last time. With what he did not know.

"He really had them, huh?"

She nodded.

"You checked them out?" he asked her.

"Like I have a fucking computer."

"I mean, they look all right? Our boy hasn't been playing swaps or anything?"

"They look all right."

The rest of the world cruised by. I guess we just looked like three happy shoppers. I could not spot any of Hunt's hired guns. Which I took as a very good sign. He was keeping the operation small. Tight.

I did not see any of Dickey's boys, either. That was not a particularly good sign. I was short of friends.

Aley turned his full attention to me. "I'm going to tell you one time and up front. Your role in all this is to keep your mouth shut. You are going to walk between me and Karen. Karen, give me the disks."

"I have them."

"Give them to me, all right? You're fucking drunk."

Corry let him take the bag. He hefted it.

"Okay. Feels righteous. We're going to take that big walk now, John boy. Down those stairs over there." He nodded toward the spiral staircases that led down to the center arcade on the ground floor. "Tourists get in the way, screw 'em. Three abreast. All the way. At the foot of the stairs, we turn out into the main hall. Hunt will be just where you wanted. With General Bootlick, in full regalia. And your drop-down redhead slut."

"Get your hand off my arm."

He let go of me. And laughed. For an instant. "Yeah? Now listen. Final instructions. Your mouth stays shut. You are decoration. Do anything funny, and the war's on. Redhead gets the first bullet."

"Fuck you, Aley. You're shaking so bad you couldn't get that pistol out of your jacket without shooting yourself."

We began to walk. Down the streets of Tombstone. To my

surprise, Corry gave my hand a quick squeeze. With her eyes on the horizon. I wish she had not done that. There was a little too much humanity in it. I did not want her real.

"Nice and slow," Aley muttered.

Almost to the stairs. I glanced from side to side. Trying hard to spot anybody or anything that looked out of place. Anything that felt off. Any pair of eyes flashing an excess of interest.

I just wanted the plan to work. This one time in my life. Just let me trade the joker disks and Hunt's delinquent hired help for Tish. And let us go. The rest of them could fight it out over the fool's gold and who had done the most cheating. Just let Tish and me get out through those big front doors.

I had warned the frogs that they might be recognized and needed to hug the edges. They seemed to have taken the warning seriously. It was a good sign that they stayed out of sight. Let them make their move after Tish and I had gotten offstage.

Hunt was supposed to be waiting by the Center Cafe in the main hall. With my think-tank buddy as the surprise game-show guest.

I wanted Hunt to react to the unexpected presence of Robert Mayhew Burns. To say just one public word to the bastard. And let the French make the connection. Then let Mr. Old Washington Blood strategize his way out of that. Or invoke his family's contribution to American history.

I would have felt a lot better if I had caught a glimpse of Dickey's whipped-hound-dog face.

At the top of the stairs, I took one last, hard look at the world around me. Aley knew street-punk tricks. But he did not possess the whole tactical framework for staying alive. Stairs, escalators, and elevators were fatal choke points. The curved staircase had marble flooring one flight down on the left, a two-story drop to a food court on the right. Once we stepped onto those stairs, we were trapped until we walked away from them at the bottom.

"What's the matter with you?" Aley said.

"Nothing."

Corry stumbled and I caught her. Feeling the brief push of her breast against my forearm. I got her straight and she looked at me. With those Hollywood eyes.

She shook her head. And said plaintively, "You just don't know."

"For Christ's sake," Aley said. "Is there a love story I'm missing here? Get a move on, huh?"

We started down the stairs. Corry's flats tapped on the marble. I could feel Aley's nerves blowing holes in his skin. I felt sick to my stomach.

I saw it coming. I think I had known it before I really knew it. Call it a premonition. I had shied like a snaked horse at the top of those stairs. If Corry had not stumbled and hit my reflex button, I might have hung there until somebody dragged me down.

Two men dressed like kids. L.L. Beaners in baggy jeans. Sports logos and earrings. They had the effect down. If you did not look too closely at their faces, you would have figured them for sixteen going on six years in Lorton. But the faces had years of grown-up trouble behind them.

Joking and jiving at the bottom of the stairs. They waited until we were almost to the middle. Then the taller one caught me looking. And made his move. Partner following.

Guns materialized from under the layers of hip. Pistols the size of howitzers. The hit men lunged up the steps toward us.

I tried to shrink myself. Crunching down like a kid who sees a whipping coming. It was a stupid, useless, and natural thing to do.

Shots. Thunder in the marble temple. Lightning flashing an arm's length away. They had automatics. Blasting fast and out of rhythm with each other.

Even professionals get the monster in their eyes when they

do the job. The act pumps them. They breathe like winded dogs and they'd sweat at the North Pole. I saw only one hit man's face after the shooting began. For a strip ripped off a second. Killing was his drug. And he was superhigh on it.

I thought it would be the last face I saw.

Beside me, Corry did a dance. Still on her feet. But jerking. A sixties go-go dancer. A wild hand slapped my arm.

Gushes tore out of her back. Flames of blood. Sprays of it. Followed by shreds of dark red meat.

I saw her face for an instant before she fell: a perfectly beautiful woman. It was a waste beyond calculation.

Aley said, "Fuck," one last time and crumpled against me. He knocked me onto my rump, hard against the lip of a stair.

At my feet, Corry twitched like a snake with its back broken. There was more of her spread over the stairs than there was left in her body.

A moment of iron silence stopped the world.

One of the gunmen grabbed the bag with the disks. They took off like Olympic hurdlers. Brilliant at their work. The job had been done with speed, shock, and just enough overkill not to mark them as professional assassins.

I had not mattered to them.

Screaming all around me. Running. I heard a whistle and torn bits of language.

I got to my feet. Rising from the dead. Running after the killers. A creature of faulty instincts and the wrong kind of training for real life.

I must have looked like the craziest man in the world. Smeared with blood not my own. Bare-handed. Chasing killers.

The pros did not have to worry about me, though. Not on any count. By the time I reached the bottom of the stairs, the gunmen were deep in the slaughter-pen crowd and I had regained my true focus. My life had not flashed before my eyes when the guns came out. But Tish had. The gunmen went for the side entrance. I cut left. Toward the main hall.

Wondering if Tish would be there. Wondering where the hell Dickey's boys were. Too dumb to realize a security guard might take a shot at any bloodstained, running male.

I crashed between two dazzled grandmoms. Eyes white, shopping bags heavy. They did not know what was happening around them. I sent one of them spinning. The other shrieked, "Lucille!"

I made it through the portal by the Godiva Chocolates stand. With the gunshots still echoing, the rush-hour crowd looked like a cockroach convention after the lights came on.

That grand hall. Great space. Under the guardianship of stone legionnaires perched up on the balconies. This time I would have preferred living cops.

Hunt was there. As promised. Standing tall. With Gabrielli beside him. Hunt looked cool. Just waiting for an invisible light to change. But Gabrielli had the jumps.

Rob, my think-tank buddy, stood a few feet behind them. Mug swollen. Body cowering.

Or so I imagined.

Tish was not with them.

And Dickey had let me down worse than I knew.

I stopped maybe ten feet away from Hunt. As if it was time to go for our six-guns. But the only gun that mattered now was the one I felt in the small of my back.

"Don't raise your hands, soldier boy," Dickey's voice commanded. "Just walk. Straight ahead."

I started moving. Immediately.

In a bitter, satisfied voice, Dickey said, "Maybe I'll start wearing better suits now. What do you think about that, smart-ass?"

I had been around enough violence to know that it blinds those unaccustomed to it. When anyone insists they can describe all the details of a crime scene, that person is either a combat veteran with a lot of survivor's scars or a liar. The little drama Dickey and I were acting out did not even register on the human cattle around us.

I was more furious than scared. At that moment. I wanted to fight back. But I did not know how. A gun in the small of my back impressed me. Enough to keep my anger just short of any further stupidity.

I wanted to land fists, and walked on like a sheep.

As we approached, Hunt looked me up and down. Then turned away and strode toward the doors. Gabrielli looked me over, too. But his eyes had the cartoon jitters. Rob Burns glanced from side to side in wonder. Amazed that this play could go on without interference. He still had no sense of the reality of this world.

"Keep moving," Dickey said.

No steel in my back now. But I sensed him right behind me.

A voice so calm it sounded mechanical came over a public-address system: *"There is a disturbance in the center hall. Please use the side corridors. There is a disturbance in the center hall . . ."*

We left the building. Through the automatic doors. A Lincoln Town Car, the serious bureaucrat's vehicle of choice in D.C., waited curbside. Upscale anonymity. Surrounded by guys in sunglasses and suits. They looked like Federal Marshals, the ultimate D.C. cover.

I watched Hunt direct Rob Burns to the front seat beside the driver. Uniform brass flashing in the sun, Gabrielli got in the left rear. Hunt waited for me. Face as bland as paperwork. He had seen a lot worse. Before breakfast.

"Nice try," Hunt said. "Get in the goddamned car."

I did. But first I turned and gave Dickey the eyes. Aching for him to feel just one tiny sliver of guilt.

"Some cop," I told him.

Hunt climbed in behind me. Pressing me against Gabrielli. A Lincoln will hold three wonks in the backseat. It's a tight fit for three soldiers.

No police escort. We just pulled into traffic behind a Red Top cab. Driving down streets I knew. From jogging, walking, driving. D.C. had become my city. Without any meaningful realization on my part. Now it was my last city. And it looked different. Familiar and foreign at the same time. I felt a tourist's hunger to see everything. One more time. Each monument and statue, every color and sign of life. My advantage over the death-row boys was that I got to go out by the scenic route.

I was scared now.

Gabrielli smelled like the rest room in a truck stop. Hunt was ice. Rob Burns looked straight ahead in the front seat. He and Hunt were still playing on the same side of the game after all. The French had let me down. But Rob did look nervous. Like a petty thief who had just blundered into a cop bar. I had done a serious number on his face back in the office.

I figured the least I could do was screw him on the way out.

The car entered the Eighth Street tunnel. Heading onto 395. The driver was good. In the heavy slop of rush hour.

I said, "So where are Rob's friends? The frogs, I mean. Didn't he tell de La Vere—"

"Shut your goddamned mouth," Rob yelled. He sounded like a girl.

"Rosencrantz and Guildenstern are dead," Hunt said calmly. "They had a traffic accident. On the way to Union Station." After a few car lengths, he added, "I think you should confine your concerns to the fate of young Prince Hamlet, John. This is the final act."

The car popped out of the tunnel. Back into the killer sunlight. And bounced over a pothole. The prospect of my death reached a new level of reality.

But you can't just fold. The rule is never give in. Never

give up. If your captors think you have already accepted your death, it just makes it that much easier for them.

"And Tish?" I asked Hunt. "Is she still alive?"

That got a little smile. "You have a nineteeth-century sensibility," he told me. "It's rare these days. But I think you should be quiet now." He liked his I'm-an-educated-culturally-astute-soldier riff, though. And he knew I got his jokes. So he said, "Ophelia is irrelevant. This graveyard scene plays differently." I felt his tree-trunk leg against mine. In an air-conditioned hearse. "Know why you remind me of Hamlet, John? Because you and he are both troublesome, meddling motherfuckers who turn everything in the neighborhood to shit. You can't leave well enough alone. You spoil things. The king should have taken care of him in the first act. For the good of the state. Now shut the fuck up."

We crossed the river. Slowing as cars crowded onto the bridges from one access ramp after another. Even the best driver could not do much.

Struggling to keep his voice calm, Rob turned his puffy lips toward Hunt. "He's . . . got rather a fantastic imagination, you know. I mean, you understand what I was doing, right, Punchy? How I had to work it? The way I explained the French thing?"

"I understand," Hunt said.

We ramped down onto the George Washington Memorial Parkway. Heading north. A pickup loaded with lawn mowers almost hit us as we merged. It could have been good news for me. Maybe a chance to run. Even a hospital bed would have been better than what I was facing.

Hunt's driver hugged the right lane. I watched the river. And the city beyond. It seemed impossible that I might never see it again. That I might never see anything again. The monuments looked white and beautiful.

"Tish didn't do anything," I said. My voice shook. There was no hiding the fear now.

"Guilt," Hunt said, "is an abstract concept I find useless. I told you to be quiet."

All of this was nothing but an annoyance to him in the end. My death was a minor chore.

The Rosslyn high-rises loomed and Gabrielli spoke for the first time. "You know, Punchy, I really have a lot on my plate. If you've got everything under control . . . you could just drop me along here and I could hoof it over to the metro stop. Get back to work."

"Later," Hunt said. With finality.

A guy in a sports car who looked like he had never had a date in his life cut in ahead of us. Hunt's driver hit the brakes, said nothing, gave gas again.

Beyond the fringe of trees, the river and the far bluffs looked beautiful. Beautiful, beautiful, beautiful. I was so scared. Paralyzed by the beauty of the evening traffic. I fought my emotions, wanting to preserve a shred of dignity. As if it mattered. I felt my eyes wet and I looked away from the landscape. I forced myself to remember every charge I had outstanding on my credit card. To keep from breaking down. I wanted to cherish every minute of life. But I could not face it.

I felt pulverized by the thought of dying. It was real and unreal. I figured it was going to be a long ride to Middleburg and Hunt's private killing ground.

I was wrong. It wasn't long at all. A few miles up the parkway, the driver snapped the car out of the stream of traffic. Onto a ribbon of blacktop that led back into the trees.

Fort Marcy. The remnants of Civil War earthworks. I had stopped once to see what the place had to offer. Nothing except a few big mounds of dirt. And trees. Two Park Service signs and an orphaned cannon pointing nowhere.

Fort Marcy was a spot where disillusioned pols shot themselves. Everybody else just drove on by.

The driver had been given his instructions in advance. He parked at the far end of the empty lot. Out of sight of the surrounding roads.

Everybody was amazingly calm about this. Rob Burns had his nerves almost under control. Gabrielli had accepted his part in things. The driver was cut from ice. Hunt was Hunt.

There was none of that small-time haste, none of the confusion that is supposed to go along with murders. The driver turned off the engine and got out. In his element now. The executioner. He walked up into the brush.

We all followed. My legs unwilling.

I should have heard birds singing. Leaves rustling. Something poetic. But the big rasp of the traffic drowned out every other sound. As it would swallow the sound of the shots. Not two hundred yards away, commuters were heading for their homes in the burbs. Listening to NPR. Or some soft-rock station running giveaways. It was a drab way to go.

Still, a part of me did not really believe I would go. I could not possibly die.

Someone had tossed a Big Mac wrapper in the weeds. When I lifted my eyes, I could just see a roofline toward the river.

My voice arrived before I had the words fully shaped.

"You . . . okay . . . you can do whatever you're going to do to me . . . but you don't have to hurt Tish." I lost it. At least partway. "*Please*. I'm *beg*ging you. Just let her go. If she's alive."

Hunt snorted. "You must have read Walter Scott as an adolescent."

The driver stopped walking just short of an earthen parapet that a hundred and thirty years of rain had not been able to melt. The fort had guarded the city against Lee and Jackson.

Maybe soldiers other than me had died here. There had been no battle on the site, but maybe there had been one of those little skirmishes that are briefly reported, then lost to history. As I would be.

"Here," the driver told Hunt. "This is good." It was a professional assessment. A spot well hidden from casual observers. You could hear the world of men, but not see it. A Park Ranger would find me when he stepped into the brush to take a piss.

Rob stopped beside the driver. He would not look at me now.

I balked at going forward. A born bully, Gabrielli gave me a push.

My heart beat so fast it was almost a constant.

I wanted a chance. Any chance. But I had Gabrielli behind me on one side, Punchy Hunt on the other. With the driver and Rob just ahead.

We all stopped.

I tried to plan a run. They would shoot me down. But I would not die passively. And there might be a miracle. I might escape somehow. I believed there were miracles on this earth. I had never seen one. But I believed in them at that moment.

Then I knew I would not run. I did not want to be shot in the back. That suddenly seemed terribly important. Ridiculously important. Besides, running would have taken a form of energy I did not have now.

I decided I would at least throw a punch at the end, to show them I was a fighter.

I wondered if my limbs would obey me.

I made up my mind. I would hit Hunt. Even if he wasn't the guy with the gun. Nobody else really mattered.

They had me penned. The driver stepped closer to Rob Burns. Gabrielli gave me another punch between the shoulder blades. Driving me into the circle.

I went mulish. Gabrielli pushed ahead and tugged me by

the arm. I jerked free. But I was surrounded now. I could see each pencil-point whisker on Gabrielli's jaw, smell medicine on his breath.

Rob backed away. As if I were contagious. He stood on the driver's flank. Blinking.

Hunt's presence swelled behind me.

A horn complained from the highway. I closed my eyes, then immediately opened them again. In panic. Afraid someone would pull the trigger before I had a last chance to look at the world. To smell it. Feel it.

I saw the blue sky through the trees.

The action of a semiautomatic clicked back and came forward again. The driver. Then a second weapon snapped. Hunt.

I began to pray. Like a terrified child. Wordless.

I could not move. I wanted to resist. Ached to fight. But I could not see a course. My arms would not do anything but twitch.

To his credit, Hunt did not expect somebody else to do his dirty work. Maybe he enjoyed killing. Some men love it.

He stepped in between me and Rob Burns and lifted his pistol. He had slipped on a pair of black gloves.

He shot Rob in the bridge of the nose.

So different than Corry's dying. So much simpler. Rob's head snapped back. Lumps of crap blew out the rear of his skull. The head jerked forward again. He fell dead.

Nothing but a car backfiring.

The driver shifted, smooth as Fred Astaire, and fixed his pistol to the back of Gabrielli's skull.

Hunt reversed the pistol in his hand. Extending it to Gabrielli. Who gave him the most confused look in history.

"Take the gun," Hunt said matter-of-factly.

Gabrielli obeyed. For an instant, his eyes strayed to me. But Hunt's force pulled his attention back. Gabrielli held the pistol as if he had no idea what it might be. An odd piece of machinery. Drooping below waist level.

"Put the gun to your temple," Hunt told him. "I'm going to give you thirty seconds to make the most important decision of your life."

Gabrielli raised the gun a few inches. Conditioned to take orders. But he did not lift it all the way.

"Put the fucking gun to your head," Hunt barked.

Gabrielli lifted the pistol until the barrel touched the skin between his ear and his ghost of a sideburn. Then he jerked it away. Hot.

But the weapon stayed close to his head.

"Punchy, I . . . what—"

"Shut up. You don't have time to talk." Hunt lifted his wrist so he could read the time. Big gold Rolex. "Here's the deal, Gabe. Thirty seconds from now . . . or sooner . . . you'll pull that trigger." He did not even look at the man with the loaded gun. "Otherwise, I'll kill your wife, the son she's watching at soccer practice, your daughter in college, and the mother you dumped in a fucking rest home. As well as you. Twenty seconds left."

"Punchy, I—"

"Shut your mouth." Hunt rammed his face up against Gabrielli's. The ultimate drill instructor. *"You scum fuck. I'll kill every fucking one of them. I'll do it slow."*

Just as abruptly, he turned his back on the man. And looked at his watch again.

"Eight seconds. Save your family, man."

I watched Gabrielli's face. There was nothing else in the world worth watching. Nothing else it was possible to watch.

He was crying. Big, sudden tears. Like raindrops on his face. A clown mask of a face. So much of everything, of every possible thought and emotion, passed over his features in those seconds. Fear. Anger. A lot of hatred. The terror beyond fear.

A flicker of sentimental recollection. Time is not a constant. But it is unforgiving.

"Three seconds," Hunt said. "Two."

I don't think Gabrielli ever considered turning the gun on Hunt. The barrel did not move even an inch in that direction. It shook in the air.

"One."

I knew he was going to do as ordered. And it looked like he would botch it, miss the aim. Just bust up his skull. Or blind himself. But not end it.

At the last instant, Gabrielli pressed the pistol firmly against his ear and pulled the trigger.

I closed my eyes.

The shot hung in the air. My ears ached. Dead meat thumped dirt.

Hunt closed a big hand around my bicep. I opened my eyes. Gabrielli's last expression was one of embarrassment. An irrelevant response of the facial muscles. His head had a lop-sided shape. The day had turned into the worst anatomy lesson in the world.

"Places to go," Hunt told me. "And things to see."

The driver knelt to test neck pulses. There were brains all over the bushes. But Hunt's boys did things by the book.

Before we left, Hunt took a last look at the bodies. And snorted. "Your pal Burns," he said. "You know he was a big player in the Washington gay scene? Not that I give a good goddamn. The bravest human being I ever knew was queer as a three-dollar bill."

No. I had not known. D.C. is the last closet.

"Serves that sonofabitch Gabrielli right, though," Hunt went on. "He was a disgrace to the goddamned uniform. Two-bit thug. *He* was the asshole behind the Mickey Farnsworth killing. Totally unnecessary. And I liked Mickey. Shit-for-brains idealist that he was." Hunt nudged the black stripes on Gabrielli's trouser leg with the toe of his shoe. "Gabe and that bastard Faust were in it together. Trying to steal my operation. Frogs did us all a favor when they took out that inflated sonofabitch. Saved me the trouble."

He glanced at Rob's body. "They look like a couple to you? Folks are going to figure it was just another love affair gone wrong. Gabe shot him, then shot himself. 'Don't ask, don't tell,' right?" He gave me a playful punch that hurt. "You see, John? There really is justice in this world. Sometimes."

"Is Tish all right?"

He thumped me on the shoulder. Happy. He had enjoyed his theater piece. Suspense to the end. For everyone except the director.

"Our white knight," he said. "Didn't think they made 'em like you anymore." Then the humor faded. He came close and I noticed he was sweating. He gave off the rich smell of the killer. "Just get back in the car. And ponder mortality. We're going to go watch some television."

CHAPTER 17

He was serious. About the TV business. His driver hustled us back toward Hunt's estate. The suburbs ran out. Small towns with Confederate hangovers huddled along the highway. The horse farms began. Middleburg drowsed in the hot evening. I did as I had been told. I pondered mortality.

Violent death shifts your cosmic house off its foundations. The pipes come loose. Plaster falls in on you. And there had been a lot of death. Death on a personal level. Ugly as a public toilet. Yet I still hoped to survive. I told myself that if Hunt meant to kill me, he would have done it back at Fort Marcy. And made it look like a love triangle.

Hope is the opium of the people. Religion is just a format. Like philosophy. At the moment, my religion was battered and my philosophy was gone. But I hoped beyond reason. That I would live. That Tish was alive. I *believed* she was still alive. With all the fervency of a snake-shaking Pentecostalist.

Hunt was right. I was yesterday's man. With a flawed sensibility. It was not just that I believed in the wrong things.

It was that I believed, period. Hunt was the man of the future.

But even his confidence had limits. As soon as the gates to his property opened, I spotted the first elements of his private army. Out in force. They were real pros and a civilian would have missed them. I picked them out in the treeline. Camouflage not quite the right shade. And the inevitable movement. If you expected them, you saw them.

At least fifty armed men. Maybe more. Little teams in one position after another. In an open swale hidden from the road, I even saw a guy crouched under a manpack antiaircraft missile. Hunt had not taken any chances.

It had all looked so smooth. But maybe the day's outcome had been a near-run thing. Maybe the French had been a real threat. Maybe there were elements involved that I had not managed to trip over. Maybe Tish and I were nothing but a footnote in this history.

Hunt caught me looking.

"I need to call them off," he said. "Show's over. 'Our revels now have ended.' Almost." He gave one of his snorts that heralded a change of tone. This time he went lighter. "You'll pardon me if I don't consider you a serious threat, John."

We parked and went in that commanding house. The Hispanic maid waited at the door like a nineteen-fifties housewife.

"Bring those drinks, Magdalena," Hunt told her. "We'll be in the library."

For a moment, I hoped that his flair for the theatrical had positioned Tish in his library. With her mouth anxious under that wonderful hair. I imagined an explosive smile and the way she would rise from her seat.

She was not there.

"Sit down," Hunt told me. "Over there this time." He glanced at his watch and opened a cabinet. Revealing a television screen. He picked up the remote. Smiling. And dropped his butt into one of those magnificent leather chairs.

"I think this is going to impress even you," he told me. "Hell, it impresses me. Bob Nechestny's the only businessman in America who could get a spot on CNN whenever he wanted it."

A familiar face warmed into focus. One of Ted Turner's gals, carefully selected to be presentable but not threateningly pretty. The drinks arrived. I accepted mine with an unsteady hand. The anchorwoman bracketed clips of a confrontation over a broadcasting tower in Bosnia. Where U.S. troops were set to remain for the next hundred years.

Then she said: "Remaining with security issues, there was a remarkable development in the defense industrial sector today. For that story, we go to Kurt Lustkrieger in Washington."

The screen filled with an earnest face positioned in front of a corporate-looking complex. "Yes, Barbie, it was a startling day that shook up the traditional way of doing business here. Robert Nechestny, CEO of Macon-Bolt Industries, made what defense analysts are calling a revolutionary announcement that will set new standards of accountability in America's major weapons purchases."

Cut to a common-looking man in a perfect suit and crimson tie. Standing behind a podium. The corporate god himself. Reading. His voice was assured, but not emotional. There was just enough warmth in the tone to suggest honesty. He wore glasses you sensed came out only for a text.

"Ladies and gentlemen, I come before you as a man accountable for a major failure. Our scientists, in the course of rigorous testing, have discovered flaws in the design of the Next-Generation Fighter-Bomber, set to be America's premier combat aircraft in the new century. These flaws are fully the responsibility of our company, and our company will fix them at no cost to the taxpayer. Further, in view of the inevitable delays to the deployment of this essential system, Macon-Bolt Industries will discount the cost of the program to the Department of Defense by nearly twelve billion dollars over the next five years. We at Macon-Bolt pride ourselves on serving our country and its brave men and women in uniform, and those interests will always come first."

The correspondent came back on-screen. "Barbie, it was truly a day of revelation and change. Mr. Nechestny went on to announce that our French allies will be given a major role in the further development and production of the Next-Generation Fighter-Bomber, which will then become not only America's but NATO's dominant combat aircraft over the next decade. Analysts were startled, since the French aerospace industry had been regarded as Macon-Bolt's last remaining competition. We're looking at a new era in international cooperation in the arms trade here. Returning to the main theme—that twelve-billion-dollar refund to the taxpayer—shortly after Macon-Bolt's *mea culpa* announcement, the White House issued a press release praising the company's integrity and its contribution to the national defense. Back to you, Barbie."

The anchorwoman returned and told us, "More on the Macon-Bolt announcement and the volatile afternoon on Wall Street coming up on Business News."

Hunt laughed out loud. And clicked off the television. He laughed again.

"A thing of goddamned beauty," he said. "And a thing of beauty is a joy forever." He drank and the hospital smell of gin sanitized the room. "Nechestny's a goddamned genius. Frogs won't know what hit 'em. He'll own the Eiffel Tower, screw their wives and daughters, and they'll give *him* nylons and chocolate bars." Hunt granted me an intimate smile. "And I'll save you any concern on his behalf. Bob isn't going to the poorhouse any time soon. Macon-Bolt's stock dropped twelve bucks a share after that announcement. Nechestny grabbed the opportunity for a major buyback. Stock closed two and a half points higher than the opening price. Made a nice pile myself, if my broker didn't dick it up. Refill, John?"

No. One drink had a lot of hitting power today. I craved water. With about six separate layers of dried sweat on my skin. And one layer of whiskey sour. The air-conditioning felt lush and poisonous.

"And don't you worry about that little discount to the country," Hunt went on. "Old Bob'll just wrap it into program costs. Macon-Bolt won't lose a nickel. And the NATO deal's going to be big." He put a hand on his knee and leaned forward. "Get my point yet, John?"

Yes. I got his point.

"You know," Hunt said, "I look at you and I just see a permanent hardhead. You're just an incurable dumb-ass idealist. You remind me of old Mickey Farnsworth."

"I take that as a compliment."

"You would. And I suppose it is one. In a useless sort of way. But let's remember that poor old Mickey's dead." He looked into his glass and rattled the ice. "The age of idealists is over, son. If there ever was one. The only thing idealists do is crap on the sidewalk and call it art. And it is a terrible goddamned waste. At least in your case. You have potential."

"Thanks."

Hunt waved a paw at me. "Now, don't go getting goddamned smug. When all the dust settles, I want you to try to think clearly. Step back and look at the big picture. I'm telling you, John, the alliance between our defense industry, our military, and Congress is going to keep this nation on top for another fifty years, maybe a hundred. Maybe forever." He swept an arm across the room, across the world. "Everything that happened this past week . . . it was all nickel-and-dime monkey business. Small-time. Sideshow of a sideshow. Now the winners keep an eye on the sideshows. But they concentrate on what's going on in the big tent."

I knew he was right. But I *still* believed in something better. Even if I could not see it, describe it, or begin to shape it.

"Tell you what," Hunt said. "We're done now. At least, I'm done with you. 'The rest is silence.' I want you to just go on home. And don't waste time and energy on those disks Mary Farnsworth has hidden away in that old PC box." He read my face. "Oh, they're the real thing, all right. But it doesn't matter now. Hell, you keep 'em. As a souvenir. And don't worry. Nobody's going to touch Mary. I promise you that."

He got to his feet. Minotaur rising.

"What about Tish?" I asked.

Hunt made the wrong face. "John . . . you came to me—so you claimed—because I'm a man who pays his debts. Well, I'm paying my debt to you. You're walking out of here alive. George is going to drive you home. But you do not have a further line of credit." He folded his arms. "It's time for you to go now."

So that was it. Tish was dead. Gone. If I had really been an idealist, or just a man worth a damn, I would have punched him. Fought him. Even if it killed me. Instead, I walked out of that library door and down the hall with an emptiness inside me that was as broad as all the prairies on the continent.

At first, Hunt just followed. But out in the twilight he took over the lead. We came around the corner of the house and funneled between a brace of bodyguards. Hunt's Lincoln waited on the spotlit parking apron.

There was a shadow in the backseat.

It was Tish.

"Next time," Hunt told me, "let's be on the same side from the beginning."

But I did not care about old generals anymore. I did not care about anything except crossing twenty feet of parking apron and getting that car door open.

We made a clumsy mess of it. Tish trying to get out, me trying to get in. She looked startled and weary. And as beautiful as heaven. We collided and she kissed me all over the face and cried. Her guitar case and a big gym bag had been stuffed in the backseat with her, making our reunion crowded and wonderful. She worried over the blood on my clothes—Corry's blood—and I told her it was nothing. I don't really remember the car starting or driving back down to the public road. I only remember holding my woman so tightly she had to ask me to let her breathe.

Our mouths were dry and we stank like two apes. But as soon as we got in the door, we headed upstairs. And almost made it. The action started on the landing. Several dynamic iterations of calisthenics later, we were on the bed. I never had changed the sheets, and it was just as well.

We had not talked. And did not talk. There was too much to say, and I guess we were both afraid of some of it. Anyway, nothing that could be put into words was important now.

We were noisy, though.

Toward midnight, in a gorge of quiet, the doorbell rang. I let it ring a second time. And a third. Before an alarm went off in my back brain.

If it was trouble, I did not want it coming up here where Tish lay. I jumped out of bed, trying to remember where my khakis might have landed.

"Don't go," Tish said.

"Just for a minute," I told her. Not sure if I would ever be coming back. It had all seemed too good to be true.

A fist began pounding the door. I jumped down the stairs.

It was Dickey. Alone in the porch light. Holding a couple of folders.

He looked at my bare chest and feet.

"Sorry about the timing."

"What do you want?"

"Can I come in for a minute?"

"Do I have a choice?"

He considered me with cop eyes.

"Yeah," he told me. "This time you get a choice."

I looked down. His suit had not improved yet. And his shoes had carried him down a lot of sidewalks.

"Come on in," I said.

He dragged the last of the day's heat in with him. I shut the door against the city night and we stood in the hallway. Letting the central air put things right.

"I don't owe you any apologies," he said.

"I didn't ask for any."

He lifted his hand. "I'm not here to screw with you, okay? And I don't owe you any goddamn apologies. Or explanations. But I just want you to try to see my side. Between two guys who maybe want the same thing but go at it in different ways." His face showed loss. Years of it. Decades. "A guy wants to be a good cop. The academy lesson plan and all that. The sacred rule of law. But it all just gets so big and fast. And bad. I mean, look at this city." He pointed through the wall. "Just look at it. We're so far from the goddamned rule of law that it's all a cop can do to try to hold back the rule of evil. And not every cop in the department wants to do that much."

He looked at me with a face sanded raw by his work. "You think we would've ever gotten a single case to court on this one? To say nothing of your dip-passport French pals who killed a United States senator. No, buddy, you just look at what we did get. We came out okay. Maybe we didn't get all the bad guys. But . . . by my working standards . . . we got a pretty good score."

"I just want to put it all behind me," I told him.

He twisted up one side of his mouth as if a hook had caught it. "Yeah. But you're going to think about it. I know your type. You'll think about it till the day you die, soldier boy." He shifted his potato-sack posture. Energizing himself to go back out of my door and face his streets. "Anyway, I don't want your stomach to get upset every time you think about me."

He thrust out his hand. Offering the folders he had brought with him.

"Here. They're a gift. City Hall won't miss them."

The entryway light was weak. I had to lift the folders to read the titles on the cardboard lips. They were police records. One for Tish, one for me. Hers was a good bit thicker.

"I'm going to marry her," I told him.

He shrugged. "You could do worse. It's all a crapshoot."

And he left.

I double-locked the door behind him. I stood dully for a moment, looking at the folders but not really seeing them. Lot of weariness to sleep away. It was no time for serious thinking. I started upstairs. Then I noticed Tish's guitar case and the King Kong gym bag she had picked up somewhere along the way. I went back down the steps stone-legged, dropped the files on the stereo stand, and picked up her baggage. I wanted to see her buck naked playing that guitar before I went to sleep.

When I entered the bedroom—our room, our fortress—Tish half rose from the sheets. That would have been a painting.

"Is everything all right?"

"Better," I said, "than I ever thought it could be. Hey, I brought your stuff up. Would you do me—"

"Oh," she said. "John. I forgot. That bag. He said it was for you. That scarred-up guy who looks like a bull."

The bag suddenly felt heavier in my hand.

Body parts? A bomb? I was weary and incautious. Anxious for closure. I put down the guitar case. And yanked open the bag's zipper. Blow us to kingdom come. At least the timing was good. Go out on a cloud of ecstasy.

The bag was full of money. More money than even bankers see in cash.

Tish gasped.

"My God," she said. "He told me . . . I mean, he said it was something he owed you. I didn't . . ."

I held up two fistfuls of banded hundred-dollar bills. Baffled. Then, slowly, I grew one of those little smiles you get when you realize the joke really is on you.

"The guy's crazy," I said. "He's got one of those warped nineteenth-century sensibilities."

Tish did not hear me. She was never a greedy girl. Except in lovemaking. But a mountain of cash like that would turn the head of a saint. She got out of bed and stood naked in front of the money.

"So," Tish asked finally, "do you, like, have to report this on your taxes?"

I took the disks from Mary Farnsworth and mailed them to the General Accounting Office with an anonymous letter. Nothing ever came of it.

The money amounted to exactly five hundred thousand dollars. It was my commission from the pile Hunt ripped off Nechestny to pay himself for the phony disks. He probably took Macon-Bolt for twenty or thirty million, not ten. Plus expenses. In their different ways, the French, Aley and Corry, and Faust and Gabrielli and Rob Burns had been set to blow the deal. Hunt had used me as bait to draw them out of their holes. I had not saved the country or the defense budget. But I had done a mighty good turn for old Punchy. Law of unintended consequences.

I was smart enough to realize the money was a reward and not a bribe. I was not important enough to bribe.

If I really had been an idealist, I suppose I would have sent the money back to Hunt. I didn't. I used my connections—the kind you build up over the years in the intelligence world—to launder it. I knew Mary Farnsworth would not have accepted a nickel, so I arranged an anonymous quarter-of-a-mil donation, in General Farnsworth's honor, to a scholarship fund for minorities. It pleased Mary—she wept with pride when she told me about it. The other half is parked offshore in Tish's name. We have an agreement. As long as we stay together, she is not allowed to touch a dollar of it. But if she ever gets restless and puts on her traveling shoes, it's hers. No matter what happens, she'll never have to count pennies in a one-room apartment again.

We're getting married next June. Mary Farnsworth is hosting the reception. She's become the mother Tish never really had.

I went back to work. Nobody wanted to pry into what happened. People made little jokes and let it go. They had no idea. And didn't want one.

As soon as I could, I took another week of leave. And flew up to Massachusetts. Habit of the tribe. I laid my flowers on Emerson Carroll's grave and saluted. In the end, he had been a good soldier. But not a lucky one.

And I went back to General Farnsworth's grave. Regularly. I talked to his headstone like an old widow. He remains my hero. But there is vanity in all of us, and it takes eccentric forms. I had to find the workman with whom I had spoken the afternoon of Farnsworth's funeral. I had to prove to him that he had been wrong. That there is still loyalty in the world. That some of us do come back.

I was certain I would run into him eventually. But I never did. Finally, I went to the cemetery's admin offices and inquired. I even remembered his name. Rickie York. Richard York, probably.

After searching the records, the personnel clerk told me that no such man had ever been employed at Arlington.

AUTHOR'S NOTE

This is a work of fiction, so it is less interesting than life. It is, however, more succinct and manageable. When it works, fiction gives the illusion of immediacy, born of compression and exaggeration. We see that which lies before us with unnatural clarity. *If* the author has luck.

The writer of fiction is the adult counterpart to the child who comes home full of tall tales. Fiction is lying, born of an old compulsion. Yet when masters write, it brings us to a greater truth. In lesser hands such as mine, this form of entertainment still may serve good ends—or so I have convinced myself.

The novel you have just finished has two purposes. The first is to be sufficiently engaging to finish in the black and keep my publisher happy. The second is to shine a storyteller's lamp on a problem of national importance.

Traitor's characters are fictional (in the case of Tish, inspired by listening to Aimee Mann's brilliant disc, *Whatever*, while driving in the rain). But the problem of massive corruption in the defense industry is real. As a serving soldier, I was appalled by it; as a citizen, I am enraged. The fact that this corruption is, in most cases, technically legal disgusts me. It should disgust you, too.

Each year, we spend tens of billions of dollars on weapons that do not work as promised and that are inappropriate to our needs. It is impossible to kill these programs. Too much is at stake. While contractors speak piously about giving our men and women in uniform "the best," and about jobs for the American worker, defense acquisition is really about fantastic profits torn from a system that lacks serious accountability. In Washington, those in power know the system is corrupt—morally, ethically, and practically. But there is no constituency for change in our capital. Defense contractors are big campaign and PAC contributors; they are a major source of advertising revenue for the media; and they hire retiring generals and admirals at generous salaries, ensuring that these officers will not speak out for reform while on active duty. My beliefs are generally the same as those of John Reynolds in this book—the plot is fabricated, but the spirit is true.

I do not imagine that a one-man crusade disguised as a thriller can change much. But it is the best I can do. I hope that readers will carry a sense of this problem with them after they have finished the book and put it away on a back shelf. One man can do little, but informed Americans pulling together can accomplish a great deal over a span of years. Defense procurement reform is an idea whose time *will* come—hopefully before a military crisis.

The current system does not serve either our soldiers or our citizens well. While we, the people, constitute the wealthiest nation in history, we cannot afford waste on this scale. We *need* a strong defense—but we are getting the wrong defense. Anyway, our national defense begins in our classrooms—not in the boardrooms of contractors. Given the deep pockets of defense industry and the genius of its lawyers, it will take time to clean up this vicious and lucrative system. But I believe it can be done. Honest men and women still can win in this country, if they do not fall victim to the cynicism that is corruption's great enabler.

There is a lighter side to this book, of course. Since my childhood in the Pennsylvania coalfields, where the world came to us through paperbacks and three black-and-white television channels, I have loved the *noir* masters of print and film. They described a great, smoky, seductive world in which the women cocked their eyebrows like Lauren Bacall and the men toughed it out to the final showdown. The dialogue was the way people *should* have spoken; the stock characters were endlessly renewable; and the same old plot was eternally fresh.

The creators always gave good value, and you sensed that their morality—it was ferocious behind the murk—was closer to the real texture of life than were the entertainments for which junior-high-school students were supposed to settle in those days. Hammett, Chandler, Cain, and all the Hollywood people right down to a boozed-up screenwriter named Faulkner, policed the fog of my adolescence. This novel is a grateful, inadequate tribute to them.

I wish more books could be this much fun to write. It was a labor of conviction and love. Even my editor's suggestions were as seductive as Veronica Lake. If the masters of the genre were alive, the incredible scandal of our defense industry would inspire them to new masterpieces—but those giants are dead. The reader will have to settle for this three-hundred-page fan letter.

I hope you found it a good read.

—Ralph Peters

WITH COMPLIMENTS

Michael Dagher

P.O.Box 942481, AMMAN 11194, JORDAN
TEL.: +962 6 568 3030 FAX: +962 6 568 4040 EMAIL: MICHAEL@UMNIAH.COM

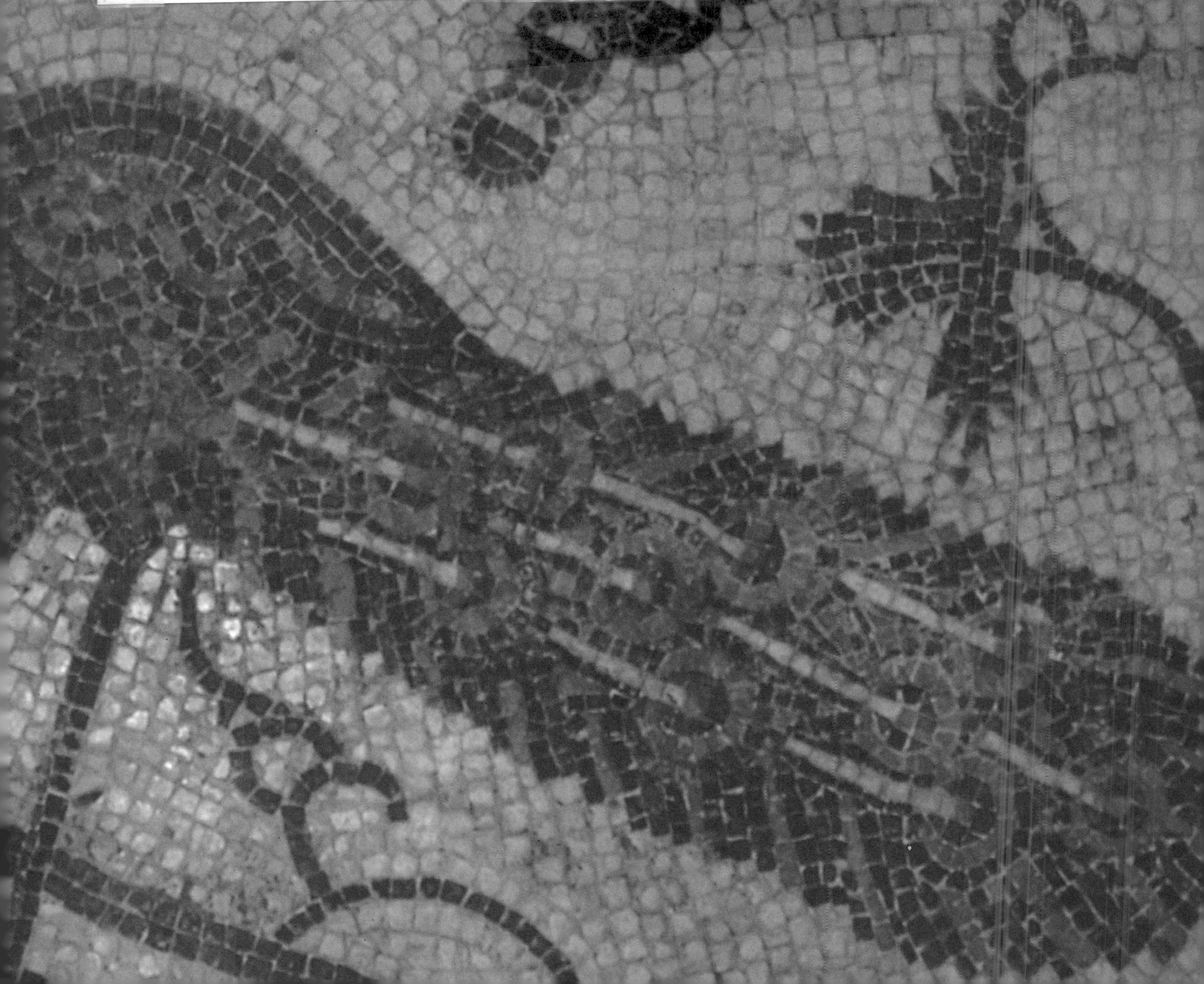

▪ JOURNEY THROUGH ▪

JORDAN

▪ JOURNEY THROUGH ▪
JORDAN

▪ MOHAMED AMIN ▪ DUNCAN WILLETTS ▪ SAM KILEY ▪

Camerapix Publishers International
NAIROBI

Acknowledgements

Wherever we went in Jordan we found only welcome and hospitality and we would like to thank the many organisations and people throughout the country who gave us help and advice in the production of this book. In particular we owe a debt of thanks to the Office of the late King, The Royal Jordanian Airforce, especially No. 7 Squadron, and the people of Jordan generally.

First published in 1994 by
Camerapix Publishers International,
P.O. Box 45048,
Nairobi, Kenya

Second edition 2001 for
Jordan Distribution Agency Co. Ltd,
PO Box 375,
Amman, Jordan

ISBN 1 874041 54 7

This book was designed and produced by
Camerapix Publishers International,
P.O. Box 45048,
Nairobi, Kenya

Production Director: Rukhsana Haq
Edited by: Robert Smith and Roger Barnard
Associate Editors: Sumaya El Hassan and Tahir Shah
Design: Craig Dodd

Printed in Hong Kong by South China Printing (1998) Limited.

Half title: The Black Iris, Jordan's national Flower, is a poignant symbol throughout the Middle East. Page 2: One of Jordan's vast valleys hewn from sheer rock creates a breathless scene with its austere beauty. Title page: Serpentine strands of sea grasses flourish amid the brilliant colours of sponges, corals and other marine growths in the calm waters of the Gulf of Aqaba. Contents page: One of the greatest of all constructions carved by the Nabateans at Petra. Known as El Deir, meaning 'The Monastery', it can only be reached after a hike through surrounding mountains. Page 6: Slender minaret of a mosque reaches upward as the sun dips towards Aqaba's jagged mountains.

· CONTENTS ·

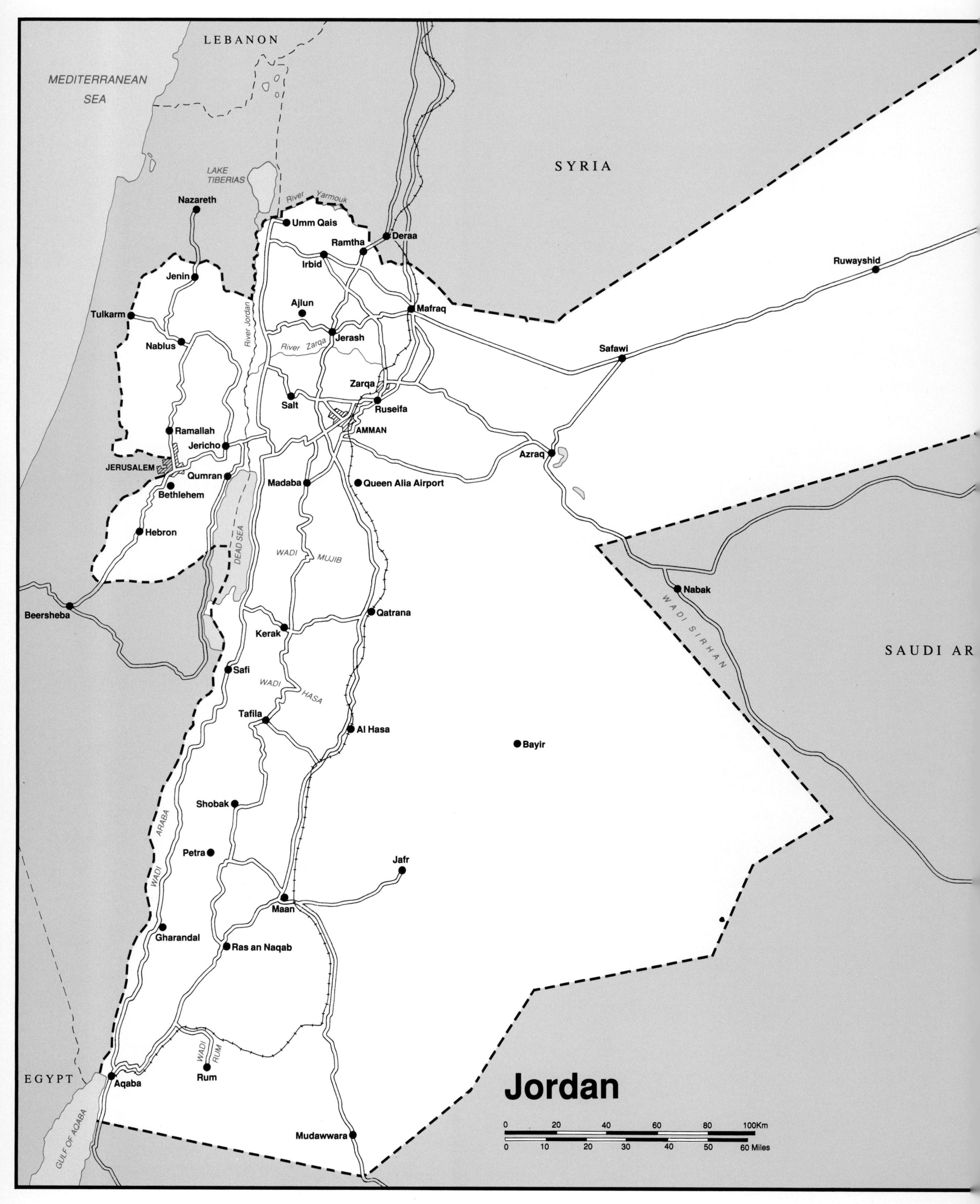

LEBANON
MEDITERRANEAN SEA
SYRIA
LAKE TIBERIAS
River Yarmouk
Nazareth
Umm Qais
Deraa
Ramtha
Irbid
Jenin
Ruwayshid
Ajlun
Mafraq
Tulkarm
Jerash
River Jordan
River Zarqa
Nablus
Safawi
Zarqa
Salt
Ruseifa
AMMAN
Ramallah
Jericho
Azraq
JERUSALEM
Qumran
Madaba
Queen Alia Airport
Bethlehem
Hebron
DEAD SEA
WADI MUJIB
Nabak
Beersheba
Qatrana
WADI SIRHAN
Kerak
SAUDI AR
Safi
WADI HASA
Tafila
Al Hasa
Bayir
Shobak
WADI ARABA
Petra
Jafr
Maan
Gharandal
Ras an Naqab
WADI RUM
EGYPT
Aqaba
Rum
Jordan
0 20 40 60 80 100Km
0 10 20 30 40 50 60 Miles
GULF OF AQABA
Mudawwara

IRAQ
© Camerapix 1993

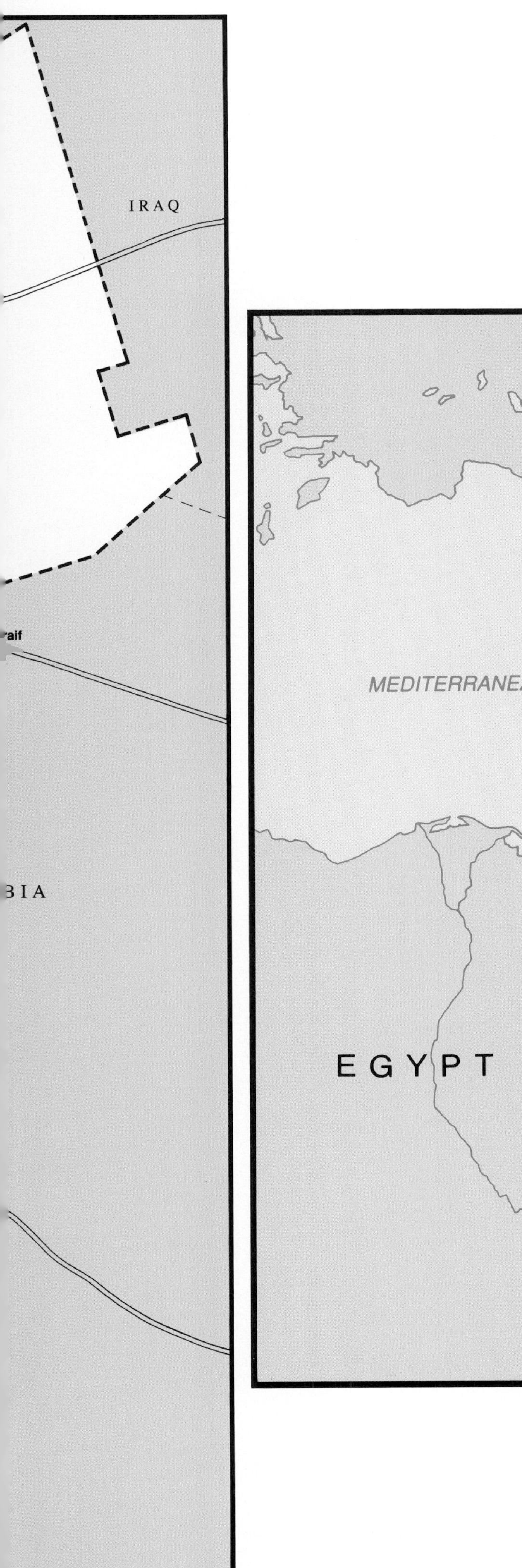

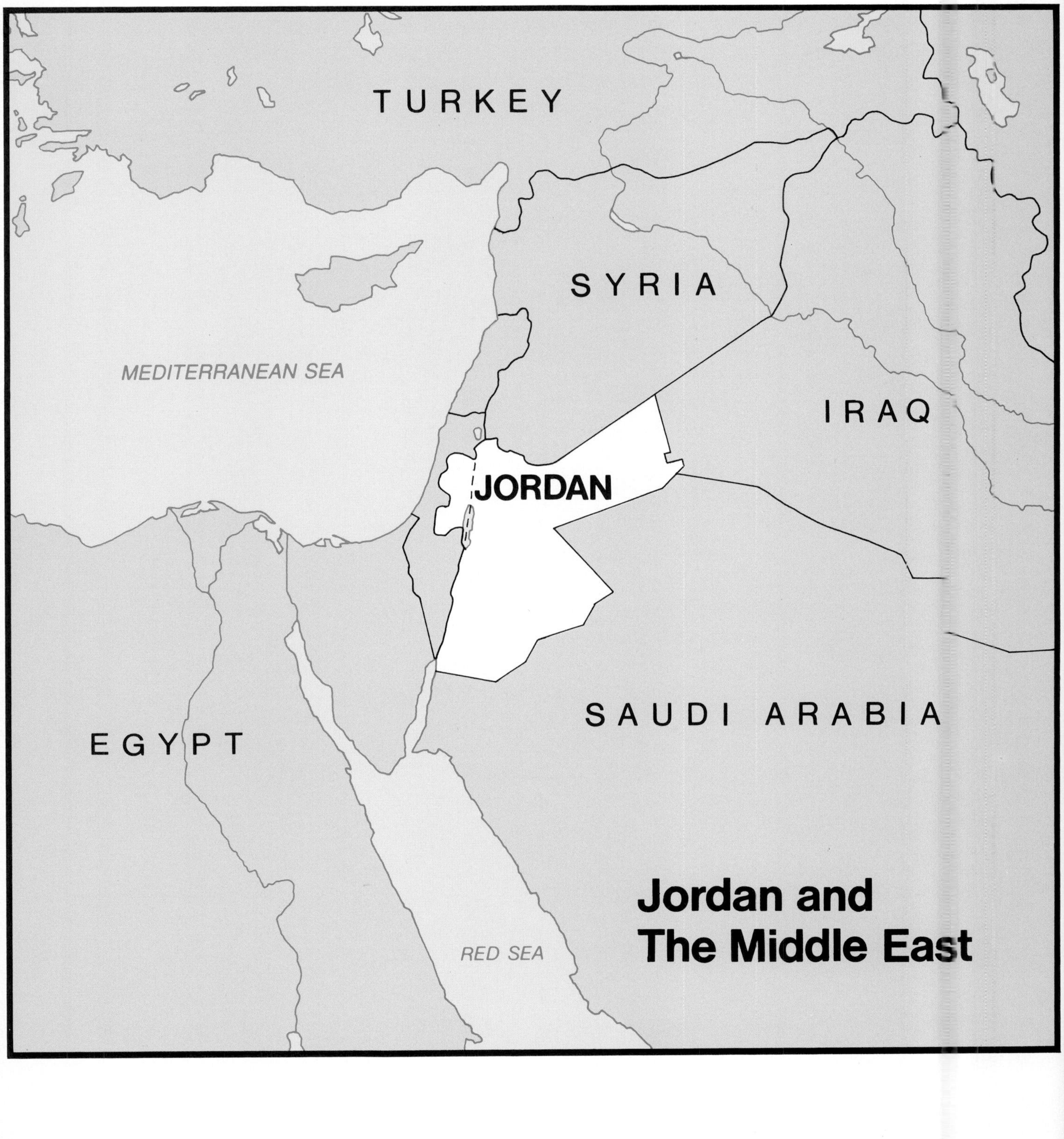

TURKEY
SYRIA
MEDITERRANEAN SEA
IRAQ
JORDAN
SAUDI ARABIA
EGYPT
RED SEA
Jordan and
The Middle East

JOURNEY THROUGH JORDAN

Previous pages: One of the Middle East's most spectacular features, Wadi Rum has earned the ethereal and apt epithet 'Valley of the Moon'.

As a modern state, the Hashemite Kingdom of Jordan is little older than three score years and ten. But its inhabitants are the guardians of a heritage which stretches way back into the dawn of history.

For Jordan geographically is the quintessence of the Holy Land. Indeed, its lineage goes even further. Spawned of this land are people from civilisations which span thousands of years.

Its strategic position at one of the great crossroads of the world, where Asia meets Africa, has drawn invading peoples to this area since before records began. All have left their mark. Written in the sand and limestone of this fascinating hot spot is a story of turbulent times contrasting with cultural and economic prosperity.

Excavations record evidence of the Stone, Copper, Bronze and Iron ages. In turn, successive civilisations have left their impression upon Jordan's soil. The Ammonites, Edomites, Nabateans, Greeks, Romans, Byzantines and many more have added to this rich cultural broth.

Above: Crimson poppy, one of many burgeoning flowers, in Jordan's Bullen Forest.

In the capital, Amman, and in Jerash are superb examples of Roman architecture while Nabatean Petra is world famous as a landmark of stubborn resistance to that very Roman dominance.

But Jordan present is no less absorbing. Its own brief history is one of torment and trial before the Kingdom finally emerged phoenix-like into its present relative peace and prosperity.

Jordan's fortune was realised, not by mere fortuity, but through the illustrious leadership of its monarch, the late King Hussein. In the interim, before Prince Hussein assumed his responsibility as monarch, his mother — Queen Zein el Sharaf — played a significant role in ensuring the orderly transfer of power.

Hailing from the distinguished Hashemite family, Hussein was the 39th (and the current monarch, His Majesty King Abdullah II is the 40th) in the line of descent from the Prophet Mohammed. The Hashemites have played a crucial part in the moulding of the Middle East's society and culture. Indeed, no other line has its history so intertwined with the shaping of the Arab World.

From his investiture as King, at the age of 17, Hussein guided Jordan through the Middle East's turbulent postwar years. Long before his death in 1999, Hussein was respected not only in Jordan but internationally for his achievements in a reign which spanned some 46 years.

Jordan lies east of the great river which bisects the Holy Land. It was the birthplace of the Arab independence movement in the early part of this century. It is not as rich in mineral wealth as its eastern neighbours, Saudi Arabia and Iraq, but the kingdom occupies a special place at the historical heart of modern Arabia. It was in the freezing winters and blistering summers of the Badia (desert) that Amir Feisal and Amir Abdullah, sons of the Meccan Emir

His Majesty King Abdullah II and Her Majesty Queen Rania.

Above: Ruins at Beidha, near Petra, date back some 9,000 years. The archaeological site, one of the oldest in the Middle East, is all that is left of a Neolithic settlement.

Hussein, raised their armies of Bedu and, with the help of the British and other allies, freed the Arab people from the yoke of Ottoman rule at the end of World War I.

But the victorious emirs who took Damascus, Aqaba and Azraq from the Turks were soon to be disappointed with the outcome of the post war Treaty of Versailles. For it was nearly 30 years before their dream of an independent Arab state could be fully realised. But the taste of freedom was bitter-sweet. Liberty for the Arabs came with provision for Jewish people to build a nation in Palestine — reigniting a conflict of interests going back to Genesis.

Amid the fighting and intrigue which are so much the story of Jordan and its neighbours, trade also wove a web of silk between successive civilisations linking the ancient Hittite with the Egyptian, Greek, Nabatean, Philistine, Israelite, Roman, Byzantine, Ummayed and Ottoman empires.

The early, middle and late dynasties of the Middle East were not established by conquest but built upon trade. Traditionally, there was no more important trade route in the middle or near east than the King's Highway. It was established in early biblical times to link Syria with the kingdoms to the east of the Jordan and the Hijaz to the far south-east. Most of Jordan's history can now be seen from a car travelling along the King's Highway for, as such a vital communications link, it was the scene of some of the most dramatic episodes in the kingdom's existence. It is less important now as a trade route, as the newly constructed Desert Highway takes much of the heavy traffic.

Strictly speaking, the northern end of the King's Highway is in Amman where it branches to all points of the compass: east to Iraq and Saudi Arabia, west to Palestine and Israel, and north to Syria. But if you begin in Umm Qais (Gadara) and travel the route its full length to Aqaba, the physical glory of Jordan is swiftly revealed.

The road starts in the rarefied atmosphere of the limestone and basalt hills overlooking Lake Tiberias and the Golan Heights. Umm Qais was both a Roman pleasure centre and an Ottoman town. Remains of both civilisations nestle cheek-by-jowl in a chaos of rocks that look down into the beginning of the valley of the River Jordan, into the deep heart of the Great Rift, peppered with wild flowers and grazing cattle.

The people of this area are simple folk, living off the land in much the same way as they have for centuries. It is not until you reach Irbid that the 20th century makes its presence felt. Industrial complexes and large farms replace the smallholdings and forests of the north. Extensive farms, producing wheat using modern irrigation techniques, roll over the high plateau above the city. But bustling Irbid is unmistakably Arabian, although not a pretty place. Streets twist and turn past hundreds of spice houses, tea shops and restaurants. The local people dress in a mixture of western garb and the more colourful clothes of their ancestors, in particular the Palestinians, who are settled in refugee camps and cling closely to their heritage. The women still prefer brightly embroidered black dresses to the glamorous fabrics of today.

Continuing south to Amman, one finds a confusing world of ancient and modern. The labyrinth of streets and roads wind up, through and around the seven pine-clad hills of the city which are covered in white sandstone and concrete houses. The architecture strikes the visitor as uniform until the eyes move down to street level. There is little hint, however, of the desert that occupies such a special place in the heart of every Jordanian.

Some way out of town you may see the black tents of the Bedu, half concealed by modern buildings and, off the main road, you will find farmers who have settled into modern agriculture yet have not abandoned their nomadic past. In fact, to them, tents are a superior form of dwelling. They take little to heat in the winter and are cool in summer. It is not unusual to see a modern saloon car parked outside a Bedouin tent. Further along the great highway are reminders of the violent history of the route, which was fought over for millennia, and never more brutally than during the Crusades when Kerak and Shobak castles were created as outposts for the robber barons from Europe.

Finally, at Petra, the road plunges into the desert and leaves the luxury of the limestone highlands behind. It was in these inhospitable wastelands of sand and shimmering light that modern Jordan was conceived by Princes Abdullah and Feisal. The Badia was ideal for their armies as it provided sustenance for the men of the desert that the Ottomans could not find, and a perfect camouflage for their daring raids on the Hijaz Railway, the main supply line for the Turks.

The modern Arabs drew upon experience in the wilderness that went back eons to the Great Rift Valley, formed as the cradle of mankind.

Tools and other deposits as well as fossil teeth and bones — the earliest pre-Neolithic finds in Jordan — suggest that mankind's ancestor, *Homo erectus*, roamed this area more than a million years ago.

Remains found on the shores of lakes Lisan — now part of the Dead Sea marked by the El Lisan peninsular — Azraq and Jafr also indicate that Jordan's Early Stone Age people spurned the abundance of caves in the limestone hills above the Jordan Valley in favour of settlements close to lakes or on dry river beds, or *wadis*.

Above: Shepherd tends his flock in Jordan's wilderness.

Between 90,000 and 40,000 years ago, these hunter-gatherers wore animal skins as they roamed the steep walls of the Great Rift Valley and the surrounding plains in search of game. They bathed in the hot springs which burst out of the ground all along the escarpment where the valley floor brought the fiery depths of the earth close to the surface. Boiling underground streams gushed out of the bedrock like natural jacuzzis.

Around 30,000 years ago the climate began to change — from temperate to arid. Man had started to learn how to plant and harvest, and raise livestock, a hint of the Neolithic change taking place as *Homo sapiens* evolved. About 10,000 years ago groups began to form communities and settle in crude stone shelters. These communities soon discovered the skills and pleasures of three-dimensional fine art.

West of modern Amman the remains of one of these communities, covering twelve hectares, are grouped remarkably close together — indicating the people had resolved many conflicts that characterise subsistence life.

About 7,000 to 6,000 years ago, the people occupying Jordan also began to build more advanced structures — walls of worked stone arranged around a courtyard. Houses on hillsides were shored by terraces and their walls thickly covered with plaster, often brightly painted. Considering that the wheel and fired pottery had yet to be invented it was an extraordinary development.

Above: A Bedouin leads his motley charges through the desert at the end of a day's grazing on the vegetation around Azraq Springs.

Doorways were raised two metres or more above the ground, with reason. Not only was it done to keep the livestock out of the central living quarters, but also as protection from the lions, leopards and wolves that roamed Jordan's thickly-wooded highlands and central valley. Thousands of years later, tiny remnant populations of leopards and wolves still stalk the area around D'ana.

Besides architecture, Neolithic Jordanians also developed sculpture. The earliest complete statues were found at Ain-Ghazal and are now displayed in Yarmouk University Museum. As the Neolithic Age became the Chalcolithic, people began to mine and work copper, as well as stone, and form ever-more sophisticated societies.

So sophisticated, in fact, that the cities of Pella in the north of the central valley and Tuleitat Ghassul, west of Amman, were built of mud-fired bricks — much like those still used across Africa and in other developing nations. But the cities had no protecting walls, suggesting that these early Bronze Age people were not yet embroiled in the wars and territorial disputes which would soon dominate much of their lives. The people of Tuleitat Ghassul made specialised tools like butter churns and drinking cups, plastered their houses elaborately and painted them equally flamboyantly. Rather than dedicate one room as a shrine, they spread murals all over their houses. These houses were remarkably similar to those still in use near the Crusader fortress in Shobak and in the ancient village which overlooks the Jordan Valley in D'ana. Thick stone walls were roofed with wood, reeds, and mud so deep that grass grew freely on top. In addition to being marvellously integrated with their surroundings these houses had the advantage of being warm in winter and cool in summer.

The people of Tuleitat Ghassul enjoyed parading on the streets. Womenfolk adorned themselves with sea shells, beads and polished stone. Men sported beards and tattoos and wore embroidered slippers. Paintings from that time show that people wore comfortable clothes, though nothing as smooth as cotton.

Soon after came the development of highly sophisticated settlements with massive 4.5 metre thick town walls six metres high. Clearly, they were built to keep out the most determined invaders. It is easy to imagine the awe-inspiring sight of the fortressed city of Jawa as seen by the marauding desert tribes after marching for freezing nights and baking days, only to be confronted by ramparts solid enough to withstand a modern howitzer, let alone their puny weapons.

In Khirbet ez-Zaraqun, on the fertile plains of the highlands (north-east of modern Irbid), the inhabitants built a town with a regular street pattern surrounded by a vast wall. Even more striking to today's observer than their sophisticated town planning is the water supply to the plateau. The people constructed a reservoir at the foot of the hill on which Zaraqun sits and carved a series of tunnels into the mountain. They then simply lowered vast buckets via well shafts to collect the water in bulk. Such ingenuity in solving the perennial problem of water in the Middle East is repeated all over the Kingdom of Jordan, especially in Petra where the later Nabateans developed a simple but efficient water supply system.

It seems clear the advent of city walls characterised the end of the internal stability in the region, for against the people came the Hyksos, the Shepherd Kings of the Bible, who spread ideas of empire all the way to Egypt, which they conquered with a terrible new war-machine — the chariot. The Hyksos appear to have had little influence on the land east of the River Jordan other than Amman, Mount Nebo and Naur. This may have been because a region so far from the sea had little attraction for the marauding Hyksos who were bent on sacking the treasures of Egypt.

The Bronze Age marks the beginning of written history, even though much of it is mythical and apocryphal. Scriptural experts estimate that the verses of

Above: Fine mosaic frieze which graced the floors of the elaborate Byzantine monastery built at Deir Ain Abata, the Cave of Lot. It is there, biblical legend has it, that the kingdoms of Amman and Moab were conceived as a result of a drunken and incestuous union between Lot and his two daughters.

Above: Like sentinels from an ancient time, the pillars around Artemis temple in Jerash stand proud against the elements, survivors of centuries of erosion and earthquakes.

Overleaf: The view over the Rift Valley from Umm Qais — where Greek and Roman holidaymakers took steam baths in the natural geysers — towards the Sea of Galilee. These lands have changed little since biblical times.

Genesis relating to the Patriarchs — Abraham and his sons — coincide with the Middle Bronze Age between 2200 and 1500 BC. Indeed, there is a convenient Bronze Age reference early in the Bible in relation to Cain's descendant six generations on. When Abraham journeyed north from Babylon along the Euphrates, and then south through Damascus to the land of the Canaanites, he travelled in lands where man was still evolving into a modern species. Vast tracts of the Middle East, especially east of the Jordan, were roamed by nomads. Some had discovered copper and iron; others lived as hunters-gatherers. After Abraham's return from Egypt his son, Lot, headed east to avoid further conflict between his herdsmen and those of his father.

Perhaps Lot stood on the western escarpment of the Rift Valley, gazing down on the verdant green of the Jordan Valley after crossing the Sinai desert and, seeing that it was 'well watered everywhere', quite naturally chose to take his chances among the Horite cave dwellers of the region. Lot's arrival in Sodom

and Gomorrah, the city states at the southern tip of the 'salt sea' embroiled him in a series of extraordinary battles and wars between rival chiefdoms. Even more interesting is the mention of the giants on the plains south and east of the Dead Sea. In the event King Chedorlaomer not only defeated the kings of the two doomed cities but also wiped out the giants and abducted Lot and his family.

Lot's dynasty is the basis of the two most enduring kingdoms to the east of the Great Rift Valley. After his release by the small army his father raised, Lot returned to Sodom and its lascivious citizens. They attempted to abduct Lot's two virgin daughters whose honour was only saved, so it is said, by angels who were staying with Lot. They struck the lusting Sodomites blind. For God the attempted kidnap was the last straw. The two cities were so decadent he rained down 'brimstone and fire' on the southern plain of Jordan, utterly destroying Sodom and Gomorrah. Perhaps leaving Sodom against her will, Lot's wife made the mistake of casting a rueful last glance at this place of attractive iniquity and was turned into a pillar of salt. Legend has it that it is Lot's wife who is still stuck in the salt stalagmites visible to the south of the Dead Sea. Her husband fled to nearby Zoar on the eastern escarpment of the Rift and hid in a cave where, as he no longer had a wife and had yet to produce an heir, his resourceful daughters plied him with wine and seduced the old man.

"Thus were both the daughters of Lot with child by their father" — (Genesis 36:20). Moab, the son of the elder daughter became head of the line which established the Moab kingdom. The son of the younger daughter, Ben-ammi, established Ammon whose capital of Rabbath-Ammon became modern Amman. The Moabite kingdom extended from the River Zered (Wadi Hasa) to the Arnon (Wadi Mojib), while the Ammonite lands stretched from the Mojib to the Zarqa (Jabbok). The kingdom of Edom was established by Esau, grandson of Abraham and son of Isaac.

Little is known about the land to the east of the River Jordan during this period, though some historians suggest that before the Exodus of the Jews from Egypt, the people there had returned to a nomadic lifestyle. This would certainly explain the paucity of archaeological finds dating from this period. But there must have a been social system, for when the Jews arrived between 1550 and 1200 BC on their long journey from Egypt, the kingdoms were united enough to do battle with the Israelites. And on all sides there was an awareness of the diplomatic niceties expected of visitors hoping to travel through territory held by others. Indeed, although the sweeping biblical saga of the Exodus and the establishment of a kingdom of Judah happened in the Bronze and Iron ages, these technologically backward people were accomplished at diplomacy and political chicanery. The arrival of Moses in Jordan also marked the beginning of an almost unbroken cycle of war, punctuated only occasionally by the

Above: Late afternoon sun bathes Petra's Temple of Gods in glorious hues of red and gold.

flourishing of indigenous cultures like the great Nabatean civilisation and the later Ummayed hegemony. Both are close to the heart of modern Jordan. In Nabateans, we see genius for compromise and diplomacy, while in the latter were the seeds of an Arab culture close to its desert roots in the Badia and to Islam.

The route Moses and the Israelites followed out of Egypt is arguable. But it appears certain that the Jews visited Kadeshbarnea, in the south of Palestine at the northern edge of the Sinai, where they found a flourishing, fully-fledged Edomite kingdom. Moses asked leave to journey north through Edom, a route which would have allowed him to head almost due east along the Wadi Hasa and there join the King's Highway, which he promised to stick to, 'not turning aside to the right hand nor to the left'. This is the first mention of the King's Highway.

His request was refused. Moses was forced to lead his people along the Wadi

Above: Detail of the magnificent Byzantine mosaic floor, at Khirbet-El Mukhayyad.

Araba to Aqaba — ancient Ezion Geber — and then across the harsh stony desert towards Maan. Their journey took them into the Badia, away from all permanent water, though ecologists believe that the desert was less barren before the massive overgrazing of recent centuries. So perhaps the Israelites were able to graze their sheep and goats while tramping, much like today's Bedouins, between oases. Fiercely independent and suspicious of the motives of the vast Jewish horde gathering on his borders, King Sihon, who had his capital at Heshbon, near Madaba, also refused passage to the Israelites. He feared they might settle on his lands north of the Mojib (Arnon) River. But weary of their peripatetic lifestyle, the Israelites took up arms. In the ensuing battle, Sihon was defeated and the Israelites, brutalised by so many years of wandering in the desert and persistent attempts to enslave them, butchered every inhabitant in each town that fell into their hands. But these primitive people, armed only with swords, daggers and spears, were unable to force their way across the Jordan to

Above: Bedouin family enjoy a picnic in a meadow overlooking the Jordan Valley.

the Promised Land in Palestine. Instead, they headed north to take on King Og at Edrei (Deraa) and then sweep victoriously south again, through the lush greenlands of the Jordan Valley, to exact revenge on the inhospitable Moabites. There they camped opposite Jericho on the threshold of the Promised Land.

During their harsh travels around Jordan the Israelites saw what the land had to offer. Transjordan divided roughly into four areas of farmland which correspond closely with biblical references to the activities of the various tribes occupying the land. The land around Irbid was known — just as it is now — for its wheat and barley fields. Among the vast coniferous woodlands in the highlands of Gilead, people cropped timber and cleared land for vines. The rolling limestone hills of Ammon and Moab were ideal as sheep pastures. But in the south along the King's Highway, the Edomites occupied less fertile land and relied on commerce for their prosperity. Perfumes, gold, precious stones and spices were traded with caravans coming from Midian, (now modern Saudi Arabia) and Sheba, (now Yemen) while exotic animals, gold, ivory, sandalwood, frankincense and myrrh from Ethiopia and Somalia came through Aqaba.

Mistrusting Jewish intentions, Balak, the Moabite king, looked down at their camp in Jericho and feared for his own realm. Swiftly he formed an alliance with the five kings of Midian as a bulwark against an invasion.

For Moses, now old and weary, the task of leading his chosen people to the Promised Land was almost complete. He surveyed the land from Mount Nebo, near Madaba. In spring, the rolling limestone hills were peppered with wild flowers and ablaze with blood-red poppies. His gaze swept on across the Dead Sea to the mountains on the other side of the Great Rift. Moses saw that it was good, and at last he died. He was buried opposite the shrine to the local god, Baal, against whose adherents he had fought so bitterly.

Now the Jews began to make their way into Palestine. But the tribes of Reuben, Gad and half the Manasseh fell in love with the fertile highlands of Gilead, Ammon and Moab and remained on the eastern escarpment of the Rift Valley. This westland movement of the Israelites coincided with the transition of the Bronze Age to the Iron Age in 1200 BC. And so began a virtually endless cycle of invasion and counter-invasion with the Israelites almost constantly at war with the Philistines in Gaza to the west.

As a result of these conflicts, Israel's power soon declined and the killing of Saul, declared king of Israel in 1020 BC, was the signal for their defeat. When David took power some years later, he consolidated his position in Palestine before attacking Hanun, King of Ammon, who was driven back to his redoubt in Amman. There he was besieged by the Israelites who cut the citadel's water supply and won the day. David also extended his kingdom to Moab and Edom by marrying daughters of the royal houses there and spread his influence over the nomadic tribes all the way to the Euphrates. On the death of David,

Solomon became King of the Israelites. Trade was vital to the development of the kingdom, especially Jordan, where the camel caravans and Solomon's fleets made Aqaba and nearby al-Khalifa prosperous centres of trade and copper smelting. But Solomon, despite his reputation for sagacity, had no wisdom when it came to the economy. His lavish spending on monumental buildings led to heavy taxes and the use of Israelites as labourers, causing rebellion in the north of his kingdom after he died. Because of the secession of Judah from Israel, and the ensuing war, the three kingdoms to the east of the Jordan were able to slip out of Israel's grasp. The entire region on both sides of the Jordan, (now called the Holy Land) sank into semi-anarchy, marked only by the insatiable appetite of the various warlords for booty. Omri, King of Israel, took Madaba from the Moabites who, according to the Moabite Stone, (a stele inscribed by Mesha, King of Moab) took the town back from Omri's son, Ahab. Mesha also defeated an attempt by Israel, Judah and Edom to throw him out.

Above: Hashemite Coat of Arms engraved into the outer wall of Aqaba Fort. The Arab Rebellion's success was largely due to the capture of the fort which opened a supply route for freedom fighters.

During the Iron Age, Moab, Ammon and Edom came heavily under the influence of Egyptian, Assyrian, and Phoenician cultures, adopting their fashions and diets. Evidence of cultural exchange in Amman and elsewhere is testimony to the advancing influence of trade in the region and perhaps explains why the various tribes and kingdoms were so anxious to dominate one another for control of the King's Highway.

Assyria began to spread its influence — and often violent power — over its neighbours, weakened by their own small regional squabbles. But an Assyrian distraction with Cairo and Luxor provided an ideal opportunity for Arab Bedu to assert their independence. Under Yatha they attacked Jordan, harrying the authorities as far as Damascus. It is the first biblical mention of the desert peoples who, two millennia later, would be responsible for the birth of an independent Arabia. Assyrian annals make note of the Nabateans who, living in the barren wilderness of Midian in the 7th century BC, had yet to move into Petra and establish their civilisation of trade and diplomacy.

The decline of Assyria in Jordan was matched by the increasing influence of the Babylonian empire of Nebuchadnezzar in Palestine. But an attempt to form an alliance against Babylon failed; some Jews were taken into captivity, and others fled east across the Jordan. While Babylon showed little interest in establishing much of a hold on Jordan, the Nabateans slowly squeezed their way into Edom. By 500 BC the Persians, who had taken control of Palestine, allowed Jews to return to Jerusalem to rebuild their temple. The land east of the Jordan fell under a Persian governor. He appears to have had little control, however, for Moabites and Ammonites continued to harry the Jews' attempts to rebuild the temple. Even then, the great shrine was seen as a symbol of Jewish permanence in the land. As such, it remains in the 1990s a potent talisman of political conflict.

Above: Surviving relic of an earthquake in ancient times, a line of stone arches still stands in Umm-el Rassas.

With the decline of the Persian empire, Transjordan and its influence faded. On his way to Egypt, Alexander the Great bypassed most of the region and on his death his own empire was divided between generals Ptolemy in Egypt and Seleucus in the Lebanon.

Meanwhile the Nabateans, who had established themselves in Petra, were making fortunes out of taxes on the trade routes. The Greek ruler of Syria, Antigonus, was keen to get his hands on the Nabatean coffers of gold and jewels and decided to send an expeditionary force against Petra. But no matter how shrewd the Greeks may have been, the swift wits of the Nabateans preserved them from the worst Antigonus could do. At first the attack on Petra, about 311 BC, was a great success and the Greeks sacked the city. But, knowing every nook and cranny of their mountain station, the Nabateans fell upon the Greeks and wiped them out.

The second Greek sortie provoked an even shrewder response. The

Opposite: A local beauty in a traditional wedding dress adorned with Maria Theresa dollars, a currency still in use in the Jordan desert.

Above: Antique silver coins decorate the exquisite wedding headdress.

Nabateans simply cleared out of the city, leaving behind a small group of negotiators who bought off the greedy Greeks. Meanwhile, the Seleucids swept through Jordan and occupied the country, a move matched by a counter-attack from Ptolemy II from the south in 284 BC. He took Ammon and Midian but left the Nabateans untouched. Thus the combined influence of the Greek kings led to a period of unrivalled prosperity, especially for the Nabateans who expanded their empire in the wake of the chaos left behind by the warring Greeks in the 2nd and 1st centuries BC. New towns rose quickly. Others were swiftly reworked to incorporate Greek architecture. The business-minded Nabateans found their skills as stone masons much in demand, while the adoption of Greek as an official language throughout the country enhanced the international standing of Jordan. Now Amman became famous as Philadelphia — and Jerash was the beautiful city of Antioch.

Despite continued strife with the Jews across the river, and wars and intrigues among the Ammonites, Edomites and Moabites, the Greek cities of Transjordan must have been havens of sanity. They formed into the Decapolis, and probably existed as commercial centres, controlling international trade routes — with the help of Nabateans — until they were sacked by the Jews who launched a massive campaign across the Jordan after the death of Antiochus IV in 164 BC.

Antiochus had sorely oppressed the Jews by banning their religious practices. Finally Judas Maccabeus led a rebellion against the Seleucids when they tried to set up an altar to their god Zeus in the Jewish temple in Jerusalem. Israel had collapsed into a decadent state of collaboration with the Seleucids by this stage and, with popular support, Judas was able to establish a dynasty and take control of the high priesthood. He soon invaded Ammon but in 163 BC, after a bitter campaign by the Syrian army, he was defeated and the Jews were massacred in Arbila (Irbid).

By 84 BC the Israelites were again on the warpath, this time with more success, under Alexander Jannaeus who swept through Transjordan, wrecking the Greek cities all the way to Wadi Hasa at the southern tip of the Dead Sea. Meanwhile the Nabateans, who were left untouched, seem to have established a parallel empire which stretched to Damascus. There is little evidence of direct rule from Petra but rather a sort of multi-national business empire built on an ability to compromise and bypass the murderous activities of the Greeks, Jews and other tribes, as they rampaged around the countryside.

By 64 BC however, the Romans, growing in confidence with the decline of the Greeks, moved on Damascus and a year later took Jerusalem, ending Greek "control" of the near east. Recognising the advantages of Greek civilisation amid the Iron Age locals and their warring chiefs, Pompey, the Roman emperor rebuilt the Greek cities and it was he who established the Decapolis. This loose

Above: One of the Dead Sea Scrolls, discovered by a shepherd in a cave at Khirbet Qumran — close to Jericho on the shores of the Dead Sea — in 1947.

alliance of Greco-Roman cities formed a commercial league, well disposed to one another, which shared common cultural, commercial, and institutional interests. There is some dispute about which cities came within the Decapolis. The earliest reference by Pliny talks of Scythopolis (Beisan on the west bank of the Jordan); Pella (Hippos on the eastern shore of the Jordan River); Damascus; Dion (possibly on the Yarmouk River); Canatha in Syria; Gadara (Umm Qais); Gerasa (Jerash); Philadelphia (Amman); and Raphana, also in Syria. Later Arbila (Irbid), Capitolia (Bait Rais), and Edrei (Deraa) were added. They did not establish a formal league as there is no evidence of their having any kind of central organization or shared administrative structure, but through them the Romans were able to spread their culture and power while allowing Transjordan almost total independence, provided taxes were paid regularly to Rome.

The Nabateans enjoyed a close relationship with the cities of the Decapolis and most of the elegant stone carving still visible at great sites like Umm Qais and Jerash is the work of Nabatean artists.

True to form, they bought independence from Rome for a lump sum. With the death of Pompey, the Decapolis had greater importance to the Romans who used the league as a military alliance to protect their interests against marauding Arab nomads, the Nabateans and the Jews. Outside the cities old enmities once again surfaced and much of Transjordan returned to tribal warfare.

With the backing of Mark Antony, Herod the Great was made King of Judea. This Jewish Roman citizen returned to Palestine in 39 BC to drive the Parthians out of Jerusalem and to take control of the lands lying east of the Jordan. Herod drove the Nabateans from the north of the country which was administered through the Decapolis. The central region fell under the Jewish kingdom of Palestine, while the Nabateans continued to hold the south.

Herod was succeeded by his notorious son, Herod Tetrarch, who married the daughter of the Nabatean king, Aretas IV, and then divorced her to marry his brother's unpleasant wife, Herodias. The insult provoked the Nabateans to attack, which they did with some success. Herod's decadent excesses at Machaerus in the mountains above the hot springs of Ma'in — where he loved to bathe in the boiling waterfalls — led to his denunciation by John the Baptist. Herod's stepdaughter, Salome, so entranced him with her dancing that Herod offered to give her almost anything she wanted as a gift of appreciation. Influenced by her mother, who had fallen foul of the prophet, Salome demanded John the Baptist's head on a platter — which was duly delivered to the horror of Herod's own court.

Finally, under Trajan in AD 106, the Nabatean kingdom was broken up and Pax Romana imposed all over Jordan. Camps built near Petra and Kerak by Trajan and Hadrian, his successor, to accommodate the Roman legionnaires can still be seen. The Romans also built a network of roads to usher in a period of unrivalled peace and prosperity in Jordan. The cities became great, while arts and culture flourished in resort towns like Gadara. Indeed, possibly the only potentially destabilising factor in the new Roman province of Arabia Petraea was the slow but steady growth of Christianity.

The conversion of Constantine in AD 333 made Christianity the Byzantine Empire's main religion and churches popped up everywhere. And although Jordan is overwhelmingly Muslim today, a large number of churches, maintained by small Christian communities, still stand. Almost every village has at least one church, co-existing with the neighbouring mosques in remarkable harmony.

But for all their devotion to matters artistic and spiritual, the Byzantine rulers were politically weak and slowly the empire began to wither. In AD 614 the

Persian princes, aided by the Jews, saw the opportunity to invade and swept through Jordan, destroying much of what the Byzantines had built. They were driven out by Heraclius (AD 610-641), who managed to bring the country under some kind of control at a time when a new and powerful force was emerging.

The teachings of the new Islamic faith, born under the guidance of the Prophet Mohammed, and the word of Allah fell on fertile ground among the desert-hardened Bedouin. Islam's combination of profound theology, rigorous piety, and strict self-discipline had an instant appeal to the tribesmen. A cardinal feature of the new religion was its egalitarianism. The equality of all adherents, irrespective of their social position or ethnic origins, ensured its popularity in the highly stratified societies outside Arabia. The Islamised Arabs led by the Prophet poured out of the desert and established an empire greater than Rome at its height — stretching from the Atlantic to the Indus River and spreading his teachings throughout the Near, Middle and eventually Far East (including the states of what became the Soviet Union), across Africa from east to west, and south to north, and over the Mediterranean and into Spain.

Above: One of the curious objects at Petra's museum is this winged Nabatean female sphinx in crouching position.

The first clash between Islam and Christianity came in AD 629 at Mu'ta near Kerak, where the defeated Muslims lost three generals. They regrouped at Medina to plan their campaigns under Khalid bin Walid — Islam's equivalent of Alexander the Great. The same year the Prophet Mohammed led an expedition into Jordan and took the Oasis of Tabuk. Showing sensitivity to the locals, however, he allowed the Christians in Aqaba and Adruh, and the Jews in Maqna just to the south, to continue their religious practises provided they paid tax in tribute.

In AD 633, a year after the Prophet Mohammed's death, the Muslims launched a massive invasion of Jordan and Palestine, first fighting in the Wadi Araba, where they defeated the patriarch of Palestine. They then swept through Palestine and Jordan, leaving only Caesarea unvanquished. Horrified by their swift success, Heraclius sent 50,000 troops who met the Arabs at the Wadi Yarmouk on 20 August, 636. The Muslims won the ensuing battle and by AD 640 Constantinople had lost Jordan and Syria. The soldiers of Islam marched on to Damascus where they established the first Muslim Caliphate under Mu'awiayah, the first Ummayed Dynasty.

Essentially men of the desert, the Ummayed Caliphs built palaces and forts deep in the Badia, an area ignored by previous rulers in favour of the more hospitable plains and Rift Valley escarpment. But the plotting of the Abbasids in their villages near Maan eventually brought the Ummayeds down in the 9th century AD. The Abbasids then transferred their capital to Baghdad. While the capital had been in Damascus, Jordan flourished because it was directly on the empire's most important trade routes. With the move east the country fell into decline, although it did remain part of the Arab empire until the 1099 invasion

Above: A finely carved lioness, its cub beneath it, stands atop Qasr al Abed, The Castle of the Slave. The castle, constructed by the powerful Tobiad family during the 2nd century BC, was partially destroyed by an earthquake in AD 362. The remains form the only surviving Hellenistic palace in the Middle East.

of the Crusaders who built the great castles of Shobak and Kerak and established the Kingdom of Jerusalem.

The invaders treated the indigenous population with savage contempt. In the name of Christianity crusader kings and dukes looked upon Jordan, especially, as a land to plunder. They appear to have been interested in controlling the King's Highway only for the high taxes they could extort from travellers and traders. When they did not tax the Arab caravans, the princes simply looted their goods.

Crusader rule was short-lived, however, for in 1187 Salah el-Din — Saladin — had re-taken Jerusalem and restored the country to the Arabs and, by the end of the 13th century, the Crusaders had been driven from the Holy Land. There followed a bloody invasion by Tamurlane's Mongols and, a century later, the Ottoman Turks took the whole of the Middle East to rule for the next 400 years with a system of government that was often *laissez faire*. In Jordan the only real

Above: Primitive milestone marks the Desert Highway.

concern of the Muslim Turks was to protect the pilgrim route to Mecca along the Desert Highway.

During the Ottoman hegemony, Palestine and Jordan remained obscure until the last century when European powers began to take an interest in the religious shrines of Jerusalem and the Holy Land, while other explorers began to search out the region's ancient history and archaeology. Most famous, perhaps, was the 'discovery' of Petra by a Swiss explorer in the middle of the last century.

World War I provided an ideal opportunity for a nascent Arab independence movement to work with the Allies to open a Middle Eastern front against the Ottoman Turks. In 1914 Sharif Hussein bin Ali, a direct descendent of the Prophet Mohammed and head of the Dhawi Awn clan of the Hashemite family took over the leadership of the Arabian nationalist movement. His family had ruled as Sharifs of Mecca for nine hundred years. With the exception of a handful of British officers, such as T E Lawrence, independence for the Arabs

Above: A symphony of light illuminates the interior of King Abdullah Mosque — constructed between 1982 and 1989, in honour of the late King Abdullah of Jordan. The mosque measures 12,000 square metres and accommodates 3,000 praying visitors.

was not a major concern of the Allies, but absorbing some of the Ottoman war machine certainly was. By June 1916, Hussein's son, Emir Feisal, had assumed command of the guerrilla armies of camel and horsemen. The other son, Emir Abdullah, also led part of the army, though Lawrence found his interest in international diplomacy and politics inappropriate in a war-time leader. Indeed, the British officer was scathing in his judgement of Abdullah which history, especially the Emir's memoirs, shows were a gross underestimation of his worth.

There was no shortage of volunteers from the free men of the desert to pursue political liberty, but as Lawrence wrote at the beginning of his epic *Seven Pillars of Wisdom*: 'They were a people of spasms, of upheavals, of ideas, the race of the individual genius.' A little later he adds: 'The Bedouin of the desert, born and grown up in it, had embraced with all his soul this nakedness too harsh for volunteers, the reason, felt but inarticulate, that there he found himself

Opposite: Four faces of modern Jordan — Bedouin woman carrying her daughter; Bedouin warrior; shepherd, descendant of slaves but now a free Jordanian; Jordanian schoolgirl.

indubitably free.' Men of such passionate individuality do not make the best soldiers in the Prussian tradition and the Arab revolutionary leaders had to skilfully massage their men into disciplined units through a mixture of threats, teasing, and the promise of great booty to be found on the Turkish trains running to the Ottoman base at Medina. But whatever the tribesmen lacked in military etiquette, they more than made up in their courage and daring and improvised raids against well-defended Turkish positions.

Only a year after entering the fray the Arabs, to the surprise of Allies and Turks alike, took Aqaba and soon after, by a gruelling journey across the desert, captured the 'shining oasis' of Azraq. Both towns became bases from which to attack the Hijaz Railway. With only minor setbacks the Arabs, together with British troops, took Jerusalem almost exactly 400 years from the beginning of Ottoman rule. But the Arabs were not entirely happy. For, having united to free themselves from the yoke of foreign masters from the Hijaz to the Euphrates, they found themselves, at the end of the Great War, placed under a League of Nations mandate.

Above: A Bedouin woman attending her flock is covered in black as protection from the intense desert sun.

Transjordan came under the British, for whom Emir Abdullah had a special affection. But by 1920 he had moved his troops to Maan with the aim of total liberation. In March the following year he took up residence in Amman and set up the Emirate of Transjordan, swiftly winning recognition from the British who agreed to Abdullah's reign under a resident British minister. Soon after, Feisal was installed as King of Iraq.

In 1922, Winston Churchill, then colonial secretary in London, divided Syria into two, the south being made up of Jordan and Palestine. Some members of the British government wanted to turn Palestine into an independent Jewish state but, as a result of fierce lobbying, Abdullah managed to head this idea off, temporarily. Transjordan was left out of the equation but, as people in search of a Jewish homeland continued to arrive in Palestine, Arabs in the region rose in revolt in 1936 fearing the Jewish Diaspora would swamp them. The British sent the Peel Commission to investigate the causes behind the revolt and to look into ways of accommodating both the Jews (wishing to return "home" after millennia in exile), and the indigenous Arab population. In 1937 the commission proposed a compromise. 'Green Palestine', the best agricultural areas, would remain in Arab hands and join Jordan under Emir Abdullah's reign. The Jews would be given a narrow strip of land extending from Tel Aviv to Haifa with land corridors to the shores of Tiberias.

Anxious to avoid a perpetuation of the biblical land wars into the 20th century, Emir Abdullah accepted Peel's proposals as a workable compromise. But hardliners among the Arabs flatly rejected it. The Jewish leadership was unenthusiastic too, as the proposal left them with a tiny area of land. But, much to the Emir's dismay, it was the Arabs who so vocally resisted any compromise.

MISS

Another attempt at finding a bloodless solution to the need to find a home for the Jews in the Near East came with a British Government White Paper in 1939. This would have granted Palestine full independence but the boundaries were drawn so that Palestinians were in a two-thirds majority. Again Abdullah seized the opportunity to head-off an Arab-Israeli conflict. Extremists on both sides ensured the plan was stillborn.

While the British scaled back their interest and influence in the Emirate, Abdullah held sway over Jordan as monarch until 1939 when he began laying the ground of consensus politics, first establishing a cabinet of advisors and later a twenty-man legislative assembly. These measures served to underline the Hashemite commitment to the Islamic concept of consultative politics which has been a major distinguishing mark of their rule. In the same spirit King Hussein embarked on the complete democratization of the Jordanian political process in the 1980s. In the Second World War he sent the Arab Legion, under British and Arab officers, to fight on the side of the Allies in Iraq and Syria against the Vichy French. On 25 May 1946, as the British mandate came to an end the Emirate was transformed into a Kingdom with Abdullah on the throne.

But with total independence came a new set of problems, which made the region politically much like it was in biblical times. In 1947, the United Nations voted to partition Palestine to create a Jewish homeland called Israel. Under the UN plan much of Palestine, including Gaza and the west bank of the Jordan, would remain in Palestinian hands. Israel would extend from Haifa to Eilat, next door to Aqaba.

Above: Schoolgirls in national dress celebrate the 40th anniversary of King Hussein's reign.

Thus most of the land given to Israel would have been barren semi-desert while the Palestinians held the fertile Jordan Valley as well as the potent religious symbol of Jerusalem. Abdullah advised his Palestinian colleagues to accept the plan. But his advice was ignored and a year later, war broke out between the Israelis and the Arabs. Almost overnight, Jordan's population doubled as thousands of Palestinians fled the fighting. In 1949 there was an armistice and, the following year, the West Bank voted to join Transjordan to form the Hashemite Kingdom of Jordan.

In 1951, however, while attending prayers at the Al-Aqsa Mosque in Jerusalem, one of Islam's holiest shrines, King Abdullah fell to an Arab assassin's bullet. Through his attempts to mediate and compromise he paid the price of being a pragmatist among Semitic people, noted more for their passion than political poise. One bullet aimed at the King also hit his grandson, Al-Hussein bin Talal, but glanced off a military bar the sixteen-year-old prince was wearing. The reign of the prince's father, Talal, was cut short by illness and he abdicated in 1952.

King Hussein was not able to take on the full responsibilities as monarch until he was 18 years old. News of his accession came three months before his 17th

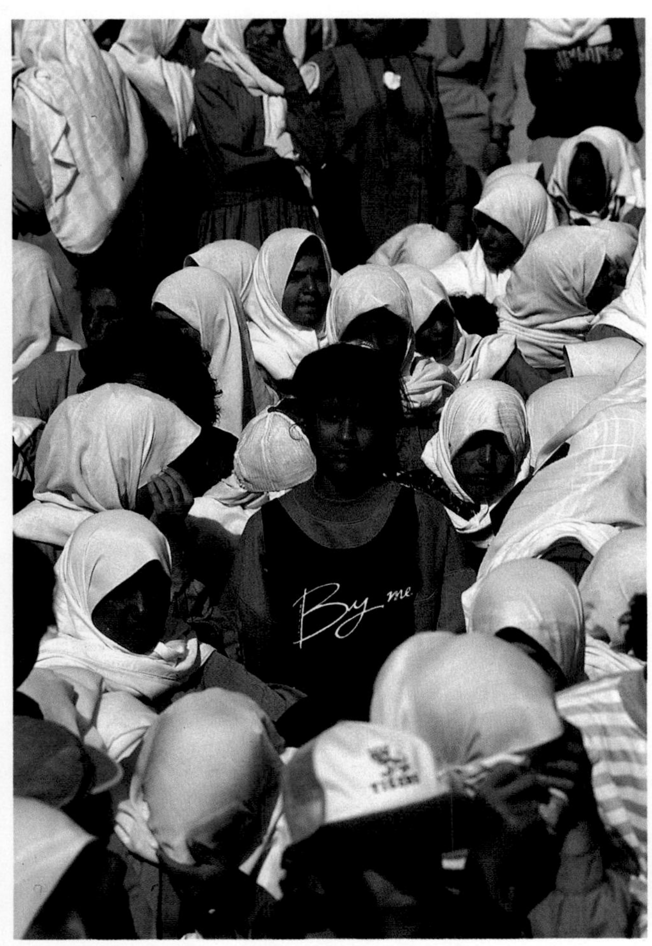

Above: Contrast of new and old: a girl's modern dress amidst friends in traditional costume.

birthday. This was, history would show, a blessing in disguise for it allowed the young king-to-be a year's respite from the problems of government which was put to good use.

Time did not allow for university but Hussein took a crash-course in military matters at the Royal Military Academy, Sandhurst — Britain's officer academy.

After the intensive training eighteen-year-old men are considered fit to lead soldiers into battle. For officer cadet King Hussein, however, Sandhurst was to provide the only formal training to prepare him for the turbulent years ahead. During this time as ruler of Jordan he was often in the thick of firefights or at the dangerous end of two-score assassination attempts. Military skills he learned, but his diplomatic finesse, which set him apart as the only leader in the Middle or Near East whose word was taken by Arab and Jew alike, came instinctively, his only guide being the Hashemite tradition of compromise and desire for Arab unity.

Until his death in 1999 Hussein's commitment to that elusive concept was the mainstay of his policies and initiatives in the region. But a lesser man would have given up on the Arabs as an irreconcilable and fractious people. Indeed King Hussein's ambition to at least persuade Arab nations to act in the best interests of the Arab peoples at large seemed to many a hopeless fantasy. Not least because the essence of the Arab character is the independence of the Bedu. In the years which followed King Hussein's assumption of royal responsibilities, however, the Bedu would prove his most loyal supporters and dearest friends in times of need.

After the 1948 war, Jordan was flooded with 650,000 Palestinians who had fled from Israel. The country was no longer the poor but happy place King Abdullah was so proud of. The influx of Palestinians strained a creaking and stagnant economy to breaking point — although many of the new immigrants brought a high level of education and proved to be a fillip for the professions and commerce. The refugee camps became seething hotbeds of political intrigue and discontent. The socialist Ba'athist movement from Syria took flame among the disenfranchised Palestinians looking ruefully west to the homes they had fled, and among the well armed Iraqis to the east.

A progressive leader, King Hussein insisted, against the advice of conservative members of his court, on allowing multi-party elections in the Kingdom for the first time on 21 October 1956. Voting took place as thousands of Palestinians and Jordanians were in a state of rage fuelled by Israeli reprisal raids on the West Bank against Palestinian infiltrators. A left wing government was elected but some of its members appeared to be close to Nasser in Egypt and the Syrians, neither of whom were well disposed to Jordan and its Hashemite King. The government of Prime Minister Suleiman Naboulsi, anxious to open relations with the Soviet Union and suspicious of the influence of the Royalist Bedouin in the army, raised tensions in Jordan. The

Opposite: His Majesty King Talal with his three sons, Hussein, Hassan and Mohammed.

Left: Her Majesty Queen Zein el Sharaf with His Majesty King Hussein in Lausanne in 1952.

Right: His Majesty King Hussein with his two brothers Prince Mohammed and Prince Hassan and their sister Princess Basma.

Bedouin regiments suspected a plot against the King by the fiercely Arab nationalist but neo-Marxist Free Officers Movement. Military manoeuvres became suspicious while mobs entered the streets of Amman fired up by Cairo Radio's support for the prime minister. Revolution was in the air and members of Hussein's household demanded to know whether they should stand and fight or pack their bags. The King stood firm.

Plotters ordered the First Armoured Car Regiment, a Bedouin unit, to enter Amman and surround the Royal Palace. This was a mistake as the officers of the regiment swore a secret oath of loyalty to the King and kept him informed of what was afoot. The large garrison in Zarqa swore similar oaths. Soon the Zarqa units rose against their officers while the Armoured Car Regiment surrounded the Palace, not to capture the King but to protect him.

Eventually what began as an attempted coup fizzled out because of the loyalty of most of the army, though a number of senior officers were court martialed and sentenced to death. In all cases, sentences were commuted by Royal command and one of the alleged chief conspirators, a general and close confidant of the King, was allowed to leave the country unmolested and a few years later returned to take up a career in the diplomatic corps.

The lack of desire for revenge would be repeated many times by Hussein. In few other countries would conspirators have kept their lives. Yet the King maintained his humanitarian stance against those who plotted his downfall. The coup attempt left Amman in a state of tension, plagued by riots and

Opposite: His Majesty King Abdullah I of Jordan followed by his brother King Feisal I of Iraq.

Above: Jordanian national flags flutter high above the crowds in Amman at the 40th anniversary celebrations of King Hussein's reign.

demonstrations. But soon order was restored by Ibrahim Hashim's new government and especially by Samir Rifai, a staunchly loyal Palestinian, who introduced martial law across the country, banned political parties, and quietly purged the army of its disloyal officers.

True to his dream of Arab unity, in 1958 King Hussein signed a unity pact with Iraq which was ruled by his cousin and former Harrow schoolmate, King Feisal. The union brought diplomatic, education, military and finance policy under one umbrella. Feisal was the head of the combined state with Hussein as his deputy. "This is the happiest day of my life, a great day in Arab history. We are under one banner of Arabism, which our great grandfather, Hussein bin Ali the Great, carried in the great Arab revolt," King Hussein ecstatically told his people on the radio after signing the union treaty on 14 February 1958.

His joy was short-lived. Five months later Iraqi officers launched a coup in Baghdad and murdered King Feisal and most of the rest of the Iraqi Hashemite royal family. Hussein wisely resisted the urge to launch a punitive raid against Iraq as it was clear that the large Iraqi army had fallen in behind the conspirators.

Meanwhile his own position looked precarious as the coup in Baghdad was supposed to happen concurrently with one staged against himself. The British sent paratroopers to his aid and, although the crisis died down, at the time few thought Hussein would survive. But he did so by energetically travelling the country and winning the support of soldiers wherever he went. In addition the US government stepped in with \$50 million in aid for the King and the British followed up with £1 million.

Above: Thousands of cheering Jordanians celebrate the 40th anniversary of King Hussein's accession to the throne.

In November of that year two Syrian jets attempted to force the King and his British pilot into the ground as they flew to Switzerland for a well-earned break. These experiences served to mature the young King and steel him for the trials which lay ahead.

During the early 1960s the Palestinian fedayeen stepped up their raids on Israel from the West Bank, causing concern in Amman that the formidable Israeli military machine would soon launch raids deep inside Jordanian territory. Hussein showed his disapproval of such acts by closing the offices of the Palestinian Liberation Organization in Jordan and demanding that its leadership base itself elsewhere. It did so in Gaza, the ancient seat of the Philistines. But this was not enough. Soon the Syrians began to shell Israeli farmers from the Golan Heights. The Israelis retaliated, not against Syria but against Jordan, south of Hebron just beyond the 1948 Israel-Jordan demarcation line. A Jordanian patrol lost 21 men in an ambush and there was an outcry in Amman where King Hussein was bitterly criticised for not allowing Palestinian armed groups to operate along the fault-line with Israel.

The debacle was seized upon by Egypt and Syria as an issue with which to convince the King that no matter how he favoured talk over fighting, he would need strong defences in the event of an Israeli attack. He was, rightly, convinced that Israel had designs on the West Bank and upon Jerusalem. But it was not clear to whom he could turn for support.

The attack on the village of Samu had been a major blow and his loyalty to the Arab cause was called into question because he refused to do battle with Israel over it.

Above: Young women perform a traditional folk dance, cloaked in the Jordanian national colours.

On 7 April 1967 Israeli farmers ploughing south of Lake Tiberias were shelled by Syrians from the Golan above. The ploughing had been a ruse to provoke the Syrians who then suffered from an air and land bombardment by secretly assembled Israeli forces. The attacks steadily increased tension in the region despite United Nations efforts to defuse the situation. On 5 June 1967 the Israeli Air Force launched a pre-emptive strike against Egypt's air force, and in less than three hours the Egyptians were left with 32 aircraft out of a total of 340 combat jets.

Although the Egyptians were supposed to keep Jordan fully informed as to the progress of a possible war they proved to be profoundly mendacious. They told King Hussein that three quarters of the Israeli air force had been destroyed and that a counter attack was under way. Jordan was asked to open a new front against Israel, while in fact the Egyptian land army was suffering heavily under a Jewish onslaught.

The Syrian air force was slow to respond while, after initial success, the Iraqi and Royal Jordanian air forces were swiftly overwhelmed. By morning the following day the Egyptians were in a state of disarray under an Israeli blitz when Jordan was ordered to join up with a fictitious Egyptian force advancing on Hebron. The result was a fiasco leaving Jordanian forces hopelessly outgunned in Jerusalem, which fell to the Israelis. It was clear to the Egyptians, who were in overall command of the campaign, that the West Bank, including Jerusalem, would be lost. The results were catastrophic. Two hundred thousand refugees again poured into what was left of the Kingdom. The war was lost and Jordan's Palestinian population was now 850,000 people.

Above: Pipers of the Jordanian Armed Forces Band lead a march past in honour of King Hussein.

In November 1967 the UN Security Council passed resolution 242 which was supposed to establish peace in the Middle East where none had existed since pre-biblical times. King Hussein gave the plan his full support and played a significant part through his diplomatic connections. But the PLO refused to accept it and the Israelis refused to abide by its demands and pull out of the Occupied Territories until the Arabs agreed on terms for a peace agreement. The latter would have forced the Arabs to acknowledge that Israel existed — a concession few were prepared to meet, though the King, in pursuit of peace and some justice for the Palestinians, was anxious to see an end to such absurd self-delusions.

Persistent problems followed this impasse. In Jordan members of the PLO's guerrilla units operated from the centre of major cities, and carried their arms openly. They harassed both Palestinian and other Jordanian civilians for 'donations' to their cause, and steadily lost the sympathy of many Arab nationalists in the country. Then, when the Hashemite government banned the open carrying of guns the PLO fighters rose against the King. And again much of the rest of the Arab world cried out against King Hussein's 'repression'. At one point the King himself was involved in a gun fight and had to shoot through the window of his own car to save himself. He received a back injury during the incident.

But his own troops were kept harshly in check. He did not want to shed Jordanian blood on his own soil. After a few weeks King Hussein managed to secure an agreement under which the PLO agreed a peace settlement. But the leadership was incapable of ensuring it. Fighting broke out again in the

Opposite: Glimpse of the Royal Box: King Hussein, Queen Noor, Prince Hassan and Princess Sarvath at the 40th Anniversary celebrations in Amman.

Above: Representing the Royal Jordanian Air Force, one of the fighter planes used in the 1960s and '70s is put on display.

Opposite: His Majesty King Abdullah II and Her Majesty Queen Rania.

streets of Amman. Soldiers in heavy tanks and armoured personnel carriers found it difficult work flushing out the fedayeen from building to building and from the ramshackle back streets of the refugee camps.

In September King Hussein was again nearly killed in an ambush. Radical Palestinian elements then staged the hijacking of three airliners and forced them to land in Jordan, close to pro-PLO Iraqi soldiers based in Jordan. A Syrian tank division invaded and headed for Irbid. They were beaten off but not before the US had put a combat fleet in the area on full alert while the Russians did the same in support of Syria. The Syrian tank division outnumbered the Jordanian force sent to block its advance, but the invaders were outshot and outmanoeuvred, and eventually driven back across the border.

By the end of September a ceasefire was agreed again. Seven months later the fedayeen were ordered out of Amman. But they fought back around Ajlun and Zarqa — the former now a tranquil tourist attraction, the latter a prosperous commercial centre. Eventually, the government won through.

Above: Arab Druze dancers in traditional costume.

In October 1973 the Jordanian armed forces were again involved in fighting, this time in support of Syria against Israeli attempts to take Golan.

Subsequently the PLO was allowed back into Jordan and changed its public image and military tactics away from terrorism and channelled its energies into the Intifada — the popular Palestinian uprising against Israeli occupation. The Palestinians no longer worked through intermediaries, nor did King Hussein accept the responsibility of representing their needs and policies.

Realising the necessity for a strong guiding force in Jordan, King Hussein appointed his younger brother — Amir Hassan bin Talal — as Crown Prince on 1 April 1965. Prince Hassan's interests stretched far beyond his own nation and for more than three decades the Crown Prince was a driving force behind efforts to ensure basic human rights for the people of the Arab World. Prince Hassan's endeavours on behalf of benevolence — between all men — made him a leading and well-respected figure in the Middle East and on the world

Above: Skydive by the Jordanian Army Special Forces at the 40th anniversary celebrations in honour of King Hussein's accession to the throne.

stage. In 1984 he founded the Crown Prince Award Scheme, which has benefitted thousands of children across Jordan.

Having survived so many attempts on his life, it was perhaps ironic that King Hussein should eventually succumb to illness at the relatively young age of 63. In the 1990s it became known that he was having treatment for cancer and towards the end of 1998 his health deteriorated rapidly. After a final and unsuccessful round of treatment in the United States, King Hussein expressed a wish to die in his own country. He was flown back to Jordan on 5 February 1999 and taken straight to hospital where he was put on a life support system. He was pronounced dead two days later and was laid to rest on 8th February in a funeral attended by kings, presidents and dignitaries from more than 50 nations, as well as an estimated one million Jordanian mourners.

Tributes poured in from leaders across the world. Typical of these was the message from President Clinton, who said: "It takes a rare kind of courage to be a peacemaker — the courage to learn from the past and imagine a better future. When peace finally comes to the Middle East, his name will be inscribed upon it. That day, King Hussein will smile on us one more time."

King Hussein's successor, the 37-year-old Prince Abdullah (Hussein's son by his second marriage to Princess Muna) was an army commander with little political experience when his father unexpectedly named him as his heir in January 1999, shortly before his death. Hussein's brother, Prince Hassan, lost his standing as heir to the throne in that shake-up.

King Abdullah II was enthroned on 9 June 1999, formally taking over from his late father four months after his death. By his side was his wife, Queen Rania, aged 28. Later, during a private reception at Amman's hilltop Raghadan Palace, the new king presented Rania with a $2 million gem-covered crown that belonged to Hussein's late wife, Queen Alia, who died in a 1977 helicopter crash. Like Queen Alia, Rania is a Palestinian, helping to cement the loyalty of Jordan's majority Palestinian population to the ruling Hashemite dynasty.

Outside the palace, Bedouin tribesmen, who form the bedrock of support for the monarchy, waved colourful Jordanian flags and Abdullah's portrait.

"Our blood and soul we sacrifice for you, Abdullah," they chanted.

Jordan's future seems secure under the Hashemite family's cloak of leadership. Its formidable lineage — which stretches back to the Prophet Mohammed — traces its descendance through Fatima, the Prophet's daughter. King Abdullah's line, known as the Sharifian House of Aoun, spawned — for centuries — masters of the Hijaz, at Arabia's heart. Abdullah II is the fourth king in Jordan's relatively brief history as a full-blown nation state.

2 · ON THE TRAIL OF KINGS

Previous pages: New blends with old at Umm Qais, once one of the ten cities in the Decapolis.

'I am from Gadara, fond of the muses,' reads an inscription on the tombstone of Apion of Gadara, whose homesick death is recorded in a small town east of Lake Tiberias. As a provincial outpost of the Greek and Roman empires, Gadara was a place for worship of the arts, blessed by a natural setting of exquisite beauty, on the top of a limestone and basalt hill overlooking the River Yarmouk and the hot springs of Hammeh. It is easy to understand how Apion must have longed for his home in what is now Umm Qais. At its height, Gadara boasted three theatres, including one at the thermal baths in the Yarmouk valley. It also had an unfinished hippodrome, as well as some of the finest wine to be tasted in the Byzantine empire. Even today, the fertile alkaline soil throws up a spring riot of wild flowers that carpet the escarpment to the bottom of the valley with deep-red poppies, dandelions, daisies, orchids, yellow-flowered shrubs and tulips.

The city was first mentioned in 333 BC when it fell to Alexander the Great's armies during the Battle of Issos River. After the death of the military genius, Gadara was settled by the Ptolemies, Alexander's heirs to the southern half of his empire. The Ptolemies developed it as a military and border post commanding the Yarmouk valley frontier with their enemies — and cousins — the Seleucids, who inherited the northern section of the Greek empire and were based in Antioch, northern Syria. The importance of Gadara as a frontier base is reflected in the change of its name in the Middle Ages to Umm Qais which, according to a German expert on the city, Thomas Weber, derived from the word *mkes*, early Arabic for frontier station. At the centre of vital trade routes, Gadara developed a cosmopolitan character that rivalled Athens in its refinement.

Above: Students enjoying a trip to the Roman ruins at Umm Qais.

Amid its ruins today, one can see how it evolved from a frontier town into a resort. Its temperate setting on top of the escarpment is given added romance on cool mornings when warm steam rises from the hot springs of Hammeh, a few kilometres below. In ancient times, Romans and Greeks would have relaxed in the sulphur-rich baths, dining on locally grown olives, fresh bread and fruit while drinking the wine produced on ideally sloping local hillsides. As dusk settled over the Yarmouk they would make their way slowly back up to the city, perhaps to watch a show — anything from gladiator fighting to poetry recitals. Or, perhaps, the occasional semi-pornographic frolics of naked young women in the baths of the Nymphaeum in the town centre.

As the city prospered it became a desirable acquisition. In 218 BC, Antiochus III marched on the mountain redoubt which he took only after a prolonged siege. Again, in the 1st century AD, Gadara was attacked, this time by the Jewish Hasmonean leader, Alexander Jannaeus who took it after ten months' siege. It finally fell after he cut off its sophisticated water supply. But with the success of Pompey's campaign to take southern Syria, Gadara soon enjoyed a renaissance.

Above: Built from local black basalt, the entrance of Roman tombs at Umm Qais is partially hidden.

After the last siege the city was rebuilt as a gesture to please Demetrius the Gadarene — one of the emperor's favourites and a freedman originally from the city. With the arrival of Pax Romana, Gadara bathed in the light of spectacular prosperity, joined the Decapolis, and became part of that commercial and cultural league. It blocked the further expansion of the Nabatean empire from Petra. Eventually, Gadara developed a fantastic water supply system, one which continues to excite much controversy today. The ruins comprise vast underground passageways that run beneath the city in all directions.

Weber, for one, is convinced that these were to channel water around the town from an aqueduct served by the Ain el-Turab perennial spring, 13 kilometres east of Umm Qais. Others, especially earlier archaeologists, believed that the water for Gadara came by aqueduct from the swamp lakes near the Syrian village of Dilli, 60 kilometres south of Damascus, via Deraa, Wadi ez-Zedi, over the Wadi esh-Shellalah by bridge, and along the Ajlun range to the

Opposite: Remnants of an ancient time — a fig tree prospers above a cluster of fallen pillars.

ancient city. Wonderful though such a theory may sound, it is the least convincing because of the wild variations in altitude the artificial stream would have had to overcome.

But the mystery of the water supply in Umm Qais deepens. The assumption is that the underground channel which runs at a slight incline from east to west ten metres below the surface of the acropolis hill was for distributing water. The sharp S-bends were perhaps installed to slow the flow to allow silt to settle before it was used for drinking and irrigation on the fertile plateau west of the city. Responsibility for maintaining the fresh water probably rested in the hands of a Roman official: the curator aquarum. Thus a giant plumbing system remains the most obvious explanation for the passageways beneath Umm Qais.

But some experts are unconvinced. Why, for example, were the walls and floors of the tunnels not sealed with tiles or plaster as was usual? Instead, the walls were striated by the tools of the excavators who worked by lamplight in the cool depths of the mountain.

Earlier innovators built hydraulic systems the envy of engineers today. And these irrigation networks are scattered throughout Jordan, especially in the north-west of the country, which was one of the most prosperous agricultural regions in the Greek empire. Its wealth came about through the ability of the Jordanians to utilise every available stretch of farm land — because of their ingenious irrigation systems.

Above: These ramshackle stone arches were once part of the impressive Roman city of Gadara.

Although Judaism held a firm grip over much of the west Jordan Valley, the north east of the Great Rift Valley was still in the hands of pagan gods. Jesus is said to have stepped ashore on the east coast of Lake Tiberias (the Sea of Galilee). There the two 'madmen' challenged the Son of God to drive the Devil out of them. When Jesus uttered the simple command 'go', the swine rushed to their death in Galilee. Soon after, 'the citizens of Gadara came to meet Jesus. And when they saw Him, they beseeched Him to leave their coasts'. Christianity took time to take root in Gadara. In fact, two Christians were martyred there in AD 303. But, by the end of the century, Christianity became the official religion of the Byzantine empire and had firm sway over the city. The word of Christianity, however, was soon swept away by the arrival of Islam. The success of the Caliphs at the battle of Fihl (Pella) and Yarmouk in AD 635 and AD 636 gave them control of north Jordan and the lucrative trade and pilgrim routes to Mecca from Damascus, as well as the routes from the east to the coast. But, in return for an annual tax, the new rulers allowed Christians and others to follow their own religions.

In the 7th and 8th centuries Gadara was hit by a series of plagues and earthquakes which caused it to fall into terminal decline, only briefly reversed under Ottoman rule.

The Turks rebuilt much of the city and added a number of elegant

farmhouses. One of these now houses the museum. Residents of the Ottoman village of Umm Qais were moved to a new hamlet to protect the monuments of Gadara but their houses have since fallen into disrepair. Although depopulation of the ancient site was intended to protect its relics, ironically it may lead to the destruction of the remaining buildings, many of which are only in use as outhouses. Among them are ancient tombs whose massive basalt-rock doors, with hinges sunk into living rock, provide ideal pens for sheep and goats.

To enter one of these subterranean caves, visitors lean with all their might against a door which has been in place for two millennia, to stumble into a silent tomb. Sunlight slants in, lighting up the interior of an ancient burial place blackened by Bedouin fires.

Although little of ancient Gadara has yet been restored, a walk through its ruined streets, especially in spring when the locally quarried black basalt and stark white limestone are offset by blooming wild flowers, is a peaceful wander back in time. This cosmopolitan area was also well-known for the sorcery and witchcraft that was practiced in the rock-cut tombs scattered on the hills around the town, especially on the northern escarpment. There visitors pick their way among the ancient tombs and modern trench defences built to guard against attacks from Israel, across the Yarmouk Valley. The madmen whom Jesus cured were said to have lived among these tombs. In the 4th century the Byzantine writer Epiphanius spoke of a ring of sorcerers working near the ancient Roman baths of Hammath Gader — modern Hammeh. There dead people were buried in wooden or stone caskets set deep inside the walls of the caves in rounded holes, called loculi.

Above: Bedouin woman, with tattoo markings on her face, portrays the traditional side of Jordan.

To the east of Gadara, next to the modern village, is the Tomb of the Germani with its basalt facade. The threshold still has the hinges which held the double rock doors, while above the portico rests the inscription dedicating the tomb to two members of the Germanus family. Inside the large square hallway steps lead up to the two burial chambers.

A few paces further on into the town stands another tomb, less flamboyant but remarkable for its doors which still function. This burial place appears to have been dedicated to the town's social secretary, Lucius Sentius Modestus. He was Gadara's 'Holy Herald', and not only responsible as such for attending sacrifices but also for organizing athletic and cultural functions in honour of local gods: a busy job in a resort city like Gadara.

After the tombs comes the acropolis hill, atop of which the abandoned Ottoman village now sits and where the Umm Qais museum displays some of the finest pieces of sculpture and mozaic floors rescued from the elements. Most impressive is the headless statue of Tyche, goddess of Gadara, which was moved from the wreckage of the main theatre in the west of the town. The museum is the home of the Rusan family, who traded between Haifa and

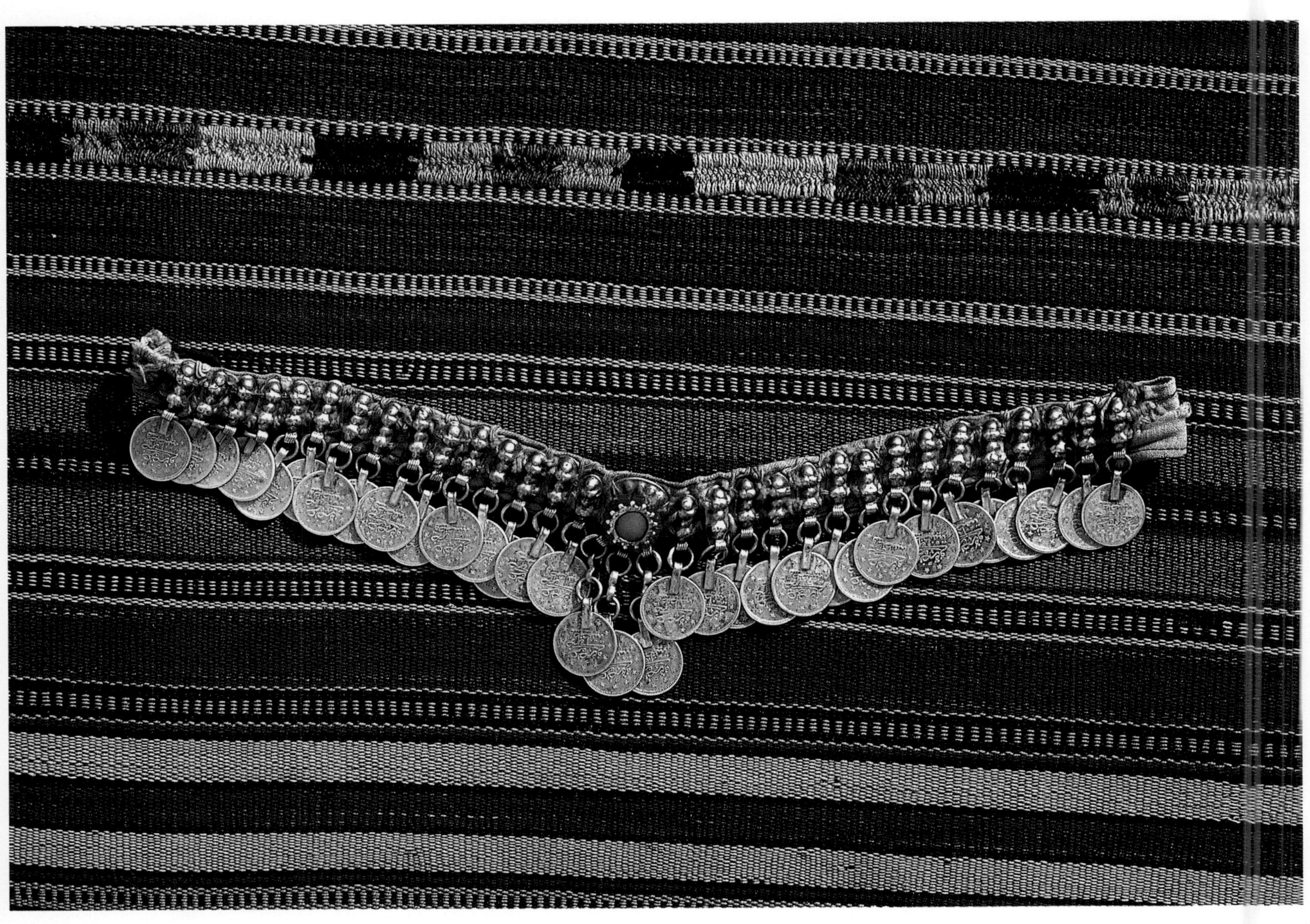

Above: Turkish coins, a legacy of the Ottoman Empire, form part of a fine headband.

Damascus at the end of the last century in much the same way as their Gadarene ancestors 2,000 years beforehand. It is easily distinguished by the dome above its courtyard. Nearby another restored building, Beit Melkawi, serves as headquarters for archaeologists working at Umm Qais. In the centre of the courtyard, which is adorned with olives, fruit trees and vines, stands a Roman-era cistern that still provides the residents of the Beit Melkawi with fresh drinking water. Both houses have magnificent views of the Jordan River Valley to one side and the Yarmouk gorge to the other.

Close to the acropolis lies the west theatre. The smaller of Gadara's two theatres, it collapsed after a series of earthquakes but is still well preserved compared with the north theatre, of which little remains. Made entirely of black basalt, the smaller theatre commands a great view over the Jordan Valley. Stone tickets dropped by punters to the regular shows have been found amid the overgrown ruins. Beneath the seats lie passageways for theatregoers,

Above: Bedouin sheikh in the cool of his goat hair tent.

underground entrances and exit tunnels built out of rock. Even the ceilings and the beams which support them are made of basalt.

Walking along Gadara's colonnaded main street, *decumanus maximus*, eagle-eyed visitors will pick out the grooves in the pavements made by chariots running through the town. Beneath the road short stretches of a drainage system still function. Just north of the west theatre is the dramatic basilica terrace — one end embedded in living rock while the other is supported by a series of arched vaults that provided street-level shopfronts. Other traders would have had wooden stalls lining the streets. The basilica was made from recycled Roman buildings of the 2nd and 3rd centuries and the circular path around the church is marked by geometric tiles. Such paths are common in Byzantine places of worship. They symbolise the change the congregation makes from matters temporal to matters spiritual as it enters the great church.

If life in the bustle of the marketplace and the chariot traffic became too much

Above: Bedouin woman pours fresh ewe's milk into a bucket.

for the Gadarenes they were able to escape to the quiet of the baths in the city. The remains of one set of baths, about 100 metres from the shops, reveal an elaborate and luxurious haven for pleasure seekers.

After changing, clients could wander through the cold bath, *frigidarium*, the warmer bath, *tepidarium*, and the scorcher, *caldarium*. Hot air and steam circulated under the floor, which was supported by short pillars, and through terracotta pipes set in the walls. When the Ummayeds subdivided the baths, some of the rooms fell into disuse until the whole lot was brought down in the 8th century by a series of earthquakes.

As the basis of all life, water was deeply worshipped by the Roman settlers and their allies in Jordan where a number of cities, including Jerash and Amman, have nymphaeums dedicated to the water nymphs. The nymphaeum in Gadara is just across the road from the main bath complex. Guides to the antiquities of Jordan are a little coy when asked what they were used for, and what went on at the ceremonies.

Naturally gracious and unwilling to offend, the guides usually reply that the nymphaeums were used for 'special ceremonies', involving some of the most beautiful women and priestesses in the town. Others remark that they were merely ornamental fountains. The detail is left to the imagination of the visitor.

However, Gadara's most impressive structure is not a place of the living, but of the dead. The North Mausoleum is almost completely intact and fills an underground chamber nine metres by eleven. A stone inscription by the great crypt reads: 'To you I say, passer by: As you are, I was; as I am, you will be. Use life as a mortal.' Despite the chilling prophecy the mausoleum is quietly beautiful. It was once reached by passing by a huge gate that straddled the town's main street as an extra-mural entrance to the city. Inside the entrance hall stone-lined tombs are stacked like nests in a dovecote. One floor was decorated with a wonderful mosaic that named three people buried there in the Byzantine period. Now this monument to Valentinianos, Eustathia and Protogenia hangs in the Beit Rusan museum in the old Ottoman village. Two sphinxes which crouched at the doorway to the original Roman mausoleum have been re-buried to protect them from natural erosion and vandals.

No Greco-Roman temples have yet been discovered at Umm Qais. Indeed, its greatest treasures still lie buried but there is evidence from coins found on the site, where they were originally minted, that the locals worshipped Zeus (Jupiter). The god is depicted on the local currency sitting in a shrine naked to the waist. The presence of the white statue of Tyche is further evidence that there might have been a temple dedicated to her. Other coins also show temples dedicated to the Three Graces. All this has an air of mystery, grace and drama. But modern Umm Qais is a mundane village filled with the unattractive bunker-like buildings that pepper the whole of the Middle East.

In the valley below, however, there is a modern triumph. The East Ghor Canal, Jordan's most ambitious irrigation project, starts near Umm Qais and leads into the Jordan Valley.

From the town, one road leads to the ancient site of Pella, the city south of Umm Qais which was a refuge for early Christians fleeing persecution in Jerusalem in the 2nd century. The road west follows the ancient trading route which links up with the King's Highway at Amman, while the junction of one of the two roads to Iraq, Syria and Saudi Arabia is at Irbid.

Irbid is redolent of spices, freshly baked bread, herbs and open-air cooking. After the sterile grandeur of Gadara, or Jerash, travellers cannot help but plunge themselves into the bustle of this modern city whose people have managed to preserve much of the best that Arabia has to offer — especially in food and spices.

Irbid sits at the centre of the fertile highland plateau north of the mountains of Gilead in the grain basket of Jordan, where endless fields of green and gold quilt the landscape.

Striking out east from the town towards the Iraqi border the road passes close to Ramtha, on the plateau south of the Yarmouk and its gorge. On a drizzly night in 1918, the leaders of the Arab Revolt suffered a severe blow. They had planned to destroy the railway bridge at Tell al Shehab on the border with Syria. But as they were making their last-minute preparations one of them, Abd el Kader, slipped away and revealed their plans to the Turks. The destruction of the bridge would have been disastrous for the Turks, cutting the east-west Ottoman supply route, and a vital victory for the Revolt. It would also have been a fine finale to months of attacks on the Hijaz Railway. To destroy the bridge meant a 140-kilometre day-and-night camel march from Azraq where, without pause, the assault — and escape — would have to be made good.

Things started badly. As the motley crew crossed the plain of Ramtha they found the ground heavily ploughed — which made their otherwise sure-footed camels slip and slide like donkeys on ice. They reached the waterfall below the bridge in the early evening with the bright moon still resting behind Mount Hermon. Pushing their way upstream they found themselves at the edge of the gorge overlooking the vital bridge. The breathless bridge-blowers distributed the volatile gelignite to fifteen nervous porters who clumsily made their way down the steep sides of the cut. They dug their bare toes into the wet soil to prevent themselves tumbling in an explosive mess straight down the hillside. Despite the tip-off from the traitor, the Turks did not make much effort to conceal themselves and were spotted resting in their tent at one end of the bridge. Everything was motionless except for a single sentry who wandered back and forth beside his fire.

Then, the still night air was broken by the clatter of a dropped rifle rattling

Above: Ruins of a once-elegant Roman aqueduct at Umm el-Jemal. The stones were toppled by an earthquake.

into the river gorge. The demolition team was discovered and the tent full of Turks swiftly emptied as they fired volley after volley into the dark. The porters assigned to carry the gelignite had been told that one bullet into their packs would blast them directly to heaven, so they simply dumped their loads into the gorge and fled. The rest of the party followed. Later, an attempt to blow up a train at Minifi, inspired more by chagrin than military strategy, nearly ended in a similar disaster. But, after hours of abortive attempts and false starts, the Arab revolutionaries destroyed the engine of a train carrying a Turkish general and his staff.

The road to Mafraq takes one out of the fertile plains of Ramtha and on to the vast black-grey basalt desert. It is good going for camels who, with their wide fleshy foot pads, can cover 80 kilometres a day without too much difficulty.

Mafraq is the regional capital and the main beneficiary of the construction of an oil pipeline from Haifa to Iraq. During the Arab Revolt the countryside around the town was semi-desert. Now, thanks to modern irrigation techniques, it has once again become the rich farmland of ancient times.

Aridity is the pattern for much of the Badia, yet early this century it was nothing like as barren as today. Formerly it was well covered with desert vegetation and herds of wild gazelle. Before the collapse of the sophisticated irrigation systems of the ancients, the Nabateans, and subsequent Arab settlers in towns like Umm el-Jemal, perfected a system of water harvesting which allowed the fertile desert soils to produce huge crops of wheat and other cereals.

At the turn of the century, the remains of Umm el-Jemal rose out of the grey sea of the desert as if it had been forced from the centre of the earth by a vast and terrifying impulse. From a distance it looked like a city after a nuclear holocaust: black, as if it had been firebombed and all its inhabitants wiped out in one awful night. Nothing could be further from the truth.

Unlike many other ancient sites in Jordan, Umm el-Jemal is no grandiose testament to the power and grace of the Greco-Roman empires or to the burgeoning egos of the men who built them. Rather it is the remains of a prosperous middle-class market town on an important trade route. Most impressive of all is the water supply system built by the Nabateans, who had learned their trade harnessing the springs near Petra. There is neither a spring nor an overground stream anywhere near the town. Its entire needs, and those of visitors and farmers, had to be met by capturing rainfall in cisterns and little dams.

The southern Hauran plain receives only 100 millimetres of rain a year but the settlers in Umm el-Jemal devised a system of canals and aqueducts which preserved enough water to produce a spring crop from natural rains and other harvests from irrigation. Since modern techniques of pumping water from underground have arrived, many of the surrounding fields are once again verdant. But ploughs have turned over many parts of the ancient irrigation systems which can been seen sticking out of the ground through the furrows in the deep red volcanic soils.

Umm el-Jemal was partly restored by the Druze who left their mountain lands of the Jebel Druze after the Great War and headed west. They briefly occupied the town, restoring parts of the enormous military barracks and some of the houses. Since then it has fallen derelict but, because of the elegant building techniques employed by its creators, much of the city is still recognisable. Its history has three main parts. Nestling on a fork of two wadis in the 2nd and 3rd centuries AD it was a small village in which Nabatean and other Arab tribes led a sedentary life. The settlers used basalt as though it were wood; building beams of solid rock two to three metres across and roofing their houses with the same. Everything seemed to have been carved from the hard, volcanic

Overleaf: Bird's-eye view of the great basalt fortress at Azraq, with a small mosque in the centre.

substance — mangers and water basins for animals, doors of solid rock held in by rock hinges set in rock, locked with cross-beams of basalt. The result is that some of the 1,500-year-old buildings still stand three stories high. The population at that time was estimated to have been between about 2,000 and 3,000 people but many more passed through on their way to Palestine, the Hijaz or Babylon in camel caravans. The great open squares of the city would have been thick with black Bedouin tents, camels, horses, and crowds of people resting, squabbling, drinking and feeding ahead of more hard trekking through the Badia. Almost all the houses in the city have lower floors designed to stable horses and camels while above them lived people, often in typical eastern courtyard houses.

With the advent of Roman rule, the city enjoyed rapid growth. In the 4th and 5th centuries, as an outpost of Emperor Diocletian's network of frontier fortifications, it was used to protect the interior of his empire from outside aggression. For a while attempt to set up a desert Maginot Line worked and allowed the city to rebuild quickly. But civilian needs quickly overtook military and many of their buildings were converted to markets or hostels as Christianity approached.

Christians built at least 15 churches in the town during the 5th and 6th centuries for a community of about 6,000 to 8,000 living in less secure circumstances, as is evident from the construction of keeps in private houses. During the Persian wars, and the plagues which ravaged Jordan almost simultaneously, Umm el-Jemal suffered badly. When the Ummayeds took over in Damascus in AD 661 they were unable to stem the tide of depopulation which struck Umm el-Jemal, though, as its name — Mother of Camels — implies, it continued to be a link in the trade routes across Arabia. The Ummayeds restored some buildings, such as the Praetorium which they decorated with frescoes.

A short distance outside Umm el-Jemal the Badia begins in earnest — a seemingly endless moonscape of baking rocks, flint and basalt hillocks ballooning out of the ground. Huge herds of sheep and goats appear to feed on the hot dust and there is little vegetation apart from the inedible broom bushes and clumps of sage. The wind is so hot it is like the blast from an oven, while above, the sun glowers down like a malevolent eye withering everything under its gaze. This is the land of the Bedu, the original Arabs, the freemen of the desert.

Driving through this arid landscape visitors may occasionally see what appears to be an unusual symmetrical black block of basalt tucked up against a rocky outcrop sheltering from the worst of the Badia's winds. Closer inspection may reveal another black speck, perhaps shepherding sheep and goats from the base of the rock. It is a Bedouin woman, dressed in her traditional *shursh*, black

Above: Young Jordanian woman wearing the brightly-coloured traditional dress of Ramtha.

cotton dress. The black rectangle behind her is her tent, *al-bayt*, the centre of her family's existence. Woven by hand from a mixture of sheep and goats' wool, the *al-bayt* is the perfect desert dwelling. Its black coat absorbs heat during the day to hold warmth and protect occupants from the freezing winds and nights. It is also waterproof, for the untreated yarns expand when wet, sealing the tent as effectively as the most modern proofing agents. All but the largest tents may be packed up and loaded onto a single camel inside an hour — though nowadays many Bedu travel by four-wheel-drive vehicles.

Lawrence, who saw the Bedu at their best and worst, fighting bravely against terrible odds during the Arab Revolt, and then abandoning themselves in an ill-disciplined horde to plunder the possessions of their foes, probably knew the Bedouin better than any other foreigner. For he knew them *in extremis*, as the children of adversity. 'This people was black and white, not only in vision,' he wrote, 'but in inmost furnishing: black and white not merely in clarity, but in apposition. Their thoughts were at ease only in extremes. They inhabited superlatives by choice. . . . . The least morbid of peoples, they had accepted the gift of life unquestioningly, as axiomatic.'

Almost unnecessarily, given the history of the Middle East and the Bible, Lawrence added: 'They were a people of spasms, of upheavals, of ideas, the race of the individual genius'. In his memoirs, King Abdullah remarks that the Bedouin are courageous and fond of oratory as well as poetry and love. Emir Feisal, later King of Iraq, and Abdullah's son, had a bodyguard of extravagantly dressed Ageyl tribesmen who marched to the music of poets singing acapella extemporised verses as they strode across the desert on their graceful racing camels.

About 40,000 Bedouin live in Jordan in their 'natural state'. The most romantic tribes are the camel herders, the tribes of the Beni Sakhr, the Huweitat and the Sirhan — all of whom fought for freedom during the Arab Revolt. Fierce fighting men, the Bedouin enjoy nothing better than a raid against a rival clan or tribe. Their most famous warrior, Auda abu Tayi, leader of the eastern Huweitat,was reputed to have killed 75 men, not counting Turks, by the time he joined the Revolt. By the end he had dispatched far more. But during the Great War massive quantities of guns were released to the Bedouin which, combined with their penchant for battle, nearly resulted in their self-extermination. The Huweitat were so anxious to fight that their numbers fell from 1,200 men to just 500, while the Rwala lost 80 per cent of their men.

But for all their fighting, which came to an end after the First World War when a central administration was able to channel their energies into the Arab Legion and the legendary Bedouin Police, the Bedouin are among the most hospitable people in the world. It is difficult for visiting men to pass a tent without being invited to take tea or coffee with the menfolk on their side of the tent — *al-shigg* — while the women peek over the top of the divide from their preserve — *al-makram* — occasionally making seditious and apposite comments on the male conversation. The greatest honour of all is to be entertained at a feast of meat served on a bed of rice on a vast dish, a *mansaf*.

Although life is hard and living conditions crude, the Bedouin value courtesy highly, along with other chivalrous virtues like honour, bravery, honesty and, above all, respect for women. It even went to the extent that among some tribes beautiful Bedouin girls would ride ahead of raiding parties shrieking encouragement and beating their breasts. If they were captured, their enemies made it a matter of honour to return them unharmed to their parents.

Subsistence is a way of life for the desert people and as a result they live close to one another. Their immediate loyalties are to their families and their subclans, then to the tribe. The modern concept of nation is somewhat alien to them although ironically the Arab nations owe much of their existence to the Bedu.

Opposite: Arabian oryx — a few years ago at the point of extinction — now flourish at Shaumari Wildlife Reserve.

Right: Ostriches at Shaumari are wary of visitors.

Right: An ostrich egg on the cracked earth of Shaumari. The reserve has dried out immeasurably since its water supply has been diverted to Amman.

Opposite: Three onagers (wild asses) roam the plains of Shaumari Wildlife Reserve, which encompasses an area of 22 square kilometres.

Above: Hamman Al-Sarakh, one of several Ummayed bathhouses in Jordan's eastern desert.

But if they are uncomfortable with the restrictions to movement which concepts of nationhood inevitably imply, the Bedu, quick though pragmatic converts to Islam, were the most loyal supporters and warriors for the first Arab nationalists, the Ummayed Caliphs. The Caliphs maintained contact with their desert heritage by building palaces in remote areas. The Bedu have also remained true to the Hashemites.

In the old days raiding was something of an art form, with magnificent Arab horses a most effective assault machine. Plunderers would ride within range of their prey on camels and then switch to their fiery horses for the final assault — shooting flintlock muzzle-loaders and carbines at a gallop with deadly accuracy. One figure in the Arab Revolt was able to hit a sprinting gazelle from his moving horse at 300 metres — and bemoaned the fact that he did so with a second shot.

Imagine these men harnessed into a reckless band of individuals, with centuries of raiding experience between them, creeping up on Turkish positions on the Hijaz Railway, or charging into Azraq at full gallop. Since pre-adolescence they had been trained in the art of stealth and surprise, carefully approaching a rival group of tents downwind, and tying their camels up behind a sand dune or a batholith. With a wild war cry, they would hurtle down upon their half-awake victims, snatching at whatever came to hand for everything — from jewels to sacks of coffee — was prized. The whole campaign would be over in a moment and the attackers vanished, whooping off into the desert with their booty. It is little surprise that in the Bedouin the Allies found the ultimate desert guerrillas — they were doing what they did best and most liked doing.

Many Bedouin have now moved to the towns but maintain a close sentimental and spiritual attachment to the desert. In southern Jordan, and on the steppes of the north-east, behind modern houses visitors often still see a black tent — now used to sleep in or to entertain. Even in Madaba, half an hour from the capital, tents are tacked onto the side of buildings. The traveller may find, however, that without the freedom of the heart that the desert skies impart, and the harsh environment of their forefathers, the urbanised Bedouin male is not of the same mettle as his recent ancestors. Arabs, and especially the Bedouin family, celebrate and indulge their children with love and affection seldom seen in the west. The contrast between the modern Arab male and the wild men of the desert could not be more extreme.

The importance of male offspring to an Arab family is shown in familial bonds so strong that they seem overpowering to Anglo-Saxons. Sadly, in modern Jordan, perhaps the most open and adaptable of the Arab countries, the family unit has started to shrink so that priorities are less focused on the *hamulah* — the extended unit — and more on immediate relationships. Jordanian society is adapting readily to the modern world yet many of the traditions held dear by members of the older generations survive.

Although patriarchal, the family unit deeply reveres women. In the home, and in most decisions, the mother is queen and what she does not order she can easily achieve by guile. Daughters are treated as 'guests' in their father's house and it is implicit that from an early age they learn much self reliance and the ability to solve problems and think independently as they help their mother with running the household — so that they will one day be a desirable catch. Marriages, if no longer pre-arranged, are always a time of great celebration, pomp and circumstance. The engagement, *khutbeh*, is a serious and elaborate business in both Christian and Muslim communities. With the assent of the fathers all arrangements are handled by the mothers. There are the groom's deputations to his future in-laws during which, if he has not met his bride before, he is indulged with an 'accidental encounter' to allow him to get to know his future wife. Other visits, especially in Muslim families, thrash out the

details of the dowry and the *mutaakhir*, a sort of deposit on the marriage if it does not hold together.

In rural communities the wedding is quick but noisy. The bride is carried to her groom on a camel or a horse, accompanied by singing and dancing members of her family and her friends. Deep in the Badia, where guns are often still carried, the bridal procession will be accompanied by plenty of shooting into the air and wild cheering and poetry.

People who are open about sexual matters are said, traditionally, to have little shame, *qalil al-haya*. But even this is changing.

The solemnity of the Bedouins' black tents is offset by more flamboyant weaving of saddlebags for camels and horses, and long, brilliantly coloured rugs to spread over cushions inside when serving guests. In the stark light of the desert the Bedouin enjoy their primary colours. These are not pastel people. The women wear the traditional black dress, *shursh*, often decorated with vivid,

Above: Desert sentinel at Qasr Kharana, perhaps the best surviving example of Ummayed architecture in the eastern sector of the country. Although built like a fortress, Kharana is thought to have been a meeting place for Ummayed leaders.

embroidered panels. Their headdresses sport gold and silver coins, shells and coral from the coast — sometimes also found on their veils. In the past, vast, double-sized dresses made of matt black cotton kept out the desert heat and cold. The dress, *thob ob*, was about five metres long and doubled up under a thick belt. The sleeves, two metres long, were wrapped about the head and tied by a headband. Although now rare in the world of nylon and drip-dry fibres, the *thob ob* may sometimes be spotted in Salt, where the women are especially anxious to preserve their traditional heritage.

Driving through the desert visitors are often struck by its silence and apparent desolation. Nothing moves apart from the occasional spectral goats or sheep grazing behind the heat haze blurring the horizon. The air is so hot one gasps for breath. Dust devils appear and circle in a soon-exhausted frenzy.

But the Badia has not always been a place of heat and desolation. The Bedouin's Stone Age ancestors once roamed steppes thick with game and vegetation. In small pockets, like the Shaumari Wildlife Reserve, where the local ecology has been protected from over-grazing, visitors may see just how productive the desert could be. Thickets of sage, grass, and broom not only provide fodder for oryx, onagers and gazelle but also protect topsoil from erosion by wind and rain. Without the binding effect of plant roots the Badia's fertile but fragile soil would be washed down to bedrock in one storm. But the Stone Age people lived off an abundance.

At first glance, in the countryside on the road to Azraq, and on the outskirts of the town itself, the walls appear to be built with deliberation but without design. These are not dwellings but Stone Age animal traps into which herds of wild ass and antelope were funnelled by hordes of 'beaters' across long distances. Armed with flint-tipped spears, arrows and bludgeons the hunters would force the game to the narrow end of a maze of walls and throw nets over the beasts they wanted to capture — or simply slaughter them. Pilots flying mail from Jerusalem to Baghdad, who first noticed the unexplained geometric walls all over the bush at the end of the First World War, likened their shape to the plans for the frame of a child's kite hence the name for these fatal images — 'betes'.

Hunting has always played a major part in the life of the Bedouin. It is perhaps why the Ummayed Caliphs built their series of retreats known collectively as the 'Desert Castles'. The first one on the road to Azraq is the ruined Roman fort of Deir el-Kahf, of little real interest except as one of the most far-flung posts of the Roman empire. The most impressive from a military point of view is the castle in Azraq — though strictly speaking it does not form part of the network of caravanserai and pleasure palaces built by the Ummayeds.

The deep, black basalt of the fort is appropriately mournful. At the headwaters of the Wadi Sirhan — once one of the greatest water masses in the desert — the fort sits on the major trading routes with the west, Iraq and Saudi Arabia. Sadly, the once blooming 12 square kilometres of oasis system at Azraq is dying. The verdant sight was once so inspiring to Bedouin, who had travelled through the Badia and survived on brackish well water, that they would sometimes run half-naked through the swamps shouting with delight. Now the demands of the 20th century are sucking it dry. The oasis, one of the major sources of water for modern Amman, is fed from the slopes of the Jebel Druze, the water seeping to the surface in Azraq. Now the oasis is being pumped dry, causing its salt levels to rise, and the water buffalo who inhabit the wetlands are in danger of dying out. Once 300 species of birds were found here, but their numbers are also falling as they, too, find other parts of the world to rest on their winter and summer migrations.

Azraq fort, one of the main rebel bases during the Arab Revolt, has been of vital strategic importance for centuries. Probably built in the late Roman era at the end of the 3rd century, it was in almost continuous use until the end of the Great War. Its great solid basalt door, exactly the same as those used in the tombs of Gadara, still swings heavily on its hinges below the keep in which Lawrence made his quarters in 1917-18. Two storeys of rooms once ranged along the entire length of the castle and some remain (in a dilapidated condition) today. The stables, however, are better preserved. Beneath a series of massive stone arches are the mangers and tethering holes cut through the basalt. The centrepiece of the structure is the mosque, sitting almost dead centre of the compound and very much ready for use. But if one reflects on the number of men who froze to death in the castle during the Revolt, the sense of desolation which the imposing fortress exudes only increases.

Azraq is an odd town. A truck stop for the convoys to Iraq and Saudi Arabia, it has lost much of the bustling raucousness which must have been the atmosphere of such an important halt on the trade routes. In the past came caravans laden with gold, silk and rare spices to lend the place an element of colour. And the plentiful water after desert crossings provoked festive joy in new arrivals. Now the air is choked with diesel fumes and the townsfolk, withdrawn and suspicious Druze, and dislocated Circassians brought to Jordan by the Turks at the end of the last century, stare blankly from their cafes at the constant flow of strangers through the town.

Not far south, however, there is relief in the form of Qasr Amra, Jordan's finest example of ancient health-club accommodation. Originally the baths, audience hall, water system, and quarters were all sheltered behind a wall overlooked by a watchtower and small barracks for the staff and troops serving the complex. With 25 hectares of well-irrigated land, the inhabitants had plenty of fresh meat and vegetables. Indeed, the little castle was an idyllic haven in the desert. Tired and hot, dusty and ill-tempered, travellers could rest in the warm

Overleaf: Exterior of Qasr Amra, used as a remote but elaborate bathing complex, with a sophisticated heating system.

Above: Frescoes adorn the walls of Qasr Amra — eastern Jordan's most extraordinary building.

baths, gaze at the magnificent frescoes on the ceilings and walls above them, and gorge themselves on good food. Perhaps some even drank wine. For while the Ummayeds were staunchly Muslim, their art on display at Amra is clearly influenced by the Romans; in particular, the large number of nude women reclining suggestively. Furthermore, many of the inscriptions are in Greek, which indicates the high degree of cosmopolitan behaviour adopted by the Ummayeds even though they were descendants of simple desert folk.

Another magnificent desert palace, Qasr Kharana, lies nearby, a short drive away along the road south-west. Although it looks like an imposing if slightly effete redoubt, Kharana is most likely to have been a caravanserai. The biggest clue to its purely decorative militarism is that the embrasures are so narrow they allow no angle of fire other than straight. The real things taper to a close allowing the archer a wider range.

Kharana is best-preserved of the desert castles and is built on two floors

around a large courtyard. In the rooms on the lower levels huge olive presses and sunken fireplaces indicate that the owners were used to catering on a large scale and many authorities look upon the castle as an ancient conference centre where Ummayed leaders could meet away from the bustle of the city. Its exterior is decorated with a facade of bricks in a herringbone-form, much like early Elizabethan buildings in Britain. Visitors pass two huge rooms on either side of the portico which may have been stables but, given the narrow width of the doors, are more likely to have been store rooms. Unlike many other desert palaces, Kharana did not have a significant permanent water supply system but relied on a cistern in the middle of its courtyard to trap rainwater. Some white plaster, which covered the walls and high vaulted ceilings of the suites on the upper floor, remains, though sadly disfigured by modern graffiti. Older scribbles reveal that Abdul Malik bin Omar, probably a member of Walid I's entourage, stopped at Kharana in November AD 710, on his way back from Mecca. This not only gives us a clue to the building's use as a rest centre, but further confirms the castle lay on a significant route, although some historians argue it was built purely as a stately pleasure dome for Caliphs trying to return to their roots.

Above: Fine carved motif decorating a stone at Qasr Hallabat hints at the former grandeur of the ruined site — which was originally constructed as a defence against raiding tribes.

Opposite: Rounded stone arch at Qasr Hallabat, a Roman fortress erected in the reign of Caracalla at the start of the 3rd century AD.

3 · IN THE HEART OF JORDAN

Previous pages: Side by side, Amman's Greek Orthodox Church lies next to one of the capital's most spectacular new buildings — the King Abdullah Mosque, completed in 1989.

Amman is a confusing city. In winter and early spring the sun, hiding shyly on a low horizon, soothes the harsh white of limestone and modern concrete with a soft brushwork of light only seen elsewhere on still mornings in the European Alps. In summer, hundreds of thousands of white blocks, like giant Lego, reflect painfully into the eye as one struggles with unmarked streets and a shimmering landscape. American-style neon atop five-star hotels burns the night sky while the air is thick with the smell of cedar, pine, night-flowering jasmine and great monuments to the Roman and Greek civilisations. It is exciting confusion. And in modern Amman one can sense the buzz of the computer-age against the glittering souk in the middle of town, a pandemonium where plastic replicas of Mickey Mouse are hawked alongside peerless Bedouin rugs brightly patterned with organic dyes.

Above: Statue of Apollo dates back to the Hellenistic Era.

The Gold Market, across the muddle of medievally criss-crossing streets from the Al Hussein Mosque, is perhaps an appropriate adjunct. But when, on a short wander east, one turns to find a fully functioning Roman Theatre seating 5,000 people, complete with special drain for the blood of those who came second in gladiator battles, the whirl of cultures is overwhelming, yet somehow unstartling.

The new arrival swiftly realises that the local people have lived among such conflicts for centuries — often symbolic of regional confrontations — and are going about their business unruffled by gold, religion and Roman splendour. At the feet of the theatre walls, on the pavement of the Forum of Philadelphia, scores of Iraqi and Syrian traders peddle goods smuggled along the ancient routes their forefathers used. There could be no better testimony to the easy-going nature of modern Ammanites and Jordanians in general.

This relaxed attitude and ability to accommodate the seesaw fortunes of the Middle East enabled Jordanians to survive the arrival of hundreds of thousands of Palestinian refugees in 1948-49. Driven or fleeing from the West Bank and beyond, the Palestinians, many of them highly educated, immediately brought a burst of energy to King Abdullah's modest capital. They rushed into the professions and commerce using the education they brought with them. Overnight Amman doubled in size. Now the picture is less rosy. Another massive influx in the 1960s trapped many Palestinians — looking west with longing — in a classic cycle of aid dependency which saps initiative and makes the vast 'refugee camps', that look for all the world like normal Arab cities, such depressing places to visit.

Until the arrival of the Palestinians, Amman was a modest capital. G Lankester Harding, author of the finest archaeological book on the country, *The Antiquities of Jordan,* arrived in Amman in 1932. King Abdullah had established the city as his capital twelve years earlier after marching peacefully in from Ma'an. But when the English archaeologist arrived in the city he found

Opposite: Aerial view of Amman, with the King Abdullah Mosque at its centre. The principal dome, which is a staggering 35 metres in diameter, is paved with 2,615 square metres of blue mosaic.

Opposite: Royal Jordanian jet refuels at Queen Alia International Airport.

Above: Legacy from Ottoman times, an ageing steam train rusts away at Amman's railway station. The capital was connected to Medina and Damascus by the great Hijaz Railway Line. Sadly, the Hijaz Railway was largely destroyed during the Arab Revolt in 1917.

Opposite: Elite carrier Royal Jordanian Airlines flies to destinations all over the world including the United States and a number of countries in the Far East.

it mainly occupied by Circassians settled in the city by the Ottoman Turks in 1880. The village had barely begun to climb the many valley sides which have now been overwhelmed by buildings. King Abdullah's 'palace' was a private house next door to the more spectacular and newly built Philadelphia Hotel

The Circassians, who were also the most recent occupants of Jerash, had built red, pitch-roofed houses similar to those they remembered from their homelands in the Caucasus, as well as the traditional flat-roofed low-rise dwellings of the Arab world. The streets were mostly earth and limestone. Dusty in summer, they turned to slithering pathways in the snow and rain of winter.

King Abdullah's establishment at Amman was the beginning of a renaissance which continues today as the metropolis expands beyond a million residents. Until his arrival, the city had dwindled to little more than an insignificant village eclipsed, like many cities in Transjordan, by the concentration of wealth

Opposite: Pretty schoolgirl provides a burst of colour as she clutches a bouquet on Palm Sunday.

Above: St. Mary's Church in Amman — one of Jordan's finest places of Christian worship.

family groups. Around the ruins they marvel at the mystery of the palace and the caves that overlook it. Eleven large hand-carved caves loom above the Qasr, which Tobiad cut deeply into the limestone — nothing more. One is huge. 28 metres deep by six wide. Inside are tying posts and troughs for 80 horses. Above it a long gallery that provides access to the other eight caves reached by a ramp down to the main road marked out by niches cut from the living rock, either for lamps or, perhaps, the funeral urns of dead ancestors.

The Qasr itself is peculiar. Although taking up no more space than an area of a tennis court, its walls were decorated with vast relief carvings of lion cut out of rocks more than two metres long and one metre high, but oddly thin. These great bricks were erected for decorative, not defensive purposes. It seems that the valley of the Wadi el-Seer has been a favourite spot for millennia. In the modern village, early Bronze and Iron Age fortifications have been found near to 1st or 2nd century BC wine presses and cisterns, showing the area was at times

Overleaf top: Ancient cannon stands guard outside the Raghadan Palace in Amman.

Overleaf: Chandeliers illuminate the banquet room at the Raghadan Palace.

Opposite: Although Qasr al Abed was built from huge blocks of honey-coloured stone, it was destroyed by an earthquake in ancient times.

Above: Mimosa tree bursts into colour.

both a desirable place to live and worth defending. Though their exact role is not clear, the Tobiad family were influential in the region from early biblical times. The Book of Nehemiah says that Tobiad the Servant, the Ammonite, was a 'governor beyond the river' and was influential enough to prevent the rebuilding of Solomon's Temple in Jerusalem. Through the ages the Tobiads seem to have been major backroom political players: perhaps what, in the Mafia, would be described as *consiglieri*. The archives of the Greek businessman, Zenon, who operated during the reign of Ptolemy II, shows that one of the Tobiads offered the Egyptians 'horses, dogs, onagers and Arabian asses' for their parks from his own estate. But Flavius Josephus gives more detail of life in Iraq el-Amir when Hyracanus, a Ptolemy supporter, fled from his father, Joseph, king in Jerusalem, and his half brothers who sided with the Seleucids during one of the inter-Greek spats which so marked the last two centuries before the birth of Christ. And he settled on the east side of the Jordan.

Josephus wrote that the young and brilliant Hyracanus 'built a strong fortress which was constructed entirely of white marble up to the very roof and had beasts of gigantic size carved on it; and he enclosed it with a wide and deep moat (which has virtually disappeared today). He also cut through the projecting rock and made caves many stades in length (a stade is about 150 metres); then he made chambers in it, some for banqueting and others for sleeping and living, and then he let in an abundance of running water, which was both a delight and an ornament of his country estate. The entrances of the caves, however, he made narrower, so that only one person and not more could enter at a time. . . . In addition, he also built enclosures remarkable for their size, and adorned them with vast parks. And when he had completed the place in this manner, he named it Tyre. . . . This place is across the Jordan. . . .'

Hyracanus' country idyll was obviously precarious. Why else go to so much trouble in building a moat and caves with restricted entrances? Despite the beauty of the surroundings and the efforts Hyracanus made to decorate his retreat, he never felt secure enough to enjoy the natural serenity of Wadi el-Seer. He lived at Iraq el-Amir for seven years before taking his own life as the Seleucids took Palestine and Syria in 198 BC.

Another legend has it that Iraq el-Amir was built by a lovesick servant to a prince in order to gain the royal daughter's hand. But the Hyracanus story at least fits with the uncertain times when men found it hard to mind the peace, and harder still to find peace of mind.

Above the Qasr and its bountiful valley, a small road winds to the top of the limestone hills where, in spring, when the sun has melted away the winter snow, the greening mountains offer up the Black Iris, Jordan's national flower, as a gift to the new season. Among these hills, just 20 minutes from the modern, high-technology capital, Bedouin continue to graze their sheep and goats as they

Previous page: Elegant lines of a reception room in the Raghadan Palace.

Above: Aerial view of Qasr al Abed, which had one small entrance, making any attempt to storm the castle extremely difficult.

have for centuries. The only significant difference is the presence of four-wheel-drive cars rather than camels and horses.

The central highlands of Jordan are a triumph of painstaking cultivation. The steep sides of the escarpment have been terraced for millennia. Low walls spread from the tops of the hills like little waves produced by a pebble tossed into a still lake. They trap water for irrigation and soil to replenish the thin blanket of earth that covers the bedrock. Often the loam has been built up by adding manure and rotting grass to a fragile topsoil which otherwise would have dried and blown into the baking valley of the Dead Sea centuries ago.

Why do more Bedouin not forsake their harsh lives for the comforts of the 20th century? The answer is simple: in the Badia, and among the mountains, they may gaze through the clear air as free men and women and look upon land they believe they have been promised. And when they look at the fields cut into the sides of the Great Rift they have the knowledge that they cannot leave the land, for they made it.

From the air Amman appears much like any other sprawling city under the midday sun. Perhaps, because of the white limestone still used in many of the buildings, its appearance is even more stark than a city in the west where the mellow reds and browns of brick are easier on the eye. But it is riddled with mystery and legend with physical monuments to intriguing tales dotted everywhere. The Cave of the Seven Sleepers sounds like something out of a fairy tale, and perhaps it is. But in the village of Rajib, alongside a busy road on the south east outskirts of Amman, the cave remains — and it does not seem long since the sleepers awoke. Part of both Christian and Islamic mythology, the

Above: Inside the Cave of the Seven Sleepers, whose story is recorded in Sura 18 of The Quran.

cellar is honeycombed with small tombs cut from the living rock. They have fine rock lids.

Seven young men, or boys, living in Philadelphia during the reign of a pagan Roman emperor — Trajan or Decius — became well-known for their Christian faith. Hearing of their commitment the emperor threatened to kill them unless they made sacrifices to his favoured deities. The youngsters refused. Rather than face the consequences they were smuggled out of the city by a shepherd who hid them in a cave with his dog for protection. Some accounts say that they were trapped in the cavern by a rock fall; others that the eight souls were deliberately sealed in by Roman soldiers. Either way they were assured of a silent death inside the hill. But God plunged them into a deep sleep.

Three hundred and nine years later they awoke, hungry — and citizens of the Byzantine empire. One wandered into Philadelphia to buy food with historic Roman coins which prompted the now Christian citizens to think that he had been brought back from the dead from Roman times. Opportunists among the marketwomen and officials took him before the ruler of the city, Theodosius. Thrilled to find such manifestations of the power of the Lord the potentate feted the seven sleepers royally. Then, inexplicably, the boys and the sheepdog returned to their cave and resumed their deep sleep.

Visiting the site is an eerie experience. A lone Bedu guard admits the visitor. The walled garden to its front is small and almost bisected by a couple of rock features at grass level.

The ruins look a crude mixture of work produced by poor architects at different times. Above the ancient, artful lintel carving of a Greek cross is the

Overleaf: Amman's Roman theatre, the largest in Jordan, can hold some 6,000 spectators. More than 18 centuries after it was built, the theatre is still in use.

Opposite: Ruins of the once formidable Ummayed castle at the Citadel, overlooking central Amman.

Above: Three teenage girls visit Amman's Roman theatre.

site of an old rudimentary mosque, itself built on the remains of a Byzantine chapel. Inside, past eight small tombs, a small glass case leans against the back wall. The case contains the jawbone of a dog. Stranger still, while seven tombs are sealed, one has a small hole through which, by candlelight, the visitor can clearly see seven small human skulls and the bones of a dog. This is one of the rare occasions in Jordan when it may be a relief not to be able to speak Arabic. The unanswered questions are all the more beguiling. The guard to the tombs completes the picture, speaking only in sign language, smiling through teeth like piano keys. His face is a ravaged map of Arabia and you can leave confident that he has been on silent vigil at the Cave of the Seven Sleepers since they first closed their eyes on the temporal world.

North-west of Iraq el-Amir is Salt, the Ottoman capital of the region of Transjordan. Today, because Amman has become the focus of attention, Salt or Al Salt, has started to rest upon its historical laurels and bask in the beauty of its 19th and 20th century Ottoman architecture. Arrival in this town in mid-morning is always greeted with the sweet smell of freshly baking bread. Unleavened loaves are thrown like pizza bases into a roaring kiln where they bake almost instantly on hot rounded pebbles, giving them a distinctive 'bubbly' shape. Torn off, the bubbles, either by chance or design, make ideal cup shapes for scooping up humus and scores of other delicious sesame, chickpea and pulse-based dips. Bakeries are a frenzy of happy activity. The bakers of Salt also produce myriads of delicate pastries, sugared and sprinkled with cinnamon, ideal side dishes for a glass of tea or coffee flavoured with cardamom. The latter gives a subtle aroma and a flavour somewhere between the bitterness of chicory and the base sweetness of the sugar generously ladled into each thimble-sized cup or glass.

Jordan's first modern secondary school was built in Salt. Non-denominational and co-educational, the institution fosters an atmosphere of tolerance. It means that children who wish to wear traditional clothes, and girls who wish to cover their faces after Islamic custom, are no more — or less — distinguished than those who have wholeheartedly adopted the street fashions of New York or London. The results are that the school, and many others like it, produce young people with open minds — the first mission of any educational establishment. One side effect of the live-and-let-live attitude in Salt is a laid-back view of life which verges on the soporific. No one bustles — they wander around the town chatting, taking tea, and mildly teasing one another. Young men imbued with this gentle spirit have a way of turning it to their advantage. As one said, while he watched the slow pace of a traditionally dressed woman from Beersheba, 'We have extended families which means, for the time being, we don't have to work. Why work if you don't have to? I prefer to look at the flowers and the pretty girls passing by.'

Opposite: Selection of exquisite Jordanian handmade pots on display in an Amman gallery.

Above: The ancient art of hand blowing glass continues at the Hebron Glass Factory, just outside Amman. Temperatures of over 900°C make the glass pliable enough to shape.

In Philadelphia, Seleucid rule ended with the ascendance of the Roman Empire in AD 63 and, for the next 150 years, prospered as part of the Decapolis under the control, successively, of the Nabateans of Petra and the Hashmonians and Herodians of Palestine. In AD 106 Trajan, made aware of the Nabatean wealth which came from control of the trade routes with the Red Sea and the Hijaz, annexed Petra and brought the routes under his control. He established the Roman province of Arabia. Philadelphia found itself at the empire's heart, benefiting from the enormous economic boom brought by the Roman-imposed peace. This wealth generated the massive Temple of Hercules on the citadel, which was once entirely covered by the city of Rabbah Ammon in the Iron and Bronze Ages. A 9th century BC Ammonite inscription dedicated the original temple site to the Ammonite God, Milkom, who came in for particular hatred from Amos and successive Old Testament prophets. A significant feature of the later Roman temple was a chamber set around a sacred rock which protruded

Opposite: Traditional ceramic painting is also carried out at the Hebron Glass Factory, one of the few in the Middle East to use traditional techniques.

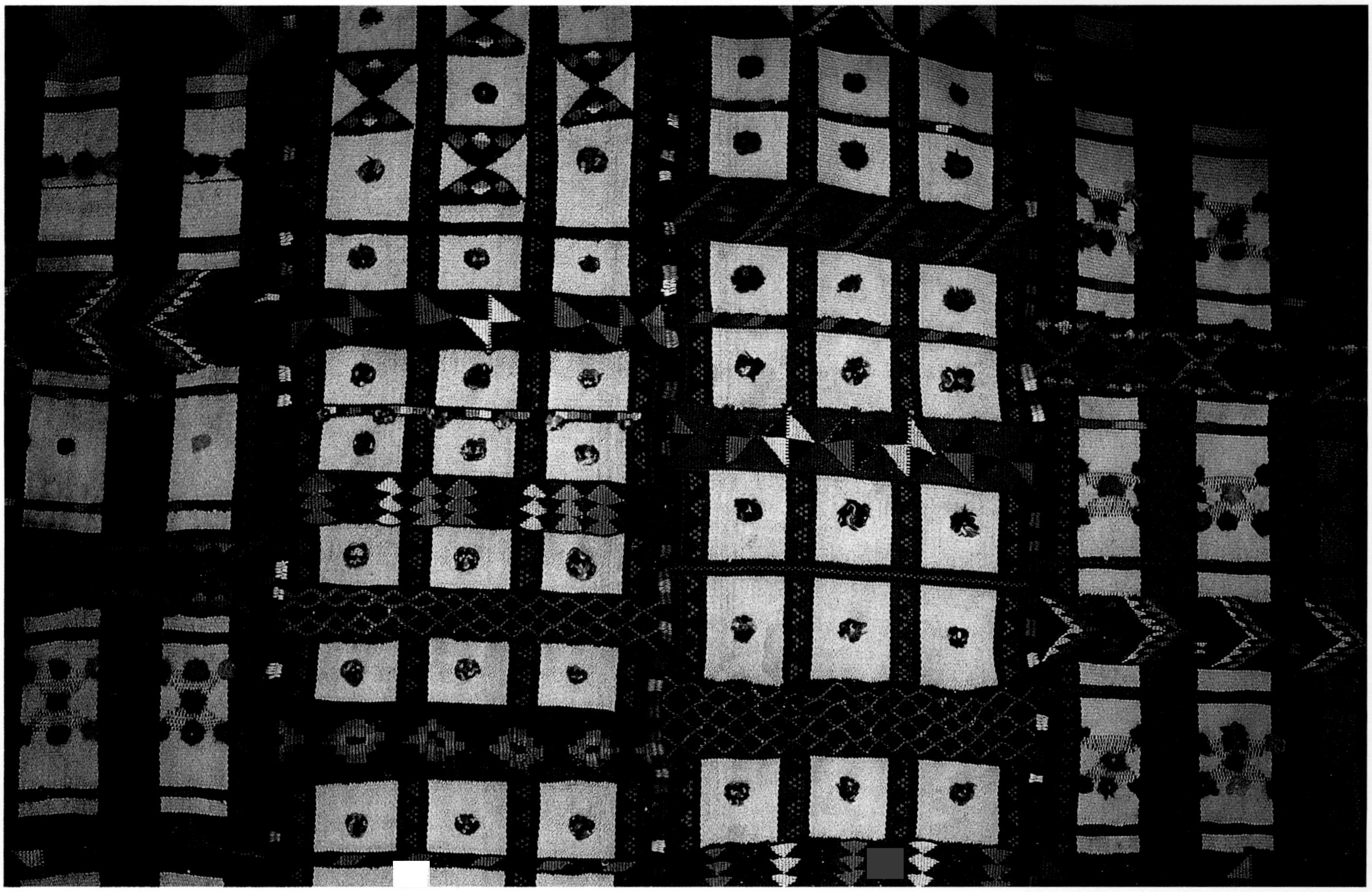

Opposite: Master weaver at work in the Jordan Trade and Design Centre in Amman.

Above: Selection of Jordanian handicrafts in bright tribal designs.

Opposite: Handwoven rug at the Jordan Trade and Design Centre demonstrates the use of traditional patterns and natural dyes in Jordan.

into the room. This has also been associated with the older Temple of Milkom. Little remains of either as earthquakes, and later developments by the Byzantines and Ummayeds, have obscured much of the distant past.

The most impressive building on the citadel is the palatial complex that served as the administrative centre between the 8th and 10th centuries AD when Amman was the capital of the Balqa Province in the Ummayed empire. During the Abbasid (AD 750-969) and Fatimid (AD 969-1171) eras it remained the centre of the region but the whole area fell from prominence with the transfer of the Abbasid capital from Damascus to Baghdad. At its height, during the Ummayed period, the citadel must have been an awe-inspiring sight as the great Caliphs wandered through the colonnaded street, which runs from north to south past 13 columns and 14 arches, to the residential palace with its throne room, frescoes and mosaics.

Much of Amman has been recycled over the years as ancient buildings were plundered for their masonry but Jerash, 40 kilometres north of the capital, has

Above: Woman weaver works at a traditional loom under the welcome shade of a canopy, near Bani Hamida's centre outside Amman.

Left: Using no more than a simple spool, a farmer's wife, from the Bani Hamida tribe spins outside her home.

Opposite top: An elderly woman of the Bani Hamida tribe continues to dye wool in the traditional method.

Opposite: Freshly dyed crimson wool hangs to dry overlooking a valley in the territory of the Bani Hamida tribe.

Left: A silver and amber necklace. Amber was believed to protect its wearer from rheumatism, internal ailments and the evil eye.

Opposite: Colourful handwoven bags on sale in one of Amman's many souks.

Above: Traditional Bedouin costume on display at the Folklore Museum in Amman.

remained relatively unspoiled. Not until the end of the last century, when the Ottoman Turks settled a few hundred Circassians there, was a significant population to be found in the well-watered valley. The Circassians, Muslims from Europe, were too few in number to ruin the great Roman town of Gerasa although they did use a number of the finest Roman blocks as keystones for their own dwellings. Jerash is perhaps the finest example of a Roman provincial town in the world. From Amman, the road there passes through the mountains of Gilead, many still covered with cypress forests that go back to biblical times. Rolling through the hills, one is taken far away from the rigours of the desert and its peoples into a softer, less demanding, world. So, in Jerash, be prepared for the sight of a large town dedicated to commerce and luxury.

The site was first occupied in the Middle and Late Bronze Ages (1600-1200 BC), and in the Iron Age up to 900 BC, but appears to have been abandoned for the next 500 years. The first major settlement in Jerash came soon after Alexander's conquest of the Middle East in 332 BC. After the break-up of the Seleucid Empire, the Romans stepped into the vacuum and established Gerasa as one of the major links in the Decapolis. Formal plans for the city, laid out in AD 40-60, were expanded as Roman hegemony spread throughout the 1st century. Trajan and Hadrian expanded the region still further. The population was a mixture of Aramaic speaking local Arabs and the elite, a mixture of Greeks and Arabs who spoke both Greek and Latin. The former was the language of arts, the latter of administration. Jerash flourished during the 1st and 2nd centuries but, by the third, the pace had slowed down. Like Amman, Jerash dwindled with the movement of the headquarters of the Islamic Caliphates to Baghdad in the 7th century but earlier, with the advent of Christianity, it had enjoyed one last fling.

In AD 330, the emperor Constantine declared Christianity the official religion of the Byzantine Empire. Many Roman temples were transformed into churches and more than 20 added to the municipality. The fortunes of the city followed the fortunes of the empire until the Byzantines lost to the forces of Islam at the battle of Yarmouk. One mosque is known to have been built in the city but, under the Ummayeds, the city lost its administrative significance. Largely bypassed by trade routes, it survived on the production of ceramics, local commerce, and agriculture. Finally, in the middle of the 8th century Jerash was almost destroyed by earthquakes which shook most of the great temples down but left many of the columns along the city's main thoroughfare intact. The columns had been reinforced with a flexible pebble foundation that absorbed the worst shocks so that, while many of the roofs collapsed, the pillars have continued to stand steady for 2,000 years.

When approaching from the south the visitor misses the full force and beauty of Jerash which, as it is steadily restored, looks less like an archeological site and more like a ghost town. The first sight to strike the newcomer is Hadrian's

Left: Triangular talisman decorated with silver coins and semi precious stones.

Opposite: Antique silver locket, decorated with coral and turquoise and silver bells. Lockets such as this were traditionally used to carry marriage certificates or amuletic charms written on a piece of parchment.

Above: Collection of hookahs for sale at an Amman souk.

Opposite top: Mensaf, the national dish of Jordan, ready to be served at a restaurant near Amman.

Opposite: Dozens of spices neatly arranged in a shop in Amman.

Right: An array of fascinating brass objects lures shoppers to Amman's busy souks.

Above: Three men while away the hours playing Mengalah, an ancient game enjoyed across Africa and the East.

Arch, built in AD 129-30 to commemorate the Emperor's visit to the city. It was supposed to have been the main gate to a new city wall which would have much expanded Jerash but the expected growth never came. Now it stands alone by the Hippodrome.

An archetypal Roman road, drawn with a ruler, leads directly into the main part of the town through the official South Gate and into the 'Oval Plaza' — a strange, distorted egg-shaped forum of columns that bends slightly to the west so that the exit from the plaza conforms to the north-south route of the main street, the Cardo.

Sewage systems run under the plaza. Cut into the paving stones is a watercourse from the Birketein pool, one-and-a-half kilometres to the north which fed a fountain structure that was built upon the foundations where the pillar carrying the Jerash Festival flame now sits.

Although only a few of the private dwellings that radiated away from the

Above: First capital of Jordan, under King Abdullah, Salt is one of Jordan's most charming cities.

centre of town have been excavated, visitors can get a firm idea of what life was like in Gerasa by walking along its colonnaded streets, grooved by the wheels of thousands of chariots. Jerash must have been a gorgeous city. And much of its early history echoed to the sound of chisels on stone as the Nabatean craftsmen carved ionic and doric columns, elaborate reliefs and inscriptions to the wealthy civic leaders who donated much money for the construction of great temples. It's difficult to pick out the most impressive of the many religious sites in Jerash but perhaps the prize is the Temple of Artemis. Thought to date from the 2nd century, it sits on a rise which dominates the ancient city. Worshippers would have had to approach the temple from the east side of the river along the Sacred Way, which took them up a monumental staircase into a long colonnaded rectangle — subsequently converted to a Byzantine church — and on into the Propylaeum Plaza.

Unlike the Oval forum, this plaza would not have been a market-place but a

Opposite: Forest of corinthian colonnades at the ancient Roman Provincial city of Jerash.

Above: Beehives in a meadow of colourful spring flowers.

venue for relaxation. Quiet recesses and fountains provide places for contemplation before the plaza flares open as it enters the Cardo. The entrance to the temple took the faithful under an arch topped by a portico made from elaborately carved stones, past the two-storey shops on either side and up the triple staircase.

The staircase is a triumph of style. Not only is it impressive in scale, but subtle in design. If you stand at the top, the seven stories cannot be distinguished. The stairs appear to fall away to the bottom without interruption. The temple precinct is 120 metres wide and the sacred precinct immediately surrounding the temple, measures 161 by 121 metres. The temple itself, however, was relatively small, just 24 by 13 metres. But it stands on a high podium surrounded by massive corinthian columns that give it a sense of intense grandeur. One column, which has stood for nearly two millennia, is now a little wobbly and if you look up you can see the top swaying. Yet there is no

Opposite: The great courtyard of the Temple of Zeus at Jerash.

Above: Aerial view of the colossal Temple of Artemis at Jerash. It was built in dedication to the patron goddess of Jerash, and was fortified by Arabs during the 12th century, before being largely destroyed by Crusader forces.

real danger of a collapse as each carved stone section of the columns ends in a taper that locks neatly and immovably into a recess in the one above.

Now Jerash is no longer a dead city. Aside from the thousands of visitors who throng its streets, the city hosts an international arts festival. There can be no better venue for the great works of the master composers, such as Beethoven and Mozart, nor for the plays of Shakespeare and Moliere, than the South Theatre. It is so finely designed that anyone who whispers in the centre of the stage can be heard in the back row as if they were sitting in the next seat. Needless to say, in a city of such wealth, an element of decadence crept in, fuelled by the products of the vineyards nearby.

The Jerash Nymphaeum was a focus for the sins and pleasures of the flesh, which are represented symbolically. This feature boasts some of the finest ornate stone carving left from the Roman age. Once it was adorned with columnettes and statues set in marble niches above. Water flowed through

Opposite: Remnants of a bygone era, corinthian columns stand like sentinels against the sun.

Opposite: Colourful spring flowers complement the stark beauty of the great Temple of Zeus in Jerash.

seven lion-head fountains beside the sidewalk and away under the pavement into a drainage system that still disposes of rainwater and some sewage. The Nymphaeum formed a complex quaintly described as a 'semi-sacred pleasure ground' by some historians. There the locals celebrated pagan and, later, festivals of a Bacchanalian nature. Among these was the annual Maiuma celebration in which naked women indulged in earthy celebrations, watched by spectators in the 1,000-seat festival theatre nearby. The festivities were banned in the 4th century after the advent of Christianity.

The fascinating history of the Temple of Zeus, south and west of the Nymphaeum, is still being uncovered by archaeologists. Standing splendid on a plinth at the top of a rise that drops into the river to the east of Jerash is the 'new' Temple of Zeus (AD 166), a more modest shrine compared with the ruined remains of a far larger and grander temple of Temenos. Little of the Temenos temple survives above ground, but below ran a series of vaults along all four sides of the great complex. Under the steps on the downhill side of the Temenos is the barrel-vault that ran around the area. It had to be raised upon another to maintain a horizontal system.

The lower vault was open to the street through great arches. This sub-vault is still intact. Locals say that it was lined with blue marble and sometimes filled with warm water as mountain herbs were tossed in for bathers taking curative waters at festival time. The Zeus complex must have been one of the most spectacular sights in the Decapolis.

In their salad days, the cities in the league tried to outdo each other in their attempts to outstrip Rome for architectural excellence. The South Theatre is an example of this competitive municipal vanity. Once absorbed into the Roman Empire, and immediately benefiting from the commercial side of the state as part of the new Arabian province, the city's elders would have happily shown their appreciation — and impressed upon outsiders the importance of Jerash as a market — by entertaining revered figures of the empire to lavish displays at the theatre. At its height the entire population of Jerash was about 18,000, so more than half the adult population could have been accommodated in the South Theatre, a massive over-capacity.

There is some debate as to whether the Temple of Zeus was an entire temple in its own right or whether it was built to be integral to the rest of the complex. Some experts believe it could have been a cultic High Place. Often referred to in the Bible, 'high places' were usually sacred places of sacrifice and part of a greater complex. This seems most likely since it would be unusual to build a discreet structure dedicated to the same god already worshipped nearby in the Temenos temple, which was built during the first half of the 1st century AD. Iain Browning, author of *Jerash and the Decapolis* and a leading expert in ancient architecture, says the actual artistic merit of the stonework on the Zeus complex

Opposite: A farmer rejoices in his abundant orange crop in the fertile tracts of the Jordan Valley.

Above: Onion plants flourish in the rich soils of the Jordan Valley.

Opposite: In Jordan, the modern and traditional live side by side, where horse-drawn ploughs still furrow the land.

leaves something to be desired, compared with the fine craftsmanship displayed by Nabatean masons elsewhere in Jerash.

But no one can doubt the class of the larger masonry work. The Zeus complex is staggering as you can see in the solid structure of the vaulting systems. The northern side of the Temenos — a holy precinct — is being excavated. Signs point to its having been an open air altar, perhaps the most sacred of all. But there are also signs that whatever was there was systematically destroyed, perhaps before the higher temple was built.

Jerash, like Petra and Wadi Rum, is a treasure. Many have spent a lifetime trying to unravel its secrets and piece together its role in the region's erratic history. But like so much of Jordan, especially the Jordan Valley, it staggered through the ages, enjoying times of extraordinary plenty and times of great recession, of high esteem and contempt in world affairs between war and peace. As with Umm Qais, Amman, Aqaba, Irbid and all the other cities and cultural centres, fortunes seemed to hang on the wings of political fate. None had the strategic minerals that would have maintained a focus of inevitable economic activity. When the Roman Empire and the Islamic Empire concentrated on the region, Jordan flourished. But when the emphasis shifted elsewhere, as it did dramatically after the Abbasids moved to what is now modern Iraq, Jordan withered, only to be rejuvenated centuries after by the arrival of the Turks in the 16th century. The Ottomans, however, treated this part of the Middle East with indifference. To them, its real role was as a conduit for the Pilgrimage to Mecca.

Today the Jordan Valley is more central to the life of the region than ever before. Its practical role has an ancient symbol in Jericho, the oldest, continuously occupied settlement in the world. Arguably, the valley was the cradle of civilisation for it was there Neolithic man first cultivated plants and domesticated animals. Strangely, however, the valley shows signs of having only been occupied for the last 12,000 years. The eastern Badia is peppered with the remains of humanoid activity going back to 400,000 BC. Artifacts dating from 20,000 BC have been discovered at the southern end of the Dead Sea. But the finds in Jerash come from a much later period.

Why the division? Why should the northern end of the valley have been settled so much more recently than the south and the rest of the country? One explanation is that the Jordan Valley was once part of the Red Sea all the way to Lake Tiberias. Dry land emerged due to silting or shifts in the tectonic plates, while a massive inland lake formed in about 100,000 BC. Lake Lisan is mentioned in the Old Testament but is also commemorated in the Lisan Peninsular. From the promontory, political boundaries aside, visitors can walk across the Dead Sea in boots like snow shoes to stop them sinking into the mud. With more silting two distinct lakes formed — the Dead Sea and Lake Tiberias. The Jordan River, fed by streams off the escarpment, flowed into the Dead Sea. The valley to the south was the Wadi Araba. This movement of the sea and formation of a freshwater river attracted human settlement.

Neolithic people settled in the valley which was ideal for intensive agriculture so long as water was plentiful. Farmers relied on irrigation from the ghors running into the valley, rather than on the Jordan itself which ran along a groove below the valley floor, making it difficult for irrigation. These primitive people tried their hands at building larger structures than their immediate ancestors, who made do with pits cut in the ground, roofed with grass, and caves. In about 4500 BC the valley people made dolmens — simple structures of stone slabs, three making the walls and a fourth the roof. It is not clear what the exact role of the dolmen was — home, shrine, mausoleum or something else entirely. They do not exist anywhere else in the Middle East and their closest counterparts seem to be at Stonehenge in southern England. A further indication of the sophisticated nature of settlements in the Jordan Valley comes from Ghassul, on the northern edge of the Dead Sea, across the valley from Jericho, where Chalcolithic peoples lived in an unfortified farming community among marshes that have long since dried up. Multi-coloured frescoes were discovered in some of the ancient dwellings from between 3750 and 3300 BC. These paintings are the second oldest so far discovered in the world — though much later than the Catal Huyuk paintings in Turkey which date back to 5750 BC. The Jordan Valley enjoyed a boom period in the Early Bronze Age but conflict came with development. From 3300 BC, fortified cities sprang up, of which the largest was probably Bab Al Dthraa. Judging from the number of people buried in its massive cemetery, just north of the Lisan Peninsular, on the road to Kerak on the southern shore of the Dead Sea, it had a population of about 25,000.

Small cities, probably organised as city-states in allegiance with others in the Jordan Valley, stretched from the Yarmouk River to the Gulf of Aqaba, taking their water from the wadis running off the eastern escarpment. The fortified towns, with walls sometimes ten metres thick, provided places of sanctuary for the nomads and farmers in the valley — either from random bandit attacks or more organised assaults of the kind so richly catalogued in the Old Testament. Many historians believe that a major Early Bronze Age trading route ran from Syria to the Red Sea, Sinai, and Egypt by way of Gilead, Amman, Moab, and Tafileh down the Hassa and Feinan wadis and into Wadi Araba. The route was both navigable and dotted with small villages all the way along.

Vital lessons have been learned from this history because when the Jordan Valley Authority set about redeveloping the region in 1979, it surveyed the ghors running into the Rift and found that the sites chosen by the ancient peoples were the same as those earmarked by the authority for resettlement and development, based on the fertility of soil and availability of water.

Opposite: Fig trees cover the verdant hillsides of the Ajlun Valley.

Opposite: Lit by shafts of light, Ajlun's vast stone stronghold was largely destroyed by Mongol forces in AD 1260.

Above: Qalaat al-Rabad, the hilltop fortress at Ajlun in northern Jordan, is one of the finest examples of Arab military architecture in the Middle East.

The southern end of the Jordan Valley began to dry up in the last two centuries BC, leaving the land suitable only for Bedouin nomads, while agriculture and permanent settlements became more concentrated in the north in Pella, Deir Alla and Tell Mazar. In 1150 BC the Philistines struck out from their homeland in Gaza and Asqualon and took over most of the central and north Jordan Valley, cutting it off from the hill kingdoms to the east. The Philistines, who brought advanced methods of iron smelting, ruled the valley for 150 years before being defeated by the shepherd boy, David, who established his kingdom of Israel in Jerusalem. After David's death, the division of the state of Israel opened the Jews to attack from Babylon, Syria and Persia. The three great empires surrounding the Middle East left the east of the Jordan, and the valley, largely untouched. Ironically, while much of the Arab world was in turmoil during this period, the Great Rift Valley enjoyed peace and prosperity. Few fortified cities from this time have been found.

The north of the valley eventually fell to the Persians who were uninterested in its potential and allowed it to decline until the Greek conquest of the region in 332 BC when some 25 Greek cities were built in the valley or the north, the most important being Pella.

In AD 63-64 Pompey cut through Syria and Palestine like a knife through butter and swiftly moved to impose Pax Romana on the region by forming, among other things, the Decapolis, of which Pella was the closest to the River Jordan. Pella was continuously occupied from the Late Neolithic period (4750 BC) to the Middle Ages — some human artifacts date back a million years — and reached its peak, along with the other cities of the Decapolis, in the 6th century AD. It had been a large Canaanite city of about 5,000 people but, by the time the Byzantines started building their churches there, it had exploded fivefold. The site was ideal; frost never spoilt delicate crops, it had plentiful water from the Wadi Jurum and the cool air of the foothills on which it sits provided relief from summer's heat.

However, when the Via Nova highway, linking Aqaba with Bosra in Syria, was built in AD 111, Pella was off the track and unable to benefit from the boost to trade the road would have brought. It had to be content with smaller links via Ajlun to Jerash and to Beth-Shan, the only Decapolis city on the west bank of the Jordan. But Pella was not to be outdone in the Decapolis competition for the most grandiose municipal structures, as the great civic complex in the centre of the city attests, though it probably fell far behind what Jerash and Amman were able to boast.

The earthquake, or quakes, which wrecked Gadara and Gerasa in the 8th century also destroyed much of Pella. It fell apart soon after the catastrophe and entered a period of decline. The advent of the Ummayeds did nothing to restore the fortunes of the Jordan Valley and Pella until the Ayyubid-Mamluk era (1187-1516), which Rami G Khouri, a leading authority on the history of his country calls the 'Jordan Valley's finest hour'.

The Ayyubid leader Saladin smashed the Crusaders at the battle of Hattin in 1187 taking Jordan back into the Arab fold. The Arab kings united Egypt and Syria allowing the Mamluks a period of stability in which to develop Jordan as an axis between the two empires. At this point, the Jordan Valley appeared to have entered a period of relatively high rainfall as sugar became the region's main crop and export. At least 20 water-powered sugar mills were built in the north of the valley and they continued to work until the 1960s. But some agricultural activity also returned to the south where there are other remains of sugar factories south of the Dead Sea. This period of plenty was disrupted by the Mongol invasions of the 13th and 15th centuries which were both repulsed but left destruction and economic chaos in their wake, allowing the Ottomans an easy invasion in 1516.

The Ottomans, strangely incompetent imperialists given the longevity of their empire, imposed punitively high taxation on the farmers of the valley who swiftly gave up the ghost. By 1600 they had abandoned the area, leaving it to bake dry in the sun so that when western explorers arrived they found it hardly credible that the valley had supported any life other than scrub bush and the occasional Bedouin herd of goats and camels which used, and continue to use, the valley for winter grazing.

The Jordan Valley remained 'dead' for 400 years, populated only by Bedu and the descendants of slaves from East Africa brought to Jordan by the Turks. Its rebirth came after World War II, especially with the building of the East Ghor Canal and other ambitious irrigation schemes, combined with a far-thinking land distribution plan for the inhabitants. Until the late 1950s and 1960s, there had been a plethora of development ideas to use the water running off the escarpment for irrigation but no sign of any implementation as the valley became embroiled in the conflict between the young nations of Israel, Palestine, and Transjordan.

In fact, in the 1950s Jordan hardly looked a going concern. After the arrival of 600,000 refugees from the Palestinian war with Israel, it suffered massive unemployment and its education system was on the point of collapse, while the roads were designed for donkeys, not motor vehicles, and tourism was non-existent. Malnutrition, along with malaria, was widespread while livestock perished from thirst in drought years. Farming was dependent on the seasons which often failed to deliver enough rain after planting and Jordan could not support its population of 1.5 million. The only way to develop the country was through the Jordan Valley by harnessing its waters for agriculture and hydroelectric power.

A plan to dam the Yarmouk River fell into stalemate after Israel demanded a scheme that would benefit all the countries of the region. Another plan, devised by the US Tennessee Valley Authority, met a similar fate although it was designed to consider the needs of all the countries affected. More plans came and went while the Arab states accused Israel of diverting waters from the Jordan to irrigate the Negev. They threatened to trap the river's flow before it even entered Jewish territory. But this would have denied Jordan access too. In June 1953, the Jordanian government commissioned two American consulting firms to produce a grand development plan for the Jordan Valley; but it was 20 years before its benefits were felt.

The principal aim was to dam the Yarmouk and drive a canal along the valley floor to put an end to subsistence farming and replace it with high intensity agriculture which would provide a surplus to meet the needs of a growing and hungry population. Lake Tiberias would be used to store water from the Yarmouk and dams would be built on the Yarmouk itself. These would link up

Opposite: Wild red poppies transform a bleak Jordan mountainside into a vibrant profusion of colour.

Above: Schoolboys at a Catholic church school pose for their picture.

Above right: Young Jordanian beauty soaks up the afternoon sun at the annual Jerash Festival.

with the East Ghor Canal, which would run the entire length of the east bank and supply another canal on the western side of the valley. By June 1966 the East Ghor Canal was built and work had started on the Khalid ibn bin Walid dam on the Yarmouk and the King Talal barrage on the Zarqa. But construction of the Walid dam was held up by another flare-up in the age-old Arab-Israeli conflict when the Israelis invaded Syria and took the Golan Heights, overlooking the project.

The June War, as it became known, also badly disrupted the agricultural development of the valley that had been stimulated by the construction of the East Ghor Canal, and which had produced spectacular results. The hostilities terrified the local farmers who had invested heavily in their new plots of land. At least 60,000 people left their homes in the valley for the safety of the eastern highlands and only about 5,000 remained behind. Though many farmers tended their fields while living in the sanctuary of towns such as Salt and Irbid, the canal was regularly bombed and was out of action for the four years between June 1967 and August 1971.

Most damaging of all was the loss of the West Bank. It had accounted for 45 per cent of Jordan's GNP in 1966, 25 per cent of the country's area under cultivation, 65 per cent of the vegetable output, 60 per cent of fruits, 80 per cent of olives and one-third of all cereals. In all, 300,000 refugees flooded across the Jordan's bridges. To cope with this King Hussein's brother, Crown Prince Hassan, 23 years old and fresh out of Oxford University, used his influence and high office to establish the Royal Scientific Society and the Jordan Valley Commission to plan how to cope with the disruption at Jordan's core.

Since the international community was unwilling to commit large amounts of donor money to reconstruction until the Jordanians were able to prove that they could plan their own economy and development, things got off to a shaky start. But by 1975 the government had raised $2 billion in development investment for a three-year plan. This was the beginning of the true renaissance of the Jordan Valley, though many more plans were to come before it reached its current productive height. However, the ecological disasters facing the world have not passed Jordan by. The farmers of the Jordan Valley rely on high input systems requiring huge amounts of fertilizer and pesticides which, in addition to damaging the environment, are also costly and a drain on foreign exchange. Plastic greenhouses not only hide the beauty of a valley in bloom but have also been shown to poison the earth. The valley's next challenge will be to come up with farming techniques that are self-sustaining enough to survive well into the 21st century.

Opposite: Golden sundown behind the ancient Roman ruins at Pella.

4 · THE GREAT HIGHWAYS

Previous pages: The modern town of Kerak jostles for space with the remains of its imposing Crusader fortress.

Opposite: Modern fresco at the Greek Orthodox Church of St. George in Madaba.

Above: Greek Orthodox priest in Madaba.

where the escarpment falls down into what was then the Land of Canaan.

At its height, Madaba rivalled the great cities of Jerash, Amman and Pella, though it was not part of the Decapolis. Alas, little but a cistern and a few bits and pieces, scattered around the town, are left of the Roman era city. Madaba was significant enough to be allowed to mint its own coins by the 2nd and 3rd centuries. Some of these provide an interesting clue to the mythical lives of the inhabitants. Along with the usual effigies of the emperors they also showed the sun on a four-wheeled chariot with the legend 'the Holy Helios of Madaba'. It may have been a nod of acknowledgement towards the Nabateans of Petra who, according to some historical sources, worshipped the sun.

Like the Gadarene, the citizens of Madaba also honoured the Roman goddess Tyche, and again there is reverence for the beliefs of the Nabateans in the inscriptions to their God 'Dousares of Madaba'.

Madaba, however, is probably most famous for its mosaics. One, a section of the 1st century BC Herodian fortress of Machaerus, which was to play a final role in the life and death of John the Baptist, is the oldest known mosaic floor in Jordan. Many fine art works may also be seen in the Madaba Museum; others are scattered around the town in private homes and Byzantine churches. The most spectacular is the mosaic map of Palestine in the Greek Orthodox church known, appropriately, as the Church of the Map. It is one of the oldest maps in the country and, because of its schematically accurate rendition of such landmarks as the Jordan River and the Dead Sea, the deep wadis of the plateau on the east of the great river, the hills of Samaria and Judaea and the Mediterranean coastal plain, it has been possible to identify most of the 150 places marked on it. The most important are picked out in red stone.

Unfortunately, since it was discovered during building operations in 1896 and badly disturbed, only fragments remain. Using an early key system, towns are shown by a gate and two towers. A church marks holy sanctuaries, while major and minor roads are clearly identifiable. The complete map would have shown an area from Tyre and Sidon in the north to the Nile Delta in the south, the Mediterranean in the west and the Arabian desert in the east. But the map's central focus is Jerusalem — seen from a bird's eye view. Given the buildings which it makes prominent, such as the Justinian New Church of the Theotocos which was dedicated to the Virgin Mary on 20 November AD 542, the map can be dated accurately to the mid 6th century.

Walking around the streets of Madaba today, there is little sense of the Roman order that must have prevailed for several hundred years from the Roman conquest of the region in AD 64. As the town is perched on a rise it feels instead more like a medieval European village with a confusing maze of streets and narrow alleys. The sensation is reinforced by the sounds of cobblers, carpet-makers, tea shops, hawkers and all manner of cottage industries clattering and

chattering as they go about their businesses. The doors to the carpet-weavers workshops at street level are always open for the light — and so that the weaver can chat with passers-by, or take a break for a glass of tea or piping-hot cardamom coffee. In Bedouin society it is usually the women who do the weaving on hand-looms set up on the ground. The Bedouin weave beautiful long rugs a metre wide which can be sewn together if they have to be used to cover wider areas. These are usually striped, as simple geometric patterns are the easiest way to bring life to a rug without highly complicated weaving.

The world-famous Madaba weavers are men. Their looms are simple. Spun wool, a mixture from goat and sheep, is strung flat in front to face the weaver who sits on a high stool and passes the horizontal threads through the vertical plane by hand. He then beats them firmly into place with what looks like a heavyweight comb. The process is slow and laborious and does not produce rugs as fine as those woven by Bedouin women but much thicker and more

Above: Byzantine Mosaic Map of the Holy Land — and much of the Middle East — was discovered in 1890 beneath the floor of the Greek Orthodox Church of St. George, Madaba. The map, the oldest in the world to depict Jerusalem, originally consisted of more than two million mosaic cubes.

Above: The small city of Madaba, with its maze of streets and alleyways, resembles a medieval European village.

lumpy — especially if hand-spun wool has been used. The Madaba carpets are possibly the hardest wearing in the world but, despite the boasts of the locals, they are by no means the finest. The endless hours visitors may spend chatting to one of the weavers is what makes them special.

Mount Nebo, a few kilometres west of Madaba is, perhaps, a perfect place for a prophet to die and has been a shrine to Moses ever since. The area was inhabited long before the Jews arrived to survey the Promised Land. Fascinating, and as yet unexplained, remains of Stone Age settlements have been found on the mountain with three peaks. Menhirs, stone circles, tombs and flint tools are evidence of very early human occupation. It is a pleasant fantasy to wander among these ancient symbols, now overgrown with poppies, giant daisies and dandelions so reminiscent of the flora on the English downs, and wonder whether the dolmens and menhirs may, in some way, be related to similar relics in Europe. Britain, especially, is liberally dotted with stone circles and strange granite blocks which, tradition has it, were set up along ley lines — invisible lines on the earth's surface of particularly potent natural power that are supposed to encircle the globe. Perhaps these ancient peoples were connected by a common force, the provenance of which has been lost in the mists of time. The explanation for the dolmens and menhirs at Mount Nebo, and elsewhere in the Holy Land, will probably remain a mystery forever. But they certainly add to the strong sense of mysticism and spirituality that descends on visitors like a gentle cloak when they first arrive at Syagha, the western peak of the mount and the site of the earliest church. It dates back to the 4th century AD.

The first mention of Syagha and the monastery which has been excavated there, revealing yet more extravagant mosaics, comes from a woman called Aetheria who made a pilgrimage to the mount around AD 394. After a vision, she found the tomb of Moses. There seems to be some substance to this; as it is unlikely the Jews would have wanted to move Moses' corpse far from where he died. Aetheria was apparently shown around the Syagha by 'holy men' and the tomb was in a small church, which she describes. The church today, a basilica, has a raised platform at the east end of the south aisle with steps beside it which correspond exactly to those of the Tomb of Moses as described by Aetheria. She may, indeed, have discovered the real tomb of the great prophet whose life is celebrated with a formidable eulogy. '(And) there arose not a prophet since in Israel like unto Moses, whom the Lord knew face to face'. Not, that is, until the birth of Jesus and the Prophet Mohammed.

Above: Bronze carving of St. George slaying the dragon, at the Greek Orthodox Church of St. George in Madaba.

The mountains of Moab rise and fall like the giant ocean waves that covered this limestone relief many millions of years ago, and a spectacular breaker plunges into the valley of the Wadi Zarqa Ma'in to the hot springs at Hammanat Ma'in. These springs have been boiling out of the ground for tens of centuries, heated and sulphurated by volcanic activity near the earth's surface, along the fault line which precipitated the massive collapse of the earth's crust into the Great Rift Valley. The springs, hot enough to boil an egg when they bubble out of the surface, are said to have profound medicinal properties. Sadly this has meant that rather than preserve the springs as a place of outstanding natural beauty, a massive hotel has been built on the site. It looks like a well-scrubbed multi-story car park — a great white concrete slab in a place filled with historical significance and myth.

But Jordan has other architecture. The restaurant, museum and rest house at Umm Qais show tasteful adaptation of ancient buildings to modern needs. So is the rest house in Petra, built, like the city it serves, into living rock.

Herod the Great was a regular visitor to the baths at Hammanat Ma'in which were said to work wonders on his many ailments. Along with today's visitors, locals flock to the boiling fountains in droves, gaily frolicking in the hot cascades dressed in underwear or swimwear — oblivious that such happiness and

Overleaf: Aerial view of Mount Nebo, with the Monastery of Syagha, overlooking the Promised Land. It was there, it is said, that Moses took his last breath.

Above: One of the finest Byzantine friezes in existence, found in the Monastery of Syagha on Mount Nebo. It depicts such creatures as ostrich, lion, camel and zebra.

abandon may be frowned upon elsewhere in the Middle East. For there, indeed, the maturity of tolerance seems far distant.

Tolerance was no major feature of Herod's world. His son, Herod Antipas, inherited that part of his kingdom which included Moab. Among the many palaces his father built was one at Machaerus — Mukawir — on a peak overlooking the hot springs of Ma'in. Now desolate, the mount is a long hot walk from the nearest road. In Herod's time it may have been more attractive since heavy deforestation and over-grazing have taken their toll on the southern mountains of Moab. The original palace may have been quite different from the barren mountaintop ruin set in hard-baked sand.

Antipas was not cut from the same cloth as his father who, despite his Jewish descent, was a non-Jew and was imposed on the Israelites as 'King of the Jews'. But he managed to combine rebuilding the Temple of Jerusalem with his own pagan worship. The fortified palaces he built offered plenty of opportunity for

the Red Sea. Those on the eastern side of the Jordan, in the province of Outre Jordain, were never intended as administrative bases for a Roman-style colonial system but more as a means of extorting 'taxes' from passing caravans. They were also to serve as an early-warning system for Arab attacks on Jerusalem. Local "administration" from castles like Kerak, extended only as far as the farmland needed to sustain the substantial garrison of several thousand men and hundreds of horses inside the thick stone walls. To the crusaders, the King's Highway became a way of making easy money while putting nothing back into the local economy. Established by King Baldwin I in 1132 to strengthen the line he had already set up between Shobak and Jerusalem, Kerak provided a huge boost to the coffers for the kings of Jerusalem.

Opposite: Sparkling falls at the hot springs Health Spa in Ma'in.

A French knight, Reynaud de Chatillon, became Kerak's last incumbent. He was a notorious sadist. His favourite means of execution was to toss his victims off Kerak's battlements and watch them bounce into the river valley below. But when he found out that many died long before they reached the bottom — from head injuries — he fitted the condemned with wooden helmets so that they would live every agonising bone-breaking second of their fall.

When Baldwin III died, his thirteen-year-old leper son, Baldwin IV was his only heir, leaving a wealthy widow, Stephanie, mistress of Kerak. Reynaud swiftly won the hand of the widow but Baldwin IV, aware that he would not live to see his sixteenth birthday and would therefore die without an heir, sued for peace with the Muslims.

Saladin gave free passage for Christians through Arab areas and traffic increased along the King's Highway. But the brief peace on the road was broken when the temptation of the caravans proved too much for Reynaud.

He plundered a caravan heading for Mecca. In retaliation Saladin captured 1,500 Christian pilgrims on their way to Jerusalem and both sides found themselves sucked into war again. This suited the Arab warrior because it provided him with the excuse he wanted to finally rid the Holy Land of the European intruders and establish Arab hegemony.

But when Jerusalem sent reinforcements to Kerak, Saladin withdrew and the truce was re-established. Once again Reynaud broke it. And when Saladin led a vast army across the Jordan, King Guy of Jerusalem was foolish enough to confront the Arabs. At the Battle of Hittin the Crusaders were soundly thrashed. Only Guy and a few aides, among them Reynaud, survived to be taken prisoner and sent to Damascus.

Saladin was so chivalrous that during the siege of Kerak he ordered his men to avoid bombarding one of the chambers in the castle as it was the honeymoon suite of Isobel, Baldwin's sister in Damascus. He told the captive Reynaud his treachery was the cause of the rout of the Crusaders. When Reynaud replied with an insult, Saladin beheaded him with one flick of his razor-sharp sabre.

Above: Detail of mosaic peacock at the Monastery on Mount Nebo.

the sort of decadence that low-grade Hollywood films have attributed to the Roman Empire. Machaerus had a walled garden filled with fig trees where vines may have dripped down upon the reclining minor potentates, languishing in the many baths with which the palace was appointed. An appropriate setting for the plot to end John the Baptist's life.

When Antipas took his brother's wife, Herodias, as a lover John took grave exception and preached loudly and publicly against the union. He was thrown in jail for his ravings but Antipas, aware of John's popular following, refused to execute him. Herodias worked her witchlike magic on the weak-willed Herod and persuaded her daughter, the lovely Salome, to dance for the tetrarch. Antipas was so moved by Salome's display he promised her anything she wanted. And when she demanded John's head on a silver platter, much against his instincts, it was delivered.

Although the Mountains of Moab are part of modern Jordan, those who

Above: Young shepherd watches over his family's flock near Mukawir.

travel the King's Highway are aware that a short wander off the beaten track will take them back down the centuries.

In spring, young wheat and barley, fed by sophisticated modern irrigation systems, cover the rounded downlands. Every inch of land that could possibly be turned to crop-bearing has been used for millennia. But the black tents of the desert nomads are still much in evidence on this border between ancient and modern civilizations — between the wanderers and the settled. All the cultures seem to meet at Dhiban, one-time capital of Moab under Mesha, where the famous Mesha stele was found and so nearly lost. Discovered in 1868 by a missionary, the earliest-known Hebrew script of that time was reported to the French consul in Jerusalem. After seeing the remarkable rock he agreed to pay the local tribesmen £60 for it. The consul rushed off to raise the money having, very luckily, first taken a cast of the work.

In his absence an argument broke out about who owned the priceless stone. The bickering ended when the rock was heated over a fire and cold water poured on it. The red-hot stone immediately shattered. Although much of it was subsequently reconstructed, many smaller shards joined the dust of Jordan — in which lie so many other secrets.

The gorge of the Wadi Mujib plunges 1,100 metres into a steep-sided U-shaped river valley where the Mujib River meanders along to empty itself into the Dead Sea. The great salt lake is in desperate need of replenishment. Every year, it shrinks and shrinks as its legendary specific gravity becomes higher. Suspended salts are concentrated by the phenomenal evaporation of summer and increased by the inflow of saline water from the Jordan. During the 1970s, as its level fell by fifty centimetres a year, the Dead Sea appeared to be dying. The dam on the Jordan — which used to deliver 900 million cubic metres a year to the inland sea — along with control on the flow of the other wadis supplying it, and the re-afforestation programmes on both its east and west banks, have taken their toll. Nevertheless, the Dead Sea will, without any improvement, exist for at least another 1,000 years.

The gasping thirst of the Dead Sea adds drama to the sight of the Mujib, one of the most dramatic valleys in the Middle East. The King's Highway continues to roll along through the limestone landscape to Kerak which stands more than nine hundred metres above the surrounding plateau. No finer example of a Crusader castle exists.

Kerak's history is also a paradigm of the treachery and intrigue, brutality and chivalry that so characterised the Christian Crusades to the Holy Land. Most of the knights were little more than thieves, racketeers and brutes who deserved their bloody ends at the hands of the Muslim armies which eventually expelled them ignominiously from whence they came.

Crusader castles were built, each a day's ride apart, from Southern Turkey to the Red Sea. Those on the eastern side of the Jordan, in the province of Outre Jordain, were never intended as administrative bases for a Roman-style colonial system but more as a means of extorting 'taxes' from passing caravans. They were also to serve as an early-warning system for Arab attacks on Jerusalem. Local "administration" from castles like Kerak, extended only as far as the farmland needed to sustain the substantial garrison of several thousand men and hundreds of horses inside the thick stone walls. To the crusaders, the King's Highway became a way of making easy money while putting nothing back into the local economy. Established by King Baldwin I in 1132 to strengthen the line he had already set up between Shobak and Jerusalem, Kerak provided a huge boost to the coffers for the kings of Jerusalem.

Opposite: Sparkling falls at the hot springs Health Spa in Ma'in.

A French knight, Reynaud de Chatillon, became Kerak's last incumbent. He was a notorious sadist. His favourite means of execution was to toss his victims off Kerak's battlements and watch them bounce into the river valley below. But when he found out that many died long before they reached the bottom — from head injuries — he fitted the condemned with wooden helmets so that they would live every agonising bone-breaking second of their fall.

When Baldwin III died, his thirteen-year-old leper son, Baldwin IV was his only heir, leaving a wealthy widow, Stephanie, mistress of Kerak. Reynaud swiftly won the hand of the widow but Baldwin IV, aware that he would not live to see his sixteenth birthday and would therefore die without an heir, sued for peace with the Muslims.

Saladin gave free passage for Christians through Arab areas and traffic increased along the King's Highway. But the brief peace on the road was broken when the temptation of the caravans proved too much for Reynaud.

He plundered a caravan heading for Mecca. In retaliation Saladin captured 1,500 Christian pilgrims on their way to Jerusalem and both sides found themselves sucked into war again. This suited the Arab warrior because it provided him with the excuse he wanted to finally rid the Holy Land of the European intruders and establish Arab hegemony.

But when Jerusalem sent reinforcements to Kerak, Saladin withdrew and the truce was re-established. Once again Reynaud broke it. And when Saladin led a vast army across the Jordan, King Guy of Jerusalem was foolish enough to confront the Arabs. At the Battle of Hittin the Crusaders were soundly thrashed. Only Guy and a few aides, among them Reynaud, survived to be taken prisoner and sent to Damascus.

Saladin was so chivalrous that during the siege of Kerak he ordered his men to avoid bombarding one of the chambers in the castle as it was the honeymoon suite of Isobel, Baldwin's sister in Damascus. He told the captive Reynaud his treachery was the cause of the rout of the Crusaders. When Reynaud replied with an insult, Saladin beheaded him with one flick of his razor-sharp sabre.

Opposite: Forbidding landscape of Wadi Mujib leads on to the shores of the Dead Sea.

Above: Aerial view of the luxurious Health Spa resort at Ma'in.

But another year passed before Kerak yielded to the Arabs. Even now its huge vaulted passage ways and phenomenal battlements remain almost impregnable. Saladin simply cut the castle off from the outside world and waited while Stephanie's forces wandered impotently around the dark, dank corridors — looking down hopelessly on the forces below.

Although the town of Kerak is now overwhelmingly Muslim, echoes of its Christian past linger in some of the family names. One group is called Matraneh, meaning bishop, while its parent clan, called Bawareesh, could be a corruption of 'parish'.

As you head south it seems as if every inch of the countryside has been fought over for countless centuries. Almost every village commemorates a battle between the Edomites and the Jews or Moabites, the Arabs and the Christians, the Turks and the Arabs, fighting for the freedom which for so long eluded them. Just south of Kerak, the twin villages of Motak and Mazar mark the

Above: Potash mine on the shores of the Dead Sea — lowest point of land on earth — looks out towards Jericho.

greatest defeat inflicted upon the Prophet Mohammed's Jihad forces in their attempts to conquer the Middle East in the name of Islam. The defeat forced the Arabs to re-group and reorganise at Medina before sallying forth, this time with as much tactical military strength as religious fervour. Three Muslim leaders, Zaid ibn Harith, Jaafar ibn abu Talib and Abdullah ibn Ruaha, killed at the battle of Motah, (AD 632) were buried at Mazar where a large, modern, mosque sits on the site of their original mausoleum. The Muslims, chastened but not broken by this experience, renewed their assaults in AD 636 and swept over the opposition, finally destroying them at the Battle of Yarmouk before pushing on to establish the first Caliphate in Damascus.

Arab patriots also fought hard for freedom in this area during the First World War at Tafileh, a village dominated by another Crusader ruin. When the Bedu wanted to attack they tried subterfuge, claiming they had a battery of guns ready to flatten it if the 180 Turks within did not give up. The response was a

Above: Sunrise over the Dead Sea.

volley of rifle shots. Auda abu Tayi, the legendary warrior with 75 dead on his account — not counting Turks — found the riposte too much to bear. Jabbing his spurs into the side of his Arab mare, he rode into full view of the enemy.

'Dogs, do you not know Auda?' he boomed in his deep bass roar.

So fearsome was Auda's reputation the inhabitants immediately capitulated, allowing the occupation of the town without loss. Tafileh was of little strategic importance but the Turkish general in the region, Hamid Fakhri Pasha, commander of the Turkish 48th Division, decided the citadel must be retaken. He collected 900 men, 100 cavalry, two mountain howitzers, and 27 machine guns for a counter attack, pressing into service all available civilian transport from Kerak. The absurd mission, the use of so many men and so much equipment to regain the position, galled the Arabs who went into a cold rage. Rather than outmanoeuvre the enemy by shifting their centre or vanishing into the surrounding hills to attack again at leisure, they set up a defence based on old military textbooks, rather than the guerrilla tactics they were perfecting. Lightly armed but effectively led, with just a handful of automatic weapons and machine guns between them, the Arabs attacked the Turks on both flanks and sent shrapnel and well-aimed rifle fire to confuse the centre. The Turkish general, with much battle experience, was compelled to deploy his staff officers in the front line.

'I have been 40 years a soldier, but never saw I rebels fight like these. Enter the ranks . . . ,' he said as bullets ripped into the flinty earth around him and men fell poleaxed by the blow of carbine slugs.

One group of Armenians with an old score to settle, rose against their tormentors and rushed the enemy positions armed only with knives. The Turks were driven back among the steep ravines and wadis which break up the Rift Valley escarpment to Kerak. But in the thick snow and ice of winter the revolutionaries, who lost 100 out of 600 men, failed to press home the advantage.

Above: High above the Dead Sea, a marker reminds visitors of the actual point of mean sea level.

Looking down into the Dead Sea valley, with its mild climate and plentiful grazing, while they shivered in their freezing camps on the top of the escarpment, morale fell swiftly among the rebel Arabs. Fights began to break out. Six men set out on a gruelling journey for money and other goods for the new garrison at Tafileh and nearly died. Only one camel survived the cold, slippery clay surfaces that made the ships of the desert stumble and stagger on the way to Guweira, north of Aqaba. There the men found the pain of blood rushing to their frozen extremities greater than the cold itself. At Guweira they rested briefly, loading up with sixteen 24lb bags of gold worth £30,000 and set off back to Tafileh.

Gold was vital fuel to the Arab revolt. To the Bedu, who remain an independent people beyond the control of any colonial master, it was the theory of nationhood that appealed, rather than the desire to rid themselves of an oppressive regime. The Ottoman Empire held sway only in the cities of Arabia. The Badia was forever beyond their reach. Nevertheless, one fringe benefit of warfare, as far as the tribesmen were concerned, was the booty from sacking a railway station, supply train, or garrison. Another was the pay. Gold, which was used to encourage and reward the brave, also paid for the supplies needed to sustain a rebel army on the move, one that had to forsake the low intensity grazing of the nomad and travel in large numbers while buying food and fodder from locals. Thus it was vital for the garrison in Tafileh that the party carrying the gold, return swiftly. The garrison was an uneasy alliance of rival tribes who, for generations, had been attacking one another. T E Lawrence, who led the re-supply party, had gone on with two others. In the searing cold they broke down. Loaded with extra bags of gold, he left them near the ruins of Odroh and headed on, to do battle with the Edomite winter. His favourite camel,

Above: Lone white flower braves the austere temperature of midday en route to the Dead Sea.

Wodheiha, once a racing beast, plunged into snow drifts, became stuck in bogs, and slid down icy mountain sides. At one point, the camel was so thoroughly stuck in a drift that she had to be dug out by hand. The ice, cutting Lawrence's wrists and ankles, caused him to bleed so that he left ice crystals the colour of 'pale, very pale, watermelon-flesh' in the snow.

At the end of the first day's ride at Shobak he gave £500 to Sherif Abd el Main and his followers, who were desperately short of money. On the second day the weather was so bad that the two escorts from Shobak slipped away from the young colonel. Eventually, his female camel, enraged by the obstacles she had been asked to overcome, hurled herself down the steep slope above Rashheidiya, with Lawrence clinging terrified to the saddle horn where he was greeted by a delighted crowd of cheering Bedu thrilled at such a dramatic entrance. His last eight miles to Tafileh were relatively smooth and he delivered the money to Sherif Zeid, commander of the garrison.

Members of the guerrilla armies of the Arab Revolt routinely made such dramatic rides, sometimes covering more than 100 miles a day. But they could have been accomplished on no other beast but the camel — nature's survivor. Indeed, men to match the camel's capacity to survive, are rare.

Further down the King's Highway, close to Tafileh, is D'ana. Seen from above it looks as though it was laid out as a chessboard because the dark, square earth roofs stand out in winter from the white buildings and snow around them. Today little has changed in D'ana although many of the Bedouin who lived there have moved to a modern concrete village at the top of the escarpment to take advantage of conveniences like piped water and electricity, and to work at the nearby cement factory. Overlooking the Wadi Arabah, D'ana village has the finest view and purest air in the Kingdom. It's only a matter of time before sharp-eyed property developers see that renovation of the houses will be both profitable and worthwhile for aesthetic reasons; not least because the surrounding area has been turned into a national park and will preserve the area from the excesses of development. The national park of D'ana is one of the last refuges of wild sable, leopard and other rare species that have been shot into extinction elsewhere in the Arab world.

D'ana almost defies description. A wander through the steep-sided valleys as the sun's angle changes the hues of the sandstone from red to purple, to green, to grey and gold, stills the heart. The air is silent. Beneath the lip of the escarpment, picked out with grey rock, the inhabitants of the region built small church caves and rock-cut villages, as well as hides for their flocks from the predators — big cats of the night. But the land below is virgin. There may be undiscovered ruins and subterranean finds that could electrify the archaeological community elsewhere, but D'ana is magical because it gives a sense that its dramatic plunging relief, wild flowers, and wind-carved landscape, unlike the rest of the country, has never been fought over. It is a small oasis of natural beauty in a landscape shaped by man which, somehow, modern history has passed by.

Opposite: Ruined Crusader fortress of Mont Realis — Montreal — at Shobak, was built by Baldwin I in 1115. It finally fell to Saladin's forces in 1189.

But even D'ana, or at least the valley below, had a major role in ancient history. This was because of its copper deposits, the engine of the incorrectly described Bronze Age. Below D'ana village, a canyon cuts through the rock to form the Wadi D'ana which is soon joined by the Wadi Khalid and the Wadi Ratiye. All three obscure valleys should be etched into the minds of any serious scholar of the Bible or the region.

Many of the hideous conflicts which erupted in and around Edom can be put down to the wealth produced where the three Wadis meet at Feinan. Two sources of copper ore are found there. First, and most important, is the two-to-four-metre-thick layer of copper minerals emerging in the Wadi Khalid. The other is found in veins and joints in the massive sandstone above the main ore horizon of the wadis Ratiye, Abiad and Khalid. The region of Feinan and Wadi Fidan, just to its north, were major industrial areas producing vast quantities of smelted copper for export all over the Near East. In fact, it was the biggest producer of the metal outside Cyprus.

The first proof of copper ore's use in this area comes from the carbon-dating of flint tools from the eighth and seventh millennia BC. Flint drills, used to make beads out of 'greenstone' — malachite — and to grind the stones into green powder — which replaced ochre as a cosmetic — have been traced to Feinan and Fidan. No ore was smelted at that time but, as the techniques for producing lime plaster and smelting copper are much the same, experts believe that they must have been discovered more or less simultaneously.

The smelting of ores did not begin until the Chalcolithic period in about 4000 BC. Small-scale copper operations existed at this time in Feinan; stone mining tools and hammerstones have been found on ancient mine dumps that produced high-quality copper. The main peak for copper production came with the Bronze Age in the middle of the 3rd millennium BC when the fluxing agent, manganese, was discovered. This allowed the miners to smelt copper out of low-grade ores and scrape off the detritus.

The volume of the slag heaps from this time suggest a production of up to 300 tonnes a year. But on the edge of the Wadi Arabah the demand for copper in Palestine and Jordan could not be met from these sources and some was imported from Catal Huyuk in Anatolia, Turkey, where mining was slightly more advanced.

By the Iron Age, the working conditions in the mines and furnaces of Feinan could only have been inhuman. It is believed the success of the mines is one reason why the Edomites spent so much time at war, especially with the Jews on the other side of the Dead Sea. Aside from any historical conflict with the

Opposite: Archaeological evidence at D'ana Village suggests it has been settled for over 6000 years.

Edomites, they would have wanted to control the flourishing industries growing up in the Arabah which attracted Solomon especially.

Even at the time of the Exodus, the copper fields would have sorely tempted Moses and his horde. During the Iron Age about 10,000 tonnes of copper was produced from 100 mines consuming 250,000 tonnes of charcoal. This may have contributed to deforestation and desertification. The massive production of copper during the Iron Age came to an end in 400 BC and the mines were not reopened until the Romans introduced technologies which allowed the miners to enlarge them and produce metal from low-grade ores. Nonetheless, Roman regard for safety and labour relations left much to be desired. Hundreds of slaves perished in underground mines which had no roof supports — or died of heat-exhaustion working the ore-producing furnaces.

In the centre of D'ana residents draw water from a spring that has cut a V in the escarpment above and is piped by gravity. Children and old women draw pure, sweet water from the perennially flowing fountains. Sitting on the steps of their houses and shops, the few inhabitants who cling to the old life in this little village, high on a spit of land jutting out over the valley like the prow of a ship, chat over a glass of tea and wonder how long this idyll will continue. With government help some houses in the village, which had fallen into disrepair, have been restored. Earthen roofs and walls of mud brick are not only prettier than concrete blocks but they are cheaper and easier to build. They also do no harm to the environment. There are many places in the Kingdom of Jordan which grip the heart with their beauty or grandeur, or both. But nowhere is the leaving as cloying as when you say goodbye to D'ana.

It is not a problem in Shobak, mother of the Crusader chain built in the 12th and 13th centuries, which now seems almost a caricature of village life. On a lone point of land overlooking a desolate landscape, Shobak was built by Baldwin I in about 1115 and besieged several times by Saladin until it fell in 1189. The Mamluks restored it and added some fine carvings in Arabic in the 14th century but it remains a testament to a brutal period. The strongest symbol of the paranoia of the Crusader era is the 375-steps down a secret underground passage through the mountain to a well.

Top: D'ana Nature Reserve, home to some of the Middle East's most spectacular scrubland, was founded as Jordan's sixth wildlife reserve in 1990.

Above: Flora at D'ana includes colourful endemic species.

5 · JEWELS IN THE CROWN

Previous pages: Wadi Rum is a favourite spot for those who want to leave the trappings of the modern world behind. The sheer rock faces, which climb upwards many hundreds of metres, attract mountain climbers from across the globe.

T E Lawrence, the cerebral Fellow of All Souls Oxford, the cold strategic planner who once had to shoot a man in the chest in the absence of an official executioner, was bewitched.

'Day was still young as we rode between two great pikes of sandstone to the foot of a long, soft slope poured down from the domed hills in front of us. It was tamarisk covered: the beginning of the Valley of Rum, they said. We looked up on the left to a long wall of rock, sheering in like a thousand-foot wave towards the middle of the valley; whose other arc, to the right, was an opposing line of steep, red broken hills. We rode up the slope, crashing our way through the brittle undergrowth.

'As we went, the brushwood grouped itself into thickets whose massed leaves took on a stronger tint of green the purer for their contrasting setting in plots of open sand of a cheerful delicate pink. The ascent became gentle, till the valley was a confined tilted plain. The hills on the right grew taller and sharper, a fair counterpart of the other side which straightened itself into one massive rampart of redness. They drew together until only two miles divided them: and then, towering gradually till their parallel parapets must have been a thousand feet above us, ran forward in an avenue for four miles.

'They were not unbroken walls of rock, but were built sectionally, in crags like gigantic buildings, along the two sides of the street. Deep alleys, fifty feet across, divided the crags, whose plans were smoothed by the weather into huge apses and bays, and enriched with surface fretting and fracture, like design.'

In truth, Lawrence confessed later in *Seven Pillars of Wisdom* he liked Rum too much. The book takes its name from the seven pillars seen on the left of the road to Wadi Rum from the Desert Highway.

Lawrence's metaphor of the street does justice only to the central valley, for Wadi Rum is one of the great untold wonders of the world. In fact, the complex of ridges and inselbergs is more like a gigantic city of rocks that exploded out of the ground. But the atmosphere of the wadi and its surrounds is gentle and serene — relieving contrast from the violence of the desert which seems to howl even when there is no wind. But where perennial springs bubble from scars in the weird rock faces it comes as no surprise that Wadi Rum was one of the earliest inhabited sites in Jordan and a holy place during the Nabatean civilisation.

The landscape of Rum was created by a catastrophic upheaval, possibly connected to the movements of the tectonic plates that caused the formation of the Rift Valley to the west. The massive, preternatural earth movements took what might have been a flat plain, broke it jaggedly, and then upended it so that the multi-coloured layers of different sedimentary and igneous rocks were exposed to the eye. And the elements carved the sandstone into crenellations and flutes, bizarre gargoyles, echoing chambers, arches, and grand flora that far

Above: Sundown draws its veil over another day at Wadi Rum, the Valley of the Moon.

outstrip anything which man has been able to produce in his great basilicas, mosques, and other monuments. The cliffs and rolling shoulders of the mountains of Rum and Wadi Ithm humble the most creative minds. Scrambling up one of the thousands of siqs, where the wind whistles and murmurs through giant sandstone organ pipes and rustles the leaves of wild figs that took root in small natural bowls of soil formed over hundreds of years, the visitor cannot help ruing the fact that Mozart never saw the wadi. For perhaps he alone could have done it justice.

The sparsely populated valleys today are occupied by traditional Howeitat Bedouin whose tents nestle against the walls surrounding the valleys, where their herds of sheep and goats graze the brush and scrub. Treated with circumspection, they often invite visitors to tea or coffee. But things were not always thus.

There are traces of Neolithic occupation — small enclosures, paved with

Left: Gorge at Wadi Rum, strangely silent but for the sound of the wind ripping across the innumerable crags.

rough hewn stones, attest to a mysterious presence. Outside the enclosures one usually finds a cairn of three stones set upright. Sometimes the enclosures occur in groups of five or six. The exact provenance of these enclosures is unknown. It is difficult to believe that people lived in Wadi Rum and its surroundings for it has such an eeriness some locals call it the Valley of the Moon. Walking through the wadis or riding astride a camel is such a dwarfing experience you find it hard to accept that people could have lived with such a sense of insignificance for long.

But close inspection of the cliff walls reveals numerous dams built to catch runoff from the very occasional rains — an average of eight centimetres a year. The dams also form open cisterns supplied by the springs that seep through the joints where granite and sandstone meet. The Nabateans would have wanted to store water in this way but the rough nature of the stonework of these ancient reservoirs indicates they were built by early Arabs before they started to settle

Overleaf: Camel riders of the legendary Desert Patrol prepare to make their way back to the small outpost at Rum.

Above: A Bedouin saddles his camel at the village of Rum, in the harsh heat of the afternoon.

in Petra, or by earlier peoples altogether. The medieval Arab geographer Yaqut, described the effects the Nabatean irrigation systems had upon Wadi Rum (in early times called Iram): 'The inhabitants of the wilderness stated that in Iram there were vineyards and pine trees'.

Scramble over almost any accessible rocks and more clues about the past of Wadi Rum are revealed. Peculiar graffiti has been etched on almost any rock or cliff face near a natural camping or stopping place, overhanging rock or under one of the few palms which grow near springs. Aside from the contemporary and vulgar scribblings of latter-day visitors, are the marks left in script reminiscent of ancient Ethiopia. There are hundreds of these marks all over the valleys where, in an idle moment, a member of the Thamud tribe resting in the cool, or leaving his camels to graze on the sweet grass of the valley's floor, entertained himself by scratching images of animals or people and signing his name — along with that of his father — to the work. Sometimes the graffiti is

Above: The Seven Pillars of Wisdom, en route to Rum, made famous by T E Lawrence who camped there.

nothing more than the two names, which interestingly seems still to be the tradition among modern vandals who have scratched their own names along with their father's on the soft plaster of some of the Desert Castles further east.

Earlier pre-Thamudic etchings can also be found in the siq of Khaz 'Ali where elongated figures wearing long tunics are depicted, one of them apparently giving birth. Wadi Rum was a favoured hunting spot and the rock carvings show a wide range of the animals which populated the area: ostrich, Arabian lion, onagers and what looks like a whale with legs.

The Thamuds were traditional camel herders and caravaneers who plied the route between their base in Madain Salih in Arabia and Petra, the nodal point for both Gaza and the wealthy cities in Syria, Palestine, and Jordan. They operated along this route from the 5th century BC to the seventh AD and the huge amount of Thamudic script that survives shows a remarkable level of literacy among such a nomadic people. This was at a time when many sedentary agriculturalists were just getting to grips with basic technologies like pottery. The script is derived from the South Semitic group of alphabets — the only surviving example of which is now in Ethiopia, where it was picked up from traders crossing the Red Sea.

The entrance to Wadi Rum from the Desert Highway is dominated by the "Beau Geste" district headquarters of the Desert Police. Formed entirely from Bedu, the police are mounted either in four-wheel-drive vehicles or on camels, given that they often spend days on patrol in remote areas. Their magnificent ceremonial uniforms consist of a full-length khaki dress, red headscarf and leather bandoliers, offset by a silver dagger and service revolver. While on patrol they also carry World War II American-made semi-automatic rifles which, like all Bedu, they love to fire, especially at night when they can see the tracer streaming into the still blue-black starry skies.

Like military men of tradition, the Desert Patrol police have become guardians of some of the finest standards of behaviour of their own culture. Just as one may expect immaculate manners and effortless charm from an officer of the Grenadier Guards, so you may expect the Bedu policemen to embody the most beguiling characteristics of their own people.

Although often inundated with gawping tourists, the Wadi Rum detachment is always happy to offer tea or coffee and answer questions they must have been asked a thousand times. Their neighbours in the scruffy little village that surrounds them, however, have somehow not been protected from the diluting influence on their spirits by the outside world. On the boundary of an ancient culture and tourism these people persuade visitors to ride their camels while offering nights with their families in slyly thrown up tents. They also litter the valley with plastic bags, old tin cans, and other rubbish which could eventually destroy the tourist market and deprive them of ready incomes. But tin cans and other rubbish from the filming of *Lawrence of Arabia* in Wadi Rum still litter the valley floor.

At the foot of Jebel Rum, not far from the police fort, are the remains of an important Nabatean temple dedicated, according to inscriptions, to 'Allat who is in Iram'. Allat was the most important goddess among the Northern Arabs and appears to have been especially highly esteemed in Rum, given the large amounts of graffiti asking for her protection. The temple, not much of which survives, was originally luxuriously appointed and was as much a place of rest as one of worship for the caravaneers on their journey to Petra. Probably dating to the 1st century BC, the temple consisted of a square courtyard with three rooms around it but open to the east. The walls were plastered and painted to represent marble. In a nearby valley, the Nabateans dammed the most productive spring in Rum and carved a niche for a deity on what was clearly a sacred place for them. Between this valley and the temple another cistern, fed

Above: Ships journey to the sapphire blue waters of the Gulf of Aqaba from across the globe.

by a channel from the spring, provided water for the small settlement that sprang up around the temple.

Southern Jordan is one of the most spectacular regions in the world and Rum is one of its great natural wonders. Nearby, Petra is difficult to categorise. Is it a natural wonder or a man-made miracle? However, in order to first understand how Petra came into being, and swung through extremes of wealth and ignominy, it is necessary to explore the surrounding areas of Rum and of Aqaba, Jordan's only sea-port.

In 1965 Aqaba began to outgrow its narrow confines on the border with Saudi Arabia so King Hussein swapped 6,000 square kilometres of desert for another twelve kilometres of coastline just south of the town for expansion. The extra coastline also gave Jordan access to the Yamanieh coral reef, rightly famous as one of the finest scuba-diving and snorkeling spots in the world. But the growth of Aqaba was a 20th century phenomenon. It gave it a renaissance after many

Above: Bird's eye view of the port at Aqaba.

centuries of torpor as a small fishing village. Before the Arab Revolt Aqaba had been a shadow of its ancient significance when it was the main port for shipments from the Red Sea to the Near East. It was also a major copper producing area and the base for King Solomon's large merchant fleet.

Whatever winter may throw at the rest of Jordan, Aqaba enjoys a year-round tropical climate never dropping much below 25°C and rising to a blistering 45°C which would be unbearable but for the clear and cooling sea breezes. The town is lucky in that fresh water only a few metres below the surface irrigates small gardens and groves of citrus and other fruits that give the town a pleasant lotus-eating air, notwithstanding the high energy hustle and bustle of the port and its lorry park a few kilometres to the north. Two kilometres from the sea and four kilometres to the west is the important ancient site of Tall al Khalaifah. Most historians agree this is probably Solomon's port of Ezion Geber.

Vicious winds howl from the north and the Wadi Arabah as they sweep over

Opposite: Shoals of dazzling reef fish explore a large and flourishing coral head seven metres beneath the surface of the Red Sea off Jordanian shores.

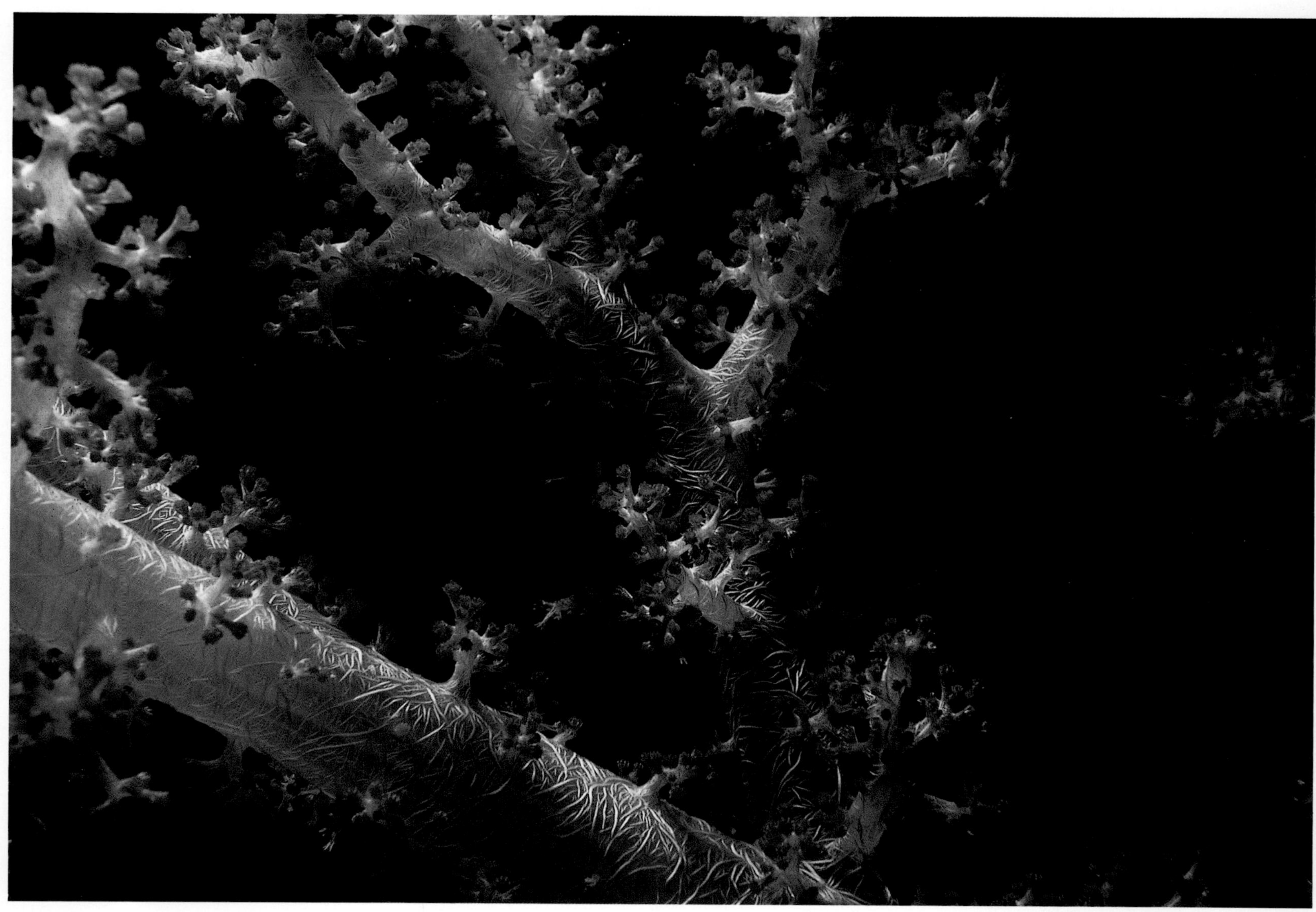

Above: Marine meadow beneath the surface of the Gulf of Aqaba.

Khalaifah and out to sea and the first puzzle is to imagine why anyone should build a town in such an uncomfortable spot. But furnaces discovered at this site on the northern edge of the town show that the wind provided a natural bellows for smelting copper, mined in the Wadi Arabah from the 10th to the 5th centuries BC. The copper processing and attendant trade brought wealth to Aqaba, though it was never a match for Petra, even during Roman times when it became a thriving settlement with the construction of the Trajan Highway from Aqaba to Damascus via Petra and Amman. By the time of the Muslim invasion in AD 636 Aqaba boasted a Christian bishop who was not removed from office at the conclusion of the Islamic onslaught, but treated with respect. Considering the degree of religious tension in this era it is extraordinary that in AD 639 the Christian bishop hosted the visiting Caliph Omar on one of his tours of the Ummayed Empire.

The Crusaders, true to form, occupied Aqaba in about 1116 under Baldwin I

Opposite: Soft corals, which colonised the radar tower of a sunken vessel in the Gulf of Aqaba, put on a dazzling display of colour as they feed in bright sunlight.

Opposite: A catamaran speeds its way across the still waters of the Gulf of Aqaba as evening draws in.

Above: Aqaba offers every conceivable watersport from waterskiing to scuba diving. The waters of the gulf are extremely calm throughout the year.

and built a fortress on the Jazirat Pharaon — Island of Graye — where the professional looters exorted taxes from visiting ships. Another garrison was thrown up in the town, probably on the orders of the Muslim Sultan Nasir in about 1320. With the decline of trade and the dwindling significance of Jordan as a result of the transfer of the Caliphates to Baghdad, Aqaba fell into sleepy decline and was only shaken back to life when it became the supply headquarters for Emir Feisal's Arab armies during World War I.

Since then, Jordan's only port — shipping thousands of tonnes of potash from the mines at Al Hasa in the Wadi Arabah — and a major military installation, is now a tourist attraction and a welcome spot to relax and reflect after sightseeing in the little Kingdom.

The Gulf of Aqaba has a unique marine ecosystem. Unlike much of the Red Sea and the Indian Ocean, the water is cool because of vertical currents of cold water. Evaporation from the surface by high winds dulls the solar heated water.

Overleaf: Sundown over the Gulf of Aqaba.

Overleaf: The façade of El Deir, The Monastery, at Petra, is overshadowed only by the surrounding mountains. Measuring over 40 metres in height, and 46 metres in width, this magnificent edifice is thought to be the largest construction ever undertaken by the Nabateans.

Opposite: Aaron's tomb, perched atop Mount Hor, just outside of Petra — one of the Middle East's most significant, yet inaccessible, monuments.

The result is ideal for the growth of coral and plant life. The reefs are a perfect environment for a spectacular number of brightly coloured fish including sting ray, scorpion fish, clown fish, iron fish, butterfly fish and occasionally a turtle, as well as the magnificently plumed lionfish — a rare sight elsewhere in the world but plentiful in the Gulf of Aqaba.

The clown fish has an interesting relationship with the anemones that catch fish using their poisonous tentacles. The clown fish is able to send a signal to these tentacles, to make the anemone hold back its sting and allow the clown fish to hide within its waving fronds.

In the 5th century BC trade was flourishing in the Wadi Araba and Aqaba. But it had not yet become centralised in Petra, the rock-hewn city of a thousand colours hidden in the Mountains of Edom.

The eastern shores of the Dead Sea provided the most ready access to fresh water. So traders from all points on the compass concentrated on this shoreline and then on running north along what became the King's Highway. The first stop for camel trains was at Wadi Mousa. There, amid the glowering red sandstone cliffs, Moses is said to have struck the ground with his rod and two springs gushed forth. The springs provided welcome sustenance to the caravaneers and their animals before they headed north to the markets in Amman, Damascus and Jerusalem. Originally no water conservation was undertaken at Wadi Mousa. The spring was allowed to spend itself wastefully in the desert after passing through a siq at the bottom of the hill overlooking what is now the city of Petra.

The most important, early permanent occupants of this region were the Edomites. A more advanced people than the invading Jews, they had prospered from the production of copper in the Wadi Arabah. Their prosperity and the copper reserves would have been a great commercial temptation to the Jews and their subsequent Judean kingdoms. This explains why Edom was so often the victim of Israelite invasions.

The conquest and enslavement of the Edomites by the Jews under Solomon provided instant wealth for the king in Jerusalem but his ambitions did not end with the immediate benefits of such riches. He developed the port at Eloth and built a navy to handle the huge tonnage of goods he wanted to see flowing through the port and along the lucrative highways. Trade with Sheba, in Yemen, and north Africa boomed as the high cultures of the Mediterranean developed a taste for expensive luxuries like sugar and rare spices, as well as exotic animals: apes, peacocks, antelope — to populate the extravagant gardens that were favoured at the time.

The goods brought to Aqaba were moved to Petra as it developed as a transshipment base for merchandise brought by sea and the greater bulk brought overland on the ships of the desert from Kuwait, Bahrain, southern Arabia and

the Yemen. These trade routes, not yet in their full bloom but nevertheless rich, were a constant temptation to the Israelites who, at one point during the reign of Amaziah (796-781 BC), caught a raiding party in the territory and wiped most of them out. They then tracked the few survivors to the village on top of Umm el Biyara — biblical Sela — where they threw ten families down to the plain of Petra below.

Above: Dazzling rock architecture of the magical city of Petra bathed in the sun's golden rays.

Various translations of the Bible say that Amaziah threw 10,000 people off the top but there are two reasons for doubt. First, it would have been a tremendous effort to get 10,000 people to walk up the mountain when they knew they would be taking the shortest route down. The second is that the word in the biblical texts for thousand 'alaf' also means family. Nevertheless, the act was one of extreme brutality, typical of the times and the way that the Jews, Edomites, Moabites and Ammonites treated one another.

But Petra did not start to evolve as anything much more than a trading post,

Above: Petra's so-called Palace Tomb is the largest of all the Royal Tombs — traditionally said to resemble a Roman palace. Beside it is the Corinthian Tomb.

nor did it develop architecturally, until the Neo-Babylonian king Nabonidus (555-539 BC) tried to shore up his crumbling empire by establishing military colonies along the incense routes in the southern desert. These passed through Medina and the oasis of Teima, south-east of Petra. The Babylonian builders passed on their skills to the local Arab population who were very quick to learn new trades so that by the time Nabonidus left the region the Arabs had started to carve the Assyrian-style facades that can still be seen on the Outer Siq of Petra. The increased military activity in the southern desert would have driven the nomadic tribes further north. Known as the Nabateans, they moved into Petra, from where trade could be controlled.

An adaptive people, the Nabateans did not confront the indigenous Edomites, but integrated with them. There is some evidence that the art of producing the exquisite pottery for which the Nabateans have become famous was actually taught to them by the Edomites. Both tribal peoples claimed

descent from the prophet Ishmael, which provided common ground to avoid conflict. Above all, the easy integration of the Nabateans was a sign of their legendary genius for compromise which, over the next few centuries, enabled them to wriggle out of the most tricky situations.

Above: The Obelisk Tomb and the Bab el Siq Triclinium are the first major Nabatean monuments close to the entrance to Petra.

Some sort of urban Nabatean development was underway in Petra by about 300 BC. Although most visible remains of the city date from the Roman period, it is likely that the Roman fabric was blended with the extant Nabatean structures built much earlier.

The most important Nabatean constructions to survive into the Roman occupation were their water systems. The complex networks of ceramic pipes and aqueducts not only stored runoff from the surrounding mountains in cisterns — an early form of water storage which the Edomites also practiced — but dammed the Wadi Mousa. When it flooded through the narrow Siq — the only entrance to the city — it did not drown the inhabitants. The dam fed a network of pipes, carved into the rock walls of the city, and central watering points reached via miniature aqueducts. The aqueducts, which have survived the centuries, provide bridges between outcrops of rock on the valley walls.

By 312 BC news of the wealth of Petra had spread to the Greek ruler of Syria, Antigonus, who sent an army against the rock city in the hope of securing it for himself. Control of the city would have enabled him to slow down the advance of the Ptolemies in Egypt. The Seleucids advanced on the city under the cover of darkness to find it deserted. The inhabitants had probably gone to one of the instant impromptu souks thrown-up whenever a caravan came to town. So they plundered what they could — including 500 talents of silver plus the expensive fragrances of frankincense and myrrh — and left.

But the Nabateans, masters of the art of raiding, followed the over-confident Greeks as they wandered home. The Greeks had convinced themselves that the Nabateans had been a walkover. But the Nabateans fell upon them, wiped out all but 50, and regained their booty. Fearful of a punitive reprise from the Greeks, these masterful diplomats then swiftly apologised for the misunderstanding. Antigonus pretended to accept while simultaneously planning another campaign.

The Nabateans were not fooled. Indeed, as they waited for the second assault from the Greek army they sent most of their families and possessions to safe hiding places in the mountains. The Greeks were easily blocked and then compensated with a range of expensive gifts. Nabatean political theory was pragmatic.

By 150 BC the spread of Hellenistic culture was serving the Greeks more effectively than their armies which had become bogged down in the internecine war between the Ptolemies and the Seleucids.

Trade suffered in both quarters so the axis shifted in favour of the peace-loving Nabateans. The vacuum left by the war enabled the Arabs to extend their empire north. In the reign of Nabatean king Aretas III Philhellen, even Damascus came under Nabatean control. Their growing might enraged Pompey who dispatched a Roman army to smash the rock of Petra in 63 BC. However, the army's supply lines became overstretched so that, by the time they arrived at Petra, the bedraggled Romans were happy to be bought off, just like the Greeks. Later, during the reign of Obadas II (30-9 BC) Augustus sent an army against Petra which Obadas' chief minister offered to guide to his own capital. He took them through the desert the back way. Before they arrived many died of thirst and those who remained were plied with gifts and sent packing.

Nabatean independence could not last forever. The nation was simply too rich to avoid the attentions of outsiders. In AD 106 the kingdom was absorbed into the Roman province of Arabia without a fight. Rome's influence brought great prosperity to Petra which swiftly gained a colonnaded cardo among other

things, the remains of which dominate the central part of the city today.

From early accounts of Nabatean culture the society seems to have absorbed a great deal from the traditions of the Bedu. It was highly democratic. The king's authority derived from his ability to listen to critics, arbitrate disputes, and reach consensus. Strabo, quoting a friend who spent some time in Petra, says that meals were prepared together in groups of thirteen. In the royal household the king would serve his guests. He was often called to account for his role by a general assembly of citizens who took a close interest in his personal lifestyle. Strabo observed that the Nabateans worshipped the sun and atop every house was an altar to their god, anointed daily and perfumed with frankincense.

But the Nabateans probably adopted the Edomite god, Dusares. Mentioned in Nabatean finds on the King's Highway, he was symbolised by a block of stone, often black basalt. Like the Israelites, they appear to have had a

Above: Petra's Lion Triclinium supposedly dates from the early Roman period. Its façade has been severely eroded, but one can still make out the pair of lions — flanking the doorway — from which the tomb gets its name.

theological objection to making images of their gods. They preferred the symbolism of a simple rock which usually doubled as an altar. With the spread of Nabatean culture, the Greeks assumed that Dusares could be equated with Dionysus, yet Dionysus was a relatively minor god whereas Dusares was the preeminent god of the Nabateans. There is some evidence that on the High Place of Sacrifice, the best preserved of the ancient religious sites in the kingdom of the ancient world, human sacrifices were made.

The sacrificial table on the High Place of the Attuf ridge sits on a platform 1,035 metres above sea level and 190 metres above the centre of the city on a peak with a stunning view of Petra. Some scholars, especially Iain Browning, whose book *Petra* is the finest guide to the city available, say that human sacrifice has been given a bad name in modern times and that in ancient civilisations the killing of a human was a symbolic and joyous ceremony in which man and God were conjoined. Nonetheless, the mechanics and cold ritualism strike most people as abhorrent.

The High Place is dominated by the sacrificial table at its centre. Carved out of the floor it rises a few centimetres above the central courtyard. With an eye to hygiene, water from a cistern feeds into a course that runs around the high altar and across the courtyard to wash blood down a drainage channel.

Al Uzza — Allat, The Mighty One — was the supreme female goddess of the Nabateans and most of the tribes in the north of Arabia, and is seen in the inscriptions and temple built in her honour in Wadi Rum.

The Nabateans could not have sustained a population of 30,000 in Petra without substantial agricultural output. Dotted all around the city and its suburbs are the remains of low walls, to trap soil and prevent erosion, and advanced systems of irrigation. Unlike many of today's agricultural systems, the Nabatean methods relied on gravity, an ingenuity that also applied to their building techniques. The Treasury which greets visitors as they emerge from the confines of the Siq is so grand it is almost ludicrous. When the Nabatean masons started building the Treasury and the great tombs they chiseled at the rock from the top down. These vast caves required no reinforcing of the roof. When the Nabateans took to building free-standing monuments, such as the Temple of Qasr el Bint, they adopted the Hellenistic techniques employed by the Romans and others involved in trade and were able to maintain a vast and high ceiling with subtle uses of arches.

Because of the incredible number of monuments, both free-standing and caved, the city feels like a museum for today's visitor. You may assume too readily that the city has always been a monument. Yet the central parts of the valleys that make up Petra were once densely populated. Recent excavations have revealed that most of Petra's citizens lived in what is now considered a typical Arab style: one- or two-storey houses built around a central courtyard set

Opposite: The blinding hues of Petra's stone are fully realised in the Urn Tomb, which leads to a chamber hollowed from the rock — measuring 17 metres by almost 19 metres.

Above: Sculpted by wind and rain the rocks surrounding the Nabatean city of Petra are tinged red by the afternoon sun.

in a complex maze of alleyways and roads impassable to anything but donkey or man. The wider thoroughfares were jammed with camels and noisy with the shouts of traders bargaining, bluffing and haggling with one another.

Pax Romana brought peace and prosperity to Petra for a while but it also took away the regional advantage the city had over other trading centres, more blighted by wars and regional differences. With an end to conflicts elsewhere, the rock city began to contract in the 4th and 5th centuries, although the Romans did everything they could to stem the tide of civic decline by organising imperial tours of the region until AD 200. Facing inevitable decline, Petra embarked on a last frenzy of construction in order to stimulate the local economy and maintain the fantasy that the city was a force to be reckoned with. Nevertheless, the merchants began to leave, seeing the benefits and rich pickings of life in one of the Decapolis cities more intimately involved with the Roman empire.

Opposite: The Treasury was almost certainly used as a place for sacrifice. Its sheltered position, away from the abrasive winds, ensures that the monument hardly suffers erosion.

Above: Topmost portion of El Khazneh, The Treasury, is peppered with bullet holes. Before Petra was rediscovered by John Burckhardt, in 1812, it was believed — by the local Bedouin — that the urn at the highest point of the structure was filled with the Pharaoh's treasure. They thought that by firing at this target the treasure trove would spew out.

Emperor Theodosius established the Byzantine Empire in AD 395 and, with the conversion to Christianity, Petra was honoured with a bishop and later a metropolitan. Like everywhere else in the Middle and Near East, churches sprang out of the ground or were established with incredible alacrity in old temples dedicated to pagan gods. Petra was no exception. There are estimated to be tens, if not hundreds, of Christian sepulchres buried beneath the sands or with their telltale frescoes hidden behind the black tar of centuries of Bedouin smoke. With the withdrawal of the Roman Legion assigned to protect the routes south to Hijaz, and the continuous infighting among the Christian churches, a lack of civic pride set in among the Petrans. Rome became disinterested in the affairs of the obscure provincial outpost at the extreme of the eastern empire. Petra began to show that it had exhausted its usefulness and by the middle of the 6th century it had sunk into obscurity.

The Arabs who moved in to the ruins of Petra, or perhaps the handful who

Opposite: The 3,000 seat theatre at Petra is thought to have been carved into the rock during the second century AD.

Above: The High Place at Petra is reached only by an arduous climb. Its flat platform was designed for sacrifices—performed at the central sacrificial tablet of stone.

remained behind when all others left, returned to their nomadic life. Yet they held the city a precious secret from the outside world. For to them it was sacred; a treasure which took a remarkable man to reveal to a world that now flocks to wonder.

As part of his training for an expedition into the heart of Africa John L Burckhardt, a young Swiss intellectual, with backing from the Association for Promoting the Discovery of the Interior Parts of Africa, based in London, learned Arabic, disguised himself as a Muslim Indian trader, and headed for the Near East. He spent a couple of years in Syria perfecting his Arabic and learning to be something of a Koranic scholar, before heading for Egypt along the King's Highway. It was while wandering through the mountains of Moab that he heard tales about a wondrous city hidden among impenetrable mountains. He knew he could not ask outright where it was but followed the trail south as the stories about Petra became more detailed until he arrived at the Wadi Mousa. Sensing

Overleaf: First awesome glimpse of Petra's enchanted legacy — the obstructed view of El Khazneh, The Treasury, at the entrance to the fabled lost city.

Opposite: The Urn Tomb was perhaps the burial place of a Nabatean ruler. In Byzantine times it was turned into a makeshift church.

he was close and aware that the Tomb of Aaron was said to have been set upon a high peak on the outskirts of the city, he claimed he had come to sacrifice a goat at the tomb in honour of the prophet.

Although deeply resentful and suspicious of outsiders, the local Bedu found it hard to refuse a pious request of this kind and so agreed to let him pass through the Siq on his way to Aaron's Tomb. As he emerged from the Siq to see the Treasury, he had to be most circumspect about his enthusiasm for the sight but made sketches and notes in a tiny book hidden beneath his cloak. In this way he was able, despite the impatience of his guide, to wander around much of Petra making remarkably accurate drawings of the main features of the city before arriving at the base of the mountain on which sits the tomb of Aaron.

To the relief of his guide he sacrificed the goat here and saved himself the bother of the long climb and left the valley. News of his 1812 discovery was not officially published until 1822 — five years after his death from dysentery in Cairo, where he was buried under his adopted Muslim name of Pilgrim Ibrahim ibn Abdullah.

Two British Naval commanders were next to visit the city, which they did in some haste for fear that the Bedu would object to their snooping. Their florid descriptions of Petra stimulated interest among the young romantics of Europe who were soon beating a path to the city.

One early visitor said that the summits of the hills showed 'nature in her most savage and romantic form while the bases, as a perfect antithesis, are worked out in all the symmetry and regularity of art, with colonnades, and pediments, and ranges of corridors, adhering to the perpendicular surface'. Lurid stuff, but it brought in the early tourists, including the Royal Academician David Roberts who produced fine and phenomenally detailed sketches of most of the city, as well as Edward Lear. His paintings are sympathetic but he has been far outclassed in his representations of Petra by the descriptive flourish of his cook Giorgio. 'Oh, Signore, we have come into a world where everything is made of chocolate, curry powder and salmon,' Giorgio exclaimed upon arriving in the city.

Lear was an extraordinary man, who revelled in the humour of limericks, the verse form he invented. But this young nation, born of an ancient holy land, demands the lyricism of a true poet, such as Rumi, Sa'di, Hafiz or Omar Khayyam to do justice to the tangible and intangible aspects of its beauty. From the Dead Sea to the shores of the Red Sea, across a nation filled with the beauty of dramatic and enchanting landscapes peopled by many colourful cultures, a *Journey through Jordan* merits no less a conclusion than the unforgettable lines of Omar Khayyam.

Alas, that Spring should vanish with the Rose!
That Youth's sweet-scented manuscript should close!